Praise for *The Witch of Babylon*

One of CNN's
"Six Most Enduring Historical Thrillers"
One of Amazon.ca's
Top Mysteries and Thrillers of 2011
Winner of the Arthur Ellis Award
for Best Unpublished Crime Novel
Shortlisted for the Crime Writers' Association (U.K.)
Debut Dagger Award

"A book so good, everyone should buy it twice."
—*National Post*

"McIntosh combines stellar research with superb writing skills. This book is the first of a planned three featuring Madison and Mesopotamia. I can't wait for the next two." —*The Globe and Mail*

"A sinuous barnburner of a story, steeped in reams of fascinating Mesopotamian history and conjecture but not derailed by it. McIntosh has taken on the (largely American) arcane masters, and beaten them at their game. Good on her." —*Winnipeg Free Press*

"Soaked in the blood of centuries, yet as fresh as tomorrow's headlines. D.J. McIntosh is articulate, literate, and scary." —Alan Bradley, bestselling author of *The Sweetness at the Bottom of the Pie*

"Is D.J. McIntosh the next Dan Brown?"
—*The Globe and Mail*

"From Iraq, ancient history and alchemy combine to terrorize us in this stunning historical thriller. A terrific read." —Louise Penny, *NYT* bestselling author of *Bury Your Dead*

"With a plot that moves like a racetrack pickpocket and a hero who has more lives than a cat and uses them all, D.J. McIntosh's *The Witch of Babylon* is one terrifying ride. Connecting the recent looting of antiquities in war-torn Iraq with Mesopotamian conspiracy contrived almost three thousand years ago, the plot ingeniously weaves the two, keeping the reader on edge and guessing to the very last page. Full of an equal amount of mayhem and erudition, this novel marks a remarkably inventive and lively debut." —James W. Nichol, bestselling author of *Midnight Cab*

"An impressive debut. The first of a projected trilogy, *The Witch of Babylon* is a well-crafted novel that will appeal to readers in search of fast-paced action thrillers. Containing puzzles within puzzles, plot twists and complex characters, it will appeal to fans of *The Da Vinci Code*—though in fairness it is much better written." —*The Sherbrooke Record*

"*The Witch of Babylon* is hard and gritty, with enough satisfying twists and surprises to please the most ardent thriller fan." —*Quill & Quire*

PENGUIN

THE WITCH OF BABYLON

D.J. McINTOSH is a member of the Society for Mesopotamian Studies and a former co-editor of the Crime Writers of Canada's newsletter, *Fingerprints*. She is a strong supporter of Reporters Without Borders and the Committee to Protect Journalists. She lives in Toronto.

In memoriam:
Major General Nicola Calipari
and Mazen Dana, a gifted journalist

D.J.McIntosh
the WITCH of
BABYLON

PENGUIN
an imprint of Penguin Canada

Published by the Penguin Group
Penguin Group (Canada), 90 Eglinton Avenue East, Suite 700,
Toronto, Ontario, Canada M4P 2Y3 (a division of Pearson Canada Inc.)

Penguin Group (USA) Inc., 375 Hudson Street, New York, New York 10014, U.S.A.
Penguin Books Ltd, 80 Strand, London WC2R 0RL, England
Penguin Ireland, 25 St Stephen's Green, Dublin 2, Ireland (a division of Penguin Books Ltd)
Penguin Group (Australia), 250 Camberwell Road, Camberwell, Victoria 3124, Australia
(a division of Pearson Australia Group Pty Ltd)
Penguin Books India Pvt Ltd, 11 Community Centre, Panchsheel Park,
New Delhi – 110 017, India
Penguin Group (NZ), 67 Apollo Drive, Rosedale, Auckland 0632, New Zealand
(a division of Pearson New Zealand Ltd)
Penguin Books (South Africa) (Pty) Ltd, 24 Sturdee Avenue, Rosebank,
Johannesburg 2196, South Africa

Penguin Books Ltd, Registered Offices: 80 Strand, London WC2R 0RL, England

Published in Penguin paperback by Penguin Canada, a division of Pearson Canada Inc., 2011

Published in this edition, 2012

1 2 3 4 5 6 7 8 9 10 (WEB)

LIBRARY AND ARCHIVES CANADA CATALOGUING IN PUBLICATION

McIntosh, D. J. (Dorothy J.)
The witch of Babylon / D.J. McIntosh.

Includes bibliographical references.
ISBN 978-0-14-317573-5

I. Title.

PS8625.I54W58 2012   C813'.6   C2011-908334-5

Visit the Penguin Canada website at **www.penguin.ca**

Special and corporate bulk purchase rates available; please see
www.penguin.ca/corporatesales or call 1-800-810-3104, ext. 2477.

ALWAYS LEARNING   PEARSON

In War, truth is the first casualty.

—AESCHYLUS, 525–456 B.C.

The Witch of Babylon is Book One
of the Mesopotamian trilogy.
It takes place in the month of August,
blessed by Shamash,
Assyrian god of the sun.

Author's Note

In 1922 a centuries-old scientific quest was finally solved. At the Sarcelles Gas Works, in the presence of two eyewitnesses, legendary French alchemist Eugène Canseliet succeeded in converting one hundred grams of lead into gold. He never shared his secret and the formula remains a mystery.

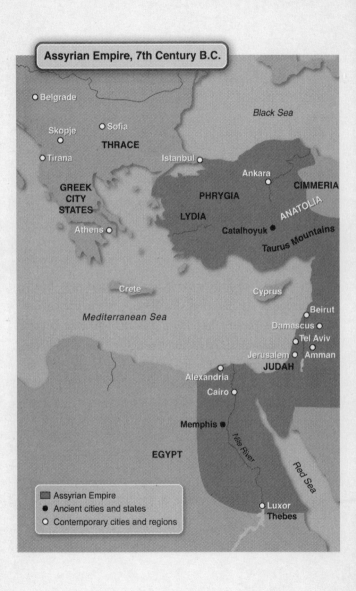

Assyrian Empire, 7th Century B.C.

Belgrade

Black Sea

Skopje

Sofia

THRACE

Tirana

Istanbul

Ankara

CIMMERIA

GREEK
CITY
STATES

PHRYGIA

ANATOLIA

LYDIA

Athens

Catalhoyuk

Taurus Mountains

Crete

Cyprus

Mediterranean Sea

Beirut

Damascus

Tel Aviv

Jerusalem

Amman

JUDAH

Alexandria

Cairo

Memphis

EGYPT

Nile River

Red Sea

Luxor
Thebes

Assyrian Empire
Ancient cities and states
Contemporary cities and regions

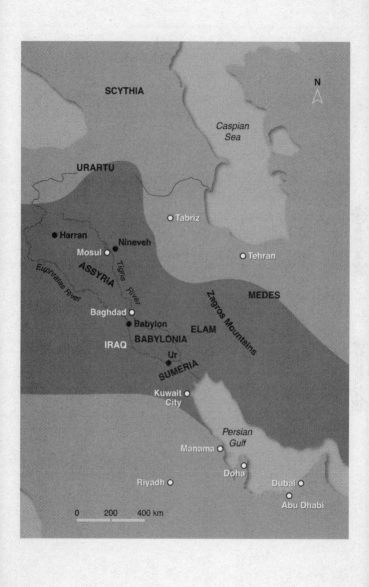

Historical Note

Perched on an arc of the Tigris River, Nineveh was once the star in the crown of the great Assyrian empire. Immense walls, six feet thick at their narrowest point and eight miles long, with fifteen magnificent gates, fortified the city. An aqueduct from the foothills of the Taurus Mountains brought water to the glorious temples, libraries, palaces, and gardens within.

Nineveh's splendor did not last. In 612 B.C., Cyaxares, King of the Medes, supported by Babylonians from the south and Black Sea region tribes, laid siege to the city. In short order Nineveh fell. It was burned, sacked, and abandoned, never to rise again.

Through the centuries, dust from the surrounding plain blew across the ruined capital to form a mound, or tell, that could be seen for many miles. Nineveh disappeared. Over time it was erased from human memory and became a lost city.

In the mid-1800s French diplomat Paul-Émile Botta, British explorer Sir Austen Henry Layard, and Iraqi archaeologist Hormuzd Rassam excavated what had become known as the Kuyunjik mound. They unearthed remarkable objects—monumental sculptures of human-headed, winged bulls, elaborate friezes, and an entire library of clay tablets.

Barely noticed among these remarkable pieces was a simple basalt engraving. Little did anyone realize then, this would prove to be the most spectacular find of all.

Prologue

The Gods have abandoned us,
like migrating birds they have gone.
[Our city] is destroyed, bitter is its lament.
The country's blood now fills its holes
like hot bronze in a mold,
bodies dissolve like fat in the sun.
Our temple is destroyed,
smoke lies on our city like a shroud,
blood flows as the river does.
The lamenting of men and women,
sadness abounds,
[Our city] is no more.

Hours before the final attack few believed the city would fall. How could the proud gates of Ishtar, those strong bridges spanning the Tigris, be breached? Were not the nation's soldiers visible everywhere? Was not the palace, mirrored by the river's serene waters, well defended? Did the ruler not promise all was well?

And yet on the ninth day of the month of Nissan, a time well chosen by the invaders to avoid the brutal heat of summer, the city did fall, crushed as easily as the delicate shell of a baby bird. Soldiers fled, threw off their battle dress, and hid among the people. Women gathered their children and cowered in dark rooms. Fires raged, turning homes to cinders. Flames gorged on the bountiful banquet of papyrus and parchment scrolls in the great library. Bodies lay everywhere, unclaimed in the streets, floating down the river like drowned and bloated livestock. Cages of exotic animals and birds kept for the people's pleasure were wrenched open, the animals stolen and butchered for food. Statues of the ruler were desecrated; the man himself was nowhere to be seen.

War's twin sister, plunder, went on a rampage. Neither the meager possessions of ordinary citizens nor the splendid hall of treasures was spared. Swarming like a colony of ravens fighting over the same piece of flesh, the pillagers stole precious ivories, necklaces of chalcedony and lapis, temple statues, and alabaster vases. One man smashed the head of a terracotta lion from Harmel's temple. Another sat cross-legged on the floor, stripping inlay from the Lyre of Ur.

By April 14, 2003, Baghdad hung its head in defeat. Its hall of treasures, the famous National Museum of Iraq, had become a casualty of war.

Threading through the crowd, a thief moved with silent efficiency, a slim man with jet-black hair and pale skin. A mark, an odd configuration the color of an old bloodstain, stood out on his left wrist. The thief allowed himself a quiet laugh at the many hands grabbing for booty. They had no idea what they were taking. The disgraced son of a diplomat, the thief had spent ten years in Baghdad and knew the museum well.

Strapped to his waist in a custom sheath hidden under his loose black jacket, he carried a Viking Tactics Assault knife, ready for anyone who dared cross the line. He'd come seeking only two objects. The first, the lifelike copper head of the goddess of Victory from ancient Hatra, he'd already deposited in his carryall. The second, even more important relic was only moments away. He kept the man named Tomas Zakar firmly in his sightline.

Tomas Zakar bent his head and pressed his hands against his ears as if blocking out the scene would stop the carnage. The visions refused to fade. Gangs of looters used machine guns to smash display cases and heaped wheelbarrows with clay vessels, chipping and cracking them in the process.

Almost all the museum records had been dumped on the floor and set alight. They burned like funeral pyres. Tomas fell to his knees to beat out the flames with his bare hands. His brother Ari, the much bigger of the two, dragged him away. "Stop this, Tomas; you'll harm yourself."

Tomas fought him off and moved toward a looter wielding a chainsaw to cut off a stone head from

Khorsabad. The chainsaw was designed to cut through pliant wood fibers. Its blade could fracture limestone and destroy the object entirely. Tomas lunged toward him. The man brandished the spinning blade. Ari grabbed his brother, clamping his big arms around his waist, and pulled him back in time. "For God's sake," he cried, "they'll kill you."

Ari cast around wildly, uncertain where to go. This was his brother's domain; Tomas knew the museum's pattern of corridors and rooms better than he. Light-skinned and ginger-haired, Ari stood out, making the two of them all the more vulnerable. Without electricity the galleries were dim, illuminated only by natural light. The place resembled a giant tomb. The largest artifacts, too heavy to move and blanketed with protective wrap, resembled bulky giants awaiting burial.

Through the haze Ari could make out the colossal Lamassu, winged bulls with human heads, forming an entrance arc to the Assyrian gallery. He pleaded with Tomas, "Come this way. Help me. I don't know where to go." Forcing Tomas against one of the stone guardians, he held him there. "Take some deep breaths and calm yourself."

Tomas tried to break free of his grasp. "I've got to go back outside. There's a tank nearby."

"The director already tried. He's been to the Palestine Hotel three times pleading with the military for help. They refused. Come, Samuel's waiting for us. We're already late."

"I can't go through with it. We'll be no better than these thieves."

"Would you prefer to leave it here for the looters?"

Tomas made another feeble effort to resist, but this time Ari was adamant. They took a convoluted route down blacked-out corridors to a small and dusty restoration room.

A diminutive older man waited for them, his face tight with anxiety. When he saw the two brothers, Samuel Diakos sighed in relief. "You're finally here. I was so worried."

Tomas pressed his lips together in a grim line. "Let's get on with it then. May God forgive us." On the floor clay vessels lay broken and in disarray, as if a whirlwind had spun across the room.

Samuel barely heard him. With a much younger man's agility he rushed over to a row of stacked shelves against the wall. Ari put his shoulder to the last one in the row, pushing it outward to reveal a small, square steel door in the wall. Samuel knelt. "I don't think the lock has been touched." He motioned for Ari to bring over a canvas sack and asked him to place it on a long table that held cotton wrap, brushes, and measuring tools used for the few tablets and fragments of engravings lying nearby.

Samuel unlocked the steel door, peering into the shadowy interior. "It's still inside. We got here in time." He slid out the heavy basalt oblong and laid it carefully on the table.

A figure dressed in black, the handles of a carryall

looped over his shoulder, appeared in the doorway. Samuel, preoccupied with the engraving, didn't notice at first, but Ari and Tomas rushed to block the man's way. The thief removed his bag and set it gently on the floor. He motioned toward Samuel. "I'll take that," he said.

"Get out of here." Tomas charged toward him.

The thief powered a kick straight to his groin. Tomas doubled over with the pain and collapsed. The assault knife appeared in the thief's hand. Ari stepped over Tomas, blocked the forward motion of the man's knife arm, and sent a hard punch to his chest. The man reeled but twisted his knife so its razor edge caught Ari's palm, splitting it open. Blood spurted between the ugly flaps of skin surrounding the wound.

The thief held his weapon lightly, ready to make a fatal strike. He believed the knife possessed its own blood scent: just as a divining rod detects water, it could sense the location of an artery and sever it instantly.

"No!" Samuel held out the engraving already sheathed in the cotton wrap. "I'll give it to you. Take it. Don't hurt them anymore."

"You're old. You couldn't stop me anyway," the thief sneered as he picked up his carryall and handed it to Samuel. "Put it inside."

Samuel complied.

A commotion sounded at the entrance, a group of looters pushing their wheelbarrow through the door. They stopped in their tracks when they saw Tomas on the floor and Ari gripping his hand, losing his battle to stanch the flow of blood.

The thief grabbed his carryall and strode over to the door. He pointed the sharp tip of his knife toward the looters. "Move away," he said.

Terrified, they dropped their wheelbarrow and backed off.

The thief disappeared into the dark hallway beyond.

Outdoors, night had fallen. People scurried in all directions, white phantoms in the gloom, arms bursting with raffia bags and cardboard boxes. One man carried a computer monitor, cables flapping around his neck like birthday ribbons. Another dragged a couch, its chrome legs carving furrows in the dirt.

When they finally reached their Toyota, Tomas slumped down angrily into the driver's seat. Ari got in, gripping the rough bandage of cotton wrap that bound his hand.

Samuel took the back seat, setting his canvas sack beside him. "It'll be all right now," he said. "The worst is over."

"What do you mean?" Tomas barked. "It's been a total failure."

"You still have your lives. That's far more important."

"Listen to him, Tomas," Ari said. "He's right."

"In any event," Samuel continued calmly, "I gave him the wrong one. Our engraving is in my bag. Start driving. We need to get out of here."

Near Tell al-Rimah, Iraq
April 20, 2003

The sun directly overhead told Hanna it was noon. Heat had turned her body into a limp rag. Her eyelids burned. She dreamt of water—the feeling of cool liquid slipping down her throat, reedy pools at the edge of the Tigris, icy moisture on ancient rock walls. She was cracking and she knew it.

At daybreak the rough hands of the men had dragged her to a hollowed-out pit. They'd pulled her arms back and bound them to a post. The spades and trowels they'd used to dig out the hole, building a pyramid of dirt the height of her waist, had been thrown down in a haphazard pile at her feet.

Hanna watched the three men return and bend down to gather stones the size of a child's fist, each one big enough to draw blood, but not so large as to bring death quickly. They dumped the stones in a small pile at the crest of the pit.

One of the men detached himself from the group and walked down the incline toward her. He was thin and had a shock of black hair that contrasted with his skin, unnaturally white for someone who'd spent so many hours under the merciless sun. A red-inked tattoo was visible on his left wrist. He pulled off her scarf, letting it dangle around her neck, bent his head until it was inches from her face, and lowered his voice so only she could hear.

"Where did they take the engraving? Tell me and I'll spare you."

Hanna said nothing, sensing a lie.

"You feel the heat, Hanna, don't you?" He reached into a pocket and brought out a green glass bottle filled with water. Pulling off the cap, he touched her lips with the bottle's wet rim. When she opened her mouth he jerked it away cruelly. "You can have all the water you want—just tell me."

She rejected this with a sideways motion of her head. Her hands were numb and her body strangely cold given the heat of the day. "I don't know," she replied. "Samuel wouldn't say."

"That's a lie. You were one of his most trusted assistants."

"Not anymore. I've heard nothing from him. He suspected me after I tried to steal it the first time."

"What did he offer you?"

Hanna wanted to spurt out a cynical laugh but her swollen tongue interfered. A dribble of spittle ran down the corner of her lips. She was so very tired. She looked at him and thought of the sand vipers that hide in the dust, waiting to strike the foot that passes too close. His eyes were like theirs: hooded, red-rimmed, so light they looked almost yellow.

Her words came out in a whisper. "Nothing. Why would I agree to join your side if I could get money out of Samuel?"

"How did he know I was coming to the museum

then? He was ready for me. That information could only have come from you."

"You know what it's like over here. Word leaks out. No one keeps secrets for long."

"Your sacrifice is a waste. We'll find it anyway."

She smelled his sweat and wondered whether some part of him, too, might be afraid. Did she have any chance with him at all? "Oh God. Let me go. I'll die out here."

In a rage he heaved the bottle away. It shattered on a rock. Splinters of green glass lay on the ground, winking in the sunlight. "Let the devil have you then." His words felt painful as a lash. He climbed back up the slope.

"Hanna has betrayed us," he shouted to the others. He raised his left hand to make the sign of the horn, extending index and baby fingers, keeping the other fingers closed, sending a terrible curse toward her. He picked up one of the rocks and walked toward the smaller of the other two men, pressing the rock into his shaking hands. "Stone her."

"You said we were only trying to scare her. She's in bad shape already. This has gone too far."

"She still doesn't think we're serious."

"Maybe she genuinely doesn't have the information."

"She knows. Just do it."

The man took aim, trying to judge where a blow might cause the least injury. The rock glanced off Hanna's shoulder with a soft, ineffective thud.

"You were trying to spare her!" he shouted angrily. "Shim, show him how it's done."

A giant of a man stepped forward. Instinctively, the smaller fellow shrank back, having seen first-hand the damage his companion could inflict. The goliath bent stiffly at the waist, picked up two stones, and whipped them full force at his target.

Hanna screamed. Her body jerked when one of the stones smacked into her face and the other tore into the soft tissue of her abdomen. After this wounding, all sense of time and place drifted away.

As if in sympathy with her agony, the light appeared to change. The sun turned burnt orange; the sky, an unnatural ochre. In the fierce heat the ground seemed to ripple as though a giant serpent wound beneath its surface. The atmosphere grew weirdly still but for a faint buzz, an electric frissoning of millions of sand particles gathering together.

The men looked north. "A shamal wind," one of them said. "Look at that."

It appeared as though a mountain had suddenly formed on the flat horizon. At first the shape was just a dim bulge, but it grew rapidly before their eyes. In minutes a wave of sand hundreds of feet high became visible. It rolled toward them like a massive tsunami. Quick flashes of blue lightning forked through the reddish dust. The Arabs called the wind *Kamasin*, derived from the word for fifty—because when they're strong, such storms can last for fifty days.

They bolted, knowing that it would be nearly

impossible to outrun the wall of sand. The smaller man stumbled and fell onto a sharp protruding rock. A stab of pain gored his knee. He raised himself up, clutching his injured leg, and staggered forward. The other two had already reached their battered GM pickup. They threw open the doors and climbed inside. The engine started up.

"Wait!" the small man screamed. "What are you doing?"

The truck doors banged shut; its tires spun on the sandy ground. The driver reversed. The wheels gained traction and the truck turned toward the south. The small man forced his legs to race, ignoring the wrenching pain. He stretched out his arms like a beggar pleading for mercy. The truck's high beams flicked on, the glare momentarily searing his eyes. His last words were drowned out by the roar of the motor and the gathering storm.

Hanna, on the edge of consciousness, caught a fleeting sense of a new wind on her face and the first assault of fine particles of grit. She drooped against the post like a broken doll, the stirring of her scarf a herald for the oncoming storm.

Part One
THE GAME

For, lo, I will raise and cause to come up against Babylon an assembly of great nations from the north country: and they shall set themselves in array against her; from thence she shall be taken: Their arrows shall be as of a mighty expert man; none shall return in vain. And Chaldea shall be a spoil: all that spoil her shall be satisfied.

—JEREMIAH 50:9–10

One

342 West Twentieth Street, New York
Saturday, August 2, 2003, 10:30 P.M.

In the weeks since the accident, I've kept away from the constellation of friends who knew and loved my brother, Samuel. If our paths did happen to cross, they managed to say, "It's a miracle you survived, John," in tones suggesting the opposite.

I wore that one dark moment on the highway like a red-hot brand.

To avoid any more chance meetings, I arrived at Hal Vanderlin's party deliberately late, hoping the crowd had already melted away. I wouldn't have bothered coming at all but Hal had proved elusive lately, not returning my calls or emails. He still owed me a significant amount of money and this party was the one sure chance I had of finding him.

As a child I'd spent hours exploring the Vanderlins' townhouse, losing myself in the dim labyrinth of its halls, opening doors to silent rooms. Most retained furniture from a bygone era—chairs upholstered in burgundy damask and framed with carved walnut, handmade lace on the arms and headrests. Wardrobes, bookcases, and desks gave off the aroma of camphor and old mahogany. A ghost house. That's how it seemed to me then.

Of all its chambers my favorite was one I called the vanishing room. A large, open rectangle on the top floor, to a boy it looked immense. Two huge mirrors hung on facing walls. If I stood dead center between them I could see myself telescope away to nothing. When I tired of those solitary games I'd run out through the kitchen to the back garden, a jungle of trees and overgrown shrubs. I'd sharpen sticks and tie lengths of string to make bows and arrows then lie in wait for a Cyclops to charge out from the bushes or a giant to swing down from a tree.

Even these innocent recollections seemed tainted now by Samuel's death.

By the time I walked into the party, only the serious hangers-on were left. Among them, Professor Colin Reed had zeroed in on a woman with white-blond hair and china-blue eyes who I assumed had just graduated and was therefore fair game. Tight pants and a clingy silk shirt showed off her firm, fit body.

Reed headed off, to get drinks I assumed. As I was

looking around for Hal she caught my eye. I sent her a smile back.

"I'm Eris," she said when we were close enough to hear each other.

"John Madison." She moved a little nearer to me.

"Are you with the bride's or the groom's party?" I asked.

I noticed her eyes widen when she laughed. They were a mesmerizing blue, so intense I wondered whether she used those contacts that enhance eye color. "Yeah, it's funny," she said. "Sometimes these university parties do seem as deadly as your second cousin once removed's wedding."

"You're at NYU?"

"No, an MIT grad. You?"

"Columbia. But some time ago. Hal and I go way back. We're childhood friends and lately, business associates."

"Isn't he a professor?"

"Yes. I'm an art dealer. He's sold some art objects through me."

"An art dealer. That's exotic. You must be a millionaire then." She chuckled to show this was just a tease.

"Millions of dollars pass through my hands. It hurts always watching them end up in someone else's bank account. Should have gone into hedge funds."

That produced another grin. "So you're a friend of Hal's?" she asked.

"My older brother and his father were friends.

Samuel would always bring me here on his visits, and whenever Hal came home from boarding school or summer camp we'd spend time together. He didn't have a lot of other friends here in the city. How do you know him then?"

She didn't answer me and I saw her flick a glance across the room. Reed appeared in the doorway, his bushy fair hair that seemed to stand up vertically from his scalp, somewhat skewed, his reddened nose suggesting this was far from his first drink. He shot daggers at me from where he stood. A signal he was not amused by my monopolizing the object of his affection.

Normally I'd stand my ground, but I had to find Hal. "Sorry I can't stay and talk." I pulled out my business card and handed it to her. "I've got to see Hal. Give me a call if you'd like to get together for a coffee or something sometime."

She gave the card a quick once-over and tucked it into her shoulder bag. "I don't drink caffeine, but I love long walks on the beach and romantic dinners."

It was my turn to laugh. "Looking forward to it," I said. I left before Colin Reed came over to break the spell.

In the kitchen, before I went out the back to look for Hal, I put David Usher's "Black Black Heart" on, turned up the volume, and opened a window so the music would drift outside. Usher wrote the song about a woman, but I'd always thought how easily the title could apply to me.

I walked outside on the stone pathway. Soft light glowed from the windows and floated out onto the tangle of garden. The heat of the August night drew the scent from the aspens and spun it through the air.

I took in a deep breath and felt almost content.

I found Hal in the small stone pavilion, sitting in the same old wicker chair his father used to occupy. An oil lamp hung on the back wall, sending out the perfume of citrus. One of his sleeves was rolled up above the elbow, a cream-colored rubber strap binding his arm so tight it made his flesh pucker.

When Hal saw me he flicked off his lighter and set a spoon down on the table beside a ziplock bag containing a grayish powder. "John, your timing is always perfect."

I stepped through the arched entranceway and took a seat on the edge of the stone wall that formed one side of the pavilion. I checked to see whether anyone else had come outside then reached up to pull down one of the blinds. A moth fluttered out, its white wings as thin as tissue paper.

You'd think it was Hal who'd just survived an accident, not me. I was struck by how frail he looked. A pattern of purple bruises dotted his bare arm, entrance wounds for old injection sites. At thirty-three, only a year older than me, he looked closer to fifty.

He frowned. "You're still a free man."

"Of course. Why wouldn't I be?"

"The papers hinted at criminal charges. They said you were way over the speed limit."

"The accident was more than six weeks ago and nothing's happened. You know they always exaggerate. I've driven that route a million times. I could do it blind."

He raised his eyebrows. "Well, it's only your word for it now. Samuel can't argue his side of the case."

"Hal. You're about to shoot up. Don't lecture me about risk."

He laughed. "There's no danger unless you have the bad luck to get the pure stuff."

His addiction was no secret to me. It had started out as a lark, but the odd occasion had become a daily event. Our commercial venture selling off his father's collection did not have a long future. We'd ripped through most of the family wealth already.

He pointed toward the spoon. "Part of a complete set assembled by Mother. Commissioned by the Spanish royals, so she was told. Sixteenth century, House of Borbón y Grecia. A wedding gift to celebrate the union of Castile, Aragon, and Navarre."

I picked up the spoon carefully, knowing Hal would freak if I spilled its precious cargo. I could see the crest on the handle: a shield in the lower half, the lion rampant and a castle in the upper two quadrants, a crown at the top. My experience as an art and antiquities dealer had taught me some hard lessons about spotting counterfeit material.

I set the spoon back on the table and sighed. "You know this set is a fake or you'd have sold it by now."

"You're right, of course. The one thing Mother

purchased with no advice from us. She was so pleased with herself. Father knew right away it was a copy. 'Badly done, too.' I can still hear him saying that; it entertained him for an entire fortnight. As always I rose to her defense. I don't have the heart to sell it."

"Hal, I only came tonight because you've been avoiding me. You owe me almost two thousand for that loan I gave you. When am I going to see it?"

"I have a long list of creditors. You're welcome to stand in line."

My voice went a notch louder. "Funny. That's not what you said when I gave you the money."

Hal winced as though I'd touched a particularly sensitive nerve. "You're so aggressive, Madison. So unlike your brother. Samuel taught me to appreciate the beauty of old objects, their stories. It's been hard to sell off my father's possessions, but with you, it's all about the dollars. It's always been like that between us. 'Me first,' that's your motto."

Our relationship had always blown hot and cold, but this time I had no patience for his bad temper and my irritation flared into anger. "I'm still trying to recover from the crash. I lost my only brother. Don't dare use him against me."

"And I'm about to lose my job. Colin Reed, who this minute is partaking of my hospitality, quaffing down my best liquor and leering at the females, gave me my walking papers late this afternoon. I found out about it too late to cancel the party. I knew they weren't going to grant me tenure, but I never expected this.

And he's got the gall to show up here. So I'm seriously broke. Even you can't suck blood from a stone."

I mumbled a few words about that being unfortunate news.

He waved my remarks away. "You'll get your money soon. I have something else, anyway, worth vastly more than a hunk of silver."

"What?" I was a little surprised to hear he'd kept something back from me. "You're not trying to sell it yourself, surely?"

He tightened the rubber strap on his arm again, ignoring me.

"Hal. Before you float off to never-never land, listen to me. You've been satisfied with the prices I've gotten for you before. If this thing you have is really valuable you could end up getting ripped off. Sell it through me and you can pay me back that way. For crying out loud, don't be so stubborn."

"You've made enough off me. This time it's my turn." Hal managed a smile and resumed his preparations, a ritual he seemed to enjoy almost as much as the high.

He picked up the syringe and pulled off the cap, dropping it onto the table. The needle looked no wider than a human hair. He drew the liquid into the syringe and cleared the air bubbles. Curling up his left fist, he jabbed the tip of the syringe into his skin, flagged it, and pushed down the plunger. A dribble of blood emerged at the puncture site.

He leaned his head back against the wicker chair

as if he wanted to rest. I walked away in disgust, leaving him there, dreamy eyed and slack jawed. Had he found anything of real value? I doubted it. But why would he want to hide it from me?

Two

Back at home I grabbed an ice-cold bottle of lager from the fridge and took it out to the balcony. The unmistakable scent of marijuana drifted up on the warm night air. This was one of the great benefits of living near the Greenwich clubs: you could get high just by breathing. An amorphous yellowish light filtered down from the signs and streetlights. Knots of club-goers passed by, calling out to each other, girls in their four-hundred-dollar jeans and five-inch spike heels, guys trying to pick them up and failing.

Although Samuel and I had shared the condo, we'd been more like two ships in the night these last years, with him so often away on a dig and me always flying off somewhere to meet a client. We'd loved the place; it was a refuge for us both. Surprisingly, given our professions, our furnishings had a contemporary look. We did have a few older pieces though—precious Turkomen rugs, the sixties Scandinavian teak furniture I'd scored from a dealer going out of business, our Eames lamps and chandelier. The high ceilings gave a sense of spaciousness, and during the day, light poured in from our large windows. On the rare winter evenings I'd spend alone, I loved to sit in front of the gas fireplace, listening to music and watching the snow drift outside. I'd put on the great Roy Orbison or Diana Krall and let their voices sink into my soul.

Just remembering the good times we'd had putting our place together over the years brought the hurt ramping back. And when memories of Samuel swamped me, as they did often, it took a long time to regain my balance. Since returning from the hospital I'd not found the courage to venture into Samuel's suite. His belongings lurked there defiantly, daring me to open the door and sort through them. Most were pieces gathered over decades of travel to the Aegean and Near East. Among them, a rare Jaf tribal rug with brocaded selvedges, the threads of vermilion and cobalt as brilliant as the day they were first woven. A bride belt of hammer-beaten silver from the Ottoman period in Anatolia. His books. A copy of *Seven Pillars of Wisdom,* signed by T.E. Lawrence, first editions of Durrell's *The Alexandria Quartet,* a set of four. I'd been a willing accomplice to the raid on Hal's inheritance, but I would never part with anything of mine.

Thinking about my inheritance took me back to my seventh birthday, a blustery November day when Samuel and I traveled to a favorite haunt, a town on Lake Ontario where a close family friend lived.

Beyond the forty-year gulf between our ages, how different the two of us were even then. Me, impetuous and demanding; Samuel, reserved and measured. I sometimes believed he'd think about it before he put his foot down to take a step. I would grow to be taller than he, with a sturdy build and the dark hair and eyes of our shared Mediterranean heritage. He had light gray eyes and the pale complexion more characteristic of northern Europeans.

There'd been almost no one around that day, just a solitary jogger and a couple with their Labradors. The dogs chased sticks thrown into the lake, oblivious to the freezing water. Samuel held my hand and I leaned in toward him as we trudged out onto the gritty sand. "You know, John," he said, "there are wonders all around us, but most people never take the time to see them. They're too caught up with their day-to-day concerns."

The parks people had already set up a rust-colored fence of wooden slats to stop the winter winds from blowing snow onto the boardwalk. A ribbon of fallen leaves ran along its perimeter. The water was steely gray. Spray shot into the air as waves collided with the rocks. No tang of salt hung in the air, nor was there any kelp thrown up at the water's edge; otherwise, you'd swear you were at the ocean.

I thought about what he'd just said and remembered a summer afternoon on the shore filling two jars with bits of colored glass worn smooth and round by the waves.

"Like the jewels I found last summer?" I asked him. It amazed me that such beautiful objects lay on the ground just waiting to be picked up. The most plentiful green ones were my emeralds, the blues my sapphires. Occasionally I'd find an amber or a rare ruby.

"Yes, like that," Samuel said. "Let's look near the rocks. Who knows? Maybe we'll find something."

It didn't take long to spot the bottle wedged between two boulders. Samuel had to help me pull it out. It was a corked glass bottle, a pale aqua colour. Inside I could see a piece of ivory paper rolled up. The cork was loose and I soon fished out the paper.

Samuel spread it out on the flat surface of a boulder. "Well, John," he announced, "I believe you've found a treasure map."

Had I been older, I'd have spotted the ruse immediately. As a youngster, I could barely contain my glee while we carefully paced off the directions on the map. One hundred steps to the blue spruce tree, forty to the drinking fountain, on to the bandstand, and back to the boathouse.

We ended up at a flower bed behind a cedar hedge, where, remarkably, one pale pink rose still lingered.

"The treasure lies under the sign of the rose, that's what's written here," Samuel said.

Falling on my hands and knees, I attacked the loose mound of earth beneath the rose plant with a stick. Samuel knelt on the ground beside me, his ancient Harris Tweed jacket flapping in the gusty breeze, dirt rimming his fingernails.

He played his part convincingly.

Using a tissue, we carefully brushed away the remaining soil and lifted out a small coffer, rounded at one end and squared off at the other. It was typical of Samuel not to fill it with kid stuff but rather with objects of real worth. I opened a little net bag containing seven gold coins. I took them out, scrutinizing the unusual images and feeling the weight of them in my hands. There was also a copper disc, green with age, an image of a bird embossed on one side; a stone cylinder seal; and a golden key. Later I tried the key in every lock in our home, but I never discovered what it opened. The chest also offered up a little enamel box, inside it a caramel-colored cameo of a lady's profile. On the back I saw an inscription in letters I didn't understand.

"Keep these in a safe place," Samuel said. "They will matter to you someday."

My cellphone chirped, pulling me back to the present. I checked my watch. Nearly twelve-thirty.

I answered, hoping to hear the blond woman's voice, but Hal came on the line, his words badly slurred. I could make out my name and nothing else. After that, a stretch of fifty seconds or so of wheezing and slow, troubled breaths.

His voice cleared up. "John, are you there? Come back to the house. I need you." The sound of his phone falling onto a hard surface sent a shock wave through my ear. The line went dead.

I could not remember a time, as adults, when

Hal had sought my help for anything personal. That he'd asked for it now was a clear sign of trouble. I grabbed my keys, flew down the back stairs to save time, and got in my car. After driving like a madman, zigzagging through the streets and ignoring every speed limit, I parked in front of the church near Hal's townhouse. The street was uncharacteristically deserted and gloomy, the large homes looming out of the darkness like giant mausoleums empty of their dead.

I got out, punched the code for the front door lock, and ran through the echoing corridor and down the stairs, through the kitchen to the back garden. A dog howled next door; otherwise, it was dead quiet.

Security monitors detected my movements and lights flashed on, sending arcs of brightness across the garden, throwing the borders into deep shadow. I saw Hal sprawled on the concrete floor of the pavilion, one arm thrown awkwardly over his forehead. His eyes were wide open and staring; his face, the picture of Edvard Munch's frozen scream.

I bent down and touched the skin at the base of his neck, searching for the tiny throbbing pulse in the soft hollow of his throat. I tried to force his mouth shut, thinking, in a panic, that if I could restore his face to normalcy he would revive. I tried pressing down on his eyelids, but in a frightening way they sprang open again when I lifted my fingers.

Reaching for his hand, already growing cold, I closed my warm one over his.

Lord, Hal. All your bravado about not getting pure heroin. You can make only one mistake with that.

As my eyes became accustomed to the gloom, I could see a nasty, bloody cut on his left hand, probably caused by his fall. I felt for my BlackBerry to call an ambulance and noticed that Hal's cell had tumbled underneath his chair. I picked it up. The top had broken, its rim a jagged outcropping of black plastic.

Hal's syringe still lay on the table next to his empty drink glass. Except for a few grains, the clear plastic bag holding the heroin was empty. The dog resumed barking, this time in a series of high-pitched, frenzied yelps, as though it had sighted quarry and was closing in for the kill.

I heard the scrape of footsteps on the flagstone and straightened up. The blond woman I'd met earlier stood staring at me, a quirky half-smile on her face. Her hair shimmered in the lamplight like pale watered silk.

She still looked as immaculate as she had earlier in the evening, with one exception: a spray of blood, visible on her right sleeve. She seemed at ease, almost nonchalant. As if it were perfectly natural for Hal to be lying dead on the pavilion floor. She took a few steps toward me.

"Hello again, John," she said.

Three

I reached into my memory, trying to retrieve her name. Erica or Erin, something like that. "Don't you realize what's happened here?"

She moved closer and trailed her fingers down my arm. "It's Eris. We met earlier, remember?"

Had she not seen Hal? Maybe I was blocking her view. I stepped aside.

As if she'd done it many times before, she knelt beside him, checked his eyes, and pressed her fingers to his throat. Sighing, she rose again. "He's beyond help now. But I think you already know that." She said this sympathetically, but her lack of alarm disturbed me.

"What happened to him?"

"I've seen enough dead bodies. He overdosed."

The sound of panting and whining came from next door. The neighbor's dog. It scratched frantically at the wooden fence. Her confirmation of my suspicion threw me into a quandary. The right thing to do was call the police, but with all the drugs around I realized the blame would stop right at my doorstep, given my own run-ins with the law in my youth.

As if reading my mind, she said, "Don't involve the cops in this."

"Why not?"

"You argued with him earlier. You left the window open. People heard you."

"That was nothing." I looked around. "Are you alone here? Where's Colin Reed?"

She turned the corners of her lips down in a mock smile. "Reed left a while ago. He was only interested in one thing and took off when I made it clear I wouldn't play. Men can be so disappointing." She said this flippantly, as if making a joke of it. "I wasted my time with him when I could have spent it with you." She picked up Hal's plastic bag and shoved it into her pocket. Her hand returned to my arm. "Look, it's unfortunate what happened to Hal. But we can do a deal. There's loads of money in it."

"What the hell are you talking about?"

She moved closer and the pressure on my arm increased. "John, it's a stolen artifact. I know that. No big deal. Surely you don't think I'm with the Feds or something?"

I stepped away and shook off her hand. "Frankly, I don't care whether you're with the FBI or Fort Knox."

The moth I'd seen earlier reappeared, fluttering near the oil lamp. Eris stretched out her hand and flicked it toward the flame. I heard a sizzle. The moth flipped around erratically, straining to fly with burnt wings, then dropped onto the lamp base.

"This is getting tiresome," she said. "Do I have to spell it out? What I'm telling you is we assisted with Hal's injection. Don't make the same bad decision he did."

"Are you crazy? Do you have any idea how stupid that was? You killed him. He'd already taken enough. I saw him shoot up the first time."

"He chose to be stubborn. He asked for it."

"What are you talking about?"

Her overly sweet tone disappeared. "Look, we know you're involved. Hal called you back here for a reason. Just tell me where it is."

My mind raced. None of this was making sense. She was either delusional or up to something truly vicious. Either way I wanted no part of it. The whole thing was spinning out of control. All I wanted to do was get out of there. I doubted she had the muscle to tackle me, and I couldn't see a weapon. I heard a sound and hoped someone else might be coming. Her glance darted to the shadowy brush at the end of the garden. A figure loomed. I glimpsed an enormous man stepping onto the flagstones. Eris smiled. This was no savior. I might be able to handle one of them. Two, no way.

An old lattice fence separated the Vanderlins' from the place next door. Through the gaps in the slats the dog growled furiously, using its teeth and paws to tear away at the rotted wood. It began to splinter.

Eris turned her head, her eyes widening in fear. She opened her mouth, revealing small, perfectly spaced white teeth, and flicked a pink tongue over her lips.

The bottom of the fence cracked. Through the hole the face and slathering jaws of a bull mastiff appeared. Eris leapt away, afraid the powerful dog would push through and attack. Lights blinked on next door. A guy's voice shouted out, "What in God's name is going on over there?" A siren wailed in the distance.

I took the opening Eris offered and whipped Hal's cellphone at her, jagged end forward, and ran through the open sliding glass doors. *Don't look back. Get out. Just get out.* I blew through the house and out the front door, got my vehicle moving before I even shut the car door. Ahead I could see police cruisers fighting their way through the intersection at Eighth Avenue.

I sped off. If the police caught me now they'd think I was running from a murder.

Four

I drove around aimlessly, checking the rear-view mirror constantly to make sure I wasn't being followed. My thoughts came in frantic scrambles. What in the hell was going on? Was Eris high on something? Did she really kill Hal? She was after some kind of artifact. The thing Hal told me about earlier? Had he called me back to help him, or to involve me in some scheme?

I checked the mirror again. Was that silver Range Rover tailing me? Could she have moved that fast? I don't know why I picked that car out; any one of them could have me in their sights. I pulled a risky U-turn and sped past the silver SUV. My body quaked and I jerked the steering wheel. Thanks only to the vigilance of the driver beside me, we avoided a crash. He leaned on his horn in justifiable rage. Add an accident to tonight's events and I'd wind up in a monumental shitload of trouble.

My state of mind was such that I hadn't been paying any attention to where I was actually headed and now I realized I'd ended up in Murray Hill. I scanned the cars behind me again. No sign of the silver one. I turned onto a side street and slid into a vacant spot just before realizing I was ahead of a patrol car. It took a slow roll past me and braked. The cop on the passenger side gave me the evil eye. He'd sensed my panic. I was finished. But to my surprise they lingered for only half a minute before speeding down the street. I rested my head on the steering wheel, the shock of the night's events closing around me like a vise.

I needed somewhere to cool down and think. Going home wasn't an option. Not yet, anyway. Eris had my business card with my address. The only other place I could conjure up was my favorite club, which had the benefit of being right across the street from my condo. I could keep an eye out for any sign of Eris.

I turned the car around and headed for Kenny's Castaways.

The building housing Kenny's had been a bar since the early 1800s. By the 1890s the *Herald* had anointed it "the wickedest place in New York." In more recent times, Irishman Pat Kenny bought the place and made it famous. Its legendary bands taught me my first lessons about great music. On one long-ago summer night I'd leaned against the rails of the balcony of our condo like a sailor transfixed by a Siren, drawn by the sound spilling out the open doors. Only eight at the time, I'd stayed there for hours until Samuel insisted I go to bed.

My love affair with the place and the songs had never ended.

Kenny's was subdued. The band was on their last set, close to packing up and heading out the door. A few people lingered near the stage nursing their drafts. I slid onto a stool, my usual spot at the end of the bar.

Diane Chen, the bartender, had short spiky hair in two shades of purple and wore makeup that made her already pale skin ghostly. She once told me she regularly waxed her eyebrows and drew them back in with black pencil. Under her long black lashes, her eyeliner had been tattooed on. A diamond stud punctuated her bottom lip, and one earlobe sported a row of tiny silver rings. Like many restaurant staff, she used her bartending income to anchor her acting career. With all those earrings, I thought, costume changes must be hell.

She waved when she saw me and walked to the front door, looking out before returning. My hands still shook. I pushed them onto my lap so she wouldn't notice.

"What's up with checking out the front door?"

"The restaurant stalker's been around again. We're trying to avoid him."

She saw the question in my eyes.

"It's this guy. He's got a regular beat and this week he's on Bleecker. He'll walk into a bar or restaurant, stand in the middle of the room, and stare. It makes the patrons jumpy. If we hand him a five he'll leave. Not a bad stunt, really. Better than parking yourself on a sidewalk with your hand out."

That brought a smile to my lips and she gave me one back.

"Hey, John. I've missed you around here. I was so sorry to hear about your accident. Did you get my card?"

Since the crash, I'd lost the will to do anything; that included opening my mail. I thanked her for the card.

"I tried to call you too but just got voice mail."

"I've been out of commission for a while. For over six weeks." The misery of the accident flooded back. "They had to cut me out of the car. My ribs got cracked up and an artery tore. The blood loss kept me in hospital so long I even missed Samuel's funeral. But I'm on the mend now."

She let out a sigh. "That's just awful. How did it happen?"

"I totally blank out when I try to picture it. I remember picking Samuel up from JFK. He'd just flown in from Jordan. We were on the Belt Parkway, the racetrack up ahead. A pickup behind us kept crowding my car, bothering the heck out of me, but when I slowed down to let it pass it wouldn't take the offer. That's my last recollection."

Only a partial truth, but I couldn't bear to tell her the rest of it. The airbag had blocked out my sight but I retained an auditory memory—the raw terror in Samuel's voice. The man who'd never raised his voice to me was screaming. I'd ignored the cutting pain in my chest, clutched at my seat belt to free myself so I could help him, and almost succeeded before I passed out.

Diane reached for my hand and gave it a squeeze. "Maybe it's a blessing you can't remember. Your brain's protecting you from a memory that's too frightening. You must miss Samuel terribly."

"I don't think I'll ever get over it, Diane."

How could I describe the black hole I'd fallen into since his death? I didn't have the words. My mind kept shifting back to the early years. His work meant long absences. There was always this sense of waiting, the way you feel in March yearning for winter to end. When our housekeeper, Evelyn, got word that Samuel was coming home, the whole atmosphere would change. I could still see her face lighting up, a slight flush to her cheeks. She'd bustle around, cleaning stuff that didn't need it, I'd go to the barber, she'd polish all the shoes and even try to bake. When the day arrived Samuel would come through the door, arms filled with boxes of gifts. Exotic things. Turkish candies; sand bottles; mosaics; Roman-glass earrings for Evelyn, handmade in Israel.

I cleared my throat to hide the fact my voice was breaking. "I keep expecting to see him again. Even though I know I never will."

She reached for a napkin and handed it to me.

"What's that for?"

"Your eyes."

Unaware that tears had begun to form, I touched my eyes and felt the wetness.

"Can I get you anything? You look totaled."

"A bottle of whiskey. Don't bother with a glass."

She laughed. "I see you've had a good night."

"You have no idea."

She poured me a double Scotch and disappeared through the door at the end of the bar. I threw the drink back and got up to check the street. From the front window I could just make out our lobby entrance. No sign of Eris or her strange companion.

It didn't take long for the caress of the alcohol to numb my nerves. I began to calm down, comforted by the familiar surroundings. I'd always loved the eclectic feel of Kenny's. Kind of like a tired speakeasy— tomato-red walls, dark wainscoting, a wagon-wheel chandelier hanging from the stamped-tin ceiling. The wall behind the bar was festooned with mirrors, beer steins, old swords and revolvers, and a massive rack of antlers in the center, dusty fedoras hanging from the tips.

Facing me was a great photo of the Boss, and under that a write-up from *Crawdaddy!* magazine:

Bruce Springsteen was headlining and there weren't a dozen people who knew who he was. Outside on the hand-drawn marquee, they'd misspelled his name. But when he began to sing it was like the ocean had calmed out and

you knew the storm was brewing by the way
it prickled your skin.

Diane slid onto her stool behind the bar, breaking
through my reverie. Under her arm she carried a
rectangular brown box. She set the box on top of the
bar and lifted the lid.

"What's this?"

"Don't you remember? You mentioned it once
when we were talking about your work. A friend of
mine bought it for me at the British Museum when
she was in London. I brought it out to take your mind
off your troubles."

When she took out the playing board, I recognized it immediately. A reproduction of the Royal
Game of Ur, the oldest-known board game. The
British Museum had a rare original, one of two found
by Sir Leonard Woolley in the 1920s at his dig in the
ancient Sumerian city of Ur.

Diane put a finger to her lips. Her long nails were
painted purplish black, each with a different zodiac
sign detailed in white. "They think the game is a
forerunner of backgammon."

"I know that, Diane. Listen, I'm not in a game-
playing mood tonight. I've got a lot on my mind."

As she shifted in her seat, the little silver hoops
and charms lining her ear jingled. "If you want to get
over your troubles you need to focus your mind on
something else. Give your emotions a rest. Anyway, I
wasn't going to suggest we play the game. After I got

it I found out it was also used for prophecy. You didn't know that, I'll bet."

"You're into telling fortunes?"

"Just a hobby. It's my new thing." Diane smiled with a glint in her eyes. "Why don't you give it a try? Another friend of mine had a run of bad luck recently. I told her fortune and everything turned around for her."

"I'm too superstitious."

"Not to worry." She took out seven red playing pieces, each about the size of a penny, and handed them to me. She set three odd-looking dice shaped like pyramids on the bar. "Sumerians treated divination as a science. They'd look for celestial omens, examine animal livers, or interpret patterns that oil made on water."

"I know."

"Your future's not fixed," she continued. "The

The Royal Game of Ur

fortune only suggests a direction, or warns about certain people or behaviors to avoid."

I was on the point of telling her to forget it when I realized I'd need a major favor from her, so I decided to go along with what she wanted.

"We'll just do a short version because it's late."

"How did you figure out the rules? No one has ever found them for the game."

"Trust me." She gave me a lopsided smile and pushed the little pyramids toward me.

I shook them and let them spill onto the bar.

Diane leaned over and peered at the dice. "Okay, move four spaces."

I took one of the playing pieces and placed it on the first space in the second row of three squares.

"You're one short of landing on a rosette."

"Is that bad?"

"You could say so. It's a penalty space. It means to expect a secret communication; the news won't be good."

"Well, that's appropriate for tonight." I picked up the dice and threw them again.

Her face blanched.

"What is it? I thought you said there were no good or bad choices."

"You threw six. You've missed another rosette and landed again on the eyes. One of the worst spaces."

"What's wrong with it?"

"It foretells betrayal and violent death."

This gave me a jolt and for a minute words

deserted me. Fortune-telling is a con, but coming after a day that had turned into a nightmare it didn't take much to unsettle me.

"There is hope," Diane said quickly. "The talisman of Sol is also associated with the space. Only the sign of the sun can save you."

"From what?"

"It protects you from murder."

This was getting bizarre. Surely she couldn't know about Hal.

My expression must have betrayed my thoughts because she added, "I'm not making this up, if that's what you think."

I cast around for something to say: "So ... why choose Sol? He's a Roman god, not Mesopotamian."

Diane seemed a bit miffed by my skepticism. "Sometimes you have to improvise."

On the next throw one of the dice fell onto the floor on her side of the counter.

"That won't count." She bent down to pick it up. "I'm curious whether the love sign will turn up. Let's see what it would have foretold. Together with the other die you'd have moved three more spaces. That position is kind of interesting. It would have meant 'happiness follows sorrow.' Kind of oblique. I'm not sure how to read it." She leaned forward, resting her elbows on the counter. "It's been a long time since I've seen you in here with anyone special."

"I go out on dates and everything seems good, but they don't call me back."

She rolled her eyes. "Give me a break. You're the one who doesn't call back. The last time you were in, two women actually offered me money to get your phone number, going on about how hot you were. So good-looking, they kept saying. It got totally boring having to listen to them. Then they bet which one would go home with you. It's those dark eyes of yours. And your beard, I guess. It gives you kind of a European look."

"So who did?"

"Go home with you? You can't even remember, can you?" She shook her head and smiled flirtatiously.

Under ordinary circumstances I'd have thought about pursuing her. Tonight I could barely keep my act together. "Diane, I really appreciate the compliment but I'm stretched too thin right now. I don't have the energy for this." I gathered up the dice and playing pieces and put them back in the box.

"Fine." She flattened her hands and pushed herself away in a huff. "Lighten up. You're not helping yourself by taking everything so seriously."

For a goth, this seemed an overreaction. She ignored me and got busy tidying up the drink glasses, wiping down the bar, and adding up the evening's take. Every time she bent over, her hip-huggers slipped down far enough to reveal the crease at the rise of her buttocks.

Her remark about the beard was flattering. I kept it cropped close to my face and it did fit my professional image, but I'd grown it for an entirely different reason. To hide the firebrand birthmark on my jaw. A source of extreme embarrassment throughout my teens, shaped like a rough letter Q, it stood out on my face like an ugly scar.

It was 4 A.M. by the time the waiter, Stan, set the locks and left and Diane finished her tasks. From the doorway I gave the street another scan, trying to decide whether it was safe to go home. At the intersection of Thompson and Bleecker, I saw a silver Range Rover stopped at the curb. Could that be Eris?

I decided not to take the chance and offered to walk Diane to the Chase Bank on Broadway to make the night deposit. Over the last couple of hours the temperature had soared. People still roamed the streets, refugees from cramped apartments with no air conditioning. A guy stood with his back pressed against a store window, holding five pet rats on his forearm, two white, two brown, and one pinto. Their long, pink, naked tails dangled below his arm and twitched when he stroked them. His baseball cap sat upturned on the sidewalk.

"He's always here at night," Diane said. "He clears out in the morning because a hot dog vendor has a permit for this spot. People give him money to pet the rats."

She put the brown envelope with the take from the till in the bank's night deposit box and closed the drawer. I took her arm gently. I needed to ask her for the favor before she left.

"Diane, I'm wondering if you could help me out with something."

"Sure, what?"

"I ran into a problem tonight. I had nothing to do with what went down, but I want to stay out of it. If anyone asks, could you say I showed up at Kenny's around midnight?"

"If anyone *asks*? Like who? The police?"

"It's possible."

"You swear you weren't involved in this ... problem?"

"I swear. Chances are no one will ask you anything anyway."

"I guess it's okay."

"What about Stan?"

"Not to worry, he's cool."

"That's good," I said. "Hey Diane, thanks a lot."

She flagged a cab and climbed in, blowing me a kiss as it drove off.

I lingered at the corner of Broadway and Bleecker, then I began walking the block to my building, and seeing club-goers still milling around, decided to take the risk. The doorman, Amir, on overnight duty this week, trotted over the minute I stepped into the lobby. "John! Did you leave town or something? It's been ages since I've seen you."

"I've been keeping my head down since the accident."

He lowered his voice. "So terrible about your brother. A wonderful man."

"He was. It's hard for me to believe he's gone. Amir, has anyone been around tonight asking about me?"

"A lady came to see you. She waited and waited. She must have asked me to call you a dozen times. I finally agreed to help her upstairs so she could knock on your door."

"You what?"

Amir held up his hands, palms facing out. "What else could I do? She was frantic. She said she'd been trying to get hold of you for weeks."

"She can be very persuasive, Amir. That was just an act. If you ever see her again, get her out of here. Don't let her anywhere near me."

"All right," he said, obviously hurt that he'd gone overboard to be courteous to someone he thought was a friend of mine. "She was in a wheelchair. What else did you expect me to do?"

"A wheelchair? What did she look like?"

"Older. Dressed in black. A black jacket and long dress. Too hot for this kind of weather. One of those wheelchair-accessible vans dropped her off at the front door."

He hadn't been talking about Eris after all but rather Evelyn, our former housekeeper.

"Sorry, Amir. I'm dead tired and misunderstood you. It would have been fine to bring Evelyn upstairs. Did she leave a message?"

"When you didn't answer she gave up and left."

I described Eris and asked him to call me immediately if he spotted her. Amir couldn't leave his desk, so we woke the superintendent and asked him to accompany me upstairs. I wanted to make sure no more surprises awaited me.

I did find something, though not the kind of surprise I'd feared. Inside I picked up a note that had been slipped under the door, a parchment-colored paper folded in half with my name scrawled on the front. It looked like something torn off a notepad. Security around here was about as reliable as a bent rifle.

> Please meet me at the Khyber Pass Restaurant tomorrow at 6 P.M. I need to talk to you about Samuel—urgently.

It was signed by a Tomas S. Zakar. Zakar? The name sounded familiar. One of Samuel's assistants in Iraq. I'd never met him, but my brother had mentioned him often enough. An Iraqi and a cultural anthropologist. "A very bright young man," Samuel had said, "a tireless worker."

I went into the living room and flipped through our photo albums. In his meticulous fashion, Samuel had labeled every picture, and I soon found some images shot at one of his sites. Several of these showed Zakar: measuring an artifact, kneeling by a trench alongside Samuel, the two of them raising a glass at day's end in their tent.

Was it a coincidence the guy had shown up on the same night Hal died? I decided to accept his invitation, hoping he could shed some light on this mess.

The adrenalin boosting me throughout the night suddenly abandoned me. A profound weariness descended. I knew I couldn't push myself any further. I lay on my bed and sank into the blessed oblivion of sleep.

Five

Sunday, August 3, 2003, 9 A.M.

The next morning I awoke with a ravenous appetite and the realization that I needed to talk to both my lawyer and the police. I'd panicked last night and would have to make up for that. I left an urgent message with my lawyer, Andy Stein, asking him to call me back first thing Monday morning.

Nothing showed up on News One, but the *Times* had devoted a couple of column inches to Hal. I couldn't find any mention of Eris or her strange companion. The item quoted a Tenth Precinct detective, Paul Gentile, who said foul play wasn't suspected. Code for when victims offed themselves. Normally, drug accidents like this wouldn't merit any coverage, but when a rich person ODs, it makes the news.

It took me three calls to locate Paul Gentile's office, only to be told he wouldn't show up for a few hours. I made an appointment to see him at noon.

I showered and put on a summer-weight Prada shirt and jacket, and pants I'd had custom-made on my last trip to Milan. Might as well look presentable for the gendarmes. I perked a pot of coffee, got cereal and milk and ate a huge bowl. The towering backlog of mail piled up on my kitchen counter threatened to topple over. I hadn't had the stomach to deal with even run-of-the-mill stuff since the accident. I pawed through it as I ate. Bills, more bills, cards of condolence. I found Diane's handmade card in the pile.

The bills reminded me I'd done nothing about Samuel's estate. That sad task was still before me. An envelope from a company I'd never heard of, Teras Distributing, showed up halfway through the pile, emblazoned with SECOND NOTICE JUNE 25TH in red type across the top. It confirmed that goods belonging to Samuel had been shipped to their New York warehouse through diplomatic courier. The package was being held in secure storage, waiting to be picked up.

After calling the number on the form, I told the man who answered that I was Samuel Diakos and gave him the claim number. He asked me to wait. When he came back on the line he said the package had already been picked up.

"Who signed for it?"

"You did." He paused. "Sir?"

I hung up to the sound of the pennies dropping.

I knew what Hal had done. He'd never returned my house keys when he stayed at my place after his mother died. He'd said at the time he needed to get away because he couldn't stand all the reminders of her. I was going to be out of town anyway and took pity on him. He must have come in while I was in the hospital, searched through my mail, and found the first warehouse notice.

Samuel kept a duplicate set of ID in his study since a theft in his Beirut hotel room four years ago. It took me a few minutes to get up the nerve to enter his rooms. Once inside I yanked open his desk drawer. He kept his ID in a vinyl case, closed with a red rubber band. The rubber band was gone. Hal's misstep told the tale. The object he'd stolen had belonged to Samuel. That explained the how, who, and approximately when. The why was simple. He needed the money.

Samuel had been like a kind uncle to Hal. Knowing how much it hurt when Hal's own father mistreated him, my brother went out of his way to bridge the gap—remembering Hal's birthday, bringing him along to the theater or on treks to museums. At times I'd felt jealous about having to share my brother's attention with Hal. And this was how the bastard repaid us!

The knowledge of Hal's theft plunged me into another black mood. A sharp reminder of how in such a short time I'd lost so much. Samuel's study had the silent air of a place shut up and abandoned.

I caught the faint whiff of tobacco from the rack of pipes on the shelf. His absence felt like a tangible force in the room. When I replaced his ID my eye caught the framed watercolor sitting on his desk, the only possession left from his family home in Greece. His mother, who'd died when the Nazis torched their village, had painted it quite skillfully. She'd given it to a local man to repair the frame, and his work shed had escaped the flames. When Samuel returned for a visit, years after the war ended, he got the painting back.

I wanted to turn the clock back to the time before the accident, to hear Samuel come in the front door the way he used to, a *Times* folded beneath his arm, carrying breakfast and a couple of lattes. We'd alternate every Sunday. One week he'd make the trek to Katz's and bring home salami and square potato knishes. The next, it would be my turn to go to Murray's for fresh bagels and Nova Scotia lox.

Samuel had relished those trips to Katz's, and not just because of the food. It gave him a reason to walk the Lower East Side, the first place he'd landed when a family sponsored him to come to America after the war. He loved the old red-brick tenements, now rapidly giving way to condo conversions, the streets wall to wall with discount stores, a spaghetti tangle of wires overhead.

I wished the thoughts away. For the first time in my life I wanted to be just like everyone else. To take the subway to a boring job. Sweat to make mortgage payments. Have a couple of beers with friends after work. To be anyone but me.

My brother could always be counted on to be my anchor in the tempests swirling through my life. I summoned up his image: small in stature, fit from decades of coping with the demanding terrain of his profession, his skin weather-beaten, his eyes almost always carrying a hint of good humor. He was cautious and punctual, with a razor-sharp memory. The antithesis of the absentminded academic.

I recalled some of those long-ago summer evenings at home. Samuel would smoke his pipe and I'd play happily with my train cars, using the iron grid of the balcony for tracks. Friends told me my penchant for acting out came from lacking a father figure. Samuel was simply away too much to fill those shoes. But lately I'd come to a different conclusion. In my eyes he'd always been close to a god. And you can't compete with that. I thought I knew what it must be like to have a celebrity for a father, a mega rock star or a sports hero. The light their sons shed on the world would always be a dim bulb in contrast.

In my younger years, the word *saint* popped up on a regular basis. "Your brother's a saint for taking you on, you know," people would say. "You're family, of course, but he didn't have to." One of my private school headmasters once said, "I'm giving you a second chance out of respect for your brother. That man must have the patience of a saint."

Now that I was older, thinking more clearly

and not acting according to the impetuous appeal of the moment, I had to face up to my talent for self-destruction. Samuel always gave me the benefit of the doubt. "That's your way," he'd say after mopping up one of my calamities. "You're young; you haven't found your path in life. You have a brave disposition, John. I often wish I were more like you."

That Samuel had died because of my actions was something I could confront only in brief moments. Had someone sideswiped my car, or was that just a trick played by my imagination, some fantasy I'd made up? I was unable to admit fault to the rest of the world. Let the pain eat a hole in my heart. I deserved no better.

I gave myself a mental shake and tried to concentrate on the new problem. What was the missing object? It could only have come from Iraq. The last time I'd spoken to Samuel he told me stolen pieces were being recovered. So if Samuel had taken something temporarily to protect it from looters, why hadn't he just given it back? It wasn't the famous Sumerian Uruk vase. That had been dropped off at the museum by three men in a car. The vase had been broken in fourteen pieces but was salvageable—it was well known in the trade that thieves would break an object and mail it to Europe or the States a few pieces at a time, reassembling it once they'd all been sent. Nor was it the Lyre of Ur. That had been ruined in the looting although its famous golden calf's head attached to the sounding board had been removed for safekeeping beforehand.

For Samuel to take the huge risk of bringing a relic over here suggested that it was a very valuable piece indeed. Mesopotamian artifacts could range in value from thousands to many millions of dollars, depending on their condition and inscriptions. Though the looting was over, for some reason this object must still have been under threat. Otherwise, Samuel would have returned it. Through a process of elimination, I thought I could narrow down the possibilities, but at least fifteen major objects and close to ten thousand small ones—cylinder seals, jewelry, and figurines—were still missing. The precious Lion of Nimrud, an 850 B.C. ivory relief, was gone, along with an exquisite copper head of the Roman goddess of Victory found in the Parthian ruins at the Hatra site. Had he rescued either of those?

In one of our last phone calls before he came home, Samuel told me about the devastation at the museum. "It could have been worse," he'd said. "Mercifully, the museum staff had the foresight to empty several galleries and conceal hundreds of objects beforehand. The American investigation team that went in afterward was brilliant. They devised a 'no questions asked' return policy and spent a lot of time publicizing it in the markets and mosques. This got really good results, but they paled in comparison to the scope of the loss."

So if the staff had hidden many of the important objects, why did Samuel feel the need to take one of them? Until I had more information, I couldn't sort out my brother's motive. When we'd talked about the museum looting he'd broken down and cried on the phone. Sacrificing his values to keep a stolen object must have torn him apart.

The phone rang. My landline. Few people had that number, and fewer people used it.

"John Madison here."

"John, it's Andy Stein. How're you doing?"

"Well, things have certainly been piling up. I appreciate your calling me on a Sunday, Andy."

"No problem. Listen, you know I'm commercial; I can't help you with your … matter, but I've been in touch with a criminal attorney. Joseph Reznick. He's one of the best. I briefed him about your situation. You should talk to him—soon."

"Sure. How can I reach him?" I scribbled down the guy's number and email address while Andy spoke.

"Oh, and one more thing. He's not cheap."

"What are we talking about here?"

"I couldn't guess. It's not a straightforward situation, is it? He'll want a retainer for a start."

"So what do you think that would run?"

"A couple of thou at least."

I had five credit cards. Only one had any space left, and not much at that. Where the money would come from was anyone's guess. My job was feast or famine, and right now I was on the brink of starvation. In the past Samuel had always been good to tide me over, but that option was lost to me until his estate was settled.

"Do you have any idea how long it will take to get Samuel's estate cleared up?"

"Under these circumstances? If there's culpability over the accident, it's unclear. I don't do estates, but you could be waiting for a long time."

The intercom buzzed as I hung up. Amir, calling to say that an envelope had just been couriered to me and he'd bring it up.

"I'm surprised you're still here," I said when I opened the door.

Amir looked wiped out. "The day man came really late so I had no choice. I wanted to get this to you before I left." He handed me a plain white business envelope with my name and address typed on it.

"Who brought this?"

"A bike courier. I'm really sorry, but he took off so fast I couldn't ask him to sign for it."

I thanked Amir and he left. Inside the envelope I found a USB flash drive enclosed in bubble wrap. No indication of who'd sent it. I got my laptop booted up and inserted the device. A page opened up on the screen.

John, greetings.

Consider this a treasure map of sorts. I've entrusted my law firm to send this to you should anything happen to me.

By now you probably know I acquired an object of great value, a seventh-century B.C. Neo-Assyrian stone tablet engraved in cuneiform. A famous biblical prophecy, as it turns out. I employ the word "acquire" with some latitude. In fact, it belonged to Samuel.

To my way of thinking, you didn't deserve it.

I set out to sell it and reap the rewards. Upon receiving a promising inquiry, I commenced negotiations. The prospect of so much money clouded my judgment. Carelessly, I disclosed my identity. I now know my knowledge of the object's existence has condemned me.

When I first became aware of the danger, I designed this little game. Solve the four puzzles in order, and you'll find the engraving.

You might well ask, why the change of heart? Wouldn't you be the last person I'd choose for a beneficiary? Put it down to my quixotic nature, I suppose. Each time you face one of my puzzles, if you listen hard, you'll hear me laughing at you from beyond the grave.

Your opponents in this game are clever. I can feel them closing in on me now. There are five of them, and I dread to think they'll win. My only solace is knowing the same fate awaits you.

Will you learn who they are in time? On the slim chance you do succeed, will greed take over, or will you do the right thing and return the engraving? My guess is you have no finer instincts and will choose the path that directly benefits you.

Feel free to prove me wrong ...

Hal

I gaped at the screen. Score one for Diane Chen. Here was the secret message.

Hal's deceit had run much deeper than I'd thought. This wasn't about Samuel at all. Hal had targeted me. Believing himself in danger, he'd purposely sent his enemies after me, actually getting off on the prospect. I hated being manipulated like this.

The faint hope crossed my mind that he'd fallen victim to a hoax. But he'd been killed for it so his foes must have believed the object was genuine. How pathetic, wasting the last few days of his life to set such an evil trap for me.

People always think the grass is greener on the other side of the fence. Hal had envied me. He'd never known how lonely I felt when Samuel was away at work for such long stretches of time. A cerebral, self-effacing boy, he'd been no match for his father. Peter had wanted an alpha male and got instead a shy, introverted boy. After one particular cringe-inducing put-down by his father, Hal had turned on me. "He said he wished you were his son instead of a pathetic kid like me." His resentment had simmered all these years.

Hal was exacting a heavy price for that now.

When I looked at the screen again, the letter had faded away and a new page came up displaying the first step in Hal's game.

I liked games, but my natural impatience didn't allow for good strategy, and I hated losing. It was Hal who'd loved the intrigue, the battle of wits. So he'd know that right off the bat he had me at a disadvantage. I grew more annoyed and angry the longer I studied it.

Crossword grid (filled letters, reading left to right by row):

```
I     C
F  O  R     K  A  B  B  A  L  I  S  M
      O           L           I     E
C     W  E        L           F  O  E  S
R  I  N  G  S     C  A  P  E  R     E
Y     S  O  P     K     I     E     V
P           A philosophy  C              E
T           M  U  T  A  T  I  O  N
O           E     T     D     N
G  O  L  D        R  O  O  T
R              W     I     L  O  W
A  B  O  V  E     H  E  X     I
P  E  N        I        L  O  S  T
H     Y        T  A  S  E  R     C
S  E  X  Y  H  E  R     A     H
      E        S     O  D  E  S
Q  U  E  S  T           U
      O     A  L  C  H  E  M  Y
```

Fill in the thirteen squares

[thirteen blank boxes]

This was another throwback to our childhood. We couldn't just play hide-and-seek like ordinary kids. Hal would insist on devising intricate games—games where he knew he'd have the upper hand. He'd once worked all morning setting up a scavenger hunt. The trail led up to his attic, where he promised a twenty-dollar bill was waiting if I could read the clues. There was no money in the end, only the desiccated body of a dead mouse. Hal had laughed uproariously when I found it.

After studying the puzzle for a few moments, I realized I wouldn't be able to solve it easily and turned my attention to the actual artifact. Hal's description gave me next to nothing to go on, but it was worth doing a search to see if I could find any references online. Interpol's database of stolen art, the Art Loss Register, and the FBI's Art Theft Program were all tools of the art trade. I knew one dealer with a bad rep who regularly checked these sources to gauge how hot an object was before he'd touch it. If it was listed, he'd triple his commission.

Nothing on Interpol remotely described a missing Neo-Assyrian engraving. This came as no great surprise because with the Baghdad Museum records burned, it would take some time, even for the top police agencies, to document all the missing objects. The FBI listed some of the most prominent stolen pieces. As I expected, the ivory plaque of a lion killing a nubian, a stunning work of art, was listed among the top ten missing works, but I found no reference to the engraving here either. I had higher hopes for the Art Loss Register because I knew it documented at least 200,000 objects, antiquities, and collectibles. But combing the site again brought up nothing resembling the piece I sought.

Glancing at my watch, I realized I'd have to leave for my appointment with the detective. Should I bring the letter to show him? I had no proof it had come from Hal and I could have made the whole thing up. I settled for printing off a copy of the puzzle and stuck it in my pants pocket, thinking I could play around with it if my meeting was delayed. I downloaded Hal's file to my BlackBerry and got a new envelope for the flash drive, scribbling my name on it.

That left one more urgent task.

Nina, who owned the condo across the hall, often looked after our place, watering the plants and checking the air conditioning while Samuel and I were away. I assumed she'd still be at home on a Sunday morning.

A quizzical smile crossed her face when I asked her to hold on to the envelope for me. Not the best solution, but all I had time for at the moment. She pressed the paper. "It's not your stash or anything, is it? I don't think you'd trust me with that." She gave the envelope a gentle shake. "I'll peek, you know."

"It's stolen jewelry. Twenty-carat diamonds. They're worth a fortune."

"Oh, no problem then." She laughed and promised to keep it safe. "You haven't forgotten about tonight, have you?"

I looked at her blankly. "Sorry, Nina, it's been a rough twenty-four hours. Remind me again?"

"My party. You've been stuck in that place of yours for way too long. It'll do you good to be social again."

"Oh, right. I'm not sure I can. Something's come up. But I'll try my best." I thanked her and walked to the elevator.

✸

After waiting for close to an hour at the Tenth Precinct station, I was finally summoned by a uniformed cop, who took me down the hallway to a clerk's desk. No sign of Detective Gentile. The cop checked my pockets and waved a wand over my body. When the clerk started asking questions to update my old file, I protested.

"Gentile ordered it," was all she said in reply. She shot another photo and confirmed the color of my eyes, my height and weight. I pointed out that my eyes hadn't changed color in the last fourteen years, and told her a woman had once said they were like dark velvet.

The clerk frowned and looked over the top of her glasses. Bending her head again, she wrote down "brown."

"You look better with the beard, though," she said. "On your driver's license, your name is spelled Madak; on your Visa card it's Madison. Why the difference?"

"Legally, it's the one on the license. It's Turkish. My brother changed it to Madison when I came to America."

"Named you after an American president, did he?" She hunched her shoulders up to her ears and let them drop. I wasn't sure whether this was a tension reliever or a gesture to show she needed more clarification. "So the correct version is on your license?"

"That's right."

"Your given name is Jonathan?"

"Yes."

"What about the second name? K-E-N-I-T-E. Is that right, too?"

"Yes. Actually that's supposed to be my Turkish given name. It's pronounced Ken-it-ee."

"If I were your mother I would have stuck to Ken." She chortled as if this were the most brilliant joke ever.

I let it pass.

The uniformed cop, Vernon, steered me to an interview room furnished with an ancient metal table and chairs, white walls the color of old eggshells, and cheap gray carpeting. The room was freezing, with the air conditioning jacked up, and smelled faintly of cigarette smoke. I guessed this place was a law unto itself, like the Vatican or something.

Vernon left the room, secured the door, and leaned against it. Through the textured glass I could see the wavy blur of his shirt. I was able to make out people passing by and hear them exchange a few words. Among other things, I learned Detective Paul Gentile's nickname was Genitalia—and it didn't have a positive connotation.

Coming here had turned out to be a miscalculation. So much for good intentions. Were they going to try to pin Hal's death on me somehow? I spent the rest of the time rehearsing the story I wanted to give them, making sure there were no rough edges to it or inconsistencies. I wanted to get the message across about Eris and her brute without admitting I'd left the scene.

When the door finally clicked open, in walked the inquisitors—two men. Vernon nodded a greeting to the first man, "Lieutenant Gentile," and shut the door, propping himself up against it, this time inside the room. Gentile and the other man took seats across from me, plunking their file folders down.

Gentile fumbled with the switches of the auto cam and turned it on, then announced the time, date, and the interview participants. The second man was Louis Peres, another detective.

In an earlier life Gentile could have played defense for pro football. Maybe his suit jacket was too small, but his muscles bulged and strained against the pinstripes. His cheeks were pockmarked, his hair cropped close to the head and stone white. He wore a Rolex Cellini Classic and a silver ring on his baby finger. He looked to be pushing sixty. Old for a cop. Gentile locked his gaze on me; Peres flipped through the material in his file without bothering to acknowledge my presence.

A female civilian clerk entered with a pitcher full of ice water and some glasses. She set the glasses in front of the detectives, put the pitcher on the table, and left.

"Okay," Gentile said. "Let's get started. Tell us what happened." He lifted his eyebrows, stared at me, and jutted out his chin like a wrestler setting me up for the first chokehold.

"Before we get into that, I came here voluntarily. Why are you treating me like a criminal?"

"We're just trying to get the facts here, Mr. Madison. A man is dead. Let's hear what you have to say."

His attitude didn't fill me with confidence. "All right. I came because someone deliberately shot Hal full of high-grade heroin, a woman I met at Hal's party. I heard her and another guy arguing with him as I was leaving the party."

"Oh? What time would that have been?"

"Around midnight. I went straight to a club. You can check on that if you want."

I knew Diane would back me up, and the time frames should easily rule me out for the murder. I gave him the name of the club and told him how to reach Diane. Gentile scribbled something down on a piece of notepaper and handed it to Peres, who left the room. I prayed Diane had already made it in to work.

Gentile continued, "So, can you identify these people?"

"The woman's name was Eris; I don't know her last name. Attractive, late twenties, fit, probably around five seven. The guy with her was pushing seven feet and heavyset."

Gentile ran a hand over his forehead. Even though the room was cold he was sweating. His face was the color of raw beef. "Colin Reed talked about a woman like that. Claimed she left the party before he did."

Of course, Reed, a married man, would say that

rather than admit he wanted to ball her. "If she left, she must have returned later. I saw her there."

More scribbles on Gentile's notepad, but I could tell he wasn't buying my story. "Are you back in business again? How did Vanderlin obtain his drugs?"

"Check that file you have. You know I was never involved with opiates."

Gentile made a pretense of opening the folder, a bullshit move because he'd have reviewed the whole thing before he even walked in here. He flipped through several pages. "Convicted for fourth-degree grand larceny, 1989, selling marijuana. In 1990, charged with third-degree criminal sale of a controlled substance, twenty-two grams of cocaine. You managed to weasel out of that one. Maybe this time you've just graduated."

"That was my wild youth. I was still a kid. I turned the corner on all that long ago. Anyway, those amounts are nothing."

"What was your relationship with Vanderlin?"

I could have answered this easily twenty-four hours ago. The friendship had certainly been rocky at times, but I'd discovered depths of bitterness in Hal's feelings about me I'd never known existed. All the same, I gave Gentile the short answer. "My brother and his father were friends. Hal and I grew up together."

"That would be your brother, Samuel Diakos, and his father, Peter Vanderlin."

"Right. Samuel was my half-brother, forty years older; more like a father, really."

"Why is your last name different?"

"That's a long story."

"I've got time."

"Samuel and I had the same father, a World War II resistance fighter with ELAS, the Greek People's Liberation Army. He and Samuel were caught by the Nazis and sent to a labor camp. When camp officials learned my father was a goldsmith, they sent him to the Deutsche Gold und Silberscheideanstalt, a re-smelting company. He was forced to sort through trays of jewelry stolen from prisoners and assess its quality."

"Obviously your father survived."

"He did. One day he found a ring in the tray, the one he'd made for Samuel. He believed his son was dead. With no family left, he fled to the safe haven of Turkey after the war ended because the Greek regime was persecuting leftists. He kept his real identity secret and changed his last name to a Turkish one—Madak. Years later he remarried and had a second son—me. Samuel had been searching for his father. When he finally learned that my parents had died in an earthquake that caused a mine accident, he went to Turkey right away to take me home with him."

"Oh, that's right. You were the poor Turkish orphan. Samuel Diakos treated you better than a natural son. You repaid his generosity by killing him."

The room turned red. The huge reservoir of guilt I carried around with me over Samuel's death funneled into a blind rage. I made a move to get up, but the uniformed cop sped around the table and clamped an arm around my neck.

I was on the verge of blacking out when I heard Gentile say, "Okay, Verne, leave him alone. Give him a couple of minutes to chill out." The cop let go but remained behind me.

Gentile poured some water into his glass and took a sip. He seemed pleased with his latest salvo. "Did you remove anything from Vanderlin's house before you left the party?"

"No." I wondered where this came from.

"Colin Reed told us he heard you arguing with Vanderlin. What was that about?"

"Hal owed me for a loan I'd given him. He told me he didn't have the money."

"So you got what he owed you some other way, is that it? You took the rest of the heroin with you?"

"Of course not."

Gentile slammed his file shut. "Mr. Madison, there's clear evidence Vanderlin died of a drug-related accident, unassisted. That information has already been made public. What interests us is how he obtained his drugs."

"Look, that's just a red herring. The woman I told you about was after something Hal Vanderlin stole from my brother, a Neo-Assyrian engraving that may have come from Iraq. It's worth a substantial amount of money."

"Could you translate that please for us humble folks?"

"It's a stone engraving made during the period when the Assyrian empire was at its height. About 800 to 612 B.C."

"Thank you, *professor*. You've been a dealer in collector's items, art objects, for what, the last seven years. Is that right?"

"Around that."

"Lucrative business?"

"Up and down. Sometimes you do well. Other times it can be very lean. It all depends on your contacts, your networks."

"And where do they come from, these contacts of yours?"

"Through Samuel originally. He was an archaeologist and had also studied Assyriology. He knew that world—the dealers, the academics, the museum bureaucrats. I've built my own roster of clients now. These last couple of years I didn't have to rely on him as much."

"Has your work focused on Middle Eastern objects?"

"At first it did because that was Samuel's specialty. Since then I've branched out. Some Renaissance art and, of course, Peter Vanderlin's collection."

"So your talents are wide-ranging. You must have a remarkable knowledge of art to cover such broad territory."

A false compliment, I thought, deliberately planted. "I know a lot about the Middle East because I grew up with an expert on those cultures. As far as the rest is concerned, I'm light on that. My skill's in sales.

I'm really a broker. The important thing is getting to know your clients well—their dreams. With the objects themselves, you can always buy the research."

Gentile paused to check the file again. "Like you did with the Livorno Madonna?"

"That ended up settled out of court as I'm sure you know. The guy who owned it was selling a fake. I had nothing to do with it."

Gentile's chair creaked when he leaned back. "Guess your researcher slipped up too."

"Even major auction houses get it wrong."

The door opened. Louis Peres entered and sat down, then leaned over and whispered something to Gentile.

Gentile nodded and resumed his questions. "I'm assuming you're acquainted with a number of prominent collectors. Some of them inclined to cross the line for an item they covet?"

"You mean art thieves who steal on order for the multimillionaire with a secret room on his estate full of stolen Chagalls and Picassos? That's just a myth."

Gentile raised his eyebrows. "Really?"

"You don't understand a collector's psychology. The whole point is to show off acquisitions, not hide them. In 99 percent of cases art thieves are brainless. They steal the stuff and then discover it's impossible to move because the work's too accurately documented."

I could see doubt written all over Gentile's face. "Doesn't seem to stop them from trying."

"Most of it ends up being passed through criminal

networks for collateral or money laundering. The big payoff comes from ransom. Insurance companies would rather look the other way and pay a ransom than ante up for the full value of the work. There've been four separate thefts of one Rembrandt painting alone. For looted antiquities, it's different. Much harder to prove origin. Much easier to cook up a false provenance. Or they'll do a reverse restoration."

"What's that?" Gentile said.

"Experts make real pieces look like fakes. Even if acquisition numbers exist, it's not that difficult to clean them off. You're looking at billions worldwide every year. That's incredible money. Samuel would see items advertised for sale he knew were stolen but could do nothing about it because he had no proof. It used to drive him crazy. The truth is antiquities markets are dependent on theft. Outside of resales, looting's the only source of new supply."

"It's really done that openly?" Gentile asked. His question seemed genuine. Maybe he'd given up baiting me.

"They usually go through smaller auction houses that aren't so particular. The missing artifact I told you about is probably from the old city of Nineveh." Gentile nodded, but I suspected he was about as familiar with Nineveh as he was with what to do with the fish fork at a royal banquet.

He pointed his index finger toward me like a courtroom prosecutor. "Mr. Vanderlin was what, a professor?"

"A part-time lecturer in philosophy."

"So he had no expertise in dealing with museum pieces?"

"Right."

"You mentioned you assisted him in selling off his father's collection, is that correct?"

"Yes."

"Vanderlin's father is still alive. Did his son have legal authority to do this?"

"He had power of attorney. Peter has Alzheimer's."

"So you're telling me that after being satisfied with your work disposing of his father's entire collection, he didn't use you for this new item?"

"Yes, I already said that. He took it from my brother in the first place."

Gentile shut his eyes as if he were meditating on my words. Finally he put his big, beefy hands on the table and rose. His chair almost toppled over when he pushed it back. He walked around to my side of the table and stood over me, making sure I felt the full impact of his bulk. I could smell this morning's bacon and eggs on his breath.

"Let's go back to last night. You told us you left Hal Vanderlin around midnight and went from there to a bar?"

Where was he going with this, switching tracks by talking about the overdose again? I glanced at Peres. He'd finally woken up and trained his eyes on me.

"That's strange. Because Diane Chen says you didn't show up until after 2 A.M. So fill in the gap for me, please."

They'd staged this whole thing beautifully, playing out the rope, letting me meander on about looted artifacts, and I'd leapt right into the lion's mouth.

Gentile managed the first genuine smile since we'd met.

I fought them off for a while longer, arguing that Diane must have had the time screwed up, but they knew better. In the end I told them I'd gone back when Hal called me and found his body. After Eris and her companion threatened me, I ran, afraid they'd kill me too.

Predictably, Gentile had followed the line of least resistance, believing I'd been Hal's supplier and that I'd cooked up the story about Eris and the missing engraving as a cover. But he had no evidence of this, just a towering suspicion. In the end, he couldn't keep me.

As I got up to leave, he said brusquely, "Mr. Madison, the investigation of your car accident is still active. And if we determine you provided heroin to Hal Vanderlin, that will get you a charge of involuntary manslaughter at a minimum. Don't be taking any long trips. I don't want to hear you're peddling your wares on some beach in Brazil."

I'd started out my sojourn with the police thinking about one woman—Eris. Now I couldn't forget another—Diane Chen. What had she predicted? *Betrayal.* The fortune teller had fulfilled her own prophecy.

Six

The glare walloped me when I stepped outside the station doors. Patches of sidewalk blacktop had turned soft. It could be 150 degrees for all I cared. I looked at the sun blazing in the sapphire sky and felt like a blind man whose sight has suddenly been restored. I couldn't get away fast enough.

I could think of only one person to turn to—Hal's ex-wife, Laurel. If the news of Hal's death had already reached her, she'd be heartbroken and need my support. As for me, I wanted to be with someone I trusted. It took a couple of calls to mutual friends before I learned she'd moved temporarily to Hal's mother's residence at Sheridan Square.

Laurel's marriage to Hal lasted a grand total of six months. Since their split over a year ago, they'd built an eccentric but deep friendship, recognizing that neither of them possessed any talent for marriage. They'd never bothered to get a divorce. A doctoral candidate in philosophy, Laurel met Hal at NYU. She was very bright but never swamped you with her intellect, unlike Hal, who loved leading people into verbal traps and tripping them up. I'd always found her attractive but kept my distance because of Hal. Had the police called her yet? I hoped to avoid breaking the bad news.

Her building wasn't too far from the station, so I decided to walk and use the time to calm down after my near miss with the police. I couldn't shake a feeling of unease. At first I put this down to the interrogation, but soon I began to sense someone tailing me. Eris? I looked back and scanned people's faces but couldn't catch sight of her. I dipped into a juice bar and watched each face as the crowd moved past. No sign of her. I went deliberately off course, turning down a residential street of four-story townhouses. One of them, outfitted with elaborate wrought-iron grates and pillars and a Spanish-style balcony, looked as if it had been uprooted from a New Orleans street and plunked down here. Despite the fancy addresses, the street felt ominous and was shadowy from the overarching trees. The high humidity and frothy greenery in the gardens gave it a tropical feel. Few people here. Eris couldn't avoid being seen. I waited for ten minutes but spotted nothing out of the ordinary. The evidence told me I was safe but my sixth sense disagreed.

It seemed totally insane that in the space of a day I'd gone from being a normal citizen to living in a constant state of fear.

I checked the street once more when I reached

Laurel's building, and seeing nothing out of place, I decided to go in. Hal had taken over his mother's home when she died last autumn. Her penthouse was an eagle's nest topping a brown-brick mesa, crowned by a gothic mélange of pillars, arches, terraces, and gargoyles. The ground floor of the building housed a bar famous for its Monday-night Latin drags.

My one worry was whether Gip would remember me, but when I entered the main foyer, he rose from behind his desk and grinned. He was spic and span in an army-green uniform dressed up with lots of gold braid, a cap, a long coat, and matching slacks. A good thing the vestibule was air conditioned. A sturdy Irishman with a round, ruddy face, Gip was the third generation in his family to hold the post. An aristocrat of doormen, he referred to himself as Gerald Powell the Third.

"Nice to see you, John. It's been a while."

"Thanks, Gip. I'm here to see Laurel Vanderlin, if she's home."

"One second, I'll check." He punched in some numbers, spoke into the phone, and handed me the receiver.

"Hi, Laurie. It's John."

"Oh, John. You've heard then."

"Yes. Can I come up?"

"Please do. I'm desperate for some company."

The elevator had been refurbished, but the original brass art deco grillwork had wisely been kept. A white-gloved, uniformed attendant slid open the door. It had to be one of the few places left in Manhattan that still offered this service. Here, you didn't ask for a floor, but simply gave the name of the resident. We sailed up to the penthouse.

Laurel waited with the door half propped open. I took her in my arms, pressed my face against hers, and felt tears slide down her cheek. I caught the bloom of alcohol on her breath. The stronger light inside showed me a face red and swollen from crying; her eyes had that glazed look people have when the shock is still new.

We entered a rotunda gleaming with Giallo Siena marble, its mirrors custom-made to fit the rounded walls, and in the center an inlaid, hand-painted credenza that had once belonged to a French king. On it sat a Tiffany lamp. In the receiving room, the floor switched to a rich herringbone oak covered with seventeenth-century silk Kashan carpets so valuable it felt like a sin to tread on them. Three sets of French doors framed by heavy brocade drapes led out to the first terrace. The place presented a face of stale elegance.

Hal's mother had made only one change, combining a hall, butler's pantry, and breakfast room to create a large family room and modern kitchen. This space was done up completely in surgical white. White broadloom, white walls, white furniture. The overall effect resembled an operating theater dropped into the middle of a museum.

I flopped down on the family room couch. Laurel asked if I wanted something to drink.

"Nothing, thanks."

"You sure?" She picked up a tumbler half full of what looked like water but I knew wasn't, waving it in my direction.

"You're drinking vodka straight?"

"The ice cube melted. If you're not going to join me, enjoy the show." She threw down the rest of the drink. I was not about to suggest she'd be better off skipping the booze. Who was I to point out moral imperatives to anyone, considering my penchant for a decent range of sins? After what happened to Hal last night, she could be forgiven for wanting to get numb.

Laurel slumped into a chair. "What bad angel has cast its spell on us, John? First Samuel and you in that terrible accident, and now this. It's unbelievable."

"I know." I felt a kind of sorrowful connection with her now that both of us were struggling with a violent loss.

"I told him so many times those drugs would end up killing him."

How much did I want to reveal? "I'm not sure it's that simple, Laurie. Hal called me after I left the party. I rushed back, but he was already dead when I got there."

"You found him? The police didn't tell me that. What happened?"

"Someone at the party administered the fatal dose. A woman. She threatened me too."

Her face went white. "You told the police about this, right?"

"I've just come from talking to them. They don't believe me. With my previous record and enough drugs circulating at the party to start a pharmacy, their guns are aiming at me. That's how they think."

"Are you telling me Hal was murdered and you saw who did it?" She swayed. I grabbed her before she could fall and helped her over to the sofa, then sat down beside her. "This is scaring me, John. I don't know who to believe."

"Why would I lie about it? Look, I know how rough this is on you. I can see that."

"It was horrible enough already, and now you're telling me it's even worse. I can't get my mind around this."

"Tell me about it. I'm having a hard time over losing Samuel and now this ... thing with Hal. It's as though a bomb has just gone off inside my head. Hal was the closest I came to having a brother."

"I thought Samuel was your brother."

"Sure, but he was forty years older than me, so he always seemed like my father. He played that role. I never knew my real father. When Hal was home from boarding school or camp we spent a lot of time together. We often sparred though. It wasn't always that brotherly between us."

Our talking calmed Laurel a bit. "I'm the only girl in the family," she said. "I have four brothers. Believe me, sparring is normal."

"But he carried it too far. Wouldn't let it go even as adults. At Columbia we'd be out somewhere, at a party or something. We'd be raising the roof, having a fantastic time, and then he'd start getting all competitive with me. Thinking about it now, I should have called him on it then."

"It goes back to how his father treated him. That's exactly how Peter would behave." She had a lovely voice. Her years in New York hadn't altered what sounded like a Midwestern accent. "I guess I'm responsible for Peter now, along with everything else."

I took her hand. "I'll help you. Samuel and I visited Peter after he went into the nursing home. He still remembered me."

She let out a deep sigh. "Why does everything have to go wrong at once? I feel like a ten-ton truck has just driven over me."

"I think there's a connection. Between my circumstances and yours."

"What do you mean?"

"Can you think of anyone who would have had it in for Hal?" I asked.

"I've found out I didn't know everything about his life. He kept things from me—I'm just starting to realize how much since he asked me to help sort out all his accounts and things. But do you mean going to the lengths of killing him? I can't imagine who would do that."

I bent my head and rubbed my eyes. "What did the police say?"

She took a minute to respond. "The detective was kind of guarded. He just said that Hal had died, probably from an overdose. A neighbor called 911 after hearing a disturbance. He's the one who identified Hal. Thank heavens I didn't have to. They aren't releasing his body yet."

"Laurie, Hal got tangled up in something. Nothing to do with opiates. He tried to sell a really valuable relic, a collector's item. That's what the woman was after. Do you know anything about it?"

"You think that's why he died?"

"Yes."

"I thought he sold everything from Peter's collection. You handled it all for him. If something was left, why didn't he go through you?"

"It didn't belong to Peter. It was a stone engraving Samuel brought over from Iraq. Hal took it while I was in the hospital. This woman, Eris, found out about it somehow. Did Hal ever mention her?"

"Doesn't ring a bell." Laurel eased herself up and walked over to a credenza against the wall. Every inch of its marble top was covered with stacks of file folders and documents, along with some dusty photos sitting beside her computer. One of these, her wedding picture, showed a bride with high cheekbones, a slight Slavic tilt to her green eyes giving her face a faintly exotic look, her shiny brown hair swept up. She was dressed simply in a white satin sheath, holding a spray of ivory roses and baby's breath. Beside her, Hal, ramrod straight in a severe black suit, looked uncomfortable, as though he already knew the marriage was doomed to fail. Like some omnipresent ghost, Hal's mother, Mina, a little blurry but clearly identifiable, could be seen in the background.

Laurel saw me looking at the photo. "Do you know there isn't one wedding picture with just the two of us? Mina always lurked somewhere, making sure she was in the shot." She ran her fingers through her hair. Usually this was the gesture of a flirt. In her case it simply revealed an overload of worry and tension. She flipped through some of the files but didn't find what she was searching for. "Somewhere Hal listed all the property that hadn't yet been sold, mostly from this place, but I can't find it."

She turned toward me. "John, there's something you need to know. Hal and I had talked about getting back together. With Mina gone and Peter in a place he'll never leave, there was finally an opening for me. Hal was brow-beaten by his father and too close to his mother. He adored her. Did you know he used to call her his jewel?"

I shook my head and let her talk.

"Things had been going well. My sublet was up and he offered to let me stay here because he'd moved back to the townhouse temporarily to care for Peter. Everything was great until I discovered he was using heroin again, even though he'd sworn that was over with. We used to see each other every day. That stopped last week when I found out. I was furious." Her bottom lip trembled.

"Junk is the devil, Laurie. It's so hard to shake. Hal once told me he'd crawl through a sewer just to get some. He got that from an expert, by the way—William Burroughs. You can't change the past. Try to just focus on the good times."

A gush of tears threatened to turn into a waterfall. "Hal was desperate for money. He had to cover all the costs for the townhouse and for here. Taxes alone were more than six thousand a month, plus paying for Peter's care."

"Why not just sell the townhouse?"

"The power of attorney forbade Hal from selling it. Peter made sure of that before he got too sick to think."

"What did Hal do with the cash from Peter's collection?"

Laurel shut her eyes for a moment, trying to regain her composure. "He went through it all. He was losing his position, too. You know he was deathly afraid of social events, but he threw that party as a last-ditch effort to get on Colin's good side—his contract was up."

"Hal told me Colin fired him." The few times I'd met Colin Reed he hadn't impressed me. "How well do you know Reed? Does he know anything about antiquities?"

"Not well. I'd see him at NYU when I'd go there to meet Hal. Or at parties and stuff. That's about it. Never liked the man much. He teaches the great German philosophers—Kant, Schelling. He's considered an authority on Hegel. As far as I know, that's about as close to the past as he gets."

"Reed was there last night. Tried to implicate me, the bastard. I'm wondering why he'd do that."

Laurel shrugged her shoulders. I noticed how graceful her movements were, even in her slightly inebriated state. "Don't take it personally," she said. "Reed's the type who'd do that just for a laugh."

"Where would Hal's computer be—at the townhouse?"

"His laptop's there. His desktop's in his cubbyhole at NYU."

I'd have to check both of them out. There had to be something on them to give me a lead on Eris's identity.

Laurel let out a deep sigh. "It feels so strange to be surrounded by Hal's family things. Now it all belongs to the bank."

"Speaking of his possessions, he still wore your wedding ring. Did you know that?"

"You mean the gold ring with the solitaire diamond? That's not his wedding ring. He had it made from an antique ring when his mother died. He was more married to Mina than he ever was to me."

An odd way to put it, but accurate. Hal's mother had always been very possessive. I could see what a challenge it would be for a new wife to wedge herself in between the two of them. "What about this place? It must be worth a fortune."

"Mina's brother left it to her. Peter deliberately held off separating from her until she'd been awarded the estate to make sure he got half the value. She had to take out a mammoth mortgage to buy him out. Everything will have to be sold just to cover the debts."

I didn't challenge her on this. Maybe she was just bad at math. Even if Mina had been forced to mortgage half the place, that still left a sizeable sum. But perhaps Peter had somehow managed to entail this place too.

I got up to stretch my legs. I wasn't sure I wanted to share Hal's letter with Laurel just yet, but I desperately needed some advice. I took the sketch of the puzzle I'd printed from my pocket. "Hal created a kind of game to show me where he hid the engraving. Does this make any sense to you?" I held out the drawing to her.

"Why would he want you to have it?" *Instead of me.* I could hear her thinking that loud and clear.

"There was nothing altruistic about it. He set a trap. He deliberately sent Eris after me."

Laurel took the paper from me and scrutinized it, then put her hands up to her face. I folded my arm around her and let her cry. After a few minutes she moved away and found a tissue, holding it to her eyes. "He expected you to figure this out?"

"Looks that way."

She let out a deep sigh. "He always beat me at these word games. Trying to solve it would make me feel like I was playing with a ghost."

"I don't think there's a lot of choice. Not for me, anyway."

"You're telling me Hal is lying in the morgue now because of this. Is that where you want to end up too?"

"He was totally out of his league. I've got a few street smarts, don't forget. The words he's used, they're unusual."

"Some of them refer to alchemy, like the *Picatrix*. It's a hand-book on magic going back to the thirteenth century. The words *black* and *white* probably refer to two of the stages of converting base metals to gold. Melanosis, the blackening, comes first to eliminate the impurities by fire and next is leucosis, the whitening. The final stage would be iosis, the reddening or achieving the pure form."

"Alchemy? Honestly? That's surprising for a committed academic like him."

I found it curious that Hal's puzzle was loaded with words relating to alchemy. How did that link to a Neo-Assyrian relic? Had the Assyrians experimented with methods to turn common metals into gold? I'd always thought alchemy originated with the Egyptians, not the Mesopotamians.

Laurel handed back the sketch. The tip of her fingernail was shredded and the cuticles red, signs that her worries had begun well before Hal's death. "Actually it's not. Come with me—you need to see something."

Seven

I followed Laurel through the kitchen into a dark corridor that seemed to stretch to infinity. Dim lights came on when she flicked a wall switch. Laurel led me to a closed door about thirty feet down the hall. "I don't usually come in here. It's too eerie." She pushed open the door. "You'll have to wait a minute. The wires leading to this room were purposely cut off; there's no electricity in here."

She shuffled forward. After a moment a match struck. Flames leapt from tall white tapers fixed into two large crystal candle-sticks, the flickering lights glittering on their facets. "Voilà," Laurel said, waving her arms, "'the spirit room.' That's my name for it, anyway."

The room was windowless and had probably once been a large pantry. Its walls and ceiling had been painted dusky grape. Lingering in the air was a scent of must mixed with a strange odor I couldn't place, like the smell of rotting fruit. There were no pentacles drawn within a circle on the floor, no goat skulls or upside-down crosses, no dripping black tapers—nothing hokey like that. Still, the room possessed an aura that was chilly and uncomfortable; it was a place you wouldn't volunteer to spend time in.

An old cabinet with glass doors held curious objects: prisms of several sizes, egg-shaped stones in different colors, an old-fashioned brass scale with weights and measures, blue apothecary bottles filled with powders. A silver statue of a horned goddess sat on top of the cabinet beside a cruel-looking knife with a blade curved like a sickle. A large tapestry hung above that, a medieval scene showing a robed and masked woman mounting steps leading to a citadel on a hillside, a wounded knight in the foreground, a raven wearing a gold circlet flying in the sky.

"This is wild," I exclaimed. "What on earth was Hal tangled up with?"

Laurel crossed her arms over her chest as if protecting herself. "This was Mina's place, but lately Hal spent a lot of time in here."

"Mina was into all this new-agey stuff too?"

"She's the one who originally got Hal involved. I know most people think it's flaky, but you can't dismiss it out of hand. The old alchemists laid the groundwork for modern chemistry."

"When Hal and I were kids Mina wasn't around a lot; usually only the staff were there—housekeepers or maids. The rare times I did see her she was pretty distant. She always came off as a bit formidable, almost scary."

"You've got that right."

I sensed there was more to Laurel's words than simple agreement. "What do you mean?"

"Hal never said anything?"

"About what?"

"Mina was a practicing witch."

I had a sudden vision of Mina drinking some potion, her image transforming before my eyes into a hag with green skin, a long hooked nose, and one tooth, sailing off the terrace at midnight to cast her evil spells. I broke into a laugh. "I know you didn't like her, but that's absurd."

Her eyes registered a quick flash of annoyance. "The last thing I'd do is make a joke about it. She took it very seriously. That knife on the cabinet is a boline, a witch's tool. Witchcraft is older than most religions, and it's become quite widespread, you know, especially here and in the UK. Mina was an eclectic."

"And that is?"

"A sole practitioner. She didn't belong to a coven. She became an authority on witchcraft practiced in medieval Germany. Well-known scholars would come from around the world to consult her." Laurel shivered and crossed her arms. "I found out about all this just after her funeral. Hal was very emotional, and one night it all tumbled out. He said he was going to make her immortal."

"How did he plan to pull that off?"

"He wouldn't say and I didn't want to indulge him in that crazy talk. I wanted to get his mind off her."

"As far as I could tell Mina was strictly Park Avenue. You're making her sound like the madwoman in the attic."

"Look at the book over there if you don't believe me." Laurel pointed to a single large volume sitting on a table in front of us. "That's the *Picatrix*, her spiritual guide."

The book's cover consisted of an intricately worked ivory relief with a border of interlinked geometric designs and a center panel of occult symbols. Fine cracks in the yellowed ivory told the book's age. Two tarnished silver clasps had been fixed into its right edge—a locking mechanism—but the hasps were open.

"It's a grimoire," Laurel said. She seemed wary of the volume and stepped away from it.

"Sounds appropriately sinister."

"A book of spells and incantations, ways to call up demons or communicate with angels. The original Arabic title was *Aim of the Sage*. It was translated into Latin from Spanish. There are supposedly only seventeen copies in existence, all under lock and key in European libraries, so where Mina got this one I have no idea."

I moved beside her and, taking a tissue from my pocket to protect the pages, opened the book.

"Are you sure you want to do that?" Laurel asked. "It's said that once you open it, the book has a hold over you."

I shrugged my shoulders and turned the first pages. "Those tales were usually circulated to discourage people from looking at forbidden material. If it's really old, it'll be worth a lot. You should probably put it in a safe-deposit box."

A little vexed, Laurel replied, "Yeah, along with the million other things I have to do."

I lifted the pages gently, fascinated by the illustrations. Framed in a circle, one of them showed a king, dressed in a multi-colored garment, sitting on a peacock rendered in radiant silver, golds, and greens. On another page a nude Hermes appeared against the backdrop of an old sailing ship. "I can't read Latin."

"It's a kind of handbook for proactive astrology and magic. If I remember what Hal told me, in those times you could die just for owning this. It has instructions for creating magical talismans and shows how to make images of your enemy to defeat him."

"Defeat?"

"Well … kill, actually."

"Nice."

She shuddered. "You know, all this talk about the *Picatrix* jogs my memory. That woman you mentioned. Hal was a member of an online group, a website for people with a serious interest in alchemy. Could he have met her through that? He talked about it several times, but do you think I can remember … Oh, I know. I think it was called Alchemy Archives or something like that."

"Let's check it out." I grabbed my cellphone and

pulled the candle as close as possible. A search for the name brought up the website immediately.

"Are these supposed to be real people?"

"Hal said so. Those symbols underneath them represent planets: Venus, Mercury, Mars, Jupiter, and Saturn. Together with Sol for the sun and Luna for the moon, they symbolize the seven celestial objects believed in antiquity to revolve around Earth. They're supposed to represent the five hosts of the website. It all feels like a lot of hocus-pocus to me."

"Why hide their identities?"

"They're professionals, not the flakes you sometimes find on a site like this. My guess is they didn't want people to know they were dabbling in this kind of stuff."

Or perhaps they had other strong reasons, like the need to hide their crimes. "So they took this stuff seriously."

The Alchemy Archives website

"Oh, for sure. You'd be surprised. Some people spend millions setting up labs trying to convert lead into gold. It's called transmutation."

"The woman I met. Could she be one? Maybe she's Venus."

"It's possible. Hal told me he was Saturn, but he didn't name anyone else." She peered at my cellphone screen. "Well, it looks like at least one woman belongs to the group."

"You can't tell from that. Those are full porcelain face masks, and anything can be digitally altered."

Laurel rubbed her eyes. I could see she was exhausted. When I closed the *Picatrix* I noticed the white edge of some paper at the back of the book. I gently slid it out. A photograph, at least part of one. The image came from our time at Columbia, one of our legendary parties. It captured me in my student days, long hair and all, passing a joint to the woman beside me. The picture certainly wouldn't help me to remember who she was because her head had been neatly cut out. My own face had been colored blood red, a crudely drawn symbol inked in above it.

I dropped the photo as if it had bitten my hand. "What the hell is this?"

Laurel bent down to retrieve it and gasped. "I don't know. I've never seen it before."

The photo had to be Hal's work, his mind far more hate-filled and twisted than I'd thought. "It's some kind of stupid curse."

"I should never have brought you in here. I'm sorry," Laurel said worriedly.

Still feeling freaked by the photo and the implications of what we'd seen in that room, I felt certain Laurel was in danger too. As we walked back to the family room I knew I had to say something. "Listen, this whole thing is getting really bizarre. I'm concerned about you. Is there anywhere else you could stay until I get this situation sorted out? Eris might try to get to you here. I'm surprised she hasn't already."

"Are you kidding? This place is locked up tighter than a tomb. I'll be fine."

I gave her my business card so she'd know how to reach me and got her cell number. "I'll call you then. Just to make sure you're okay."

She hugged me. "Watch out for yourself. Don't worry about me."

"You didn't get much sleep last night, did you?"

"Next to none."

"Why don't you try to rest? Do you have anything to help you sleep?"

She shook her head but took my advice and curled up on the couch. I bunched one of the pillows under her head and tucked a mohair throw over her. She smiled her thanks. I heated up some milk in the kitchen microwave and brought the cup to her.

On the way out I gave Gip a description of Eris, warning him to be on the lookout for her.

I headed over to the Khyber Pass Restaurant, still feeling shaken. It took me a while to organize my thoughts. Hal had stolen an engraving from Samuel. What made it so valuable? His message referred to five antagonists, and he'd set them after me. It was his idea of a vindictive joke, I guess, to include himself as one of them. Did Eris also belong to the group, and if so, who were the other three? Why would people running an alchemy website have any interest in an Assyrian engraving? I hoped Tomas Zakar, the man I was about to meet, could give me some answers.

Still pondering this, I stepped across the street to the triangle of park facing Laurel's building and immediately stopped short. A heavyset man lurked near a corner, his back turned to me, his fist closed around something. Eris's strange companion? As if reading my mind, he whipped around and launched himself at me.

Eight

The man threw a tennis ball along the sidewalk, grinning as he moved past. A little dog skittered behind him to take up the chase. I cursed Hal once more for wrecking my peace of mind and left for my meeting.

St. Mark's Place in the East Village was rambunctious as usual on a hot summer evening, crowded and slightly frenetic. A couple of uniformed cops stood next to their cruisers trading stories with two beefy men in street wear, the local undercover squad, no doubt. The Asian fusion and sushi restaurants were already busy, the smoke shops doing a brisk trade. I always got a laugh out of one store sign that read UNISEX—24 HOURS A DAY, SEVEN DAYS A WEEK. Down the sidewalk, a group of Hare Krishnas swayed toward me, bald-headed and saffron-robed, chanting the familiar mantra and beating their big drum. The sixties all over again. Some things and some places never change.

The Khyber Pass, an Afghani restaurant, was a favorite of Samuel's. I'd never paid much heed to its name, but after my recent experiences, the fact that we were meeting here was a bit unnerving. Its name came from the famous three-mile-long pass through the treacherous Hindu Kush range—a British officer had once said that "every stone in it has been soaked in blood." A bad sign for the encounter I was about to have? I hoped not.

I arrived late. The times I'd been there with Samuel the place had been hopping, but I'd always gone late in the evening. Today, only one customer sat at a small table on the postage-stamp-size patio out front. He pushed back his chair and rose, giving me a slight nod. Shorter than me and with a slender build, Zakar was conservatively dressed. He had a formal, ascetic look, with sharp features, dark hair and eyes, and olive skin like mine.

"You're Tomas Zakar?" I extended my hand.

"Yes." He returned my handshake and murmured, "Thank you for coming." He'd obviously recognized me immediately. I felt a touch discomfited that he had an edge on me.

He gave his watch a cursory glance. "Not too late, I hope," I said.

He waved away my remark. "You're here. That's the important thing." He indicated the entrance. "Shall we go in?"

Inside, we walked down a few steps into a room redolent of the Orient. Afghani music wafted from a nearby speaker on the wall. The place was richly decorated in a cacophony of reds, from deep burgundy to scarlet. Each table was covered with a handwoven rug, a sheet of glass placed over top. The hostess directed us to a banquette beneath the bay window at the front.

"This is the best table for our discussion—the most private," Tomas said after we were seated. "Would you care for a pipe?" He waved toward a collection of large narghile pipes in ruby-red and cobalt-blue cut glass on the bar. A menu had been placed on our table with a choice of fruit-flavored tobaccos.

"No thanks," I said.

His dark eyes registered a hint of surprise. "Samuel loved to take the pipe."

I'm sure he didn't intend it that way, but his statement came out as something of a put-down. As if I couldn't quite measure up to my brother.

"A drink then?" he said.

I passed on alcohol for the time being, wanting my wits about me, and chose instead an espresso. He ordered mint tea and smiled ruefully. "Mint tea. The only thing in America that reminds me of home."

"Speaking of home, how did you know where to find me?"

"Oh, I've been to New York a couple of times before with Samuel."

I suppose my brother had no particular reason to

introduce us, but somehow this felt like another bolt from the blue. I wondered how trustworthy the guy really was. "I hate to ask, but since we've never met, do you have any ID?" I already knew what he looked like, but I didn't want him to think he could take my trust for granted.

He seemed taken aback by my request but leaned down and reached into a pocket on his backpack, handing me his passport and a picture of him and Samuel at some gathering, the two of them smiling into the camera, palms and potted plants filling out the background.

He told me he'd grown up in Mosul and had received his degree from Oxford. We found a bit of common ground when I learned he'd taken some exchange courses at Columbia. Samuel had employed him as his assistant for the past three years, their work focusing on the Nineveh site. He'd come to America in search of the engraving. Hence the urgent plea to meet with me.

The waiter brought our drinks. I added sugar to my espresso and gave it a stir.

Tomas blew on his tea to cool it down. "My condolences to you," he said.

"Thanks. It's been hard."

"Yes. Even now I can't believe he's gone. Samuel was so much more than my employer. He financed my last year at Oxford and helped out my parents when they lost their home. I can't describe the sadness I felt when I got the news. It made me ill."

I felt a touch of jealousy listening to this. He'd obviously grown very close to my brother, but I was also reassured to hear that his motives were genuine. The shock on his face was plain when I told him Hal had died after stealing the engraving. "Do you know anything about it? It was Neo-Assyrian and it looks like Samuel shipped it home from Iraq."

"Exactly why I've come over here. To bring it home. But surely you know what it is? You must have had it assessed when you found it."

"There's a problem. Hal hid it, and I have no idea where." For the time being I omitted any mention of Hal's game. Tomas folded a napkin around the tumbler of tea and sat silently, wrapped up in his thoughts, digesting this turn of events.

I gave it another try. "The engraving. It may somehow be related to the old science of alchemy—do you know anything about that?"

He toyed with his napkin and mumbled, "I'm sorry. What you've told me is very upsetting."

Was this an attempt to avoid answering me? I decided it was better not to press him too hard right away, and asked how he'd met Samuel.

"On my first job at the National Museum. As you know, your brother consulted for them regularly. The staff totally trusted him. They couldn't afford to pay him, but he always found research money from somewhere. Did he never speak of me?"

"The last while he didn't talk a lot about his work."

Once again I held off plunging right in with the

questions I most needed answers to, afraid of putting him off. I wanted to read the guy a little better, so I tried to come up with something to get him to open up a bit. "Were you able to get out of Iraq before the war?"

"No, we couldn't leave until after the Americans entered Baghdad. The entire city was in a state of extreme denial. An orgy of wishful thinking that was. People bought into the delusion that last-minute diplomacy would deliver a miracle. Then the bombs started dropping. It was the most bizarre thing. Until we lost power we could actually see the buildings around us exploding on CNN. Unbelievable. I was watching a disaster happen while I was actually in it."

I sensed a few cracks opening in his armor. An experience like that would shake anyone up.

"Once I visited Amiriyah, an air-raid shelter bombed by the American military during the Gulf War. You could still see the bodies of the poor souls who'd been clustered in there, imprinted on the walls by the heat of the blast, like shadow people. A modern version of what we see in excavations. Forgotten battles brought to light, once-great cities destroyed, mounds of bones, broken up and burned. You've seen Pompeii?"

"Yes."

"The shelter reminded me of that. Corpses frozen in time. When this war started it felt the same, as if our entire population had suddenly been vaporized. No cars on the roads, none of the usual buzz of the city.

Then we'd see the sky light up. That eerie, phosphorescent green on the TV screen. We could hear the blasts from the real bombs outside and feel the floor shake, like earthquakes hitting over and over again."

What could I say to this? War was completely alien to my own experience. I felt the same stumbling incoherence I'd shown when a friend told me he had cancer and I'd responded with only vacuous, limp-wristed reassurances.

Tomas took a hesitant sip of his tea. "At times the oxygen seemed to vanish and we breathed in soot. Our bodies were covered with it. We kept coughing it up. Without water, we had to use old cooking oil to clean it off. It was impossible to sleep. We never knew where the next missile would hit. Like an assassin waiting for you—you can't tell from which dark doorway or hidden wall he'll suddenly appear. We lived in perpetual fear." He set his glass down. That sounded convincing enough. I had the strong impression of someone who kept his distance, who wasn't one to wear his emotions on his sleeve, but a tautness around his mouth and eyes told me that talking about the experience cost him something.

I murmured some words to convey my sympathy. "You're bringing back memories for me too—of 9/11. An artist friend of mine had a son who died in the towers. I spent a few days trying my best to console him. The impact of it spread so far. In my friend's case, his family ruptured. He and his wife ended up getting a divorce."

"A terrible event to be caught up in."

"I wasn't here. I was in Miami that day. Like everyone else, I was mesmerized by the TV, watching over and over again the planes hit, the towers crumple, people materializing out of the clouds of chalky dust, the wrecked bones of the skyscrapers jutting out of the ash. Being away when my city was under siege felt like a sin of omission."

He grew thoughtful. "If you've suffered through some kind of trauma, they say you should talk about it, but that only seems to make it worse."

"Thank God you survived the invasion. Samuel told me he was in Jordan, in Amman. Did you meet up with him there?"

"What do you mean? He was with us all the time."

"You're telling me he was in Iraq?"

"Didn't you know? He came the week before the invasion because he'd learned the engraving was at risk."

I felt a momentary surge of anger. Samuel had lied to me. Why would he do that? To keep me from worrying? "That's why he brought the engraving to New York, then? To keep it safe?"

"Yes."

"The minute he took it off museum premises he'd effectively stolen it. I can't believe my brother would do something like that."

This struck the wrong chord and Tomas bristled. "Many people did this. Antiquities are being returned now. Things people took to protect them from the looters."

"These days all Iraqi antiquities are suspect; dealers won't touch them. If I get my hands on the engraving, it's going right back to the museum."

By the look on his face I could see he believed my remark extended to him. "It's easy for you to judge. You can't imagine what it was like during the looting. I came close to being killed."

So far his story sounded credible. "No criticism intended. It must have been pure chaos."

He gave me a dark look. "It was intentional."

"That sounds like a conspiracy theory."

He waved his hand back and forth as if clearing away cigarette smoke. "Explain then, out of all the government buildings, why one of the very few protected buildings was the Ministry of the Interior. It housed Saddam Hussein's secret service documents. They said the looting was impossible to stop because of Republican Guard snipers at the museum, but it carried on for two full days after they fled."

"It generated a lot of bad publicity for us though."

"Have you ever heard of that shocking treatment? It's used for the mentally ill."

I was disconcerted by this and couldn't imagine what his question was leading to. "You mean electro-convulsive therapy?"

"Yes, that. The war planners wanted no reminders of the past. Their idea was to create a new society with no history, like a blank slate."

Again I had the impression of a tightly wound coil ready to spring loose at the slightest pressure. I decided to cool the conversation down. I'd gain nothing by alienating the guy. "Samuel was in Iraq during the bombing and everything, then?"

"I was quite worried because of his age, but he held up surprisingly well." Tomas paused as if unsure how much to reveal. "It was our only option, you know. You've heard of the treasures of Nimrud? The tombs of the three great Assyrian queens?"

"You mean the gold headdresses and necklaces?"

"Our country's crown jewels," Tomas said. "Only we had no Tower of London to keep them in. We were afraid they'd been stolen too, but they were eventually found in an underground vault in the Central Bank. A long time ago it had been flooded with half a million gallons of sewage water. That prevented any theft. The Baghdad batteries are missing, though, another terrible loss. Our people discovered electricity eighteen hundred years before you did. Did you ever see them?"

I shook my head.

"They were tall terracotta jars with copper rolls connected to an iron rod. When an acid like vinegar was added they produced an electric current. What a travesty that they've been taken."

"A lot was saved though, I understand."

"Thanks only to the museum staff who hid thousands of objects beforehand. They're national heroes, those people."

Our server interrupted to ask whether we wanted to order food. Tomas and I both declined, and I took the opportunity to switch the conversation back to the missing relic. "What does the engraving look like?"

"It's a large tablet, oblong, two feet by fourteen inches. The words on it are in Akkadian, cuneiform chiseled into the stone. Only a few people knew about the engraving, or so we thought. Samuel, of course, me, and Hanna Jaffrey, an intern from the Asian and Middle Eastern Studies program at the University of Pennsylvania. That's one of the problems."

"What is?"

"Jaffrey. After we closed our camp at Nineveh she left for the town of Tell Afar near the archaeological site Tell al-Rimah. She had a boyfriend, another U of Pennsylvania intern, there. We were told she returned to America before the outbreak of the war, but I haven't been able to contact her since. She's simply vanished. I can't find out if she's really back here or still over there."

"Surely she'd have left before war broke out?"

"Some on the archaeological team decided to remain and try to protect the sites. She may have been one of them."

"She was at Nineveh, then, when you found the engraving?"

"Yes, last December. We were working at Kuyunjik mound." He hesitated, in mid-sentence. "That's—"

"I know where it is."

It suddenly struck me that part of his stiffness had to do with nervousness about meeting me. We were circling each other like two male dogs, neither ready to trust the other.

"Nineveh is one of the legendary lost cities of Assyria," he continued. "More than a hundred years after its discovery, there's still an enormous amount to excavate. You've been on digs with Samuel, I assume."

"Of course." *A lie*. I couldn't admit to Zakar either my lack of knowledge or my regrets. I'd begged to go on fieldwork trips with Samuel but had always hit a stone wall of excuses. "Wait until you're older," he'd say. When I was a teenager he found other reasons. At some point I gave up asking. He'd been generous about trips abroad. We toured Florence, the Louvre, and Berlin's fabulous Pergamon, but I'd never set foot in the Middle East.

"I envy you that, being so young and traveling to foreign lands. Touching the history, not just studying it in school. You were lucky. Your memories of Nineveh are probably hazy after all this time. You'll recall there are two mounds, Kuyunjik, the principal site, and Nebi Yunus, the old armory. Excavations at Nebi Yunus presented a lot of difficulty because houses have been built on some sections."

"A shrine to the prophet Jonah was also built there, wasn't it?" I asked.

"Yes," Tomas replied, "another reason access to the site is limited. The shrine is sacred to Islam. But Samuel got permission to take another look at the old workings on Kuyunjik. The Antiquities Board agreed because some of the mud-brick and stone walls had become badly eroded. We had foreign financing, and part of our mission was to protect the ruins.

"For me there's always a sense of awe when I first catch sight of the Nineveh mound. You'll remember it's on a flat, barren plain, and the hill rises suddenly out of nowhere. The eye can tell immediately it's not a natural phenomenon. It has an almost spiritual presence, even now, after millennia have gone by."

I let my mind slip back to the accounts I'd read about Nineveh, in its time the largest city in the world. Sennacherib's magnificent palace, with massive stone statues guarding the doorways and decorative limestone panels depicting each step of the palace construction. Waterfalls, carp ponds, and eighteen canals adorned the parks where elephants, camels, and monkeys wandered free.

"What's the condition of the excavation now?" I asked Tomas.

His thin lips turned down into something approaching a grimace. "Very poor, I'm afraid. Dirt piles and holes, mostly. It was extensively looted in the nineties. When we set up operations last year we concentrated on terrain near the Shamash and Halzi gates, areas both Layard and Hormuzd Rassam investigated."

I knew that in Layard's time, in the mid-1800s, archaeological excavations differed little from whole-sale plunder. Early explorers focused on the flashy stuff and cut whole sections out of palace reliefs, taking what appealed to them most or what they could easily remove to ship home. Not until the early twentieth century when German archaeologists like Robert

Koldewey and Walter Andrae came did photography and careful documentation of sites become standard.

"It was hard work. Our men spent most of their time constructing new braces and shoring up walls. We had to sift through large deposits of debris. The winter rains filled our trenches with water and disturbed the markers we'd so carefully laid out and photographed. A lot of it had to be redone."

"Why pick that time of year then?"

"Our funding was good only until the end of December. We had no choice. It was one of the greatest thrills of my life. My first major project and Samuel made me a supervisor."

"Did you find anything?"

"We made an incredible discovery. There'd been a couple of dry days, and I used them to work through a small hill of rubble. The surface was damp, but with careful troweling and brushing I made headway. That's when I unearthed the first bone. I knew immediately that I'd found something phenomenal."

"A burial ground?"

"No. We brought the entire team in at that point. It took us ages to uncover everything. Whole skeletons, flattened by the weight of the earth. No sign of armor, shields, or that sort of thing, so they weren't soldiers, and of course any clothing would have disintegrated long ago. But along with a lot of ash, wood char, and bone masses we found bronze jewelry—armbands, earrings and the like.

"By that we knew we'd discovered the remains of

citizens who fled as Nineveh burned. Amazing. As if we'd traveled back thousands of years. All the evidence of the catastrophe lay before us. You could almost hear the people's cries as they choked on the black smoke and clouds of ash and as hot embers struck their flesh. Many had lethal wounds, hacked by the swords and daggers of the Medes."

"Were there any other artifacts?"

"A few small guardian statues and cylinder seals, things people wanted to rescue from the fires."

"Is that where you found the engraving?"

"Close by. One evening we'd worked later than usual. The sun was low in the sky. The land had beautiful reddish hues, deepened by the fading sunlight. A certain scent of the earth hangs over these old sites. I don't know what it is—I'm sure some geologist could explain its chemical composition. But I like to think it results from the freeing of things that have lain buried for centuries, when they are released from their graves and restored to the world."

So Tomas has a romantic edge to his soul. He's not so strait-laced after all.

"Samuel was about forty feet away from me," Tomas went on. "It had been a long stretch. I'd been swatting away clouds of flies all day; I was tired and thinking only of getting ready to pack up and go. I heard him yell. Hanna Jaffrey and I rushed over, afraid he'd hurt himself. Even in the weak light I could see he'd turned pale. He told us to look down. He'd been working a cavity that extended horizontally into the earth. At first I couldn't see anything significant. I bent down. The protrusion just looked like a chunk of rock, part of the volumes of detritus we were accustomed to finding in these sites. Then I realized what I was looking at. A tooled piece of stone extending from the debris wall, with clearly visible cuneiform markings on it. We all felt re-energized then. For the vast number of hours of work you put into these places, discoveries are often thin indeed. It set our hearts racing.

"Hanna and I rushed to get our battery-powered lights and our cameras. We set them up, and the three of us spent several hours carefully removing the surrounding material. We cheered when we finally eased the slab out. It was a very large piece, the entire surface covered with writing. Best of all it was intact, and because it was stone, not clay, well preserved."

"Was Samuel able to identify it right away?" I asked.

"Within a day he'd understood the first lines. Of course you're aware several stages are needed to transcribe cuneiform symbols into meaningful words in our language? It's nothing like simple translation."

"Sure," I said. "It takes a lot of patience."

He gave me a quick look. Lurking in that glance was the suspicion that I knew a lot less than I'd claimed to, but he didn't call me on it. He continued. "Within a week Samuel was sure of what he'd found. He was elated."

"So you know what it says?"

"Only what he told us. My skills are still developing so it would have taken me quite some time to decipher, and Hanna Jaffrey, she barely knows it, the script."

He had a formal way of speaking that lapsed only occasionally into a misplaced word or grammatical mistake. It matched the restrained, almost cold edge to his personality.

Tomas seemed on comfortable ground here. He probably taught in addition to his fieldwork. "Scribes devoted their lives to learning the ancient languages because it took so many years to master the hundreds of characters in early alphabets. How amazing to think of the Canaanites in the Sinai turquoise mines. They first came up with the idea of associating symbols with sounds rather than images. That's why the Phoenician alphabet was revolutionary. Its twenty-two characters meant, theoretically anyway, everyone could learn to read and write.

"Because the engraving was made on stone, we knew it was important. Royal inscriptions and oracles of special significance were often recorded on stone due to its permanence. Less lofty documents were written on clay. Scribes would sometimes put water on them to use them over again."

I wanted to be polite, but now he really was telling me stuff I already knew. I held up my hand. "I'm aware of that."

He gave me a faint smile. "Ah, sorry again. I forget."

"What did Samuel say about the text?"

"He couldn't contain himself. 'One of the greatest finds in all of Iraq's history,' he told us."

I thought of my brother and how much this would have meant to him. His joy would have rivaled George Smith's, the amateur Assyriologist who discovered the story of Noah and the Flood in 1872. Smith interpreted cuneiform tablets at the British Museum during his lunch hour. His eureka moment arrived when he discovered the famous story on a tablet, part of the Epic of Gilgamesh. When Smith realized what he'd found, anecdotal reports told of him dashing about and flinging off his clothes in front of his fellow scholars. Samuel had a more restrained personality, but he would have been jubilant all the same.

"Someone tried to steal it," Tomas carried on. "The next day Samuel took it to the Baghdad Museum and concealed it there."

"He could do that without anyone knowing? I checked the sources—FBI, Interpol, and the Art Loss Register—and there's no mention of anything like the engraving."

"In the museum itself many tablets and cylinder seals still have not been transcribed. That's also true for foreign museums. It's one of the great tragedies of this looting. Much was never recorded. Even if objects resurface, there will be no way, if identification marks have been erased, to show they belonged to us."

Tomas paused, signaling to our server that he'd like more tea and motioning to my cup. I shook my head. "The scribe signed his name, Nahum. Does that mean anything to you?" he asked.

"No."

"Nahum was one of the twelve minor prophets of the Hebrew Bible. The Book of Nahum, called the Burden of Nineveh, prophesizes the destruction of Nineveh. The city was burned in 612 B.C."

This new information hit me like a thunderbolt. He'd just made the connection to the prophecy Hal referred to in his letter. "You're trying to suggest the engraving I'm searching for is an original version of an Old Testament book?" My pulse quickened in anticipation of his answer.

"Yes, exactly. Can you imagine its significance? They've found quotations from the Book of Nahum among the Qumran Dead Sea Scrolls, but only fragments. The engraving contains the original words, intact. It's a phenomenal find—I can hardly think of a comparison. We can only dream about its value to history."

The server set a fresh cup of tea down before Tomas. Thanking her, he continued. "A Mesopotamian statue recently sold in Switzerland for twenty-two million. That had nothing like the importance of an original book of the Bible. I couldn't even guess what it would be worth."

The initial thrill faded as I came to my senses. "And I'm sure you were all thinking it would be front-page news. How could Samuel fall for that? It can't be genuine. And Hal was murdered for the thing."

Tomas shrank back as if my words were actual blows.

"Claims like this are made all the time. Remember the limestone ossuary they made public last year? It supposedly held the remains of James, brother of Jesus. Experts think the surface patina was manufactured. There's a sucker born every minute for this kind of stuff."

"You haven't even seen it and you're saying it's a fake," he shot back. "It's entirely possible for a Hebrew scribe to have lived in Assyria."

"I know, but that's a far cry from an original book of the Bible being written there."

"He was likely a highly educated scribe taken in tribute to work for the Assyrian king. Nahum means 'comforter' and probably wasn't the scribe's real name. He was *originally* from Judah, and even though the Assyrian state was on its last legs, the author of a tirade against Nineveh like the Book of Nahum would have been killed. So the prophet had to hide his identity. The engraving is real, I assure you."

I was starting to piece it together. "So, an enslaved Hebrew scribe writes a diatribe against what he believes is a godless city. Fine. But if the engraving was found buried in the lost city of Nineveh, how did it ever become a book in the Hebrew Bible?"

Tomas considered this for a moment. I could tell he didn't want to tip his hand and reveal too much more.

"Papyrus was beginning to be used around that

time; they must have smuggled papyrus copies out of Assyria."

He could be right. A Hebrew might have been forcibly deported to the Assyrian capital, and multiple copies of the book spirited back to Judah. "It's just … I've seen people caught up in the excitement of a major find only to have it turn out that some entrepreneur manufactured the thing. All the major museums have been fooled."

"But not Samuel. He checked it very carefully. We got wind of another attempt to steal it during the looting. That's when he made up his mind to bring it here. "

I cursed silently. Protecting another country's history had grown into an obsession for Samuel.

Tomas saw the look in my eyes and assumed I disapproved. "We could never have talked him out of it, you know. We did try. It's ironic—the looting also gave us the cover to get it away. Without Samuel we'd never have made it across the border."

"Why not just keep it in Jordan and wait out the war?"

"The walls have ears over there. American collectors lobbied their government to relax the rules on exporting Iraqi antiquities in the fall of 2002, right before the invasion. They said Iraq's policy forbidding the export of antiquities was 'retentive.'"

"I wasn't aware of that."

"Archaeologists counter-petitioned to make sure thousands of historic sites would be protected and were promised nothing would be damaged. What a farce. Rumors have surfaced of massive theft and even the use of advanced infrared imaging systems and ground-penetrating radar. Before the war is over everything will have been strip-mined."

I could see the pain written on his face. His feelings seemed genuine. "Was he suspicious about anyone in particular?"

"An American dealer and his associates."

I mentally ticked off the most prominent American dealers in Mesopotamian antiquities. Not a large group, and I knew virtually everyone. "Did he give you any other description? Any idea of who it might be?"

"I don't think he knew any more than that, or perhaps he didn't wish to accuse someone without clear proof. But he did mention an office on West Thirty-fourth Street, a block or two from the Hudson River. He said some other items he suspected had been stolen from the museum were sent there from agents in Baghdad."

"That sounds promising. What's the address?"

Tomas sighed. "I'm sorry. That's all I remember him saying, although he did find out the identities of two of the dealer's associates, a man and a woman. The woman who threatened you, you said her name was Eris?"

"Yes," I said, thinking again about her name. *Eris, the Greek spirit of strife, war, and pain. It suits her.*

"She's the one." Tomas snapped his fingers. "Her full name is Eris Haines. She's a former employee of the Department of Defense, research division. They develop advanced weaponry, carry out scientific research with an impact on national security. Before that, she worked as a private security consultant in Bosnia."

"And the man?"

"George Shimsky. Reportedly, a brilliant chemist. He suffered some kind of accident. Terrible scars on his face."

I drained my espresso. "The two of them were terrifying. They may be linked to a website called the Alchemy Archives. Do you know anything about that?"

"Not about any group. You mentioned alchemy before. It's from the Arabic *al-kimia*. A gift of the science of chemistry from the Arab nations to the West. Alchemy is supposed to have originated in Egypt, but you could make a compelling case that the earliest sources are Mesopotamian."

"Why would alchemy have anything to do with the Book of Nahum?" I slid the question in again, determined to get a real answer this time.

He shrugged his shoulders. "One can find many hidden meanings in biblical scriptures. Samuel may have had an answer for you on that. But if so, he took it to his grave."

He let that remark dangle for a moment before changing the subject. "I understand you were born in Turkey. Samuel said you were only three when your parents died in a mine disaster."

The sudden switch in conversation convinced me Tomas knew more about the significance of alchemy than he was willing to reveal, but he persisted. "Did you never try to seek out your relatives?"

"They'd made it pretty clear they didn't want me. Why would I?"

A slight flush on his neck indicated he knew he'd overstepped the bounds of politeness with someone he hardly knew. "You had some good fortune, though—you got Samuel. He never married. I find that curious."

"He was married, ages ago. His wife passed away before he learned about me. That helped to make up his mind to take me under his wing. Her death left a gap, and he found out about me at just the right time."

It was so humid you could practically see steam rising off the pavement outside. I ordered a glass filled with ice and a bottle of Lauquen, a crisp artesian water. When I offered some to Tomas he declined.

The heat didn't seem to bother him at all, even though just looking out the window at the people sweltering made me uncomfortable. I grappled with his revelation. Samuel had discovered an original book of the Bible. If true, the find would be sensational. But pieces were deliberately missing from the story, and that troubled me.

"Anyway, back to what you were saying. Samuel had ties with most of the major museums and a number of options for safekeeping. So why bring the engraving here? I don't think you're giving me the whole story."

Tomas took a breath, and in the gap I saw a flicker of concern in his eyes.

"There's something else to this then?"

He shifted uncomfortably in his seat. "I'm not at liberty to say."

"You don't trust me?"

He tried to avoid my eyes. "You've seen what can happen. Until the danger has passed you're safer not knowing. That's probably why Samuel didn't tell you himself."

My patience finally hit the wall. "If you want to find the artifact, you need me. Tell me everything or I'm out of here."

A few minutes passed in silence while he struggled with what to say. "Samuel believed it contained a concealed message."

"You're saying Nahum used some kind of code?"

"Not exactly. Not a cipher. It's something to do with the way he wrote the book. Signs in the text the prophet left for his confederates."

He could read the disbelief on my face. "It is possible. You've heard of the copper scroll they found at Kirbet Qumran with the Dead Sea Scrolls? It listed a number of sites throughout Israel. Hiding places for gold and silver."

"That was written centuries after Nahum. There were no hidden messages. The locations were described; contemporary interpreters just can't understand them. Don't you think that if there was a secret message in Nahum's prophecy, over thousands of years someone would have figured it out?"

"No." Tomas's voice dropped, and I sensed we were finally getting down to it.

"Why not?"

"Because the words on the engraving differ from even the most original version of the Hebrew Bible we have."

Tomas's voice was barely a whisper, his black eyes leveled at me. "You must admit I've been forthcoming with you, John Madison. Now it's your turn. If you have some kind of lead I want to hear it."

"Nothing concrete yet. I haven't had a chance to follow anything up."

"I expect to be kept informed. It's the property of my country."

"It will go back to Iraq through the proper channels."

Keeping a lid on his temper seemed to be more and more of a challenge for Tomas. "My experience with valuable antiquities is that things can get derailed even through what you people call proper channels. An original book of the Bible? This would be something hard to let go of, especially when there's no proof of where it came from. Samuel trusted me. You should too."

Was he suggesting I intended to sell it myself, in the same breath as he invoked my dead brother? What a prick. I certainly wasn't prepared to just hand it over to him. "We're getting ahead of ourselves," I said icily. "Let's see whether I can find it first."

We ended in a stalemate. Clearly, neither of us had any intention of volunteering more information. He checked his watch and said he had to go, scrambling to pick up his backpack. He scribbled a number on his business card and stood up. "You can call me at this number. The bill's taken care of. How do I reach you?"

I gave him my email address and phone number. After he left I waited for a minute or so before following him. Rounding the corner onto Second Avenue, I spotted him leaning into a car, his arm resting on the open window of the driver's side, talking to whoever was inside. He walked around to the passenger side and got in. The driver gunned it and took off. I walked away knowing he'd given me only a sliver of the truth. But I was determined to get the whole story.

Nine

I'd planned to head for home and take another shot at the puzzle, but a better idea surfaced and I ventured instead back to Hal's townhouse on West Twentieth. The street felt relatively safe, with people coming home from the restaurants sauntering along the sidewalks. It was a perfectly unremarkable evening. And yet the feeling of something malevolent at my back crept over me again.

I leaned against the iron fence of the school opposite Hal's house and surveyed my surroundings. St. Peter's Episcopal Church, with its handsome gray limestone, bright red doors, and graceful clock tower, lay just to the west. The tall, black iron church gate stood open, as it often did when some arts or music group had an event on. Beside the church was the brick facade of the Atlantic Theater.

Seeing nothing out of place, I crossed the street to Hal's townhouse. It was a typical four-story home, less elaborate than most, with a plain stucco finish in faded rose and black trim. The first floor was at street level, not half a story up as in the grander brownstones. Yellow police tape stretched in an X over the front door. I glanced around to make sure no one was watching and punched in the numbers to the lock code. Peter had once installed a much more elaborate security system, but Hal had let it drop, along with a lot of other things he could no longer afford. The door clicked open and I slid under the tape, closing the door behind me.

I'd decided to come because there had to be some kind of trail among Hal's papers pointing to the hiding place, even an outside chance he'd actually stashed the engraving in a location I knew about.

The interior was dim, but I knew the place as a hare knows the dark tunnels of its warren. I moved around the ground floor, the rooms still reeking of booze and weed from last night's party, and made sure the windows and doors were locked. I was glad to see the police had done their job well. Everything appeared secure on the second floor too. A stale smell hit me as I passed by Peter's bedroom, with its accumulation of spilled food, dust, and nocturnal accidents. Hal had been no housekeeper. He'd probably not even bothered to change the bedclothes after his father went to the nursing home.

Hal's study occupied a windowless alcove midway on the second floor, so I had no concerns about clicking on the desk light. The room was furnished with a heavy, Dutch-designed oak desk, no doubt belonging to one of his illustrious ancestors, and a matching wooden chair. An IKEA bookshelf stood in odd contrast against a side wall, crammed with tomes on philosophy, physics, and game theory. I rooted through them and found several volumes on alchemy.

The walls had been stripped of the valuable paintings, pale rectangles signaling their absence. The one picture left, a Dürer reproduction print titled *Melencolia 1,* wasn't worth enough to bother selling.

Hal's laptop was missing. I hunted around his papers, looking for some kind of trail pointing to the engraving's hiding place. Just as I'd guessed, a copy of the first notice from Teras Distributing sat near the top of an unruly pile littering his desk. Clipped to the letter was a note from Walter Taylor, a cultural attaché in Jordan and an old friend of Samuel's.

Samuel, I've sent your package through our diplomatic carrier as you asked. It should arrive at Teras Distributing in June. If I didn't know you so well, I'd say all that arak you've consumed over the years has finally taken its toll. But seriously, you may well have uncovered a rare find. What a fitting denouement to your career. Let's discuss this further when I'm back home on terra firma. Keep some gin on ice for me. Don't even think about returning to Iraq, my friend. The place is set to detonate.

So Samuel had confided in someone other than his assistants. In Jordan it would be after three in the morning. I'd have to put off calling Taylor for now.

Stuck in a drawer was a computer printout:

Neo-Assyrian stone engraving originating from Kuyunjik mound, Nineveh. Seventh century B.C. Full description upon expression of interest. Rare antiquity.

A contact number underneath had been scratched out. A draft, perhaps, of the advertisement Hal circulated to sell the engraving. So amateurish. No legitimate dealer would touch an item like that without at least a full description, an indication of the value, and some guarantee of provenance. If Hal thought he could get away with a sale, he was crazy. Whatever address he came up with, Interpol could trace it in minutes. He might as well have put up a billboard in Times Square. Ever since the Baghdad Museum was trashed they'd been watching all the Iraqi-origin stuff closely. His lack of judgment was stunning.

For the next half hour I pawed through the rest of Hal's bills and letters. He was far deeper into credit than I'd realized, letting even basic things like phone and cable payments slip. I pitied him. The months before he died must have been dismal.

When I found nothing in Hal's desk I climbed the stairs to the top floor. Almost all of it was taken up with the place I called the vanishing room. It had been used by Hal's grandfather for fencing practice. "His fencing teacher was badly wounded, right over here." More fable than reality. I remember Hal relating this story with gusto when we were boys and me staring hard at the floor, trying to spot old bloodstains among the grooves of the blond hardwood, imagining the fencing master falling, his sword clattering to the floor, a flare of crimson on his white shirt, the way it happened in *Zorro*.

The slatted wooden blinds on the two front windows were closed, so I could safely turn on a wall light. It cast a soft buttery glow, the light glancing back from the mirrors. The room was bare of furniture; I'd never known it to have any aside from the cabinets flanking the rear wall where Peter had housed the bulk of his collection. On the front wall beside the window, fencing masks and swords hung from a custom-made rack—lightweight dry foils, épées, and the deadlier sabers. Hal and I were caught playing with them once and were banished from the room for months afterward.

The cabinet shelves were bare now and thick with grime. I groped for the switch hidden in a curl of decorative wood at the top of the first cabinet and heard the snap of the lock releasing. The back slid behind its neighbor, revealing a large closet. I felt a surge of anticipation—I was almost certain Hal would have stored the engraving here, as his father had with his most precious pieces. A couple of large cardboard boxes sat against the back wall of the closet, their flaps open. The boxes were empty. I swore out loud.

The only other object was a small bronze urn sitting on a shelf about two feet below the ceiling. I brought it down and opened the lid. Inside were some yellowish gems. I took one out. Precious stones of some kind. Why had Hal kept them in here? They were quite small and uncut so wouldn't be worth much.

Upset and preoccupied by my failure to find anything, I relaxed my vigilance as I left the house. That was all it took. As I passed by the recess between a townhouse and the churchyard a figure lurched out of the shadows, locking his thick arm around my neck. He gripped my jacket, pulling me hard against his chest, so tight I could actually feel his diaphragm rise and fall.

I jerked my body away and felt his grip slacken slightly. I swung my arm around and struck out, hitting him with all my strength. My jacket came off as I tore myself away. I was free.

With only a split second to react I opted not to run down the street, thinking Eris might be waiting there and armed. Instead I charged through the church gate and flung open the wooden front door, hoping whoever was inside might help. But the interior was dark and silent.

I darted up the stairway of blackened wood that led to the second-story galleries. Tucked into one corner of the landing was a small door, like the entrance to a monk's cell. I pressed against it, felt it give, and slammed my body into it, hard. It sprang open.

Shutting it as quietly as possible, I found myself in a tube of yellow brick so narrow I couldn't spread out my arms. I felt for my cell to call the police and realized it was in my jacket pocket. Only one option left then—to hide.

A black iron spiral staircase curled up the tower's center. Sconces fixed into the rounded walls produced a weak, yellowish illumination. My shadow preceded me as I corkscrewed up the stairs. I couldn't see more than six feet ahead and had no idea how high it went. The air inside was warm and close, and my head buzzed with the turning motion. At the top of the stairway a plank door painted battleship gray opened onto a large room, about fifteen feet square. The space soared to a crumbling plaster ceiling. In places the plaster had fallen out, exposing the wood lath beneath.

A steady pulsing sound off to my left turned out to be a huge iron pendulum enclosed in a wooden frame. Above this a collection of gears and pulleys whirred away. The drivers for the church clock. The pendulum swung back and forth with the slow sideways swish of a reaper's scythe.

Poe's story surfaced. I imagined the walls and floor sliding in, crushing me flat.

A full-dress army uniform, dusty with age, and Second World War military colors hung on one wall. Ghosts of dead soldiers whispered into the silence.

I listened for any sounds of pursuit but could detect only the steady stroke of the clock, a soft boom, like the heartbeat of a giant. Flimsy steps led up to a closed hatch on the ceiling. I climbed them and pushed at the wooden covering. Something fell, and I pulled back as though it had been aimed at my head. A dead sparrow landed on the floor with a tiny thud.

The hatch opened into an empty, dark space. The sour smell of bird droppings and mold lingered. I could hear the swish of wings. Pigeons? Bats? I felt gingerly around the wooden frame above the hatch to see whether enough secure flooring existed for me to clamber up. When I pulled my hand back it was covered with dust and the furry wings of dead moths.

Could I hide there?

Footsteps rang on the metal stair treads below the room, steadily gaining, interspersed with the ticktock of the giant pendulum, as if the clock were counting out the seconds left in my life. The door creaked open.

The man's leg extended over the threshold and then his entire body came into view. He could barely squeeze in. He tottered into the room and stopped.

When he spotted me a tremor of excitement seemed to ripple through his body. Tortured sounds came out of his mouth, as though his vocal cords had corroded. Like a stone statue, he took slow, deliberate strides toward me. This I knew in my gut was the burned chemist. He was like some primeval creature who'd taken on human form, as if a god had fashioned a giant sculpture and breathed life into the stone. The ancient Greeks chained their statues to prevent them from escaping, believing they were alive. I realized now they did this out of fear, not to stop them from running away.

His face was broad and abnormally flat beneath a completely shaved head. His skin had a grayish quality, like dried putty. He glared at me out of one eye. It filled me with revulsion. For an instant it seemed as though the Cyclops of my youthful imagination had come back to claim me.

He turned his head and now I could see that he actually had two eyes, but the left was severely damaged and masked with scar tissue. Over the vacant space where his left eye should have been, waxy skin had been clumsily grafted back on.

I had a couple of advantages. The guy was powerful but slow moving. My reaction time was much faster and I was above him. Always a good position to be in if you want to beat someone.

He had trouble with the stairs, the weak wood of the steps sagging beneath his great weight, and his balance seemed off. I did my best to judge the optimum distance. When he got within reach, I gripped the rails to take the weight of my body and kicked his chest. He lost his footing and crashed down the stairs.

It would have been a successful move, but when I grasped the frame of the hatch to pull myself into the cavity above, the worm-eaten wood splintered and came away in my hands. I plunged down a few steps, close enough for him to grab me. He caught my lower legs and pulled me the rest of the way down. This time I couldn't break his grip.

He forced me out of the room, down the twisting stairwell to the main floor of the church, and out the door. At the curb a Range Rover revved its motor.

Someone opened the side door. The brute threw me face down on the floor, where the second bank of seats had been removed. Inside, I could make out the form of another man. When I tried to lift my head a heavy boot smashed my face into the floorboard. Blood flooded into my mouth as my incisors cut through the soft flesh of my bottom lip. I spat out dirt and motor oil.

A hand dug into my trouser pocket. "Look up," the guy said. "Where are your keys?"

I wasn't about to help him out. "Must have lost them in the tower."

The ploy didn't work. He opened the window and said something to the thug outside, calling him Shim. That had to be George Shimsky, whom Tomas Zakar had mentioned. A minute later my jacket was thrown into the front seat. The keys were extracted and we took off, leaving Shim behind.

If they were taking me back to my place, it was on the tip of my tongue to point out they'd never make it past the doorman. But I held back. Let them walk into their own trap.

A ringtone. I heard the driver answer. "Yes?" A woman's voice. "We have him and we're on our way. Just a minute." I heard her rustling for something. "Okay, I've got it with me. Yeah, we're nearly there." A space of silence while she listened. "Not this time," she responded, snapping the phone shut.

The voice belonged to Eris.

We stopped in less than ten minutes. The interior lights came on. "Sit up," the man ordered.

The driver's door opened and slammed shut again. *Click, click, click*—the sound of pumps on the asphalt. They tapped around the front of the vehicle and came to a halt opposite my door. When it opened Eris faced me. Her platinum hair shone under the streetlights.

She scrutinized me. "You've got blood on your face. I can't take you in like that." She reached into her handbag and extracted a tissue, bending toward me. For an instant I considered making a grab for her, but the odds of failing were too high.

I could smell the faint, spicy scent of her perfume as she leaned over. "Okay," she said. "You're going to put your arm around me and escort me to the elevator. The two of us are coming back from the clubs. We're slightly drunk. When we see your doorman you'll smile. Don't bother trying to get away. You're not tough enough to go against us."

"Really? I did last time."

That didn't lighten her mood any. She tossed me my jacket, ordered me to put it on, and pulled out her gun, keeping it pressed against my side, too close to be visible to anyone else. We proceeded into the lobby while the second man drove away.

I glanced toward the desk. No sign of Amir. On a slow night he'd duck out for a coffee. He couldn't have chosen a worse moment.

Eris moved abruptly away the minute we got on the elevator and leaned against the wall, aiming her gun at me. I tried to put on a brave face, but inside my heart flipped around like a broken bird's. I consoled myself with the thought that this was happening because she wanted something from me. All I had to do was cooperate.

We stepped off the elevator into an empty corridor. Passing Nina's door, I could hear Jay-Z booming out of her sound system, the chatter of party voices raised to full volume. If I yelled no one would hear. It seemed my entire building was in a conspiracy to defeat me.

She handed me my keys to open the door and herded me straight into my bedroom. Out of the corner of my eye, I noticed the balcony door still open. I had a brief, crazy vision of flinging myself through it, ducking the inevitable bullets, swinging over the rail, and dropping to the balcony below. They did this in movies and somehow always survived.

Eris got something out of her bag and walked toward me. A spray atomizer. I remember wanting to say something and opening my mouth as the mist hit my face. My chest tightened and the world slipped away.

Ten

"Move your legs," the doctor ordered.

I tried and could not.

"You're paralyzed; I was afraid of that."

It wasn't the voice of the grim-faced surgeon who'd stitched me up in the hospital, but an angel doctor's. Her hair shimmered silver in the light; her ice-blue eyes, fringed with blond lashes, were clear and beautiful.

The angel's face morphed into Eris's.

A wave of horror crashed through me.

I lay prone on my bed, naked from the waist up, both wrists clamped onto the steel bed frame with handcuffs like giant twist ties. I tried to heave, roll over, move my legs, or even a toe. I urinated and couldn't stop myself. From my pelvis down, my body lay like a dead weight.

I tried to talk but my words came out like the bark of a dying seal. I cleared my throat a couple of times before I could manage to whisper, "What have you done to me?"

"We need to talk."

"You bitch."

"Don't use foul language around me."

"Tell me what you've done."

"You've been disabled. Like a car engine with a few spark plugs pulled out."

"Is this what you used on Hal?"

Eris frowned. "We're not here to talk about Hal. You can still use your arms. Tell me where the engraving's hidden or I'll yank out a few more plugs."

I deliberately lowered my voice even more to force her to draw nearer. If she got close enough I could try to hit her head with mine and do some damage.

She didn't take the bait. "Talk louder. I can't hear you."

"I told you I don't know. My brother, Samuel, brought it over. Hal stole it from a warehouse and stashed it somewhere. You killed him so you've screwed yourself."

"Tonight you met with a man, Tomas Zakar. I believe the two of you talked about retrieving the engraving. There's no point in lying." She peered down at me closely but maintained enough distance that I couldn't touch her. "Are you taking all this in?"

"I want to know what you shot into me," I rasped.

"You're soft, John. You have no idea what it really means to be afraid." She was seated in a chair beside me, angled so I could see her easily. She'd taken off her cardigan. On her upper arm was a green-inked tattoo, a circle with a cross extending from the bottom like the sign for female. The symbol I'd seen for Venus on the alchemy website.

I watched as she tugged her top up to the line of her breasts. Her entire stomach was criss-crossed with a network of angry red welts and scars. Not one square inch of normal flesh was visible.

She rolled her top back down. "I know something about pain. I can teach you, if you want."

"How'd that happen?"

"Fighting in Bosnia. Now start cooperating. You don't have a lot of time left."

"This is a lost cause. I told you I have no idea where it is." I'd obviously miscalculated her age at the party. If she'd seen action in Bosnia she was much older than I'd thought.

Was some sensation crawling back into my limbs? I thought I could feel the silkiness of my bedsheets and a flare of pain running up my legs.

"You're getting tiresome," Eris sighed. She took a syringe filled with a milky liquid out of her bag. "This is called China Cat. It's heroin that's been tinkered around with to strengthen its purity. If I inject it, you'll die." I felt the prick of the needle tip crease my skin as she leaned toward me.

I had to give her something. "All right, I'll tell you. Just take the needle off me."

She pressed it deeper into my flesh. "Talk then."

"Hal did leave an indication of where to find it."

Eris hesitated.

"Listen, I don't want to die over a hunk of rock. Believe me."

I could feel the sting of the needle as it pressed even deeper. "That's not good enough."

A flicker of feeling stole back into my legs, a cold burn traveling from the soles of my feet into my shins. Was it my imagination or was the drug wearing off? But that wouldn't matter if she used the needle. Fear punched through my gut. Then I thought of the copy of Hal's game.

"You didn't know Hal. If he had a choice between dating Beyoncé and playing board games, he'd choose the games. He left a map revealing the location in the form of a puzzle. So far I haven't figured it out, but I will."

"Where is it?" Her eyes lit up.

"Look in my back pocket."

She withdrew the needle and dug inside my pocket. I was relieved when she pulled out the piece of paper—I hadn't been entirely sure it was still there.

Eris fixated on it as if it were a map to King Solomon's mines. "We're going to keep this. Maybe we don't need you after all."

Did this mean I was free, or would I now be getting an armful of heroin? "You do need me," I said. "Only someone who knew him well can solve it."

"You mean it's some kind of code?"

"Something like that. A word code. Probably a series of anagrams."

"Show me."

I tried to raise my head but was still too weak to hold it up for any length of time. "I can't right now, but you'll never find it without me. You'd be kissing a fortune goodbye."

"We have other options …"

When I tried to look at her she kept slipping in and out of focus.

Voices registered outside my front door, followed by loud knocking. "John … John, are you in?" A volley of giggles. It was Nina, emerging from her loud party like a badger out of its nest. A male voice next. "He's not there. Let's just go in and get it, babe."

Nina again. "He said he'd come to my party. What if he shows up now?" More giggling. "Maybe we shouldn't go in."

Nina, you have to come in. Don't leave, I prayed.

Eris bolted up in alarm, took a few steps toward the bedroom door, and listened.

The male again. "Give me the key. I'll go in and get it."

Open the door. God help me, just open it.

"No, I'd better. In case he's there—he doesn't know you." Scraping sounds. The crack of the door being pushed open. Whispering.

Eris glared and signaled for me to keep quiet. She tucked the puzzle into her bag, tousled her hair, and undid a couple of buttons.

Nina spoke again. "I'll be totally freaked out if he's in there asleep."

"Where does he keep it?"

"In the dining room."

Their feet shuffled over the carpet. Eris stepped out into the living room. "Hi," I heard her say. "Your timing isn't the greatest."

Nina gasped.

I tried to yell, but the drug was still playing havoc with my vocal cords.

"Oh!" I heard Nina say. "I'm so sorry. I didn't think anyone was here. I'm John's neighbor."

I gathered all my strength and channeled it into my voice. "Nina, don't listen to her. She's lying."

"He's drunk," Eris said quickly.

"I'm not. Nina, come here. In the bedroom. I've got to see you."

"Hey." The guy's voice. "What the hell?" The front door slammed. Nina and a man materialized in the bedroom doorway. In seconds, Nina morphed from an expression of shock into an explosion of tipsy laughter. Her boyfriend wore an irritating smirk.

She put her hands up to her face to stifle her sniggers. "Oh, John. I just wanted to borrow some wine. We ran out. I really apologize."

"Where's Eris? The woman?"

The guy lost his smirk. "She took off. She's gone."

Nina had trouble suppressing another smile. "I'd never have guessed"—she gestured toward me on the bed—"that you were into this, this … sort of thing."

"I'm not even going to try to explain. Help yourself

to a whole case of wine, just cut these things off first. There's an X-Acto knife in Samuel's desk drawer."

She found the knife and returned. Her escort had to do the cutting because the plastic ties were so tough. When they finished I tried to lever my legs over the side of the bed but managed only to flop around like a dying fish. A wave of dizziness and nausea hit me. Nina, finally realizing something was very wrong, asked if she should call the police.

"No, there's no point. Would you mind just making me some coffee? Triple strong."

Her boyfriend made a few perfunctory remarks about hoping I was okay then hightailed it back to the party. I practiced sitting up and succeeded by the time Nina returned with the coffee. She said she wanted to stay and make sure I was all right, but I insisted she go back to her guests.

I chugged the coffee down and massaged my legs, getting them to the point where I could wobble to the living room. I made sure the front door was locked and saw my keys on the hall table where I'd tossed them. I staggered into the washroom and stood under the shower for half an hour.

I heard the whine and the crash of the garbage trucks emptying metal trash containers outside. The howl of a siren trailed off into the distance. Four in the morning. I closed my eyes. What a strange hole I'd plunged into. And it didn't seem to have a bottom.

Eleven

Monday, August 4, 2003, 8:05 A.M

A bizarre nightmare woke me up. I lay face down on a city sidewalk, the concrete like molten steel in the afternoon sun. Eris was closing in. Each time I put a hand down to drag myself forward to escape her, my palm burned as if I'd just touched a hot stove.

I shuddered, coming fully awake, and got off the couch. This time my legs did everything they were ordered to. Another brutally hot shower helped to clear away the fuzziness still meandering through my head. I clipped my beard so I looked presentable again and applied some salve to my lip, the pain tapping out a constant drumbeat. I tore off the bedsheets, walked down the hall, and stuffed them into the incinerator. I thought about knocking on Nina's door to thank her for the rescue but could hear no noise from within and assumed she was still sleeping it off.

When I contacted Joseph Reznick, the criminal lawyer Andy had recommended, his assistant told me he was in court, unreachable until later in the day.

"Could I make an appointment for this afternoon? It's urgent."

"Not even if you're facing a firing squad. But I'll tell him you called."

The time was right, however, to call Walter Taylor in Jordan—it would be afternoon there. But when I reached his office his secretary told me he was on leave for two weeks. She'd forward a message to him but couldn't promise anything. I had to be satisfied with that.

I put on some music, got the copy of Hal's puzzle, and sat with a coffee at the kitchen counter trying to solve it with new eyes. The first music selection was R. Kelly's rendition of "If I Could Turn Back the Hands of Time." A great song by a master vocalist; I once flew halfway across the country just to hear him perform live. But the music wrecked my concentration.

I turned it off and focused on the puzzle. The word pattern on the board was wrong. Two groups of words were completely separated. In these games at least one word has to bridge the two sides. If I put an *s* onto *quest* on the bottom row and an *i* above the *s*, that would create a bridge. But the completed word had to fit the thirteen squares, so that didn't work. I scrutinized the rest of the board. The theoretical game player missed good chances to build words off a *t* that appeared on the eighth row from the top on the left side.

A spark went off. I reached for it but it lingered like a half-remembered dream, teasing me before it faded away altogether. I toyed with various combinations of words for another half hour and got nowhere.

I got up, stretched, and with another coffee wandered into Samuel's study. His door was ajar. Eris had no doubt stormed through here while I was out cold. I wanted to read the Book of Nahum, but when I opened the door my eye fell on books that had been thrown in a heap on the floor. I looked up and saw that the section on his bookshelves allotted for his journals was empty. I got down on my hands and knees and combed through the books and papers scattered about the floor and found them. Thirty in all. A lifelong record of his wanderings, observations, and private thoughts.

Samuel's journals were not diaries but rather a hodgepodge of observations, records of events or notes he'd made during his travels, personal comments, and sometimes even sketches. In bound volumes of forest-green leather, each was labeled with the time period it represented. I sorted through them, putting the nearest dates on top, and found the most recent one, from January 2001 to December 2002.

The first page surprised me. A picture he'd pasted in, an Assyrian relief from Sennacherib's palace. I'd seen it in the British Museum. It showed soldiers

flaying Hebrew prisoners of war, the quilt-like stria-
tions in the background meant to depict a forest.

Below the image were some notes he'd made
based on a book called *The Bible Unearthed* by Israel
Finkelstein and Neil Asher Silberman:

> In 722 B.C., Sargon II lays waste to Samaria.
> End of the Israelite kingship line. Samaria
> utterly destroyed. Israelites deported to
> Assyria.

The records also described how Sennacherib took
revenge on Judah.

> As to Hezekiah, the Judahite, he did not
> submit to my yoke. I laid siege to 46 of his
> strong cities, walled forts and countless small
> villages in their vicinity, and conquered
> them by means of well-stamped earth ramps,
> and battering rams.... I drove out of them
> 200,150 people, cattle beyond counting, and
> considered them booty.

So did all this fit in with the engraving somehow?
Would Nahum's ancestors, grandparents maybe, have
come from Samaria and experienced this? The case
for Nahum being deported to Assyria as tribute and
forced to work as a scribe was getting stronger.

I knew Assyrian kings established the true first
empire. Former vassal states like Judah were converted

Stone relief from the southwest palace of Sennacherib, 704–681 B.C.

into provinces with appointed governors under direct Assyrian control. Resistant states were burned, looted, and subjected to mass deportations—the first ethnic cleansings.

In Assyria's defense, Samuel once told me, "It's who gets to write history that counts. Our image of Assyrians and Babylonians came from the Old Testament, and thus, their history, written by their enemies, cast them in a totally negative light. Only in the late nineteenth century when interpretation of cuneiform tablets began did a different picture emerge."

Samuel revered the Assyrians but recognized that some kings were tyrants. Sennacherib laid waste to Babylon so thoroughly that only reed beds and thickets remained. On the other hand, his son Esarhaddon spent much of his reign restoring Babylon to its former splendor. Ashurbanipal was a great scholar who assembled the famous library of clay tablets found at Nineveh and helped the Persian Elamites stay alive by sending them food. But he had a dark side and took delight in vicious punishments. He had leashes of chain fixed into the lips of prisoners of war with a cruel iron ring. I could recall reading one account where he feasted under a tree hung with a particularly gruesome fruit. Ashurbanipal had beheaded an enemy, spit on and slashed the face, and then suspended the head from the tree.

I flipped through more of Samuel's journal and saw that he'd identified kings of several obscure states: King Aza of Mannea and King Mitta of the Mushki. Why was he interested in these little-known rulers?

I picked up the copper plaque on his desk. My brother had had it inscribed with an Assyrian curse from King Ashurbanipal.

> Whosoever shall carry off the engraving or shall inscribe his name on it, side by side with mine own, may Assur and Belit overthrow him in wrath and anger and may they destroy his name and posterity in the land.

Samuel used to joke that this was the first copyright and said modern publishers would love to have the power of an Assyrian king. As I looked at it now, the curse took on ominous overtones, and I wondered whether it had retained some of its power through the centuries. Nahum's engraving had indeed been "carried off." Twice, I had learned. And Samuel and Hal were dead because of it.

Samuel's small collection of relics consisted almost entirely of rescued objects, items he'd culled from dealers that would have ended up in private hands anyway. His career had been set in motion by his desire to restore cultural histories. "Names are important," he'd once said, "they shape who we are. As a boy I was intrigued by my namesake, the prophet Samuel, who recovered the Ark of the Covenant. I decided then that my life's work would be to rescue artifacts, our reference markers for history."

A laudable goal, but one he'd taken too far this time. And who knew what repercussions lay ahead?

I found Samuel's Bible and looked up the prophet's book. The rare times I'd read the Bible I'd always had difficulty with its antiquated language, but I found Nahum surprisingly easy to read.

The Book of the Vision of Nahum the Elkoshite
Chapter Two

2:1   Behold upon the mountains the feet of him that bringeth good tidings, that announceth peace! Keep thy feasts, O Judah, perform thy vows; for the wicked one shall no more pass through thee; he is utterly cut off.

2:2   A maul is come up before thy face; guard the defences, watch the way,

make thy loins strong, fortify thy power
mightily!—

2:3 For the Lord restoreth the pride of Jacob,
as the pride of Israel; for the emptiers
have emptied them out, and marred
their vine-branches.—

2:4 The shield of his mighty men is made
red, the valiant men are in scarlet; the
chariots are fire of steel in the day of his
preparation, and the cypress spears are
made to quiver.

2:5 The chariots rush madly in the streets,
they jostle one against another in the
broad places; the appearance of them
is like torches, they run to and fro like
lightnings.

2:6 He bethinketh himself of his worthies;
they stumble in their march; they
make haste to the wall thereof, and the
mantelet is prepared.

2:7 The gates of the river are opened, and
the palace is dissolved.

2:8 And the queen is uncovered, she is
carried away, and her handmaids moan
as with the voice of doves, tabering upon
their breasts.

2:9 But Nineveh hath been from of old like a
pool of water; yet they flee away; 'Stand,
stand', but none looketh back.

2:10 Take ye the spoil of silver, take the spoil
of gold; for there is no end of the store,
rich with all precious vessels.

2:11 She is empty, and void, and waste; and the heart melteth, and the knees smite together, and convulsion is in all loins, and the faces of them all have gathered blackness.

2:12 Where is the den of lions, which was the feeding-place of the young lions, where the lion and the lioness walked, and the lion's whelp, and none made them afraid?

2:13 The lion did tear in pieces enough for his whelps, and strangled for his lionesses, and filled his caves with prey, and his dens with ravin.

2:14 Behold, I am against thee, saith the Lord of hosts, and I will burn her chariots in smoke, and the sword shall devour thy young lions; and I will cut off thy prey from the earth, and the voice of thy messengers shall no more be heard.

Chapter Three

3:1 Woe to the bloody city! It is all full of lies and rapine; the prey departeth not.

3:2 Hark! the whip, and hark! the rattling of the wheels; and prancing horses, and bounding chariots;

3:3 The horseman charging, and the flashing sword, and the glittering spear; and a multitude of slain, and a heap of carcases; and there is no end of the corpses, and they stumble upon their corpses;

3:4   Because of the multitude of the harlotries of the well-favoured harlot, the mistress of witchcrafts, that selleth nations through her harlotries, and families through her witchcrafts.

3:5   Behold, I am against thee, saith the Lord of hosts, and I will uncover thy skirts upon thy face, and I will shew the nations thy nakedness, and the kingdoms thy shame.

3:6   And I will cast detestable things upon thee, and make thee vile, and will make thee as dung.

3:7   And it shall come to pass, that all they that look upon thee shall flee from thee, and say, 'Nineveh is laid waste; who will bemoan her? whence shall I seek comforters for thee?'

3:8   Art thou better than No-amon, that was situate among the rivers, that had the waters round about her; whose rampart was the sea, and of the sea her wall?

3:9   Ethiopia and Egypt were thy strength, and it was infinite; Put and Lubim were thy helpers.

3:10 Yet she was carried away, she went into captivity; her young children also were dashed in pieces at the head of all the streets; and they cast lots for her honour-able men, and all her great men were bound in chains.

I put the book down, disappointed. The passages shed no light on the central question—what great secret had Samuel found in Nahum's words?

The last time I'd checked my email was before Hal's party—far too long. I scrolled through the messages. After deleting all the spam and saving the nonurgent stuff, I was left with two, the first from Diane:

"John, that problem you mentioned. How could you ask a friend to lie about something like that? A guy died! I told the truth."

Short and to the point; fair enough, I guess.

The second message came from Eric Nolan. A Holbein was coming up for auction this week. The last time the piece sold it had broken the million-dollar mark. Eric wanted me to represent him; the commission would be mouthwatering. His last message, posted this morning, gave me until this afternoon to reply. It was 1:40 now. How could I take the time to research the work's provenance and show up at an auction with this threat hanging over my head? I punched in a message to Eric giving my regrets and cursed my bad luck.

Twelve

Continuing to work on Hal's mindbender was top priority, but I still felt sluggish from the drug and needed to find some space to think, breathe some decent air. I wanted to get away from the rumble of the city and the constant buzz of traffic. Feel the sun on my face.

Leaving my building, I was struck by a wall of heat. It felt hot enough outside to grill burgers on the sidewalk. The air had a heavy quality as if it were pressing down on my shoulders; the sky was buff-colored at the horizon from the effluent of thousands of vehicles. A sulphurous odor rose through the sewer grates, reminding me that like an ancient city, another metropolis lay under Manhattan: a network of pipes, lost subway tunnels, ancient quarries, underground streams, all long buried.

I got my car from the parking garage I used on Thompson and fought with morning traffic to reach

Coney Island, mulling over Hal's game as I drove.

As I headed for a quiet square of lawn overlooking the beach, I saw a mermaid poised on the boardwalk handing out flyers. She wore a pale, flowing Lady Godiva wig that tumbled down her backside and accentuated thick black lashes as long as her baby finger. Her upper body was swathed in chiffon, showing off her breasts without laying bare the whole story. A long, sequined fish tail completed the outfit; green satin shoes peeped out from the bottom. The Coney Island Mermaid Parade took place in June. She was a little late.

I found an unclaimed bench and sat down. Throngs of young women lay on beach mats, played volleyball, sauntered along the water's edge. The scent of coconut oil and vanilla drifted on the breeze. One of the volleyball players wore only bright red bikini bottoms and a micro top with loosely knotted ties. Every time she jumped for the ball, her breasts popped out. She seemed quite skilled at hitting the ball and pulling back her top before her feet hit the ground again.

Not a good location, I thought, for a guy who needs to concentrate.

I'd turned my attention back to Hal's game when my cell chirped.

"Is this John Madison?"

"Yes," I said. "Who's speaking?"

"It's Joseph Reznick. You talked to my secretary earlier. You said you wanted to speak with me urgently."

"Thanks for getting back to me. Andy Stein said I should get in touch."

"Right, I remember you now."

"Is there any way we can meet to talk about my situation?"

"How about around five? Will that work?"

Would I have solved the game by then? Could I afford even an hour away from it? No. I had to keep going. "Is there any chance we could do it tomorrow?" The guy had to be thinking I was a total ass, pleading for an urgent meeting and then putting it off. If so, he didn't let on.

"Well, that's better for me actually. Around the same time?"

"That sounds fine."

"Have you been interviewed by the police?"

"Yes, it was pretty rough."

"No one represented you?"

"No."

"Don't volunteer if they want to interview you again. If they charge you, give them your name and nothing else. At some point they'll have to let you call an attorney. You don't want to say anything until we've had a chance to talk. No interrogation unless I'm sitting beside you." He gave me the number of his personal line and said to call him immediately if I heard from the police again.

"Thanks very much. By the way, Andy said you might check out my situation."

"I have some pretty good contacts, yes. There are

two issues, your accident and Hal Vanderlin's death. On the second, things are up in the air; they don't have much, but it's early days yet. About the crash, the police are feeling pretty pumped up. Only one thing is keeping them from charging you with reckless endangerment. But let's save that for our meeting. You can reach me overnight if you need to."

I terminated the call, glad I had at least one person on my side. If they did charge me and made it stick I'd be seeing jail time. The thought of that made me sick.

The news unsettled me to the point where I couldn't concentrate on Hal's game as I'd intended to do. I looked around at the sights and sounds, trying to get my mind off it. At a neighboring bench a man and two boys were eating their lunch, a jumble of fast-food containers piled around them. The kids, dressed identically in striped T-shirts, oversized blue shorts that just about reached their knees, and sandals, seemed around six years old. They sparred with each other throughout the meal. One would steal a fry, the other would throw ketchup packages at him. I assumed the man was their dad because he ordered them around with the kind of bossiness that's the exclusive territory of fathers. Most of his remarks were aimed at the dark-haired boy, the thrower, who, I must admit, was more of a pest. Their bickering was annoying.

I turned sideways and stretched my legs out, tipping my head back to soak in the rays. I thought about the many days in childhood I'd spent here with Samuel, and I wondered whether anything in the small chest he'd given me would have relevance to my quest. I was thoroughly familiar with its contents, having handled them many times over the years: the seven gold coins with their mysterious images, the copper medallion, the golden key. Nothing seemed to connect to the engraving.

Yells broke through my reverie. The two boys had meandered away, their sparring escalating into all-out war. The light-haired kid was taking whacks at his brother with an orange plastic baseball bat. The dark-haired one would duck and pull away and then rush back with a kick. One of his sandals had fallen off. Both of them were yelling at the top of their lungs. Dad had remained behind, mesmerized by the red bikini. The kids' yells brought him back to the real world. He charged over like a bull aiming for a toreador. He grabbed the dark-haired boy and gave him a slap on the behind with enough force that I could hear the blow from where I was sitting. The boy howled and burst into tears. I cringed on behalf of the second kid, who had to know what was coming.

But no. The man crouched down and gave him a hug, talking quietly to him. He picked up the baseball bat, held the kid's hand, and walked him over to their car, putting him inside. The dark-haired child lingered.

The guy just sat in the car, motor running. Finally, still crying but more quietly now, the boy made his way over to the car and got in. As they drove off, a breeze came up, scattering the fast-food containers and papers.

That's how it starts, I thought. Favoring one son over the other. That child will grow up with a hate-on for the whole world.

I turned my attention back to the engraving and went over the facts again. Samuel had recognized Nahum's text as a prophetic Old Testament book called the Burden of Nineveh. After someone had attempted to steal it, he refused to let anyone see it. He believed that not only was the text genuine but it contained a hidden message. Pointing to what? Something to do with alchemical processes to make gold. Was this just the product of an old man's imagination, or could there be some truth to it?

Another call cut into my train of thought.

"I'm so glad I reached you," Laurel said when I picked up.

"Is everything okay?" Her voice sounded shaky, as though she'd been crying again.

"No. That woman you described—Eris?"

"That's her name."

"She tried to get to me. I ran out of breakfast stuff. On my way back from Gristedes I had an odd sensation of being followed, and Gip just caught her trying to get upstairs, pretending she was a courier. She left when he confronted her."

"She probably searched the townhouse and came up with nothing, so now she wants to ransack your place."

"Good luck to her. I've spent the last couple of months sorting through Mina's things, helping

Hal decide what to sell. I think I'd know if he hid something here."

"He could have done it when you weren't home."

"I suppose." She didn't sound convinced.

"Listen, how about I come over? You shouldn't be alone."

"Could you? I'd feel better."

I turned the radio on for the drive back. Dire Straits' "Money for Nothing" came on. Whether the music helped to clarify my thoughts, I don't know, but as I pondered what hidden meanings Nahum's prophecy might have, the spark went off again and this time ignited a fire. I'd solved Hal's puzzle.

When I got upstairs Laurel greeted me with a kiss on the cheek. I can't say I minded the role of savior.

"What's wrong with your lip?" She touched the swelling on my face.

"It's nothing. I'm more concerned about you. And some good news. I may have the answer to Hal's game."

"Really?"

We went into the study off the family room, where I drew a sketch for her.

"Four letters are missing: *r, a, n, s*. Hal purposely didn't use all the letters available. All the words on the board should be linked, but the groups on the left and right sides of the board aren't joined. I needed to look for a connecting word. Putting the missing letters in

Melencolia 1 by Albrecht Dürer, 1514

between the *t* and the word *mutation* produced the correct word: *transmutation,* the one meaning to transform base metals into gold."

"Oh brother," Laurel said. "I'm embarrassed I didn't see that. That wasn't very inspired. Hal was usually a bit more inventive."

I'd already saved the image of the second puzzle on my BlackBerry, so Laurel couldn't see how I'd made the transition. I opened it and showed it to her. "Recognize it?" I asked.

"Of course. *Melencolia 1* by Albrecht Dürer. It's hanging in Hal's study."

Only two squares to be filled out this time. I tried the obvious answer, Dürer's initials, *A* and *D*, and then the numeric equivalent of his initials, one and four, but neither worked.

"Did Hal mention anything in particular he liked about the picture?"

"I'm not sure. He loved Dürer and M.C. Escher because they understood the mathematics of space and the connection between numbers and visual art." She thought for a few minutes. "Nothing comes to mind about anything specific he liked."

"What did he really intend?" I felt desperate. "I don't have time to fool around with this. Is he just going to keep stringing me along?"

"Knowing Hal, there's more to come. He didn't just pluck these puzzles out of thin air. They point to a meaning, some kind of underlying theme. How did you make the switch from the first puzzle to this one?"

I sidestepped her question. "You're giving him far too much credit. Hal was no better than a thief. Thanks to him my life is now pure hell."

Laurel bristled. "And all the money you made selling off his father's collection, you conveniently forgot about that."

Her reaction caught me off guard. "All I got was 20 percent. That's lower than a lot of dealers ask for. And I'm still owed money from the loan I gave him."

"You're whining about the world not treating you right. That's your problem, John. With Samuel or Hal, anyone who's been good to you, you just take whatever is on offer. And when that stops you throw a tantrum."

I was on the verge of losing my temper big time when I remembered that as his legal wife, Laurel would have inherited his wealth. With Peter's collection sold off and the properties in limbo, she'd have nothing left. Part-time teaching hours and grant money don't stretch far in this city.

She whipped around to face me. "Why are you doing this anyway? For the money, right? You said that thing was really valuable."

"It's not about money. I want those people off my back. And yours too. I have to find it. When I do I'll make a very public show about handing it over to the FBI. That's the only way they'll leave us alone."

"Someone will locate it eventually. Let them deal with it."

"I can't. Eris attacked me last night. She's convinced I know where the engraving is. She wants my scalp."

This shook her up a bit. "Tell the police then—they can take care of it."

"You're kidding me, right? After what that detective already put me through? He won't believe a thing I say."

Laurel slumped onto the couch, put her head in her hands, and drew her legs up. I sat down beside her. "Laurie, you're going through a difficult time. I know that."

"How am I supposed to plan for a funeral, John? The police sent some things over they found on Hal and don't need for forensics. I couldn't bear to look at the stuff. They won't even tell me when they're releasing his body." Tears filled her eyes.

"Listen to me. You need to get out of here. Is there no one you can stay with? What about your parents? Where do they live?"

"In North Dakota. They have a poultry farm outside Bismarck. But that's not even a last resort. I'm not welcome there. You could say there's a bit of a lifestyle clash."

"It would be a good place to stay, short term anyway. You'd be safe."

The look on her face told me what she thought of that idea. "Sure, trot home, hanging my head in shame. My mother was always on my case about Hal. I had to beg him to make even one trip to meet my parents. I shouldn't have bothered because she couldn't stand him. 'Too many airs and graces,' she said.

"She never wanted me to come to New York in the first place. I can still hear her. 'We have a decent university in our own state, why isn't that good enough for you?' She made some lame excuse for not showing up to the wedding. When the marriage fell apart, do you know what Mom's comment was? 'Well, Loretta, at least he's finally out of your life.' She actually laughed. I can just imagine what she'd say, given how Hal died."

"You're going to have to hang out with me then, until we can figure something else out." I put my arm around her. "What's with Loretta?"

"I could never stand my name. I started using Laurel the minute I left home."

"I'll remember that next time I'm mad at you."

She smiled. "I'm sorry for getting temperamental. I know you're doing all you can. I'm just so stressed out. It's bad enough with what happened to Hal and then coping with all the problems around the estate. Now I have to worry about some weird group of killers. It's insane."

Teardrops clung to her long lashes. She reached for a tissue to pat them away. She had beautiful eyes, grayish hued indoors but green in the sunlight.

"I woke up last night with the worst feeling," she said.

"I had a nightmare too."

"It wasn't a nightmare. Just a sense that everything's going seriously wrong, like I'm caught in a web and can't break free."

"You should move out, for a while anyway. I'll figure something out. In the meantime, let's visit Reed at his office at NYU and see if he can tell us anything. After that we'll stop by Phillip Anthony's gallery. He's an expert on Renaissance prints who can advise us about Dürer."

"All right. Can you wait while I shower and get some stuff together?"

Laurel's frame of mind wasn't helped by her surroundings. She seemed lost in Mina's place, swallowed up by it. It had a depressing, worn-out feeling in spite of its luxurious furnishings. Almost four thousand square feet on two floors and all of it unoccupied, except for her small domain in the family room.

Looking out the French doors, I could see one of the gargoyles stationed on a cornice over the terrace, a winged figure with a snarling lion's head, a lion's body, and a dragon's tail, not unlike an Assyrian demon. Gargoyles protected against evil spirits, which is why they were used on European churches. But this one seemed to draw the evil in.

When Laurel returned she looked like a different woman. She'd put on a dress, a green floral print with a tight bodice and flouncy skirt, a kind of hippie-chick number that showed off her curves admirably. Her rich, natural brown hair fell in silky coils to the base of her long neck. I liked the fact that she didn't touch it up.

We left the moody atmosphere behind.

✴

I decided not to bother with the car. NYU was just around the corner, and Phillip Anthony's gallery not much farther away. Besides, I didn't want Laurel to think I drove a rental by choice. My Maserati coupe had been totaled in the crash. It killed me to even think about that.

The philosophy building, a handsome turn-of-the-century structure in red sandstone, was just a few minutes away from Washington Square Park. Laurel showed her grad-student pass to the guard, allowing us to get upstairs without alerting Reed to our visit. We went to Hal's office first. It was small enough to qualify as a broom closet. One look told us we'd wasted our time. The place had been swept clean. I pulled all the desk drawers out. Empty, every one.

"That was fast," I said.

Laurel glanced around angrily. "What about his papers, and the computer? Where are they?"

"Only one way to find out."

Although I'd called earlier to make sure he'd be in, I purposely hadn't told Reed we were coming to see him. Caught unawares, he'd be more likely to spill something.

Reed masked his surprise at seeing us with a hasty smile, scraped back his chair, and rose. "Laurel," he said, "how are you? I was shocked to hear about Hal. I'm so sorry. Can I do anything to help? Just say the word."

He went to hug her and she thrust him away. "You were shocked, Colin? If Hal had been drowning you would have held him under. You know how vulnerable he was, and you still took away his job. I count you responsible for what happened."

Seeing that false sympathy wasn't working in his favor, Reed reverted to his usual abrasiveness. "I don't recall agreeing to an appointment with you two." He threw an unfriendly glance my way. "Hal was drug addled. He wasn't even able to handle the limited classes we gave him."

I couldn't argue with that, but I wasn't about to give him the satisfaction of letting him know. "Glad to see you care so deeply about Laurel's feelings. Where are all of Hal's things? His desktop's gone. Nothing's left in his office."

"The computer is university property. We wiped the files and it's already been given to someone else." He motioned toward the door. "Outside are a couple of plastic boxes with his papers and other stuff. Laurel, you're welcome to them."

"You're a wretch, Colin." Laurel spun out the door and bent down to sort through the material.

"Well?" He glared at me openly now. Bluster didn't suit the man. His squat nose wrinkled unattractively and his fleshy lips stretched into a grimace.

"That blonde you were romancing at Hal's party—Eris Haines. I need to get in touch with her."

"Wouldn't have the foggiest. I'd never met her before. She kept pawing at me all night. I had a tough time shaking her off."

I broke into a laugh. "Colin, *come on.*"

"I have nothing more to say to you, John."

"What would your wife think about that, I wonder?"

"You asshole. You are capable of that, aren't you?" He turned and searched among some papers lying on his desk and picked up a card. "This is all I have. Be my guest." He held it out for me.

The logo on the card read TRANSFORMATIONS in large gold lettering. Underneath that, in black, Eris's name, phone number, and fax. Nothing else.

"One other thing. The stone engraving Hal kept in his office, did you take it out of his desk? It was stolen from my brother. I've already talked to the FBI. Best to give it up now."

I struck out on that one. The look of sheer astonishment on his face told me he knew nothing about it.

Thirteen

Phillip Anthony, a British import who'd settled in the city twenty years ago, sold prints and paintings from his gallery on East Tenth Street, just past University Place. He'd started the gallery with Claire Talbot, who became successively his business partner, his wife, and his ex-wife. You could still see her name spelled out ever so faintly on the brick where he'd removed the brass letters. I'd known Claire first. She'd drifted in and out of our group of friends at Columbia. The two of us had kept in touch only because our professional lives brought us together. I'd applauded her when she made the break from Phillip. He was insufferable even for short intervals.

Phillip used his gallery primarily as a showcase—he made most of his sales to private clients for substantial sums. If I lacked the knowledge to solve Hal's puzzle, I'd have to seek it from people like him.

His assistant told us we'd find him on the second floor. Phillip normally used this space for storage and picture restoration. Today the room was bare, making it appear much larger. The walls had a fresh coat of white paint and the floors shone. Stretched across the entire ceiling was a canvas depicting Michelangelo's Sistine Chapel frescoes.

Laurel didn't know what to make of it. "Well," she said, searching for something polite to say, "if you can't see the real thing, I suppose it's better than looking in a book. It's surprisingly well executed."

I wouldn't have been that complimentary.

A voice behind me broke into my thoughts. "Rather adventurous, don't you think? It took fifteen art students two months to complete."

Behind us stood a tall, angular man with a receding cap of gray hair and watery blue eyes, extra large, like a baby's, magnified by the thick lenses of his glasses.

"Phillip." I stretched out my hand. "This is Laurel, a friend of mine."

He gave me a brief, cool handshake and bestowed a warm smile on her.

I explained that she was a doctoral candidate in philosophy. Phillip liked people with lofty credentials.

"What brings you here?" He turned to me. "We usually see you only when there's something to gain. Like an event where you can score some clients."

"I'm researching a Dürer." A cutting remark he'd just made. Then something clicked. I'd been in such a fog of sorrow over Samuel's death that I'd missed it.

The steady drop-off in the number of party invitations and work offers.

Like courtiers in a royal circle, the movers and shakers in our world could close ranks in an instant. I got work because of my connection to Samuel, and they adored him. People blamed me for his death. You could be on top of the crowd, but if you stumbled they'd fight over who got to make the final twist of the knife. Not only had Samuel's death produced a hard knot of grief that felt permanent, but it could very well end my career.

I pretended not to notice his frostiness. Phillip had never really warmed up to me, nor had we gotten off to the best start. I'd gone out power drinking with a couple of other dealers after an auction. One of them celebrated his big win by treating us to pricey shots of twenty-three-year-old Evan Williams bourbon. As the evening wore on we all got pretty hammered. Phillip, boasting about his sexual performance, told us he'd once lasted an hour and five minutes. I asked him whether that was on daylight savings time, when the clocks went ahead. It didn't go over too well.

I tried to think of something positive to say about the Michelangelo reproduction. "This is an unusual display for your gallery."

He smiled. "A fundraising project. Each panel is sponsored by a different corporation. We had the event last night and did damn well out of it, actually." He pointed vaguely in the direction of God touching the hand of Adam. "IBM shelled out ten thousand for that panel alone. We had to talk them out of covering Adam's nether parts with their logo, though."

Laurel gaped at him, wide-eyed, the shock palpable on her face. He grinned to show this was just his little joke. I joined in with a laugh I didn't really believe in. "How much longer will it be on display?" I asked.

"Oh, at least until summer's end." He directed his gaze toward me. "Ghastly news about Hal Vanderlin."

"It was terrible." I stole a glance at Laurel. A slight reddening of her face was the only clue that Phillip's comment had upset her.

"I heard rumors about a drug problem." He cocked his eye.

I had no interest in turning up the heat under the rich stew of art world gossip and changed the subject. "Tell us about your project."

Phillip lifted his thin arm and pointed again to *The Creation of Adam*. "There's some interesting speculation about Michelangelo's meaning here."

"You mean the pop analysis," Laurel said. "It's not about God creating Adam at all but the reverse. Adam, who stands for mankind, imagining God in *his* own image."

"Yes." Phillip gave her a smile that verged on a leer. "But I believe that's too simplistic. An American doctor, Frank Meshberger, said Michelangelo had, through the shape of God's image and his swirling robes, meant to depict the labyrinthine spirals of the human brain. Renaissance painters knew what the brain looked like because they dissected cadavers.

God's head is presented to us from the left profile, and the left hemisphere is the active speech center. His head is juxtaposed over the *arcuate fasciculus,* or the locus of speech in the human brain." He gestured dramatically toward the ceiling.

I had to stifle a laugh.

"So here's my theory," he continued. "While appearing to faithfully depict the Old Testament fairy tale about creation, Michelangelo's seditious brush was really saying that the sacred ability of man to speak, to imagine, to think in symbols and abstract concepts, represented his emergence from the profane—the animal world. And because of this, divinity lies within humans, not outside them. Adam is reaching out for the power of the word, not to a mythical god."

When he took a pause Laurel broke in. "Would a sixteenth-century sculptor have known something like that—where the center of speech was located?"

"Perhaps we don't give the artist enough credit." Phillip rubbed his fingers absentmindedly over his chin, warming up to the subject. "A jolly old subversive, that's what I call Michelangelo."

"That's a stretch, Phillip," I said. "All you have to do is look at the art. Adam's figure is flaccid, languorous, as if he's just coming alive. All the energy and force are in the portrayal of God. Michelangelo had his differences with the religious hierarchy, but he was still devout."

"Look at the rest of the ceiling, then," Phillip persisted. "What are pagan soothsayers doing in the midst of what is arguably the most famous Christian work of art? The Oracles. Astounding, really. A Libyan sibyl is placed next to the Creation panel. He's put pagan priestesses on equal footing with Old Testament prophets."

"You're saying Michelangelo promoted paganism?" Laurel said.

"Precisely. The church ruthlessly attacked pagans, but ironically they're still celebrated at the very heart of the church through the genius of Michelangelo."

I'd had enough of his pontificating. "Listen, Phillip, Laurel and I have been discussing Dürer's copperplate engraving—*Melencolia 1*. Can you shed some light on it for us? You're the expert here."

I'd struck the right nerve. He preened like a strutting peacock. "Ah, *Melencolia 1*, one of the three *Meisterstiche*—his master drawings. I've always felt Dürer rivaled Leonardo. He was a remarkable painter as well, and mathematician. He wrote two books on geometry. In order to appreciate his work, you must see the man in his cultural context."

Here we go again. Could he not just get to the point?

"Dürer was tutored at the knee of his father, an acclaimed goldsmith, and became the foremost artist of woodcuts and copperplate engraving. Six hundred years later no one has bested him. His father moved to Nuremberg in 1455." He raised an eyebrow. "Stop me if you've heard all this; I do tend to run on."

I motioned for him to continue.

"I said we need to be aware of the context. It's not

possible to fully appreciate Renaissance art without understanding Hermeticism, a Greek and Egyptian philosophy from Alexandria in the first century."

Don't tell me we'll have to listen to two thousand years of history just to get some answers.

"Alexandria burst with life; it was, overwhelmingly, the beating heart of world scholarship. Cross-currents of many philosophies, religions, beliefs swirled through the city."

He rubbed his hands as he gave us his little lecture. "Egyptian soothsayers, Jewish mystics, and Greek Platonists all gathered there. The priests of Cybele, who castrated themselves in honor of their goddess, paraded through the streets in bright orange cloaks, jewels, and long hair, clashing their cymbals and drums. Hermeticism first flourished in that city."

"Hermeticism. That's related to alchemy and transmutation, isn't it?" I hoped this would give him a gentle nudge to move on to the topic we really wanted to hear about.

The man literally looked down his nose at me, his glasses sliding awkwardly to rest on its tip. "John, why is it you have such a penchant for reducing everything to the lowest common denominator? Alchemy is like an applied science, only one aspect of Hermeticism, and certainly not the most important."

He pushed his glasses back and threw another indulgent smile Laurel's way, then carried on. "One phrase is central to Hermetic thought: 'That which is below is as that which is above, and that which is above is as that which is below, to perform the miracles of the one thing.' That's a translation of a key line in a tablet, *The Secret of Hermes*, from which all succeeding Hermetic works draw reference. The tablet was attributed to the Egyptian sage Hermes Trismegistus, but it's thought now that it's apocryphal. Like the Bible, it had numerous authors whose names may be fictitious. *As above so below*, as it came to be known, meant that all elements of reality were related and in harmony. The material and the spiritual were one. Patterns seen on earth mirrored those in the sky. Modern physics supports this view by showing us that the solar system is configured the same way as an atom. You're familiar with the five-pointed star, the witch's pentagram?"

"Sure."

"In the upright position it signifies good, but when it's turned upside down with its two apexes pointing skyward, the pentagram is considered the sign of the devil. But take either the Mesopotamian eight-pointed star or the six-point Seal of Solomon. Both look the same whether they're turned upside down or not. They symbolize the phrase I just mentioned and stand for the harmony of all things."

I'd had no idea Phillip was so knowledgeable on the subject. We'd veered a long way from Dürer, but his knowledge of hermetic thought caught my attention. I toyed with the idea that he might actually be the unscrupulous American dealer Samuel had suspected, but that seemed a stretch.

Laurel, picking up on my discomfort, jumped in

again. "Christianity separated the material world, the dark and sinful flesh, from the spiritual realm."

Phillip patted her shoulder. "Yes, their goal was not to know nature but to transcend it. To make room for the Christian church, pagan beliefs had to be either subsumed or crushed. As the church gathered strength, Alexandria, the seat of ancient paganism, crumbled."

He stopped rather abruptly and turned again to Laurel. "Mesopotamians enter the picture here."

"You mean Harran?"

"Just so." He beamed at Laurel as if she were his prize student. "The flow of people and ideas gravitated there. When Harran declined, scholars migrated to Baghdad, the supreme center of learning in the eighth century A.D. There, Sufi schools greatly added to the body of Hermetic knowledge. One man in particular, Jabir ibn Hayyan, earned himself the title of father of chemistry because his accomplishments were so brilliant. He perfected distillation, invented the alembic still and the processes used to make hydrochloric and nitric acid."

Phillip turned his watery gaze on me. "And here's where your alchemy comes into it, at least as it concerns the poppycock of turning base metals into gold. An eminent Sufi mystic in Baghdad of that time made the claim 'It is we who through our glance turn the dust of the path into gold.'"

The insults to me were certainly piling up.

"Scholars focus entirely on Egyptian sources, but it could easily be argued that Mesopotamia gave birth to alchemy. The knowledge incubated in Harran and Baghdad spread to Cordoba under Moorish rule. When Europeans took a pause from the looting and massacres of the Crusades, they brought many texts and Hermetic concepts home. As a humorous aside, our own King John of England was so enamored of these ideas that he secretly petitioned to become a Muslim, with the intention of turning his kingdom over to Islam. And can you believe it, they denied him the honor!"

"Fascinating, Phillip. But I wanted to know about the Dürer print, *Melencholia 1*."

His voice floated on as if I hadn't said anything. "Hermetic thought and practice re-emerged in the great academies and secret societies of Florence under the Medici. When the Medici empire fell, Hermeticism took root in Venice. There, a gentleman named Manutius, one of the first publishers, produced Hermetic texts. In 1503 he greeted an honored guest—Albrecht Dürer."

"Dürer actually visited the city several times," I corrected him. I'd learned this while researching some pieces in Peter Vanderlin's collection. "His eyes were opened in Venice. He loved Bellini's work."

Phillip directed another beatific smile Laurel's way, as if she'd been the one to point this out. "He did. His exposure to Italian Renaissance culture fundamentally changed his artistic vision. The gothic stiffness of his early work gave way to more natural forms.

"Hermetic thought was absorbed by the great cultural and scientific minds of the Renaissance."

Once more, Phillip's arm swept toward the ceiling. "My own artists, Michelangelo, Raphael, Botticelli, and Tintoretto, among them. Like them, Dürer was captivated by Hermetic philosophy."

That was nice. Phillip owned the major Renaissance artists.

I waded in, still anxious to get back to our original question. Phillip, anticipating me, held up his hand. "Yes, the picture." He walked over to a Mylar cabinet, selected a book, flipped it open. It was a catalogue raisonné. He held it out, pointing to the upper right-hand corner of Dürer's engraving. "The symbols in *Melencolia 1* are Hermetic. The bell, for example, represents the correspondence between all things. The bell's ring swelling outward can also be a shape. Dürer could never have known how profound his image was. Our own planet functions like a bell. The earth literally sings. Friction between sheets of the earth's crust produces ringlike waves that can be heard in space. They even know the scale—B-flat major."

Phillip pointed to the top left-hand corner of the engraving. "The rainbow illustrates the same principle: white, which transforms to the spectrum of colors. Have you heard of a condition called synaesthesia?"

"Where some people see music as colors?" Laurel said.

"That's one type. A perfect example of inter-changeability. In Dürer's picture the ladder symbolizes the connection between heaven and earth. Renaissance masterpieces were regarded not simply as images but also as actual talismans with magical properties."

Phillip flashed his pearly whites at Laurel again. "There's a long list of notables—Dante, Mirandola, Dürer, Goethe, and my own English Edmund Spenser—who carried forward the fundamental notion of the 'one.' The great Isaac Newton was the last before that heretic Descartes drew down the dark curtain of rationalism."

"Can you explain some of the other symbols?" she asked.

"It would make more sense to consult someone better versed in that field. I do know, however, that Dürer played a few tricks on his audience."

"Tricks?" Laurel raised her eyebrows.

"It was not at all typical for Renaissance artists to sign their work. In fact, many were forbidden to, so they were forced into subterfuge. In *The School of Athens*, Raphael hid his initials on the collar of one of the figures. Dürer often used a monogram on his works, but in *Melencolia 1* he hid his name."

He stretched out long, bony fingers to give Laurel a friendly pat on the cheek. "You have until tonight to figure out how he signed the work. If you're successful, dinner's on me."

"Any first-year art history student knows that," I said. "You're talking about his magic square. All the rows and columns add up to thirty-four. On the bottom row are a four, fifteen, fourteen, and one. The one and four stand for *A* and *D*, Dürer's initials. Or alternatively, A.D. 1514, the date he completed the work. Picasso was so impressed by that he hid the date of *The Unknown Masterpiece*, 1934, in his own picture."

This failed to wipe the smug look off Phillip's face. "Your origins are dubious, John, and your manners show it. That's only the first. There are actually eighty-six ways Dürer signed his name, but I suspect anything deeper will elude you. You'll need help. Claire was just here for our fundraiser. Why not call on her? She'll get it sorted out for you."

Laurel did not look amused. "If it's all the same to you, we'd appreciate knowing now."

This time Phillip waggled his finger at her. "Ah, what's the rush? I guarantee you I'm acquainted with some of the best dinner spots in town."

Fourteen

At Laurel's suggestion, we headed for Washington Square Park to work on the Dürer puzzle. The park had a good cluster of people, and we'd be safe among the throng.

"What an ass Phillip is," I said. "He's got a rep as a total loser with women."

"It shows. Who's Claire?" Laurel asked.

"Phillip's ex-wife and an old friend of mine. I'm surprised he suggested her; I thought they were on the permanent outs. She co-owned the gallery with Phillip, and later started her own. She's a curator at the Museum of Modern Art now with a long trail of creds—degrees from Cambridge and the Sorbonne, that kind of thing. Her father has one of the most important collections of occult literature in the country. If she senses some interesting gossip she won't let it go, so let's see if we can figure this out on our own. I'd rather not call her unless I have to."

We wandered through the Waverly Place entrance and into the circle of chess players. We stopped to watch two men playing, their heads bent over the board, focused on the match as if their lives depended on it. I leaned over to the one nearest me and whispered Knight f3. The guy didn't even blink.

"Do you play chess a lot?" Laurel asked when we moved away.

"Once. I never played again because I didn't want to destroy a perfect record."

She gave me a pretend slap.

We sat on a bench near the dog runs. In a truly civilized gesture the park offered separate enclosed runs, one for the small guys and another across the path for the big boys. We stopped to watch a Yorkie wrestle his ball away from a longhaired dachshund.

Farther on, people cooled their feet in the fountain. Park workers zipped past in golf carts. Washington Square had lost most of its zing since the sixties, when Pollock and de Kooning had studios nearby and Allen Ginsberg and Dylan were the local bards. The way I heard it, back then pot practically grew on the lawns.

If Dürer really had signed his name eighty-six different ways, I despaired of ever finding the correct one. We took another look at *Melencolia 1*. A couple of websites we searched on my BlackBerry proved helpful. "In the upper right-hand corner, what do you see?" The image was furry and grayed out, although still clear enough to read.

"The bell," Laurel said, "and the magic square. Magic squares were originally Chinese, weren't they?"

"Yes, Babylonians had them as well, fifth- and sixth-order squares used for astrology. In Dürer's magic square, the two numbers of the constant, three and four, add up to seven. Multiply them and you get twelve. Seven and twelve are the most sacred numbers." I checked another website and read the text aloud to Laurel. "'Seven was revered by Mesopotamians because of the seven celestial bodies visible to the naked eye: the Moon, Mercury, Venus, Sun, Mars, Jupiter, and Saturn. Pythagoras believed seven to be the ultimate expression of harmony, and Judaism considered it the perfect number as reflected by the seventh day— Shabbat, the day of worship.'"

"There's music too," Laurel added, "seven notes on the diatonic scale."

"Right. And you've heard of the seventh heaven? It's the Muslim concept of supreme heaven, the one of absolute purity. But this doesn't help us," I said. "Seven won't work with only two spaces to be filled in."

"What does Dürer's entire name add up to?" Laurel asked.

I counted out the numeric value of each letter in his name and added them up. "A hundred and thirty-five. You'd need three squares for that, and we have only two."

"I guess there's no point trying the constant, thirty-four, because that would stand for the letters *C* and *D*," Laurel said.

I nodded absentmindedly. After another half an hour we'd gotten nowhere and decided to leave. The sun had disappeared behind a heavy bank of clouds, turning the late afternoon sky to mottled purples and grays without taking the heat away. Rivers of perspiration slipped down my spine, pooling in the hollow at the small of my back.

Laurel stopped as we neared the park's west exit. Two figures caught her attention. She half turned toward them and I followed her gaze. The first was a silver Elvis. Gelled and silvered hair slicked back at the sides, silver face, flashy sequined suit, chrome-rimmed sunglasses. Every minute or so he would pivot, thrust out his hips, and assume a new Elvis pose. The other performance artist, a few feet away, wore a jester costume. Gold and black hat with bells and a black bodysuit with a white collar. On each flap of his collar was a symbol for a suit of cards: spades, hearts, diamonds, clubs. His face was completely hidden by a white porcelain mask. On his left wrist I saw a red tattoo.

Laurel put a hand to her lips. "Who's that?"

"Good question. The Elvis is probably a legitimate performance artist, but the jester's got to be from the alchemy website."

We were in a crowded park so felt safe enough. We waited to see what he'd do. His gaze wandered to Laurel's ample breasts and locked on. I put my arm around her to send him the clear message that she belonged to me, then held up my other hand and flipped him the bird.

"Let's take off," I said. "I don't want to hang around this guy."

So that made three of them—Eris, Shim, and this jester. And they posed a danger not only to me but now to Laurel too. The only solution I could see was to counter their numbers with allies of my own. That meant giving Laurel more of the story and enlisting Tomas's help. I'd wanted to learn what else Tomas knew anyway, and this would furnish the pretext. I could involve them while keeping something in reserve. Hal's flash drive was safely, I hoped, with Nina. The only other existing file was on my BlackBerry, and Eris and her friends wouldn't be getting their hands on that. I told Laurel about the Book of Nahum and what Tomas had revealed of it.

"I see why they're so desperate to get it," she said after a moment of astonishment over the immense find. "No wonder it's worth a fortune. What did you say his name was—Tomas Zakar? Are you sure about him?"

"Samuel employed him in Iraq. That checks out."

"How do you know it's not just some story he gave you? He could be anyone. What if he has terrorist connections?"

"There's no chance. Samuel would never have associated with someone like that. I'd like you to meet him; another pair of eyes might help us crack this thing, and there's no point working at cross purposes."

"All right. But if you sense anything negative about him, back off. This game of Hal's is sucking us under and I don't think you see that. You worry me by rushing headlong into things."

I lost my cool over that remark. "Laurel, my life has been directly threatened. And look at what just happened. Those freaks will show up out of the blue, even in a crowded park. They have no fear. And how are they finding me? You're quite right I'm rushing. I have no fucking choice."

"Why are you getting mad? I'm just looking out for you." She linked her arm through mine. "We'll get it sorted out."

The condo would be at the top of their list of places to find me. I had to get out of there. Laurel waited for me around the corner at Caffe Dante while I stopped by the condo to pick up a few things. But before I went anywhere near my place I stood in the doorway to Kenny's and made sure there was no surveillance.

Once inside I threw a change of clothes, some toiletries, and Samuel's last journal into a small case. I shoved my treasure chest into the back of his closet, folded a blanket around it, and tossed some shoes on top. I stuffed Samuel's billfold with his American Express, Visa, and about two hundred dollars, returned to me after the crash, into my pocket.

As I was about to leave a call came.

"Darling, what have you become embroiled in this time?"

Claire. She never bothered to introduce herself, assuming the entire world knew who she was. "Funny you should call me."

"Phillip passed along a message. He said you wanted to speak to me. Something about alchemy and Dürer? You do get mixed up in the quaintest things, dear."

"I'm just doing some research on a Dürer print, but I think it's under control. Can I check in with you later if I need to?"

"Of course. But now I'm intrigued. You're chasing a big fat commission, aren't you? I hadn't heard of any Dürers being available right now."

"Everything's always on the market, Claire. You know that. Listen, I appreciate your call but I've got to split."

She hung up abruptly, feeling cheated, no doubt, because I'd held out on her.

I got in touch with Tomas, and he suggested we meet at his room at the Waldorf. Before leaving, I took out the precious bottle of 1985 Barolo I'd saved for a special occasion. On the back of my business card I wrote a thank you to Nina. There being no answer when I knocked, I left it propped against her door. She'd earned it.

Fifteen

Before going up to see Tomas, I suggested to Laurel that we wait in the Waldorf lobby to make sure no one had followed us. When we reached the hotel we settled into plump chairs.

Our housekeeper, Evelyn, taught herself English by watching old movies, so I grew up transfixed by Cary Grant captive in the Plaza, King Kong teetering from the Empire State Building, Lana Turner vamping at the Waldorf Astoria. Fantasy and reality not yet being distinct in my young mind, on one school visit to the Empire State I'd stubbornly refused to make the trip to the observation deck, afraid that a giant, hairy hand would curl around me and fling me off the top. Some of my strongest first impressions of the city came from those films. They gave New York a varnish of glamour no other place possessed, one of the many reasons I loved it so much.

On special occasions, Evelyn would bring me to

the Waldorf. For her, walking into the lobby was like entering a king's palace. We'd tour the place the way others would a gallery or museum, finishing off our visit with lunch at Peacock Alley—a Waldorf salad with candied walnuts for her, and for me an indulgence, strawberry napoleon with white chocolate mousse. The Waldorf had undergone a long process of recovery from the sixties, when many of its fabulous art deco designs had been concealed under carpets or behind heavy drapes. The work of Louis Rigal—his twelve remarkable murals, and the mosaic disc on the floor made of 150,000 pieces of marble—shone on full display. A focal point of the room, the tall clock from the 1893 Chicago World's Fair, still rang its Westminster chimes every fifteen minutes.

People drifted through the lobby, going about their business. No one seemed to be paying any special attention to us. I glanced over at Laurel. She was looking down, fidgeting with a tissue, fright at seeing the jester still occupying her mind, I guessed. She had a lot on her shoulders already, and the news I'd brought her might well have been too much for her to handle. In the short time we'd spent together, I'd felt an attraction for Laurel that I hadn't experienced for a long time. She caught me looking at her and gave me a half smile. "Let's go up," I said. "I think we're okay here."

The elevator stopped at the second floor to admit an older woman wearing heavy, oversweet perfume. Her hair was a frightening helmet, stiff and overly bright, speaking of decades of applied color. She strode in and commanded center spot, forcing Laurel and me to retreat to the back wall.

Tomas's door swung open after the first knock. A friendly lion seized my hand in both of his huge paws, insisting, "Come in, come in, John. You are most welcome here." I noticed a deep welt on the man's palm when he took his hand away.

Tomas looked up from his perch on a chair in the corner and gestured toward the lion. "My brother, Ari."

Laurel greeted them politely when I introduced her; she appeared duly impressed by the surroundings. When Ari stepped aside, we could see the room was actually a large two-bedroom suite with a living area done up in faux Chippendale, fresh flowers on gleaming tables, ornate draperies, carpets and walls in soft coffee and cream tones, all of it designed to project an air of inoffensive gentility. The high ceilings soared to elaborate cornices. A camera like those used by TV photojournalists sat on one of the chairs beside a beaten-up backpack. The suite occupied a premier position in the hotel, its windows looking out onto Park Avenue.

I thought they'd been burning incense until I noticed a cigarette smoldering in the ashtray, a package of Gitanes Brunes open beside it. The coffee table was covered with takeout containers. The presence of someone else was disconcerting, and I was annoyed with Tomas for failing to mention his brother when

I'd called him. Nor did Tomas seem particularly welcoming. I felt like a moth fluttering into a hornet's nest.

The lion gestured toward Tomas, signaling for him to give up his seat. He did so with an audible sigh. Whether Tomas didn't want to move or just hated being ordered around wasn't clear. I thought about the two boys I'd seen earlier at the beach.

I reluctantly sat down. What else could I do? It would have been rude for us to make an excuse and walk out again.

I'd never have guessed that Ari, with his caramel-colored mane, freckles, and profusion of curly hair on his arms and the back of his hands, was Tomas's brother. He wore Levi's and a jean shirt and had pale green eyes that crinkled at the corners when he smiled, which seemed to be almost constantly. Both in looks and temperament, the contrast between him and Tomas was striking. I took an instant liking to him.

"What may I offer you to drink?" Ari asked. "We have a whole cabinet full of things." He flipped open a bar full of miniature bottles. I thanked him but said I'd pass. Laurel asked for a bottle of Poland Spring.

"Please, eat, eat, help yourselves," he urged, beaming at us. "It is all from Khyber Pass. That's where you met with Tomas, no?"

I nodded.

"The best food there." Ari pointed to the containers. "The mantoo is most delicious, we have two kinds of hummus, dumplings, yogurt with mint, ashak, baklava—it drips with honey and nuts. Please help yourself."

We selected samples of food and munched away.

Twenty minutes or so. I would stay exactly that long, then make my excuses and go.

Ari turned to me. "Please may I say how terrible it is about Samuel. Our great friend. We cannot believe he's gone."

Every expression of sympathy still stung like an accusation, but I expressed my thanks.

We chatted about whether he liked the city and how long they were expecting to stay. Tomas said little, but I watched him steal the occasional glance Laurel's way. We learned Ari was a photojournalist covering the Iraq war for the BBC. Despite Ari's efforts to put us at ease, our conversation had a stilted, uneasy tone that mirrored an underlying tension in the room.

Finally, Tomas joined in. "John, you can feel free to talk. Ari and I share everything."

It was perfectly reasonable he would take his family into his confidence, but it still bothered me.

"What happened to you?" he asked, indicating my lip.

"Eris Haines paid me a visit last night. She almost killed me."

Ari walked over and rested his hand on my shoulder. I could feel the warmth spread from his palm through the thin fabric of my shirt. "Our friend, you are not alone now. Samuel would have done anything to protect you. We will take his place. Please honor us by believing me."

He probably meant this sincerely, but I wondered whether his brother shared the sentiment. I got the feeling Tomas would rather throw me to the wolves than welcome me into the flock.

"Tomas has told you the story?" Ari affirmed this with a nod of his head. "I didn't tell Haines anything because I don't know where the engraving is. Hal left a kind of trail, a puzzle that needs to be solved in order to find it."

Tomas spoke up. "Why would he do this? It makes no sense. First he steals it from Samuel, then he gives you a map to get it back?"

"A nasty trick he played on me. I think he told Eris Haines I knew where the engraving was hidden, then he created the game, believing I wouldn't work it out in time to save my own life."

"He deliberately set you up? Why would your friend do this?"

"Hal was damaged and abusing drugs. He turned on me. And now Laurel and I could use some help." With a paper furnished from Laurel's purse and my pen, I drew a perfect square, dividing it into four rows and four columns and writing in the numbers. I held it out so Ari could see. "Does this mean anything to you?"

Ari shook his head and beckoned to Tomas.

"That's Dürer's magic square," Tomas said. "But I can't see any relevance to the Book of Nahum. Hal was a science professor, correct?"

"He taught the science of philosophy. A Dürer expert told us the artist hid his name in the picture, perhaps by using the magic square."

Laurel asked me to pull up Dürer's bio again. "There," she said once the text came into view. "Halfway down the page it says his father changed the family name from Thürer to Dürer."

"That won't do it either. Even if we substitute a *th* for the *d* and assign numbers to the letters and add them up, including his first name, we get one, five, and nine, and there are only two spaces."

We spent some time concentrating on number–letter combinations. I found the whole exercise really frustrating and felt close to tearing my hair out when Laurel spoke up again. "Didn't Phillip Anthony say Dürer's father moved to Nuremberg? Was he German or another nationality?"

"I don't know; let me check it out." The bio confirmed what Phillip had told us. "Hungarian."

"And what was the name in Hungarian?"

"Another sec ... Ajitos. It means doorway, like Dürer."

"Does that work?"

I added up the numeric values of the letters. "Ajitos without his first name would total seventy-four. Let's give it a try." When I entered the numbers the page failed to move.

I was just about to pack the whole thing in when I thought of something else. "Are we looking at the wrong alphabet? Dürer might have used the old Latin alphabet. There's no *j*."

"That's interesting. Think of the common roots: *Dur* and *Tur* both mean door, don't they?" Laurel said. "So what would that be in the Hungarian using the old Latin alphabet?"

"*Ajto* means door in Hungarian. And in numbers, using the old Latin alphabet, without the *j*, that would be expressed as … thirty-four, Dürer's magic square constant."

"That makes sense," Tomas said. "I remember it now. I read somewhere that the square had eighty-six possible combinations of thirty-four."

I recalled Phillip's earlier challenge: *There are actually eighty-six ways Dürer signed his name, but I suspect anything deeper will elude you.* Phillip had virtually given us the answer back in his gallery.

When I keyed the three and four into the two squares, the page flipped to reveal the United States Senate Seal. Beneath it were squares for an eight-letter word and a three-letter word.

I checked out the seal on the Web and found that it had been designed by Louis Dreka in 1866. It was circular with the words "United States Senate" around the exterior circumference. A shield with thirteen stars and stripes occupied the center, with the Latin words *E pluribus unum* across it. Above the shield was a strange-looking conical cap, and below, crossed fasces I recognized as Roman.

The quotation in Latin, *E pluribus unum*—"Out of many, one"—was far too long to fit the spaces. Neither the crossed Roman fasces at the bottom nor the cap at the top fit either. We had no idea what Hal was getting at.

Ari addressed a question to me. "Tomas and I appreciate your coming to see us. You could have kept this to yourself and then we would have no idea about the fate of the engraving. We appreciate that you are being honest. So I take it this means we'll be working together?"

"More or less. Everyone gains that way, but I want full disclosure."

Tomas knew right away what I was getting at. "That's privileged information. I can't divulge any more."

I got up. "You're giving me no choice. I'm leaving then."

Ari walked over; his hand returned to my shoulder. "You should stay with us. You know now how dangerous those people are. We can't help you if we don't know where you are."

"I'll be okay if I can just get through this game. I'll be in touch."

He dropped his hand and made a plea to Tomas. "It makes no sense. Just tell him the rest of it."

A heated discussion ensued between them in what I assumed was an Arabic dialect. Tomas finally gave in. "The information stays only with you?"

"Of course."

"We honestly can't tell you much more. Samuel believed the Book of Nahum revealed the location of plunder seized in the seventh century B.C. during one of King Ashurbanipal's military campaigns into what is now the region of Anatolia, in Turkey. He discovered this when he came across an Assyrian inscription, an account of booty Ashurbanipal took and hid somewhere in Assyria."

That was possible, I suppose. It was commonplace for Assyrian records to list in great detail the spoils they'd taken after successful battles. "What was it?"

"We don't know. Samuel wouldn't tell us. He only hinted at something. He said the treasure was connected to an ancient witch and a famous legend that had a supernatural element—something beyond normal human experience."

"Was it a Greek legend or Middle Eastern? Did it have anything to do with transforming base metals into gold?"

Tomas shrugged his shoulders. "I have no idea. The engraving has explicit signs that don't exist in the biblical scriptures. Without it, we don't have the text Samuel was working with."

"And the American dealer who's after it, is he aware of this?"

"Samuel thought the dealer knew at least that much. The value of the engraving goes beyond the intrinsic. He believed Nahum intended it to be a guide to the location of Ashurbanipal's plunder. Since Hanna Jaffrey has made herself scarce, I'm assuming she was the conduit for the information to the dealer."

My mind swirled with this new information. Had Ashurbanipal seized a motherlode of precious objects? The engraving itself had to be worth at least twenty million. If it led to plunder taken by an Assyrian king, the value would be incalculable. And yet Tomas's story, especially when he couldn't give anything more than a vague description, hardly seemed credible.

Tomas could see the skeptical look on my face. "The Anatolian states were rich in gold, silver, and precious stones, and they had superb craftsmen. It's quite possible the king found a gold mine of artifacts."

"Ashurbanipal's son was king when Nineveh was sacked, right?" I asked him.

Tomas nodded yes.

"When it was clear to the king that he'd lost the battle, he gathered all his precious objects, his queen, and his concubines and had his retainers build a massive funeral pyre and set it on fire. All his possessions burned with him."

Tomas's scowl practically reached down to his knees. "That's just a fairy tale. There's never been any proof."

"But you're asking me to believe there's still some treasure trove out there? What is it? Let me guess—the Queen of Sheba's lost jewels?"

"You're the one who wanted to know. Now I'm telling you and you heap scorn on me."

Ari, the peacemaker, stepped in, worried that our

fragile accord was splitting apart. "You can't be sure of that, Tomas."

"Give me some credit." Tomas flung words at him with an implicit criticism of me. "I'm the only one here with any real knowledge of Mesopotamian culture, I might add."

I raised my hand. "All right, point taken. But you're asking us to believe it has remained hidden all this time? That's absurd."

"There are twelve thousand archaeological sites in Iraq," Tomas snapped back at me. "Those are just the registered sites. Many haven't even been explored yet."

Laurel and Ari exchanged glances as the conversation grew more heated. Finally she took my hand. "You're both arguing about phantoms. When you have the engraving, it will likely all become clear. Anyhow, I'm dead on my feet. I want to turn in now."

Downstairs, I used most of the credit left on my Visa to book rooms for Laurel and me for two nights.

"Come in for a drink?" Laurel asked me as I walked her to her door. "I don't feel like sitting in a lonely room by myself."

"Sure. Why not?" I flopped on the bed while she went to the bar and got two miniature bottles of Scotch. "Straight's fine," I said. She handed me my glass and sat down beside me.

I took out my phone and started removing the battery cover.

"What are you doing?"

"How did that guy dressed up like a jester find us?" I said. "It was no coincidence—I've tried to be careful."

"They must have some kind of surveillance on us."

"I'm not going to spend the rest of my life being hunted by those lunatics." I slid out the battery and looked into the compartment. "Damn. This looks okay. I thought Eris might have slipped some kind of tracking device into it."

She sipped her drink quietly for a few minutes. Just as the silence was beginning to get awkward, she said, "You might as well get undressed."

Although it seemed a somewhat cold approach, the speedy transformation from small talk to open invitation broke some kind of record. I happily complied and took my shirt off.

"Turn your back to me."

She obviously felt modest about nudity, so I turned around. "If you prefer the lights off I'm fine with that."

"No, that's okay." She ran her hands under my jaw and down my neck. I took one of her hands and kissed it gently. She murmured something I didn't catch and coyly pulled it away. This did nothing to deter my lust. I could feel myself getting harder than a rock. She moved her fingers to the base of my skull. The tense network of muscles in my neck and upper back surrendered. For the first time in a long while, I relaxed.

I leaned back a little. Strands of her long brown hair brushed my shoulders. She ran her hands down my back, caressing it with her fingers. Better to let her be the pursuer. After all, things had progressed very well without me pushing anything.

Her next words had the same effect as a sudden plunge into freezing water. "There's something implanted underneath your skin in the middle of your back where you'd be least likely to see it. Eris probably inserted it when you were unconscious. We need to take it out."

I'm not sure what was more of a downer: realizing Laurel's finger work was not a prelude to sex, or having missed the fact that this thing had been stuck into my back.

"With all the injuries your body has suffered lately, I guess you didn't notice that one little spot of pain."

I sat on the toilet seat while she used tweezers and scissors from her manicure case to pry it out. A pinprick or two and it was over. She deposited a small object that looked like a grain of rice into my hand.

"Just flush it down the toilet and then it's done," she said.

I got some tissue and carefully wrapped the device inside. Sticking it into my pants pocket, I walked into the bedroom and put my shirt back on.

Laurel stood in the bathroom doorway, a worried look on her face. "Aren't you going to get rid of it?"

"No," I said. "I have a better idea."

Sixteen

The evening sky, a low gray canopy of clouds, trapped the heat and made the city feel like a compression chamber. The atmosphere cried out for release—an explosion of thunder and a deluge of rain. Drivers yakked away on cellphones, cool as ice cubes in their frosty interiors while pedestrians wilted. With the number of people milling about, it was almost impossible to spot my pursuers, but I was sure they'd be keeping their eye on me. My first stop would be Corinne Carter's.

Corinne, raised in Harlem, had made a permanent move south; she'd been part of our inner circle at Columbia. She was the only one who'd ever gotten away with calling me Johnnie. At school, she'd been the centrifugal force that held us all together. When someone crashed after a major bender, she was there. If a disagreement ramped up into something damaging, she'd be the one smoothing the ruffled feathers. It was a surprise to all of us that she ended up living like a hermit.

From her home office Corinne specialized in developing and testing advanced security systems on contract for banks and Wall Street firms. She could negotiate her way around the Web as well as any hacker.

Her building was a yellow-brick monolith at the corner of Eighth Avenue and Twenty-third. Days went by without her ever knowing whether the sun shone or the rain poured down. Her blinds were always closed. She once said she could tell it was fall because the heating system cranked on. I don't believe she even owned a proper winter coat. The building's front entrance was a few steps from the subway, where she could connect to all the services she needed. Right across the street, a Dunkin' Donuts and Dallas BBQ provided sustenance. She ate a lot of ribs and cherry crullers.

Corinne was as cloistered as any medieval nun.

Sure enough, she answered when the doorman buzzed her.

I had no idea whether the evil chip could read elevations as well as coordinates, so outside the elevator I stuck it into a wad of gum that I fastened under a ledge.

As soon as I stepped across her threshold I was wrapped in a long, enthusiastic embrace. "How are you? I tried to visit you ages ago, but the hospital wouldn't let anyone near you and you just seemed to vanish after that. I must have tried to call or email a dozen times." She touched my lip. "Did your mouth get hurt in the accident?"

"Sorry for not getting back to you. I couldn't face talking to anyone for a long time. I'm better now, physically anyway." Telling her about the attack would just upset her more.

She gave my hand a squeeze, shooed the cat off a chair in the living room, and offered me a seat. Her cat, a colorpoint Persian, mewed his displeasure. "And now this happening to Hal. I totally caved when I found out yesterday."

"He got careless I guess," I said.

"It's not that hard to do. I've seen it enough times. That stuff just rips the shit out of people."

"I knew you'd be really depressed about it."

"Well, thanks for coming to see me. I know we don't get together as often as we used to, but I'm always thinking about you guys." Corinne's best feature was her gorgeous brown eyes. Right now they were getting a little teary. "I used to envy Hal, growing up with all that privilege. It always surprised me that he hung around with us."

I felt a flash of guilt. Had I not been facing this labyrinth of trouble I would have touched base with her right away. I didn't want to cause her even more distress by telling her the real reason for Hal's death.

"Can I get you a drink or something?"

"A coffee would be good."

"Black, right?" She said this as she walked to the kitchen, more a rhetorical question than anything.

When she returned I could see she'd put on a few extra pounds since the last time we'd been together. She'd always been pleasingly plump with ample curves, and had carried it well. Guys found her easy laugh and warmth appealing. It mystified me that she kept herself hidden away like this.

She handed me my coffee and sat on the couch opposite, her mug in her hand. "Do you know anything about arrangements for Hal?"

"No. Apparently the police haven't released his body yet. So Laurel tells me."

"How's she taking it then?"

"Not well. And there are mega problems with the estate to clear up. Both Mina's and Peter's."

Corinne let out a sigh. "That mother of his. She kept him trapped like a fish in a bowl. At her funeral Hal could barely stand, he was so distraught. Incredibly strange, what he did with her. Peter's in a nursing home now, isn't he?"

"He's in really poor shape. Can't feed himself anymore, doesn't recognize anyone."

"At least he won't know what happened to his son."

"Yeah. A weird kind of blessing." I sipped my coffee. "Corrie, there's something I was hoping you'd help me with. Do you have any time right now?"

"I'm just finishing up some work. How much of a hurry are you in?"

"Huge."

"What's it about?"

"Some people have been giving me a bad time. They want to get their hands on an artifact that belonged to Samuel and they won't identify themselves. The only lead I have is an unusual website with a forum about alchemy."

"Alchemy? You mean black magic, Satanism, that kind of stuff?"

"Not that weird. They're serious. Apparently the website links to articles about Renaissance and medieval documents that describe esoteric methods to convert base metals into gold."

She let out a laugh. "You're kidding me."

"I know it sounds crazy. But these people are rough. They've actually threatened me twice. To make matters worse, Hal was mixed up with them. I've only just found this out. And I need to know who they really are."

"Do they show up on this website?"

"Only through masks and astrological signs. But I do have two names. Eris Haines and George Shimsky."

"Well, let's check things out on the screen."

She asked me to get a kitchen chair and bring it into her study. In contrast to the homey clutter in the rest of her apartment, her office was spartan. No books anywhere, no files, just a couple of ballpoint pens and some scratch paper. The only exception was a jumble of cat toys on the floor. The cat wandered in behind us. He grabbed a mouse with rips in the fabric and proceeded to claw out the insides, strewing white cotton stuffing everywhere, his yellow eyes fixing on

Corinne with a mean glare. She laughed. "He's just mad at me for making him get off the chair." The cat began to purr and brushed against my legs. I put my hand down and ruffled his fur.

This amused Corinne even more. "Now he's trying to make me jealous."

Three monitors sat on her desk, each with a different screen saver. On one, strains of Bartók played to rain falling gently upon a field of wildflowers; on the next, ocean surf caressed a coral beach. The last monitor showed a forest blazing with autumn colors.

"That's as close as I ever get to nature," Corinne joked. She took a seat in a chair so technologically advanced it looked like something you'd see in a fighter jet. "It's custom-made. Sitting for hours on end does unspeakable things to your back. Now, do you just have names? No birth dates, licenses, anything like that?"

"Only this." I handed her the business card Colin Reed had given me. "The phone and fax numbers are duds, so the business name probably is too. Other than that, Eris Haines may be an MIT grad and she was fired from the Department of Defense. George Shimsky was a chemist."

"That should get me started."

I sat beside her while she searched through sites.

"Okay, I can't find anything on Haines. There's a good chance that's not her real name. Ditto for the company name. Shimsky graduated summa cum laude also from MIT in 1984 at the age of twenty. One year later he had five patents to his credit. Bright boy. Worked for Dow Chemical and FMC. Didn't appear to last too long at either one. Set up his own consulting company and then disaster hit. Good Lord!"

"What?"

"It says here he was trying to convert metals into gold." She shook her head. "How freaky can you get? He suffered major physical trauma and stroked out. After that, I can't find anything on him. What was the website you mentioned?"

"Alchemy Archives dot com."

She brought up the site and spent a few minutes checking it out. "There's some interesting stuff here, but it will take me a while to really get into it. Listen, Johnnie, I really do have a damn deadline to meet. Can I get back to you? I'll make it soon."

"Sure. It's great of you to help."

"I'm here whenever you need me—you know that."

"Oh, there's one more thing, another name— Hanna Jaffrey, a U of Pennsylvania student. Could you try to find something on her too?"

"There's someone else? It's beginning to sound like you've got the whole world mad at you."

Seventeen

After saying goodbye to Corinne and retrieving the chip I hailed a cab and soon reached the area Tomas had mentioned at the extreme west end of Thirty-fourth Street. It was a bleak terrain, a dark little corner piece in the glittering jigsaw of Manhattan.

I asked the driver to slow to a crawl. On my left the wide plain of the West Side rail yards stretched into the distance. Opposite it was a church with a red brick facade, a Romanesque arch in white limestone, and a gothic window above that, closed up with cement blocks. This wasn't a commercial building, but I asked the driver to stop for a minute anyway—I could see the Hudson from here so we had to be close. A sign by the doorway read ST. MICHAEL'S CHURCH, WORSHIPING IN THE ROMAN CATHOLIC TRADITION SINCE 1857.

A statue of Jesus stood outside the church. Full-size, encased in clear Plexiglas like a see-through coffin, he stood on a pedestal, gazing down on the passersby. He was fashioned entirely of white plaster, one hand outstretched, the other touching a large gilt filigree over which was superimposed a golden cross and a white human heart. Above the case, in Roman capitals, were the words "Come to me all you that labour and are burdened. I will give you rest."

It could have been written for me.

In the next block I found it, a nondescript stucco building about five stories high. At street level was a chalky blue door of wooden slats that appeared not to have been used for years, and farther on, a ribbed metal square the size of a garage door. Beside that I saw the five planetary symbols etched on a simple brass plate affixed to the wall.

The driver spoke up. "If we go any farther we're going to hit the highway. What do you want to do?"

"I've seen enough. Take me to the Port Authority."

He growled what I took to be an assent, jerked his vehicle around, and sped off.

He dropped me off at the Port Authority Bus Terminal, where sidewalk vendors still had their wares out—used books, women's purses, fragrant oils. One of them uncorked a bottle and held it toward me. A faint scent of jasmine floated through the air, colliding with the odors of sidewalk blight.

A homeless guy approached me with his hand held out. He had on a pair of torn gym shorts, Nike sneakers, and a baseball cap crowning long dreadlocks. His pale eyes centered on me. His smile revealed the rotting teeth of a meth head. I handed him a couple of quarters. He doffed his cap as I moved on.

The last time bus travel resembled anything close to upscale had to have been between the two world wars. No matter what the city, all bus terminals had that same sad, left-behind look. The Port Authority was a champion of the breed. A skin of sludge-brown ceramic tile surfaced the floor, walls, and massive square pillars. There seemed to be a conspiracy to keep the light as dim and forbidding as possible. The exception was a giant artwork of glittering aluminum and multi-colored facets on the south wall. It hung there like a beautiful child abandoned in a public washroom.

I made my way to a ticket counter, thinking I could save cash by test-driving Samuel's credit card. The agent gave me a baleful stare. "Can I help you?"

This was the standard phrase taught to all sales reps before they got ready to skin you alive.

"A ticket for the next bus to Philadelphia, please."

"One way or return?"

"One way."

"That'll be twenty-three dollars."

I thrust Samuel's American Express through the wicket. The woman swiped the card and waited. Making slits out of her eyes, she peered at her screen. She turned back to me. "I'm sorry, sir, this card's no good. Says the cardholder's deceased." She eyed me. "You don't look too bad for all that."

I mumbled an apology and asked where the bus bays were located. She rolled her eyes and pointed to a cluster of signs. "That's what the signs are for. Read that over there."

My idea had been to leave the tracking device somewhere on a bus so that my pursuers would think I'd left town. I never got the chance. On the way to the bus bays I spotted the man I'd seen ogling Laurel in Washington Square Park—a sharp-featured guy with skin white as a cadaver and jet-black hair, a red tattoo on his left wrist. Not a coincidence to see him here now.

He came after me. The bus bays suddenly seemed deserted and no Port Authority police were around. I charged out of the building and sprinted down Forty-second. At Tenth Avenue I caught the tail end of a yellow light. By the time the jester reached the inter-section, the light had turned red and traffic surged in front of him. When I reached the West Side Highway I headed north before turning up Forty-fourth, gasping for air, knowing I couldn't keep this pace up much longer.

Where the street breached the West Side tracks a band of jagged black rock fringed the steep banks, creating a man-made gorge for the railway. The sheer drop of about twenty feet to the rail lines and the solid-block wall of buildings across the street reduced my options. Barbed wire enclosing a truck storage lot gave me no opportunities either. Behind me, the *Intrepid,* a massive gray ghost of a battleship, loomed on the Hudson. Beside it was anchored a black subma-rine, and behind that a smaller ship crowned by half a Concorde. The mélange of old ships and planes offered plenty of hiding spaces, but at night the site would be closed off.

My insides threatened to burst from racing so hard. Seeing the jester turn the corner, I searched for some way to get off the street. It was a minor miracle I'd kept ahead of him this far. To my left was an area with broken and bent sections of fencing. I squeezed through a gap and tried to lose him in the thicket of trucks. The wire bit through my shirt, slashing my shoulder as I passed through. I wove between vehicles, trying to dodge him.

The sound of his pursuit stopped abruptly as if he'd suddenly taken flight. Was he circling around or had I lost him? I emerged onto Forty-fifth, down the street from a white low-rise. The building's cavernous entrance gaped open. I whipped inside. It was, of all things, a stable, stinking of damp, manure, and old oil. Off to one side I could hear the rustle of hooves and the swish of tails. Rows of ornate white and brightly colored carriages stood empty. It looked like a gypsy convention with all the drivers on lunch break. The carriages they use in Central Park, I thought, that must be what they were.

I crouched behind the fourth in a row of five carriages on the greasy floor, breathing in the straw dust, listening to the soft nicker of the horses. I couldn't risk using my cell. If he'd tracked me inside, he'd hear my voice immediately and know my exact location. A new sound alerted me. Footsteps moving among the carts. I pulled in my breath, hoping he'd wander in another direction, but the tromp of his boots came from only two carriages away. I ran for it.

A heavyset guy with big wet patches staining the armpits of his work shirt looked up in amazement as I bolted out from behind the carriage. Not the jester after all. My luck held.

Once on Tenth Avenue, I checked to make sure he was nowhere in sight, hugging the little storefronts to be less noticeable. Right before I reached an outdoor café filled with people socializing on the warm summer night, something that felt like the butt end of a screwdriver jammed into the small of my back. One black-sleeved arm gripped me.

"I thought you'd pull some dumb shit like that, Madison."

I tried to yank myself away. He pushed me against the glass window of a bakery. None of the passersby took any notice.

"You're going to shoot me right here? In front of all these people?"

"No, we're going across the street to the deli where my car's parked."

"And what if I won't?"

"You ever been shot?"

"No."

"I have. At first you can't feel anything. Just a punch. Like someone took a shovel and rammed it into your back. Then you get a weird burning sensation. After that, your legs won't hold you up any longer."

"So when we get to your car, she'll be waiting, right?"

"Eris? Oh yes she will. With open arms."

Before I could respond, I heard a sound like a tire exploding. The world slowed to a crawl. I felt the guy pull away from me. My legs began to melt. I pressed against the window glass, trying to hold myself up. I waited for the burning sensation to assault my lower back. A wail built deep in my throat.

A woman at the café table nearest me lurched out of her chair and screamed. A yellow cab braked hard. A guy passing by pulled out his phone and started punching in numbers. The café tables emptied. People ran away from me. I stretched out my hand. No one reached back.

Eighteen

The crowd collected around something at the curb. I curled my hand behind my back. Nothing out of the ordinary. No burning, no gaping hole, no sticky ooze of blood. My legs felt stronger. I pushed myself away from the window and found I could still walk.

The first of the sirens began to scream and a fire truck steamed in, stopping in front of the café with cruisers right on its back. After that I lost count of the number of emergency vehicles. I pushed to the front of the crowd and saw a graffiti-scarred cargo van stopped at a strange angle to the curb. In front, a man lay flat out on the pavement, his shorts torn and one of his sneakers ripped off, blood welling around his torso, streaming down his legs.

Uniformed men formed a circle around him. One of them leaned over, hands clamped together, and began to apply the steady push and release of life-saving chest compressions.

I peered at the crowd for any sign of the jester but he'd disappeared. Understandable that he wouldn't want to conduct his business that close to half the NYPD. I remained there for some time, feeling protected by the group. What had happened? Was the accident a pure stroke of fate? Had my assailant's shot gone wild, hit the van, and caused the collision?

People scattered when a couple of cops walked up and ordered the onlookers back. I checked for the jester one more time before climbing into a cab stuck in the gridlock. The accident that had saved me brought the memory of my own crash rushing back. Exhaustion overwhelmed me, but the sharp edge of panic wouldn't let me rest. I sensed myself slipping, afraid I could no longer cope with the turmoil Hal had plunged me into. I needed help. Somewhere in the precinct of Penn Station, Rapunzel, an old acquaintance of mine, ran a catering truck. There, I hoped to find at least temporary salvation.

Rapunzel was so named because his hair was cropped short except for a blond tuft at the back of his head hanging down to his butt. He'd never heard of the fairy tale, so when he learned Rapunzel was a woman's name he shortened it to Rap. He'd been in business for more than a decade. In that time his locations had changed but not his service. He'd stiffed a couple of people I knew and sold one guy some stuff with impurities nasty enough to put him in the ICU.

I found him standing next to his truck, listening

to music pounding out from the speakers. "Hey, Rap, I see you still have bad taste in tunes."

He grinned and put down the sandwich he'd been chewing on. "Good to see you." He checked out my torn shirt and the bloody cut on my shoulder. "What's up with that? You been dating rough trade again?"

"Very funny, Rap. Listen, I need to make a purchase."

"I've got some cool turkey sandwiches. Mom cooked the bird and wrapped them up herself."

"You're a joker, Rap. You missed your calling."

"I make too much coin doing this, even though I work like a dog. Speaking of which, this heat is a bitch."

"I'm light today. Can you be my banker for a spell?"

"A spell?"

"Maybe a week or so."

"Do you see me wearing Armani? There's an ATM right over there." He pointed vaguely to the north.

It wasn't a big stretch from drugs to weapons, so I thought it a good bet he'd have what I wanted. No one was looking over our shoulders but I lowered my voice anyway. "Look, a situation has come up. I need a gun."

His eyes widened.

"And some uppers—I need them too."

"I never read you as a gangster, Madison. Art business not going well?"

"You don't want to know," I said. "How about it?"

"I've got some serious stuff in. You know what I'm saying? How much do you want?"

"Enough for a week or so."

"Hold on." He grabbed his cellphone, half-chewed sandwich, credit card machine, and cash box, then motioned for me to follow him into the cab of the truck. He reached down and pushed my feet away to lift a polyethylene mat off the floor. Underneath was a lid crudely cut out of Masonite. In the depression below lay a couple of pistols.

He slapped on some latex gloves and picked one out. "It's a Glock. I take it you don't know how to shoot."

I shook my head.

"This is the best for people like you. You've got seventeen rounds." He showed me how to load it. "If you're really planning to whack someone you've got to get close."

"How come?"

"You'd need a thousand practice shots to be any good longer range. You're looking at a grand and a half for this. Ammunition's free."

"I'm good for it. Just not right this minute."

"You're kidding me."

"What about the bennies? Come on. I used to buy exclusively from you."

"Got some Dexedrine. Just as good, really. That's around three hundred."

"Just for a few hits of it? Any truck driver has that stuff."

"Don't see any truck drivers around here at present. It's pharmacy grade. I'm not some *charity*, Madison."

I took off my watch and held it out to him. "Omega Speedmaster. Worth a couple thousand. Take it on loan for the two of them, the Glock and the stimulants."

He picked the watch up and turned the stainless steel band around in his hand. "Watch looks in pretty good shape. I'll keep it for the pistol only. And final sale, no loan."

"You're not serious."

"It's human, man. We all need money. It's a human thing."

"So I should take my business elsewhere?"

That produced a belly laugh. "We're running out of time here." He pulled a ziplock bag out of the glove compartment and dropped in the Glock, then peeled off his gloves.

"Haven't you got anything to put it in? I can hardly walk around carrying it in my hand."

He shook his head and rooted around behind the driver's seat, pulling up a small canvas satchel. "Should charge you more for this. Take it," he said. "Now beat it."

When I got out I left the door open a crack. Rap's half-eaten sandwich sat on the dash. I waited until I could see him walk to the open panel of his truck and engage in a heated conversation with another customer, his lanky body framed by the backdrop of chocolate bars, wrapped white-bread sandwiches, soda cans, and juice cartons.

Stealing back into the truck, I took out the evil seed Eris had planted in my back and stuck it between the lettuce leaves in Rap's sandwich and walked away.

I found a hole-in-the-ground restaurant near the ass end of Penn Station and drank two cups of muddy coffee that tasted like it had been boiled all day. I hoped that had concentrated the caffeine and indeed it took away most of the tiredness, even though it set my nerves more on edge. My ship was sailing again and ready to plow the rough seas.

I went to check my watch, forgetting for a moment it had been confiscated by Rapunzel. My phone told me it was almost 11 P.M. I walked away, uncertain what my next move should be. In a rage over missing out twice, Eris would be setting the dogs loose now. My life had taken such a bizarre turn. To be hunted in my own city, unable to stay in my own home, my life run by Hal's game. I hated the whole situation but could see no way to extricate myself.

I called Laurel. The message center came on, indicating she wasn't in her room. After a few moments of quaking alarm I tried her again. This time she answered.

"Where did you go? You promised to stay in your room; don't scare me like that."

She laughed in that loose way people have when

they've been drinking for the better part of the evening. "I couldn't bear staring at four walls. The Zakars and I went to the bar. A couple of drinks drowned my boredom beautifully."

Male voices spoke in the background. "Is that Ari and Tomas?"

"One moment. Tomas is saying goodbye now." I could hear Laurel's higher-pitched tones blending with theirs. A minute or so ticked by.

Laurel came back on the line. "I feel totally dumb now, suspecting them. They're Assyrian."

"Oh?"

A rush of words followed. "Ari's won tons of awards for his photography. And Tomas once planned to become a priest. He'd entered a seminary before he went to Oxford."

"Why the change?"

"He fell in love but the woman ended up with someone else. Kind of bittersweet romantic, actually."

"Well, I'm glad you feel reassured." I didn't mean this sarcastically but she took it that way.

"Is there no way to please you? I thought you wanted me to like them."

"Of course. I didn't mean it to sound like that. I'm just on edge. The guy we saw in Washington Square, the jester, tracked me down."

I could hear her sharp intake of breath. "Oh shit. John, you've got to get away from this. You've used up your quota of narrow misses."

"That's a good idea—for you. I wanted you to do

that before, remember? For me, there's only one way out I can see. Find what they're after and get it over with."

The line fell silent and for a minute I thought she'd hung up. "You're right," she finally said. "I'm going to put in a few calls to friends, see if I can find somewhere else to stay."

"Laurel, if you're still here tomorrow I'm going to try to get all of us an appointment with Claire Talbot at MoMA."

"You want to see her after all?"

"I'm not getting anywhere with working out the meaning of the Senate Seal. May as well give an art expert a try. And I'd rather not talk to Phillip again."

"Tomas wants to see a professor, Jacob Ward, tomorrow morning. He's a biblical scholar at Columbia who knows Hanna Jaffrey. He's an expert on the Minor Prophets."

His name wasn't familiar, so he must have begun teaching at Columbia after I left. "Does he have any idea where Jaffrey is?"

"Apparently not."

"I thought Tomas wanted to keep a low profile. Does he trust this Ward guy?"

"Yes, he does. I'll tell him to change the time. Ward in the afternoon and Claire in the morning."

I said goodnight to her and hung up feeling a bit cheated. While I'd been the knight errant out doing battle, Laurel and the Zakars had gone partying.

✸

Back in my hotel room I ran a washcloth under hot water and dabbed at the cut where the wire had bitten into my shoulder. I lay down on the bed but sleep eluded me. I was restless and on edge.

I checked out Jacob Ward on my cell and found that he was quite the star in his particular scholastic universe, with academic credits up the yinyang, articles published in all the best journals, and ringing endorsements from his students. Some of his colleagues disputed his views, but other than that, I couldn't find one negative comment about him. It would be interesting to actually meet the guy and see for myself. No one was that perfect.

Next, I leafed through Samuel's journal, as much for the comfort of reading his handwriting as for finding clues. I hoped something might pop out. And something did.

Samuel had pasted in a picture of the Dürer woodcut *Woman of Babylon* from his Apocalypse series. Underneath it he'd written,

> Note Dürer's portrayal of the Whore of Babylon, lower right-hand corner of the picture. She is the cupbearer and originally the goddess Ishtar—prototype for Aphrodite, Venus, and Ashtoreth. The Bible converts her from a goddess to a witch and a whore. Dürer's beast does not match the Book of Revelation's description.

Woman of Babylon by Albrecht Dürer, 1498

A few more pages on, another image had been pasted in with a further note.

Like the Seal of Solomon (the six-pointed star), Ishtar's eight-pointed star represents the conjoining of heaven and earth—the symbol for transmutation.

I'd never known my brother to have much interest in religion. Yet here was direct evidence, in Samuel's own hand, linking alchemy with an Assyrian deity. What did Ishtar's eight-pointed star and the Whore of Babylon have in common? How was a hidden Assyrian treasure connected to this?

I closed the journal and sat back, mulling it over. All I had right now was fragments. I felt deeply frustrated at my inability to knit the whole picture together. Was Tomas still holding information back, or had all the talk about treasure simply been a decoy to steer me away from the truth? Samuel had referred to transmutation. Perhaps the final destination my brother had in mind was not treasure at all but a formula to convert base metals into gold.

Nineteen

Tuesday, August 5, 2003, 7:30 A.M.

As it turned out, on Tuesdays MoMA was closed to the public. I reached Claire at home. She said she could meet us around noon at MoMA's temporary site in Queens.

I put in a quick call to Laurel, who said she'd barely been able to sleep after talking to me last night. She hadn't made a connection with any friends yet so would remain in town. She assured me she'd spend the morning with Tomas and Ari, and we agreed to regroup at MoMA.

While I dressed I turned on NY1. An intro about the Iraq war reported that bodies of civilians were being found at a rate of twenty per day and the kidnappings and executions were expected to get a lot worse. A few items later, I caught a story about gunfire erupting near Penn Station. The camera zoomed in to a catering truck with bullet holes scored into its aluminum panels, panning out to show Rapunzel being led toward a police van, a chain criss-crossed around his back pinning his arms to his waist. As I'd hoped, Eris and the jester had tracked the transmitter to Rapunzel's van. The news piece reported that Rap was charged with sale of a controlled substance and criminal possession of a weapon. No mention of Eris or her thugs.

Finally a piece of good news.

I had a debate with myself about whether to take the pistol with me. I'd gained a certain measure of comfort knowing that Eris had probably lost me, and unlicensed guns were illegal in New York—I couldn't afford to be caught with it. Even if they did pick up my trail again, I could hardly stage a shootout and run the risk of harming innocent people. I reluctantly wrapped the gun in a towel and shoved it in my suitcase before heading down to the lobby.

Outside, the morning air was fresh and clear. I bought a *Times* and headed to the Westway Diner for breakfast.

Emblazoned above the window, a banner ad boasted that the diner had been voted best in Manhattan. Doubtless, tourists would be impressed since New Yorkers knew their food, but only until they walked past other diners and discovered those too had been voted best in Manhattan. The details were in the who, what, and when of the vote. I had no quarrel with the breakfast, though, and the fresh coffee revived me.

Recalling the questions I'd mulled over last night, I sensed something hovering just outside my awareness. As I ate I let my thoughts flow, helter-skelter. Then it came. I felt as if instead of handing me the bill, the waiter had just tipped a bag of gold onto my plate.

It was Corinne's remark about Hal's mother's funeral. Although I'd been out of town at the time, I knew that Mina's funeral had been held at the Church of the Intercession in Hamilton Heights. If there was a family mausoleum, Hal would have had unlimited access to it. It would make a brilliant hiding place.

I threw some cash down on the table to cover my tab and ran to the subway. I got off at the 155th Street station and rushed the two blocks to the Church of the Intercession.

A wall of dove-gray limestone closed off the cemetery from the street. Stationed inside the entrance, a tall Celtic cross with birds and animals sculpted in relief had been installed as a tribute to John Audubon, who'd once owned the land. The grounds had a serene, parklike feel; ancient elms shaded the lawn, still quite green despite the prolonged heat. The gravestones ranged from prominent headstones surrounded by picket fences to simple markers. Many were so old, the names had blurred into the stone. No one else was around.

Seeing all those headstones reminded me I had no family left. With Samuel gone, the nearest person I had to a relative was Evelyn. I should have gone to see her by now. Only in her mid-fifties, her arthritis had worsened to the point that she needed extended care. She'd come to us a few weeks after my fourth birthday. It was a surprise Samuel had lasted that long. A studious older man with a penchant for quiet and order could not have coped easily with a boisterous toddler. The story of Evelyn's origins remained a mystery to me because she never spoke about growing up in the Middle East. Children are hypersensitive to secrets withheld, but somehow I always knew that questions about her early years or why she'd fled her country were forbidden.

During grade school, every morning she'd carefully wrap a homemade lunch in waxed paper and a brown paper bag she'd saved from shopping, tuck it into my knapsack, and walk the five blocks to school with me. When I was older I grew to resent this. She always wore black, and like a great black crow fluttered around my shoulders, never letting me out of her sight. Even in winter, which she hated, on would go her oversized galoshes and she'd set out beside me, moaning all the way about the slippery ice and mounds of snow. I couldn't bear the contrast to the other kids' mothers and tried everything to get rid of that plodding presence by my side, but despite her quiet nature, I could never shake her off.

It was only when I went to boarding school in my teens that I realized how much she meant to me. Of all people, she'd been the hardest one to face after Samuel died.

A circular path led to a group of large mausoleums. Only these were big enough to hide anything.
Like miniature mansions, they sat in a row around the
walkway. Two of them caught my eye but they had
the wrong names: Garret Storm and Stephen Storm.
Garret's resting place was an elaborate gothic folly with
a lacy wrought-iron door and a pitched roof flanked
by spires and topped with a cross.

I looked for Mina's tomb under Vanderlin, her
married name, and Janssen, her maiden name. But
fifteen minutes of searching proved fruitless. One of
the largest mausoleums, built of aged brownstone the
color of milk chocolate and mossy with age, had no
name at all. Its door was fastened with a rusty padlock.
If Mina was interred in a mausoleum, this would have
to be the one. I took a few steps forward to see whether
it had been recently opened.

"Hey there."

A man marched toward me. He wore a black
leather vest, blue jeans, and a satin shirt. Chunky
necklaces flopped around his neck.

"Sir," he said, "you're not supposed to be in here."

"I thought it was public. The gate was wide open."

"Don't you read signs? It says you need permission
from the cemetery office. Appointments only."

"I'm sorry. My great-aunt died recently while I
was out of the country. She's supposed to be buried
here."

"I see." He crinkled his eyes, trying to take my
measure. "What was her secret?"

"Pardon me?"

"Her secret to a long life. People would pay serious money for that."

He was making some kind of joke at my expense. I waited for the punch line.

"The last person buried here was born in 1836. Now, that would put your aunt at a ripe one hundred and sixty-seven years old. I just hope for your sake you got her genes." He burst out laughing.

"I must have been told the wrong location."

Tears glinted at the edges of his eyes, but not of sorrow. "Did they say Trinity?"

"Yes, that's what they told me."

"Go to the columbarium. We're the only cemetery left in Manhattan carrying out active interments, but it's all cremations now. You'll probably find your aunt's remains there."

A niche in the columbarium would be too small to hide anything of significance, but I'd check it out anyway. Maybe Hal had left a note or other directions.

The clerk on duty at the columbarium told me I'd need an appointment even for that viewing. When I explained I had to leave New York that afternoon she relented. "What was the name?"

"Janssen."

She tapped a few words into the computer and checked the screen, then shook her head. "No record of a Janssen. Maybe in the cemetery but not here in the columbarium."

"Okay. Could you look up Minerva Vanderlin?" I spelled it out for her.

"Oh yes, here it is. The niche is no longer assigned to her. Her son picked up the remains."

"When would that have been?"

She peered at the screen again. "January 25—six months ago."

The urn I'd seen back in the closet at the townhouse had likely once held her cremation remains. He'd scattered her ashes, probably over some favorite spot of hers as people often do, and used the urn to stash the gemstones.

I headed over to the subway, pissed as hell. Hal had trumped me once more. I was so sure I'd been on the right track. The disappointment weighed heavily on me.

I waited for the train, hoping to get one of the cars with functioning air conditioning and a welcome blast of cold air. Even the short hike from the cemetery had me dripping with sweat. A few paces away, two kids were putting on a show for the waiting crowd. They both wore pants that had to be size XL, though neither one was heavyset, and oversized Ts, one with Tupac Shakur's image silk-screened on the front; the other was a Sean John. The shorter kid had a pair of Air Jordan 18s that must have set him back two hundred bucks.

I watched their moves, appreciating their skill. One kid suddenly grabbed the ankles of the other and flipped himself up. His partner caught his ankles in turn so that they formed a human O. They somersaulted down the platform and back again with a prowess that would have left professional acrobats gasping. The crowd clapped and threw quarters, the kids scooping up the change just before the train came shooting into the station. We rocked and rolled along the tracks at warp speed. I savored the meat-locker cold of the car.

Twenty

MoMA's temporary site was located in a former Swingline staple factory. The good citizens of Queens had cheered when they found out the top prize in culture would hop over the East River and settle in their burg. They'd painted the building a rich blue.

Near the front entrance, Ari stood taking nervous drags off his Gitane. Laurel, appearing a bit frail and worn, waited beside Tomas. On the one hand, knowing that he was watching out for her took a weight off me, but on the other, he looked proprietary and it got under my skin.

Claire Talbot met us after we signed in. She gave me an emphatic double kiss and Tomas and Ari a handshake. Laurel received a frosty smile. She and the guard escorted us through the display of impressionist paintings from the permanent collection. We passed by *Starry Night*. The actual painting resonated all the more in the face of its many inferior reproductions. Van Gogh's trademark style was on full display: violent brush strokes, turbulent spirals, strident ultramarines and apocalyptic blues. His moon stood out in vivid yellow, the sun, visible in the same sky, a pale and watery contrast. The dark image of his cypress pointed into the sky like an ancient obelisk.

"There's always a crowd around *Starry Night*," Claire said. "No one ever seems to tire of his work. Imagine how many posters and prints must be scattered around the globe. All those sunflowers!" She gave a little trill of a laugh. "This period is not my specialty, as you know, love." She lightly brushed her fingers on my jacket sleeve. I caught Laurel picking up on that.

Claire had an intriguing look—alabaster skin; a mass of wiry copper hair just brushing her shoulders; hazel eyes; long, artistic fingers; and a body aesthetically thin. She loved wearing artsy, bold-patterned clothes and eye-catching handmade jewelry. I remember her wearing a dress made from fabric that was a direct copy of a Mondrian painting. After she broke up with Phillip our paths crossed many times at receptions and launches, where she'd go out of her way to shower me with compliments. I took the bait, once, until it became clear that her real goal was to steal one of my top clients.

To people she judged her equals, Claire was a panther. Seductive and velvety smooth. And she didn't hold grudges. "You never know," she once told me, "when people can come in handy. It's no use making enemies out of them." This calculated social advice apparently did not apply to her staff. With them, her temper tantrums and diva-inspired put-downs were legendary. Mercurial. Hot one moment and cool when it suited her.

Once in her office she settled us in chairs of shiny plastic in white, citron, and black. I showed her a print of the Senate Seal. She scrutinized it for ten long minutes, went to her computer and tapped on the keyboard, then sat back and smiled.

"I haven't forgotten everything I learned at Daddy's knee. See the conical hat above the thirteen stars? It's called a Phrygian cap. The Phrygians came from Thrace, primarily from the area known today as Bulgaria. Around 1000 B.C. Thracians migrated to the region of Anatolia in Turkey. That became the kingdom of Phrygia."

I sneaked a look at Tomas. Last night he'd suggested the treasure stolen by King Ashurbanipal came from Anatolia, home to the Phrygian kingdom. This gave us another link.

"The Phrygian cap proved to be enduring," Claire continued. "You can trace its history through art. It's on a second-century Greek bust of Attis, the lover of the goddess Cybele, and you often see the Persian god Mithras wearing it. Mithras evolved into a Roman warrior god, so for Roman freedmen the cap symbolized liberty."

Laurel said it reminded her of the hats worn by French revolutionaries.

"Of course," Claire responded, with a touch of condescension, I thought. "Because of the association with freedom. As I've already explained."

"Is this getting us anywhere?" I addressed this to the rest of our little group.

An uncomfortable silence ensued. Ari sighed. "It is complicated for me."

"What exactly are you looking for?" Claire asked.

"We're after a word associated with alchemy, specifically the concept of changing lead into gold. But I don't see the relevance of a Phrygian cap."

"I thought you told me it had something to do with Dürer."

"Phillip helped us work that out. Tomas is writing a paper on Mesopotamian origins of Hermetic thought. He came across the Senate Seal image in the course of his research."

"How is my ex, anyway?" I was sitting closest to her. She reached out and gave my hand a squeeze. "Bet he charged you for his time," she said.

Everyone laughed but Laurel. She clearly wasn't impressed by Claire's witticisms, nor by her pointed attention to the males.

"Well, you were on the right track." Claire now threw a glitter-ing smile in Tomas's direction. "There's a strong connection. Just a sec."

She searched through more sites, then invited us to look at the screen.

"This comes from a seventeenth-century manuscript called *Atalanta Fugiens* by Michael Maier.

From *Atalanta Fugiens* by Michael Maier, 1617

The section of the book this image appears in is a guide to transmutation. The oddly shaped funnel over the alchemist's head is part of the distillation apparatus where the lead is deposited to be purified. Finished gold coins lie in a basket on the stump. Descriptions of alchemical processes were common in medieval and Renaissance manuscripts."

"He's wearing a Phrygian cap," Laurel remarked.

"That's right. The cap was strongly associated with alchemy."

Claire ran a hand through her wiry curls, the light bouncing off her hair so that it too seemed spun of copper and gold. "The Greek myth of Jason's golden fleece originated in Phrygia, where legendary gold deposits were found. The myth arose because sheep-skins washed in the gold-rich river Pactolus became saturated with tiny nuggets that adhered to the wool."

She browsed for another page and pointed to a new image. "Here's another famous folio from the same time period called *Mutus Liber*—The Silent Book. It's French. With the exception of a few lines at the beginning, the book has no script, only pictures. Like a textbook, a manual on turning base metals into gold. Goodness knows how many poor souls paid dearly for those experiments. They ended up dying from chemical poisons, hideous burns, or worse. The Russian czar Fyodor I Ivanovich once forced two alchemists to drink mercury after they failed in their promise to make gold."

I thought of Shim, who'd chased the same daydream and suffered horribly as a result.

"European heads of state feared alchemists because if they succeeded, large volumes of manufactured gold would devalue their currency. At the same time, they coveted that power for themselves."

"You mean they opposed it only if the formula fell into someone else's hands?" I broke in.

Claire smiled. "Yes. Nothing ever really changes, does it? You probably think alchemy was no more than a huge scam, but is it actually possible? The short answer is yes. Russian scientists turned lead panels into gold at a secret research facility near Lake Baikal in 1972, and ten years later an American, Glenn Seaborg, converted bismuth atoms into gold.

Doing it on a large scale, though, would be outrageously expensive."

Claire was right. Looking back on those experiments from the perspective of modern science, the early chemical explorations seemed almost laughable. And no doubt a significant number of alchemists who promised an easy way to create gold or elixirs of immortality were no better than snake-oil salesmen. And yet I found myself beginning to wonder again whether some of those early practitioners really had found a formula. Many respected scholars in those times thought it possible.

Claire tapped the image on the screen. "Hermeticists believed all matter was composed of the same elements; they needed only to find the right key to shift the balance and make the change from one material form to another. My father thought alchemy was really an allegory for stages of spiritual purification."

"Who wrote *Mutus Liber*?" Ari asked.

"A Huguenot," Claire said. "The French Protestant Huguenots endured severe persecution, so the author had to hide his name. The book's title page listed a line in Latin: 'Cuius nomen est Altaus.' The author's name, Altaus, had been anagrammed to conceal his true identity. His real surname was Saulot."

Twenty-one

After saying goodbye to Claire we headed back to Manhattan, where we found a Thai restaurant near Jacob Ward's residence. Laurel looked up at the sky before we entered. "I wish it would just rain," she said. "This is what my mother calls a soggy day. It's so oppressive."

We got a table. The waiter took our order and returned with our drinks. Tomas nursed a coffee. The rest of us had asked for ice-cold Sing Tao beers that slid beautifully down our throats. I plugged the words *Phrygian cap* into the spaces. A new page greeted us.

Laurel sighed. "There seems to be no end to this."

"No," I corrected her, "we're close." Underneath the squares Hal had typed *You are at the finish line.*

"I have no idea what the man intended. This whole thing is a colossal waste of time," Tomas said angrily.

Ari, always the peace negotiator, broke in. "From

what I remember, John, when you showed us the preceding steps there was nothing too complex."

"I thought the acrobatics with the last one were pretty tricky," Laurel said.

"Perhaps for you, Laurel. But he wasn't thinking about you when he assembled the thing. It was all meant for John. Why didn't he leave this for you? You're his heir, are you not?"

Nice dig, Tomas. Divide and conquer if you can. "As you well know, the engraving didn't belong to Hal in the first place."

The four of us sat in silence, trying to work out what appeared to be an anagram. Ari, whose command of English was the weakest, found the exercise particularly frustrating. "I'm still thinking all the time about my work. It's hard for me to concentrate."

"The story you were following up in Washington?" Laurel asked.

"Yes."

Realizing that I'd been left in the dark, Ari turned to me. "In Washington, before I came to New York, some contacts confirmed rumors circulating about Abu Ghraib."

"What's that?"

"A prison in Iraq. Occupation forces are sending interrogation squads in to torture prisoners. It's going to happen outside the regular military command. This news is astounding. If it gets out, the whole Middle East will ignite."

"You know this for a fact?"

OWL LA MEMOIR

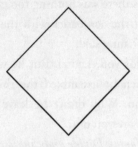

TRANSMUTATION

"That is what I'm working on, yes."

Tomas barged in, his impatience directed toward his brother this time. "Why are you bringing this up? We've got to concentrate on this damned game."

Ari responded simply, "Not all of us can live in the past."

Tomas flung some words back at him in Assyrian.

I broke the impasse by interrupting to ask Tomas about the accounts I'd found in Samuel's writings. "Samuel's journal mentioned a couple of obscure kings, one called Aza, the other, Mitta. Does that mean anything to you?"

The bad mood he'd been nursing flared into rage. He slapped the table with his hand. "You'd get a lot further if you concentrated on finding the engraving instead of sifting through every word Samuel wrote.

And there's one thing we've never resolved. I want it turned over to me when it's found."

"I'll be taking it to the FBI," I responded flatly.

His lips turned down in an ugly frown. "I won't agree to that."

What little patience I had left vanished in a blur of exasperation. "After all I've gone through, you expect me to hand you a stolen artifact worth millions? They'd jail me for that. All my efforts to build up my business would be destroyed."

Tomas laughed bitterly. "From everything I've heard, you don't know the meaning of hard work. You lived off Samuel. You actually killed your golden goose."

My fist clenched and Ari clamped his hand down on my arm. "May we act like grown-ups here?" he said. "People are looking."

The restaurant manager glanced toward our table, lifting her delicate, dark eyebrows. I notched my voice down. "Explain something. So far I've been carrying the heavy load. Laurel and I, our lives are in danger; my brother is dead; Laurel's husband is dead. What exactly have you contributed? Why can't you at least be more positive?"

Tomas threw me a look cold enough to paralyze a rattlesnake. "You think I'm getting a free ride? You don't know the slightest thing about me. The danger we're in now is nothing compared to the risk I'll take to get the engraving home. Someone needs to take care of that end of things."

Laurel scrunched up her napkin and threw it down. "That's enough. This is getting out of hand. It's time to see your professor, Tomas, anyway."

Outside it felt as if the atmosphere had grown hotter. August in New York. Everybody who could had left the city. As for the rest, you could actually see steam rising out of their ears if you looked hard enough.

Jacob Ward lived on West Forty-fourth Street on a block lined with four-story brownstones, fancy black grates separating their pint-sized front gardens from the sidewalk. The Actors' Studio, where Elia Kazan and Lee Strasberg developed method acting, stood out prominently on the street. Legions of stars, Brando, De Niro, and Monroe, to name just a few, had honed their craft there.

When we arrived Ward ushered us into his generously proportioned hallway. He spoke genially to Tomas. "You're lucky you got me at home. My kids are in Westhampton with my wife and the housekeeper. I only came back for a couple of meetings."

"I was wondering whether you've heard from Hanna since we talked," Tomas asked.

"No, I'm afraid not. But that's not surprising. We didn't correspond regularly."

He shook my hand. "I'm told you're Samuel Diakos's brother. I knew him by reputation. I was so sorry to hear about the accident." I mumbled my thanks. He took us downstairs to the garden level and suggested we sit outdoors.

Some people approach life with sheer energy, outshining those surrounding them. Ward, an undisputed star in the lecture hall, channeled much of this into his teaching. He looked more like a stock promoter than a professor. He had a beefy, florid face, handsome even if it carried a bit too much flesh. His suit and shirt were custom-made, ostentatious but expertly cut. He wore a Duchamp tie and a Ferragamo caramel leather belt. A rope of gold chain circled his wrist. His fingernails shone too brightly to be natural and I realized they'd been manicured.

In the garden we settled into comfortable lounge chairs, glasses of Perrier with lime twists in hand. A waterfall of ivy covered the wall of the neighboring townhouse. Overhead, a paper parrot floated in the tree branches. A cluster of large plants with broad, dark green leaves and trumpet-shaped white flowers mushroomed like jungle plants in the side beds. Two urns on either side of the kitchen doors were filled with double petunias, giving off a powdery, overly sweet scent like an old lady's perfume.

Ward gestured toward the tree with his glass. "Would you believe we have a pair of cardinals here? Right in the heart of the city. I still think of this neighborhood as Hell's Kitchen, even though they've changed the name to Clinton. A real estate promo. How wishy-washy is that?"

"After your former president?" Tomas asked.

Ward chuckled. "No, he's hiding away in Westchester." He leaned forward, resting his drink on his knee. "I grew up two blocks away from here. A humble third-floor flat. My wife, Miriam, got a generous inheritance. The kids were older and she wanted to do something with her time, so we took our capital and picked up a couple of these properties. We own the one immediately behind us. And one on Forty-seventh. Miriam renovated the heck out of them. In a couple of years real estate will peak and we'll unload the other two." He laughed. "When the cookie jar starts to look empty. But not this one. I want to hang on to it."

It seemed overly personal information to be sharing with people he'd just met. But I sensed this was one of the ways he had of making people feel comfortable. By my estimate, the cookie jar had to be pretty full. He was talking upwards of twenty million dollars' worth of real estate, not counting whatever they had in Westhampton.

He picked up his glass and crossed his legs. "Before we get into Nahum, may I ask why you're interested? He's pretty obscure. Daniel or Ezekiel, on the other hand, much juicier fodder for archaeological pursuits there."

Tomas smiled. "I'm from Mosul. Nahum spent most of his life in that area so I have a particular interest in him."

"I see. A word first, then, about biblical interpretation. It's basically all guesswork. Despite that, it's grown into a small industry. I use the Masoretic text of the Hebrew Bible. That's what the Christian Old Testament is based on. In addition to direct archaeological evidence, I cross-check with other accounts—Mesopotamian records, Roman and Greek historians—to verify interpretations." Tomas nodded his assent.

"Let me give you some background. The first complete version of the Hebrew Bible wasn't assembled until sometime around 560 B.C. in the years following the Babylonian exile. That's a gap of at least three hundred years until the earliest text in existence today—the Qumran Dead Sea Scrolls. Fragments of Nahum appear in 4Q169 of the scrolls, so I've been fortunate to be able to use those too as a partial guide."

We were in the hands of a master here, and he savored an audience. "Do you know what a *muraqqa* is?"

"It's a Persian album, isn't it?" I said. "Beautiful folios in continuous sheets made of patches of paper pasted together, decorated with images, calligraphy, and intricate borders."

"Those are the ones," Ward replied. "I like to think of the Bible that way. Old Testament stories were originally oral; conversion to script didn't begin until the seventh century B.C., when literacy blossomed in Judah. Like a *muraqqa*, the Bible is a collection of pieces; over time, sections were removed, altered, or replaced by new ones. The original wording and meanings changed." He laughed. "I've seen colleagues argue for years over the meaning of a couple of sentences."

"In some cases, wasn't it purposely changed?" Laurel asked.

Ward agreed. "Some of that was intentional. The Bible's authors wanted to express a theological viewpoint, and events like the fall of Nineveh were written about to illustrate those values rather than to document history. The Christian Old Testament itself is full of editorial miscues. *An eye for an eye*, as an example—what do you generally think of when you hear that?"

"The punishment should fit the crime," Ari said.

"Correct. But originally it meant *no more* punishment should be meted out than the crime warranted. Almost a reverse of the commonly accepted notion."

"Like the old party joke," I said. "You form a line and the first person whispers a sentence to his neighbor, and by the time you reach the end, the sentence totally changes."

"You've got the idea. Here's another one: Armageddon. What does that mean?"

"The end of the world?" Laurel threw in.

"No. It's a real place, a Greek word referring to an actual location—Har Megadon, the mount and plain of Megiddo, where the final battle is supposed to take place. A more subtle shift in meaning, but it illustrates my point all the same. No story survives intact for more than a few generations. What's old is new again. I often think that statement is an almost perfect reflection of reality."

"You're talking about the Mesopotamian myths," I said.

"Exactly. Take the original tale of Cain and Abel. Have you ever wondered about its inconsistencies?"

"Can't say I've spent a lot of time thinking about it."

"We have Abel, the shepherd, and Cain, the farmer. Why was God so offended over Cain's gift? Would it not be natural for Cain, a farmer, to offer the 'fruit of the ground'? Why was that a poorer gift than Abel's, the shepherd who gave the first of his flock?"

Tomas, not to be outdone by me, offered his opinion. "Sheep were more valuable because they were used for sacrifice?"

Ward drank some Perrier and stood up. He liked to gesture when he spoke, and sitting down obviously cramped his style. "You have to put the story in its social context," he said. "Most of the Judean Hebrew people of that time were nomads, shepherds. Their natural territorial enemies were city dwellers. Cain is a farmer and therefore linked not with the nomadic life but with settled communities. Later in Genesis you'll notice that, after his exile, Cain became the father of cities. He symbolized the cities that Genesis described as cesspits of sin—a notion, by the way, that carried through to modern times. 'Nature' is celebrated and cities are regarded as a necessary evil."

Ward remained standing with his back against the patio table, forcing us to look up to him. "I'm taking a bit of artistic license there. Authors of the Hebrew

Bible wanted to forge a great nation. They succeeded brilliantly. But that necessitated emphasizing the menace from their enemies—Canaanite and Assyrian city builders."

"I think you're taking a lot of liberties. It's all open to interpretation. You can't prove any of that." Tomas seemed miffed by Ward's claim. If he'd once studied for the priesthood, his faith in traditional teachings probably remained strong.

Ward gestured with his glass. I could hear the ice cubes tinkle as the water sloshed. "Genesis is a parable written by a nomadic people threatened by city-states. Read the earlier Mesopotamian version of Cain and Abel. It's completely different. In it the two protagonists were a shepherd king and a farmer king. But the dispute was over a woman, not gifts to God. A much more believable reason for a fight."

I knew Samuel had ascribed to this view. He believed myths were not made up but originated from real events, the flood tale being a perfect example. Before the advent of writing, information could only be passed down orally, and the raw information that was vital for future generations had to be expressed in the most dramatic way possible—through poetry. The rhymes and tempo of poetry made the stories easier to recall.

Ward broke into my thoughts. "Getting back to Nahum, when I began my study of his book, I asked a writer friend to review it for me. It's not that well known; he'd never heard of it before. So he approached it with a completely fresh viewpoint. The first surprise was how much he loved it. He said it was poetic, utterly convincing. But it also confused him because the whole tone and thrust of the work changed significantly after the first chapter. That confirmed what I believe and what other scholars have argued."

"What would that be?" I asked.

"The entire first chapter and the first two verses of the second chapter were written long after the original work and not by Nahum at all. Interestingly, the King James Bible supports this by beginning the second chapter at what is the Hebrew Bible's Chapter 2:2."

A few raindrops fell. The sky turned slate gray. A deluge threatened. We scrambled to get up and rushed into the kitchen. "I guess sitting outside wasn't the best idea after all," Ward said. "Let's move upstairs to the library."

Ward ushered us into the front room on the first floor. The rear wall of his library was stacked with books: tomes on art and New York photography; old volumes smelling of must, gilt Hebrew script on their spines; an entire shelf devoted to symbolism in religious art; the odd novel. I picked out *The Great Gatsby* and leafing through it saw that it was a signed first edition.

I took advantage of the break in the conversation to find the restroom on the second floor. It was furnished with a separate tub and shower, the shower head fastened to the ceiling to let the spray flow like a waterfall. An arty ceramic basin, electric tooth-cleaning gear a dentist would envy, hand-decorated Milano ceramic tile, wide pine plank floors, spotless white towels.

I glanced at the time and swore out loud when I realized I'd forgotten the appointment with Reznick, the criminal attorney. There'd simply been too much on my mind. I hastily put in a call to his office, but getting no answer, had to be satisfied leaving a voice mail.

As I turned to leave I glanced out the window. A silver Range Rover was parked directly across the street. Its tinted windows prevented me from seeing who was inside. My stomach dropped. I cranked open the window and could hear the motor running and smell the exhaust. I had to think of a way to check the vehicle out without disclosing the problem to Jacob Ward.

When I returned, I found him standing in front of the fireplace in full performance mode, expounding on some fine point of biblical lore.

"I think one of the guests for your next meeting might be about to arrive," I said. "I hope we're not taking too much of your time."

He glanced at his watch. "If they're here, they're far too early; I've got over an hour yet. How do you know?"

"There's an SUV idling outside your house."

He walked over to the front window, peered out, then laughed. "It's five-thirty. That's my neighbor Lawrence Barry. My kids call him Larry Barry, the thirty-minute man. He shows up every day at this time and sits in his car for exactly half an hour."

"Just to get a parking space?"

"You can't park until 6 P.M. A guy on our block once made the mistake of taking that spot about five minutes before Larry showed up. The man had just moved in; he had no clue what a bad idea that was. Every morning he'd notice some kind of new insult. A scratch near the door handle, a Coke can thrown on the hood, dog dirt on the bumper. Every day, always something. After a couple of weeks he wised up and it's been Larry's spot ever since. I leave my car at Columbia and take the subway home. I can't be bothered with all that nonsense."

Ward left to refresh our drinks and returned with a pitcher of ice water and a plate of cookies. He handed them around. "These are the best. Dark chocolate peanut butter chip. Levain's Bakery. It's always nice to have something sweet to nosh on when you get that late afternoon hunger jag."

He had an undeniable talent for putting people at ease. I could see why he was a popular lecturer. But I picked up on a lot of false notes. He was putting on an act. I wondered what kind of person hid beneath.

I glanced over at Laurel. She looked pale and seemed restless, didn't smile when I caught her eye. I asked her how she was feeling. She said she was getting a headache but could hold out for a while yet.

Ward appeared not to notice and carried on. "Nahum means 'comforter.' That's a little sly. Whom is he comforting? Not the Assyrians. You might think Judahites were reassured to hear how their enemies met such a terrible fate. But the work also carried a veiled warning for them, terrible threats about the consequences of worshiping foreign gods."

Ward looked around to make sure he still held our attention. You could almost hear the drum roll in the distance. "I believe the Book of Nahum was not a prophecy but an eyewitness account of the siege and destruction of Nineveh by the Medes and Babylonians. As I said before, the first chapter was added on much later.

"You can imagine that's not a popular opinion, but I have an interesting ally," Ward continued. "The King James version of the Bible puts the entire Book of Nahum in the future tense. Probably its translators felt that the Hebrew text, much of it in the present tense, didn't sound 'prophetic' enough. And there are a number of other cues that reveal Nahum's direct knowledge of the battle.

"The first two lines of 2:4 refer to red shields and to soldiers wearing red. This specifically describes the Medes. According to Babylonian accounts, Cyaxares, King of the Medes, led the battle supported by the Ummamandu, a tribe of Scythians from the north, and the Babylonians. The Medes were fierce fighters, known to wear red to hide their battle wounds. This kept the morale of their own men up and projected an image of invincibility to their enemies.

"Nahum's line in verse 2:7, 'The gates of the river are opened and the palace is dissolved,' is often quoted as proof that the book is a prophecy." He turned to Tomas. "Maybe you can help us out here."

For once Tomas seemed pleased to be included. "So far, no material evidence of a flood in Nineveh has been found. Fire, yes—the city was extensively burned. Only five of Nineveh's fifteen city gates have been excavated: Halzi, Shamash, Adad, Nergal, and Mashki. Armaments and skeletons found at the Halzi and Adad gates made some archaeologists jump to the conclusion that those locations represented the main thrust of the attack. But we know two gates existed on either side of the point where the river Khosr entered the Nineveh precinct. It's entirely possible these sites—the river gates—were breached first, allowing the armies to invade the city proper. That's probably what the line means."

"Something that specific suggests a hands-on account, not a prophecy," Ward agreed. "To sum up, here's who I think Nahum was, whether or not that was his real name. A gifted Hebrew scribe deported as a young man to Nineveh to work for the notorious tyrant Ashurbanipal. The king had assembled the great library of tablets excavated at Nineveh, the vast majority of which were copied from Babylonian texts, so we know he needed many talented scribes. The Book of Nahum borrows Assyrian words, providing further proof. Nahum's own ancestors probably went through the terror of Assyrian attacks on Samaria. That alone would explain the almost personal sense of hatred in his writing."

I jumped in with a question. "When Nineveh

fell, wouldn't Nahum have been an old man by the standards of the day?"

"Yes," Ward said. "Probably over sixty and without many years left." He used his fingers to tick off his next points. "First, on one level, the book is a letter giving Nahum's contacts in Judah an eyewitness report of the battle. Second, it sends a message to the people of Judah warning them against worshiping idols and foreign gods. Third, it has another function—to counter the enormous power of the goddess Ishtar over people's hearts and minds. Fourth, the book satisfies Nahum's own need to express his feelings of revenge. He positively gloats over Nineveh's downfall."

None of us, of course, mentioned the fifth purpose: Nahum's hidden message about the location of Ashurbanipal's treasure.

Twenty-two

After thanking Ward for his time we left the house and walked toward Ninth, each one of us lost in thought, mulling over what he'd told us.

Tomas broke the silence. "I'm not sure I agree with all his points, but Ward was right about one thing: the engraving was written after the fall of Nineveh."

"How do you know?" I asked.

"It dates to 614 B.C."

"I didn't think dating methods were quite that precise."

"Samuel told us the inscription at the bottom of the engraving states the date—in Akkadian terms, of course."

Still chafing at Tomas's earlier attitude, I tried to think of a way to avoid spending time with the Zakars. Unexpectedly, Laurel supplied the excuse.

"I'm getting a migraine," she said. "It was all I could do to sit there at the end. My vision is blurry.

When the pain hits I'll be a train wreck. It's this heavy humidity."

"Can you take anything for it?"

"My pills, but they're at home."

"Can't we go to a pharmacy?" I said.

In less than a minute her face had gone from pale to chalk white. "I'd have to get a prescription."

"Best you go," Ari said. "We can hail a cab for you on Ninth. We'll go to the Waldorf and meet you both there later."

I escorted Laurel back to the penthouse, keeping my eye out for any sign we were being followed. When we reached the building, Laurel headed upstairs while I stayed behind. I leaned against the fence of the little triangle of park across the road; the location gave me a good view of the stretch of sidewalk and surrounding area. I stayed for a full twenty minutes without detecting any sign of Eris. Laurel was stretched out on the family room sofa when I walked in.

"Any better now?"

"My head is, thanks to the pills, for the time being anyway. Now my feet are killing me. I should never have worn these heels."

"That's something I can fix. Do you have any lotion?"

She fished in her handbag for a tube of cream and held it out to me. Closing her eyes, she leaned back on the pillows. Her feet were bare. I could see bright red marks threatening to turn into blisters around her heels and baby toes. I squirted the cream into my palms. It had a pleasant, fruity smell like ripening apples. Her skin felt damp and hot to the touch and I took care to use slow, gentle movements. The corners of her lips turned up with pleasure. Without opening her eyes, she said, "You have no idea how wonderful that feels, John."

She sighed and swung her legs down to the floor. "Detective Gentile left a message for me. They're releasing Hal's body tomorrow, so I've got to make arrangements and get the lawyers to lever out some funds for a funeral. There's a lot to do."

"That's fine. Why don't you start while I work on the game? It may not take as long as you think."

I undid the first couple of buttons of my shirt, still feeling hot from being outside. Laurel had set the air conditioning to a perfect level; there wasn't a hint of chill. I spent the next hour struggling with Hal's words before peeking in on her. She was still on the phone, toying with something on the desk while she talked. A ring, it looked like.

In the kitchen the stainless steel stove still had the original cellophane wrap over its knobs. I knew Hal had lived on takeout, and I guessed that on the rare occasions she cooked, Laurel was strictly a microwave artist.

I found a teacup full of moldy sprouts, a wheel of Camembert, and a carton of Perrier in the fridge. My intention had been to whip up some salad, so I discarded that idea. I got out the cheese and put it on a fancy crystal cake plate. In contrast to the refrigerator, the cupboards were stocked full of popcorn, tins of cashews, jars of Greek olives, Russian Sevruga caviar, capers, smoked Malpeque oysters, packages of cookies and crackers, tinfoil bags of tostada chips, some dark chocolate.

The wine cooler supplied a nice bottle of Schloss Lieser Riesling. Dry and crisp. I opened two different packages of crackers and arranged them around the cheese. A glass bowl matching the cake plate was just the right size for the olives. I opened the oysters and put them in a bowl, set the chocolate on a plate.

In the dining room I filched sterling silver forks and knives from one of the drawers and a linen table-cloth and napkins with an inscription in Latin, the initials HRH embroidered around the edges in gold. I added a candelabra with three ivory tapers. With all the dinner things piled on a tray, I went to the terrace and laid out a nice spread on one of the tables.

Touches of lavender tinted the evening sky. I wiped the table and chairs, still wet from the afternoon rain, and held my hand around the candles to light them. Mercifully, they didn't go out. Some solar lamps, a few shrubs, and potted plants were arranged near the balustrade. As I turned to go, I noticed an emperor moth fluttering over to rest on a lamp globe, its wings beating a slow harmony, folding and opening. Only the females fly at night. Astounding that a moth was able to fly to these heights.

Laurel didn't seem to notice me when I came back into the study. "Join me for dinner on the terrace?"

I held out my arm and led her outside. Her face flushed when she saw the table. "How sweet of you." I poured some wine and we clinked our glasses.

"To you," I said and put my glass down. A little wine dribbled down the side and left a mark on the tablecloth. I heard Hal's mother shriek from her grave.

"Did you make any headway?"

"I found a funeral home to look after things, and the lawyers are releasing enough to pay for it. That's a huge chunk off my mind. Now I'll have to let people know."

She walked over and leaned against the railing. Lights were coming on all over the city now, a million stars in the urban galaxy. Farther out, the flat, murky expanse of the Hudson made its presence felt by the absence of light. Tall buildings glowed gold in the waning sunlight above ribbons of luminescence marking the verticals and horizontals of the avenues and streets; acid scarlets, blues, and greens shone from the neon signs. The street noise floating up to us was greatly subdued. The gargoyle, coiled in deep shadow, surveyed the city from its perch as though summoning its strength to spring on unsuspecting bodies below.

"John, I'm leaving. I need to get away from this game of Hal's. It's your issue, not mine, and I'm tired of it. There's so much on my mind, I don't have the energy for anything else. Wherever it leads has nothing to do with me anyway."

"Unfortunately, the alchemy group believe you're involved."

"I won't let them run my life. Last time I checked I was a twenty-four-year-old woman capable of making her own decisions."

"But we already agreed you can't stay here."

"I know. My friend finally got in touch. She'll put me up for a couple of days."

"That's great. Where does she live?"

"Near New Haven. She commutes to the city a couple of days a week. She's picking me up later tonight."

I would miss spending time with her, but things would be a whole lot easier if I had only myself to worry about.

"You've gotten obsessed with this whole thing. You should drop it. Can't you find somewhere to go away for a while too?"

I thought back to the chase at the Port Authority. "They'd find me anyway."

She ran her fingers through her hair and sighed. "I think you secretly like the adventure. You said you'd hand the engraving over to the FBI. Is that really true? The money you could get—it must be pretty tempting."

"Tempting for a fool. The thing's hotter than a branding iron. A dealer with a long history and very discreet international clients might pull off a sale like that, but I'm not there yet."

"Everything in Peter's collection is gone. Is that right?"

"As far as I'm aware. I sold all the items we'd cataloged."

"You should see the mess the records are in. That wasn't just Hal's doing—his mother's files are totally chaotic too." Tears drifted down her cheeks.

I wasn't sure what she wanted me to do. I moved beside her just to let her know I was there, not wanting to add any pressure. "What's wrong?"

"I wish Hal and I could have made a go of it. I really got my hopes up after Mina died. People said they could never get the two of us. But there was a side to him no one knew. He never tried to control me. He always appreciated my view of things and supported me, even if my choices ended up bombing."

Her head was bent ever so slightly. She rubbed her hand across her cheek as if to suppress her impulse to cry. I wrapped my arms around her, intending to comfort her. My consoling gesture quickly morphed into something else. Her breasts pressed against my chest. I buried my face in the rich silkiness of her hair, kissed her neck and then her lips. I tried to hold back on the steamroller of my lust, but any pretence of taking things slowly quickly vanished into thin air.

She pushed me away reluctantly. "Look," she said, "part of me would like to do this but I'm not ready. Hal isn't even buried yet and right now I need some space. We won't lose anything by waiting."

I muttered something in response about that being okay, even though the words clashed with my real feelings like a hammer hitting a windowpane. When she left to go back into the study I grabbed the bottle of wine and downed the rest of it, feeling rejected, although I knew I had no good reason to react that way. I attempted to focus on Hal's game again but found myself drifting off.

I'm not sure what woke me. It could have been the gusts of wind blowing raindrops in, pinging onto the floor. I checked the time: 9:15 P.M.

I struggled over to the French doors. The terrace was dim and bleak looking, the remains of our food drowning on their plates. The candelabra had fallen, and a candle had burned a black hole into the table-cloth before it sputtered out.

I closed the doors with a smack, almost falling on the slippery floor. I felt chilled and, to tell the truth, a shade embarrassed about falling asleep. I checked the powder room. It was clear. No Laurel. I called her name. She didn't answer.

Why were the lights out? I remembered lowering the family room lights, but I hadn't turned them off. Laurel must have, seeing me asleep. I fumbled along the wall for the switch and flicked it on. A cold fluorescence flooded the blue white of the kitchen.

Had she gone into the spirit room? When I opened the door the odor I'd noticed before wafted into the hallway, but the room itself was dark and empty. Along the corridor was a second set of stairs: in Mina's social heyday, the staircase used by the domestics. It led to a vast upper floor of bedchambers, baths, closets, and anterooms.

Laurel must have gone there, probably to avoid disturbing me. Finding no light switch for the stairway, I stumbled up. The wooden steps groaned. I emerged into the dark canyon of a hallway and stopped, cocking my head like a dog, listening for sounds of her.

Hearing nothing, I called out again. My voice echoed and bounced off the walls like a mountain yodel. I moved ahead, hands outstretched, until I made contact with the wall. Using the wood paneling as a guide, I slunk down the hallway.

A switch presented itself, and when I flipped it a series of antique sconces sprang to life. I proceeded farther, opening doors, calling Laurel's name. It was clear that no one had ventured up here for some time. The place had a silent, empty aura. I brushed the ledge of the wainscoting; my hand came away coated with dust. My apprehension grew by the minute. I continued the search long after I knew in my gut she wouldn't be found. When my brain finally caught up with my heart, a wave of sadness folded around me. I felt a sudden hatred for this place and wanted to get away from it.

What had she done—fled into the rainy night? Surely she would at least have left a note if she'd already gone to New Haven. The first inkling that something had gone wrong presented itself when I went into the rotunda. I saw a narrow opening, a seam in the panels where the marble met a strip of wooden inlay. Of course. There had to be some exit other than the elevator. But unless you actually moved your hands over the surface, when the door was closed you'd never know it was there. It was wrong, the door standing open like that.

I called her cell and got her voice mail. My email showed a new message, sent minutes ago from an unfamiliar address. No text, just a video attachment. What I saw put the fear of God into me.

Twenty-three

The video opened with a gray and grainy background, everything out of focus, then cleared up and zoomed in on Laurel. They'd bound her to a standing pipe in a room with tiled walls and floor. There was no audio. The film had the jerky, amateurish quality of a bad wedding video. Her body had slumped, her head lolling as if her neck was broken. I tried to see if I could detect the rise and fall of her chest, anything to give me a scrap of reassurance. Someone off camera must have issued an order because she jerked her head up. Her face was white and slack, in her eyes a mixture of dismay and terror. She spoke but I couldn't tell what she said from the movement of her lips.

I bolted down the stairs, falling a couple of times, not even feeling it. I had the presence of mind to straighten myself up right before the exit to the lobby. Gip would not be on the desk. I pushed open the door and gave the night doorman a nod. "You know Laurel Vanderlin?"

"Yes," he said.

"Did you see her go out?"

"Almost an hour ago, yeah. Her friend took her to the hospital. I asked whether I should call emergency, but the friend had a car right outside. A good thing because she had trouble making it that far."

"Her friend. A fairly hot-looking blonde?"

"Can't really say. Why? Don't remember who you were with?"

He kept a poker face but I could tell what he was thinking. A threesome done up with a lot of booze and designer drugs that had gotten out of hand. He'd seen it enough times before. He watched me every step of the way out the lobby without saying another word.

I ran for blocks up Seventh Avenue. The rain came in sheets; I didn't care. I needed to raise a shield between me and this last terrible hour.

When my lungs began to sear every time I reached for a breath, I took shelter under an awning. Every inch of me was wet, my clothes plastered to my body as if I'd gone swimming in them, water streaming down my face. The image of Laurel in that room drilled holes through my brain.

I stumbled along, hardly aware of where my feet were taking me. The cascade of horrors paraded in front of me like ghouls from a graveyard—the car crash, Hal's murder, Shim and Eris hunting us, the grinning jester, and now Laurel. Every one of my actions had a dark edge. My brain exploded with anguish.

My cell went off. Another email. Short and to the point.

> Meet us at the High Bridge water tower tomorrow at 9 P.M. Laurel for the engraving. She'll die if you bring the police.

I wandered around, desperate to figure a way out of the situation. I ended up sitting in a pocket park; the benches were wet from the rain but I barely noticed. Even at night, the smokers were out in full force, leaving a trail of butts under every bench. A guy next to me dressed in a smart pinstripe suit threw his still-burning cigarette on the ground, picked up his briefcase and helmet, and walked over to his motorcycle. A stone-black Ducati S4R, splendor on two wheels. He straddled it and revved the motor. I'd have given anything to be able to take off into the summer night like him and leave the cesspit of my life behind.

The High Bridge was built in the 1840s to hold a pipe bringing fresh, clean water from the Croton River into Manhattan. The oldest surviving bridge in Manhattan, it had fallen into decay and was closed after the cops caught kids dropping rocks onto the Circle Line boats. I'd seen photos of it and thought at the time how much it reminded me of Roman empire architecture. Originally built of stone, the classical series of arches spanning the Harlem River conjured up images of the ancient aqueducts bisecting the Tiber valley. Underneath the flat surface, an enclosed hollow ran the entire length of the bridge to carry the pipe. In those days, even the most functional spaces were beautifully designed, and this one had elaborate pillars and arches.

The tower stood at a desolate point in the park. Someone had been murdered there last year. Walking into that situation would be tantamount to strapping myself into an electric chair and pulling the lever. I had to find some other way to negotiate saving Laurel.

A rumble of thunder sounded as I entered the Waldorf. The earlier rain had made no dent in the humidity; the air was thick with oppressive heat like the inside of a volcano ready to blow.

In my room, I rooted around in my bag looking for the gun. I needed all the help I could get now.

It was gone. Had someone alerted security to search for it? If so, I was dead meat; they'd have called the police by now. If someone had complained security would have to act, but it was unusual for a hotel to invade a patron's privacy. And who'd have told them? No one had access to my room. I quickly changed and made my way over to the Zakars'.

Ari gave me his usual enthusiastic welcome when he opened the door. "Ah, John, we wondered when we'd see you. We expected you hours ago. Tomas gave up waiting and went down to the bar. Where is Laurel?"

"They've taken her, Ari. What in God's name am I going to do?"

He sank down on the couch and put his head in his hands. "It is bad. You may not get her back, I fear."

"What a fucking bastard Hal was for doing this to us."

Ari raised his head. "Yet it is done. We just go forward, that's all. But I'm afraid there's something else I must say." He got up and went into his bedroom and returned with a plastic bag.

I wondered what was coming next.

Ari cranked open the window and asked whether I'd mind if he smoked. He reached into his jeans pocket and pulled out a little silver dish with a flip top. A portable ashtray. He got out his package of Gitanes, selected one, and lit up. Holding the cigarette sideways between his thumb and his forefinger, he took a steep drag and blew the smoke out with a sigh. Then he opened the bag, reached inside, and brought out the gun.

"Tomas found this in your suitcase. You don't have permission for it; we saw that the serial number was filed off. He's very angry you kept it around us."

"Are you kidding me? He had no right to go through my things. How did he get into my room, anyway?"

"He should not have. But it's also wrong for you to keep it when you are with us. Tomas is here on false papers. If we're together and you're caught with this, or even worse, if you use it, there will be terrible trouble for everybody. Tomas disabled it anyway. You can't use it any more."

"What I choose to do is none of your business. And, I might add, because of the decisions your brother and Samuel made, Laurel could die."

"I agree, but we're all bogged down in this, this … mire now. I'm trying to do what I can to pull us out. The only reason I came here was to watch out for Tomas, and now I have to fly to London early tomorrow. I don't want to leave unless I know there is peace between the two of you."

"You didn't answer me. How did he get into my room?"

"Trying to survive in Iraq through two wars and much treachery in between can be a great motivator to learn skills people like you have no need for." He put the bag down on the bed beside him.

"Why do you have to go to London?"

"I've made more progress on the story I told you about. That is also the problem—it's been a little too successful. Some highly placed officials in the U.S. government got wind of it. Serious threats have been made against me, and I've been called back to London. They want me to take some time off until I'm reposted."

"Your bosses are ditching the story then?"

"No. They'll probably look for some local freelancer who's less well known than me to cover it, someone who can dig things out without being as noticeable. They want to protect me."

His cigarette had burned halfway down. He sighed and stubbed it out in his ashtray. "What's happened to Laurel, you see horrors like that every day in Iraq. People kidnapped, blown up, killed for no reason at all. Just before I came over here another reporter and I left Baghdad to cover a story in al-Nasiriyah. Heat like a furnace and pretty much a wasteland on that trip. Often we'd meet American supply vehicles going like bats out of hell.

"About twenty minutes after we passed one of the convoys we saw something ahead. At first, just a glimmer by the side of the road like a piece of white cloth flapping around. Closer, we could tell it was a teenage boy wearing a dishdasha. The boy would take a few steps into the road and then waltz back, like there was some invisible line he couldn't cross. All the while he was crying. Shrieking, actually. Crying and waving his hands.

"Our driver braked hard. A dark lump lay in the center of the road, a little girl, what was left of her anyway. She'd been hit full force by the convoy. We found out later that when she'd seen the supply trucks coming she'd run up because a couple of days earlier, soldiers had stopped to give them candy. I doubt they even knew they'd hit her. They travel incredibly fast to avoid attacks. Her brother was terrified to go to her out of fear that the same thing would happen to him."

The murmurs of thunder grew closer. I thought about closing the window. "I guess you've learned to cope with danger. You know what to watch out for. I got into some scrapes when I was younger, but nothing remotely like this."

"We," Ari said. "We're in this too. You're not alone—don't forget that."

"Even so, I'm caught up in something I don't fully understand. My life has been threatened more than once and now God knows what they're doing to Laurel. I thought I'd figured out Hal's hiding place this morning—a mausoleum at the Trinity cemetery where his mother was interred—but I couldn't get into it. I have to follow Hal's game through to the conclusion, whatever that is. To be honest, I can't even finance the rest of the search."

Ari reached over and rested one of his big hands on my arm. "I can't promise it will end well, but I'll do everything possible to make it so. Don't worry about money—we'll take care of that."

I looked closely at him. "Where's all this cash coming from? You're a journalist, Tomas is an anthropologist. Someone else must be funding you."

"A portion was donated." His gaze swept away as if he was keeping something from me.

Laurel's warning flag about terrorism resurfaced. "Who?" I insisted. "Is it some militant group? I need to know or I won't continue."

Ari pulled out another cigarette and rolled it between his thumb and forefinger, not lighting it.

Buying himself some time, I figured, trying to formu-
late a story I'd accept. He smiled. "We Assyrians
have enough on our hands just trying to survive. We
were glad to see the end of Hussein, but now more
and more of our people have to flee the country. It is
becoming very dangerous for us. The money does not
come from us."

He studied my face. I got the impression he was
trying to decide whether I could handle the truth.
"Samuel gave us the money. It came from him."

Lightning flashed right outside the window. I felt
as though it had just struck me. "That's impossible.
My brother didn't have that kind of money."

"He sold some things, from what I understand."
Ari hesitated. "I believe your property, the condo-
minium, was one of those things. To an investor in
Dubai. That's what he told us. Apparently the purchaser
agreed to a long closing, four or five months."

"That's impossible."

"He intended to tell you. I guess he never got the
chance."

I could see from his face that he was telling the
truth. After all, he had no reason to lie. With Samuel
I'd always had a special reserve of trust. Ari had just
blown that to pieces.

A strange hiss whistled through the air. On its
tail, a bright arc of lightning illuminated the night
with a cold luminescence, as if a floodlight had
suddenly been trained on the window. Ari rushed
to close it. I sat, dazed by this new information. I'd

lost Samuel, and possibly Laurel, and now the home I loved had gone with them. I put my head in my hands. My grief gave itself a voice and blew out of me in jagged sobs.

Ari didn't try to quiet me but moved closer. He waited until I calmed down and brought a towel he'd dipped in cold water. He handed it to me with a sigh. "It seems I'm always the one to deliver the bad news. No wonder I decided to be a journalist.

"You've always thought of Samuel as a little naive, haven't you?" he said. "You think Tomas maybe talked him into the whole scheme. That is wrong. Samuel spearheaded it from the beginning. He was well aware of the hazards and made it very clear if anything happened to him we could rely on you in his place."

"I can't imagine why he said that."

"Are you giving yourself enough credit? Sometimes the people we're close to see strengths we don't even know we have. Tomas proves that to me all the time. Think about it. We stand a good chance of recovering the engraving thanks to your efforts."

"I'm not sure I have the guts to carry on with this. For the last two days I've been constantly looking over my shoulder, wondering when the next attack will come. It's pure luck I'm still alive. By tomorrow night, Laurel may not be."

"Let me give you something." Ari reached inside the collar of his rumpled jean shirt and pulled a chain over his head. A golden charm dangled from one end. I could feel the warmth of his skin on the metal when he handed it to me. One face of the medallion was embossed with a winged disk, Assyria's most famous symbol.

"A *ktiwyateh*. An Assyrian talisman. The emblem of Shamash, god of the sun," Ari said. "It's protective. We Assyrians have lasted for over four thousand years, so it's proved its worth. Before you laugh, it's kept me safe through two wars, three gunshots, and numerous near misses. There's a bullet with my name on it somewhere but so far I've escaped it. So the medallion has been tried and tested. I want you to have it. We're bonded now. Brothers in arms?" He paused, then continued.

"And please don't take what Tomas says personally. He's under big pressures like we all are. That's not to excuse his behavior. I wouldn't be able to go now if I didn't think he was in good hands. He too will be sick when he hears about Laurel. He really liked her."

Don't talk about her in the past tense. I can't stand the thought of that. "Tomas gives you a rough time as well."

Ari chuckled. "What do you expect? I'm the older brother. There's a lot of history for us to overcome. In my father's eyes, I did no wrong. With Tomas, just the opposite. I've been paying for that for a long time. I can deal with it. I have, what is it you say in English, big arms."

"Big shoulders."

"Yes." Ari laughed again and touched his shoulder. His aura was so strong that when his smile faded, as it did now, the light in the room appeared to grow dimmer. "Something else. I'm break-ing a secret, but it helps for you to know. Tomas's fiancée died recently."

I looked up at him in surprise. "Laurel said they'd separated, that she'd married someone else."

"Tomas is too ashamed to tell it, the real story. He's taken the blame upon himself."

"What happened?"

"Did Laurel tell you my brother once planned to become a priest?"

"Yes, and that he changed his plans because he wanted to marry."

"Tomas could only have gotten away with that excuse over here." He shook his head in a kind of world-weary gesture. "Assyrian priests are permitted to marry; that's not what happened.

"His fiancée lived with her parents in Baghdad— Karradah District. When the bombing started she became terrified and begged Tomas to let her stay with him, but he was too busy helping Samuel and thought she would be safer at home. After we got the engraving Tomas and I went to see her." Ari's face sagged. "We found a disaster. The family apartment block crushed. Half was still standing. We could see the guts of the building's insides. But the rest? All metal rods sticking up, hills of broken concrete.

"You see Tomas as a restrained man, and usually he is. But on that night he went berserk. The one time I had to stand to the side. I could do nothing to help him. They never found her body."

"I know how bad it feels."

"Of course—Samuel," Ari said. "And also, I want you to know I won't forget about your inheritance. I'll see that you're treated fairly."

Ari made sure I'd truly calmed down before going to get Tomas. He took the gun with him. In truth, I think he wanted to give me some time alone to regain my composure.

I took advantage of the opportunity. I had no compunction about rifling through Tomas's suitcase after his raid on mine. In it I found two passports, the Iraqi one in his own name he'd shown me at the Khyber Pass and a second stating that he was George Anapolis, a Greek citizen. Clothes, toiletries, an extra pair of shoes, nothing else of interest. I found a book zippered into a side pocket and flipped through it. Ovid's *Metamorphoses*. Adhered to the middle page was a white paper rectangle the size of a business card, and on it, an address in Baghdad. The fact that Tomas had hidden it like that told me he attached a lot of importance to it. I found a scratch pad, scribbled the address down, and shoved it in my pocket.

Thunder boomed again in a series of crushing blows alternating with spear shafts of lightning. Like giant hands, sheets of rain beat against the windows.

Despite the pain it caused, once I got back to my room I replayed the hostage video a few times in case I'd missed any sign about where they were keeping Laurel. The background consisted of standard tile walls and floor. It could be any bathroom, basement, or commercial building in the city.

I switched on the hotel radio, hoping to take my mind off my troubles. Songs from Dwight Yoakam's aptly named *Last Chance for a Thousand Years* CD came on. It felt like both our last chances, mine and Laurel's, had vanished that long ago

Twenty-four

Wednesday, August 6, 2003, 7 A.M.

Whether because of the intense workout my emotions had gone through last night or the simple urgency of needing a solution, I decoded the first part of Hal's puzzle in short order the next morning.

Owl la memoir converted to *low memorial*. As in Low Memorial Library, the Columbia University administration building. While the words didn't fit seven spaces, I was convinced they led to the solution. The answer would be waiting for me on campus.

I checked my email again but there were no new messages. I sent one to my lawyer, Andy Stein, asking him whether it was too late to do anything about the sale of the condo.

Much as I would have preferred to avoid Tomas, it was still safer for the two of us to go to the library together. By now Ari would have told him about Laurel, and I counted on him being motivated to help her. I flung my things into my suitcase, phoned to warn him to be ready and got the message system. A knock on his door went unanswered.

At registration I hurriedly paid for our rooms and asked to leave a message for Tomas Zakar requesting that he meet me at Columbia.

The clerk looked him up. "He already checked out, sir, earlier this morning."

"Are you sure?" Had the news about Laurel so scared him that he'd abandoned both us and the search? Had he left with Ari? Another mystery to wrestle with. A call to Ari's phone got me nowhere. He wasn't answering either. Likely he was already winging his way over the Atlantic and unreachable. I had no time to worry about Tomas. Laurel was all I cared about right now.

A clang of metal signaled the city coming to life. Big trucks lifted the garbage bins, vans at curbside unloaded produce, store clerks rolled back metal window grates. I passed an entrepreneur getting ready for the day's trade, lounging on a doorstep of one of the grandiose buildings lining Fifth Avenue. Two cats lay at his feet, a silver tabby and a coal-black Persian, each on a round blue bed with an open can of cat food beside them and a hastily scrawled sign reading PLEASE HELP. Judging from the expensive Kodiak boots the guy sported, people had been generous.

A Statue of Liberty waved flyers in my face, a man dressed head to toe in rubbery green latex, his flowing robes flapping in the breeze. His face was coated in matching green greasepaint, and on his head he wore a seven-pointed crown. The cats stared in amazement.

I joined the throngs crowding into the subway for the ride uptown and got off at the 116th Street stop and made my way over to the heart of the campus. I told myself that Laurel would be all right. They wouldn't make any serious moves without the engraving. Still my anxiety mounted, dimming the swell of nostalgia that surfaced at the sight of Low Memorial. How many times had Hal, Corinne, and the rest of our friends gathered on those steps to joke around and hang out together? I'd had many good times at Columbia. In hindsight, too many.

A neoclassical beauty, Low Memorial was a temple at the crest of an imposing staircase. The architects had been inspired by Rome's Pantheon. Ten Ionic columns soared to a vast granite dome.

I passed bronze renditions of Zeus and Apollo and stopped just inside the entrance. What was I looking for? Many classical elements had been incorporated into the interior. Which one was Hal pointing to? Circling the famous bust of Pallas Athena were the twelve zodiac signs. None fit the seven spaces of Hal's puzzle. I reviewed the original words: *owl la memoir*. Perhaps Hal had used them simply to generate the building's name, but I believed they had a further meaning.

The reference to *owl* tugged at my memory. Hal had intended the game for me, so something I would have known about had to relate to the answer. And then I recalled what it was. The statue of Alma Mater outside. The contest we'd taken part in as freshmen to find the owl carved into her cloak. The statue was modeled after the Greek Athena, the Roman goddess Minerva. The seven letters of Hal's mother's name.

I sat on the steps outside and filled *Minerva* into the seven spaces. Minerva's name and the anagram faded, leaving only the diamond and the word *transmutation,* confirming that my answer had been correct. So what did that mean?

I remembered the funeral urn I'd found in his townhouse and the dull gems inside. They could have been low-grade diamonds, but the urn had contained nothing else, no directions to a hiding place. I pondered this for ten minutes or so until something Corinne said came floating back to me.

Incredibly strange, what he did with her.

At the time I'd thought she'd simply been referring to their rather perverse relationship. Had she meant something different? She picked up right away when I called.

"John, I'm glad you phoned. I'm sorry I haven't been in touch yet."

"No problem, Corrie. Listen, I've been wondering about something. When we talked before, you mentioned how it was strange what Hal had done with Mina. What did you mean by that?"

"Hal never told you?"

"No. He cremated her body, didn't he?"

"For the first stage, yes."

"The first stage?"

I heard her sigh through the phone. "I'm not surprised he didn't want to broadcast it. It was so weird. Talk about being chained to someone. He had her ashes compressed and converted into a diamond, the solitaire on that ring he wore. So she'd have a kind of immortality, he said."

"Are you serious?"

"They can do that now. An adult human body has enough carbon to generate dozens of small diamonds. The gems are synthesized from the ashes."

"My God."

Words deserted me.

Corinne broke through the silence. "There's something else I have to tell you. About Hanna Jaffrey."

"Did you find her?"

"Something came up on an Iraqi news blog. The picture it showed would have never made it into the mainstream media. It was stomach turning. Have you ever heard of a place called Tell al-Rimah? It's somewhere in Iraq."

The destination Tomas mentioned where he'd expected Jaffrey to go after she left their camp at Nineveh. "Yes, I know of it."

"Apparently she and her boyfriend had gone missing from an archaeological team staying at Tell Afar. This was in April. A sandstorm hit the area, a big one apparently. After the storm cleared they searched for them. They found Hanna first, bound to a post. It was so brutal. She'd been stoned. One of the team members was quoted as saying her face was no longer recognizable."

I felt sick listening to this. "Lord, that's terrible. Did they catch who did it?"

"Her boyfriend's body was recovered too, not much farther away. He's suspected. His knee was damaged but they assumed he killed her and then got caught in the storm. Apparently they'd been fighting about something back at the camp."

Or did the boyfriend have some help? It took me a few moments to feel calm enough to talk.

"Are you still there?"

"Yes. Just thinking."

"John, I don't want to pry into your business but this is really horrific stuff. Are you all right?"

"I'm being careful."

"I hope so. I've dug out some other information too. It's not much but maybe it will help. That woman—Eris Haines. Her real name is Eris Hansen and she wasn't fired. She was a specialist in trans-humanism and left the DOD in good standing."

"Trans-humanism. What does that mean?"

"Technologies to enhance the physical or mental abilities of humans. Think the bionic man or woman."

Haines had said she'd attended MIT, so that fit. "Corinne, thanks for all this. You've really helped."

"Not a problem. Keep in touch. Don't be a stranger, okay?"

"You've got my promise."

After I hung up I thought about the transhumanism angle and wondered whether it had anything to do with the motherlode Nahum's engraving led to. I'd assumed transmutation meant converting base metals into gold, since that was the most common application of the word. But it could refer to any form of change, even evolution. When I'd researched the word I'd learned that Darwin had initially been called a transmutationist. Hal's play on words: from human flesh to a diamond. From the human animal to an entirely new form of being. Was this the supernatural element Tomas had hinted at? These questions led nowhere and left me as much in the dark as ever.

I had to make it back to Sheridan Square, the last place I'd seen a ring. Before I left the library I checked my email, hoping to hear from Tomas. There was nothing from him, but my lawyer had responded:

John,
First off, what happened with Reznick? I set you up with one of the best criminal lawyers in town and you didn't bother to show up for your appointment. Reznick is totally po'd and I'm not too happy either. As far as the

condo's concerned, a New York firm acted
for the purchaser so I got in touch. The sale
has been executed and is final. Nothing can
be done on that end. I explained your situation and they're willing to let you stay until
August 26th. Under the circumstances, this
is generous. All your possessions have to be
cleared out by then or they'll be forfeited.
That's the best I could get out of them. I'll
send you a confirmation letter along with my
invoice.

My last shred of hope died like a rained-out fire.
I could scare up some money by selling off Samuel's
collection, something I hated to even think about.
Otherwise, I was bankrupt, hunted, and completely
alone.

Part Two

THE SECRET OF NAHUM

Upon the eleventh day,
When Lucifer had dimmed the lofty multitude of stars,
[The King] and Selenius went from there,
Joyful together to the Lydian lands.

There [the King] put Silenius carefully,
Under the care of his beloved foster-child,
Young Bacchus, he with great delight,
Because he had his foster father once again,
Allowed [the King] to choose his own reward.

—OVID, *METAMORPHOSES* XI:85–146

THE SECRET
OF NAHUM

Twenty-five

Andy's note made my next call ten times harder. The situation was out of control and I could no longer cope on my own. I would have to tell the police about Laurel, but I needed someone with me they'd believe. I dialed his private line and he answered right away.

"Reznick here."

"It's John Madison calling."

"Well. You're only a day late. There's a long line of people wanting my help, Madison. I'd bumped you up strictly as a favor to Andy."

"Look, I really apologize for missing our appointment. A friend of mine is in serious trouble. She's—"

"Legal trouble?"

"In a way."

"If she wants an appointment I hope she has better manners than you."

"It hasn't actually reached the legal stage yet. She's been threatened and now she's missing."

"Don't tell me you want to go to the police on her behalf?"

"Yes, that's what I was thinking."

"Ever been in the Tombs?"

"No."

"You soon may be and I'll tell you, they'll eat you for breakfast in there. I warned you last time we talked not to contact the police voluntarily for any reason, and that was before I got the new information."

An alarm went off in my brain. "What new information?"

"A warrant will soon be out for your arrest."

"Why?" I could feel my heart sinking.

"Apparently a neighbor of Hal Vanderlin's found some drug paraphernalia thrown over his fence. A silver spoon. The police have it. It has traces of heroin on it and your fingerprints."

He took my silence for an admission of guilt. "I'm willing to offer you another chance. Come into my office to give me a full statement and I'll accompany you to the station. You'll be charged and probably have to spend a day or so in the lockup, but I'll get you—"

"I can't do that. You don't know the whole—"

"Then I'm not able help you anymore, Mr. Madison. Goodbye."

I felt like I was caught in the middle of eight lanes of expressway traffic. All my potential moves had just been cut off. Every cop I passed by now would be a threat. Once I had the engraving, I'd have to find some way to negotiate with Eris and her crew entirely on my own.

Gip greeted me when I entered the lobby of Laurel's building. "Good morning, John. Nice to see the weather's cleared up. You're here for Laurel, I assume. Is she okay? I understand she took ill last night."

"Turned out to be just a bad migraine. She's fine now but not at home. She's meeting with Hal's lawyers and needs a document she forgot, so I've come to get it for her. Is that okay with you?"

Concern darkened his expression. "I hate to tell you, but the board is strict about these things. She should have called me to authorize it. Can you get hold of her now?"

Hell. I'd counted too much on him trusting me. "They're buried in that meeting, and you know what receptionists are like, not always willing to break in."

Like a granite boulder settling into a riverbed, his face told me he was not to be moved. How to get around this?

"Gip, do you have security in the building? They could go up with me."

"We only have a service on call. Look, since I know you I can be a little flexible. Our maintenance guy is here fixing the air conditioning. Let me get him to accompany you." He spoke into his cellphone and made the request.

"Thanks. Laurel's been so upset about Hal it's no surprise she's forgetful."

"A very sad business. I watched him grow up."

"I know. It's been hard on all of us."

The elevator pinged and the maintenance man leaned out and waved. I trotted over and got inside. Thankfully, I remembered the penthouse entrance code.

A flurry of nerves hit me when we walked in. I thought I'd seen Laurel toying with the ring in the study off the family room, but I couldn't be positive. The view out the French doors showed the plates and soggy dinner things still sitting on the terrace table.

"What a mess," the maintenance man said when we entered the study.

It looked like it had been hit by a force-five hurricane—files and photos dumped all over the floor. Her laptop was gone.

He gave me a suspicious look. "What's happened here?"

I shrugged. I didn't have to manufacture a look of shock; I was as surprised as he. "I don't know. She was probably getting ready to sort through this stuff when something else came up."

He didn't seem convinced. "I'm going to have to call this in." He took his pager off his belt and punched in some numbers.

I sensed my opportunity to find the ring slipping away. I thought I'd seen it in the study, but where? I opened the desk drawers, thinking Laurel might have put it away. Memo pads, paper clips, things like that—but no ring. And then a rare piece of good luck—sitting on a recessed bookshelf over the desk were a man's watch and wallet, and beside them, Hal's ring.

I heard the chirp of the maintenance man's cell. In the few seconds he turned his attention away to answer, I pretended to reach for a book, then grabbed the ring and slipped it on my index finger. I bent down and rooted among the file folders on the floor, found one labeled Property Administration, and searched through it. I drew out an invoice for property taxes and straightened up. "This is it. This is what Laurel wanted."

The man held out his phone. "Gip wants to talk to you."

"Hi, Gip. Listen, everything's okay. There's a wallet and watch on the bookshelf in here. They weren't taken, so I don't think you need to worry about a robbery. It's probably just a case of lax housekeeping. She's not the most domestic person. I'll ask Laurel to talk to you about it when she comes back."

I handed the phone back to the maintenance guy. He spoke to Gip, terminated the call, and looked at me. "Okay. He says to leave it for now. He'll make out a report for the householder."

Before I left the building Gip noted the document I'd taken. I felt ecstatic about getting the ring, like a great weight had just rolled off my back.

My hands were bigger than Hal's and his ring was so tight I couldn't get it all the way down my finger. It was a heavy, clunky piece, and I made my left hand into a fist to ensure it didn't fall off. The minute I got a safe distance away from the building I took it off. A basketball game was in play on the West Fourth Street courts; a sweaty, raucous crowd of fans bunched along the wire-mesh fence. I'd spent many happy times at the Cage watching the tough, fast-moving action. I drifted over.

I found an empty spot at the end of the fence and turned my attention to the ring. It looked old, with elaborate designs worked into the gold frame encircling the solitaire. I thought it was an antique, possibly a Victorian copy of an ancient Celtic poison ring. The goldsmith's stamp on the inside of the band confirmed this—a mark not seen on contemporary rings. The diamond winked in the sun as if Mina's spirit lived on inside it. It creeped me out.

Thinking it might be a hinge, I put pressure on some scrollwork at the crown of the ring. I heard a faint click and nudged the face of the ring outward. A tiny piece of folded paper lay in the pocket underneath. I unfolded it with shaking hands.

Hal's spidery writing stood out in blue ink: *Trinity—Janssen Tomb.*

I'd been right yesterday. I'd been so close! Hal had hidden the engraving in the cemetery mausoleum beside the Church of the Intercession after all. Even though Mina hadn't been buried there, Hal would have still had legal access to it any time he wanted.

Although I'd narrowly missed the engraving yesterday, finding the ring gave me a measure of peace.

My best guess was that the Alchemy group had trashed Laurel's study hunting for the engraving or new information leading to it. Probably because she told them to look for it there. Not knowing the answer herself, but hoping to buy some time, she'd tossed them a red herring. A clever detour on her part. That also meant she was not too far gone to think rationally. My cell showed 11:48 A.M. Nine hours left to free her.

I stopped in at Garber's Hardware and bought a penlight and a battery-powered hacksaw to cut the padlock. The hacksaw was only about two hand lengths long and therefore easy to conceal. I dumped my clothes into a trash can to make room in my bag for the engraving. Taking another look around to check for Eris or her people, I flagged a cab.

Inside the cemetery I scanned the grounds for the caretaker, but there was no sign of him. There wasn't a soul to be seen. Luck might be on my side for once. I walked straight up to the unnamed mausoleum, assuming this had to be the Janssen Tomb by default. When I tugged the padlock it fell off. The hasp had been cleanly cut through. The doors swung open easily, unimpeded by dirt or debris, another sign someone had been here before me.

I pocketed the padlock and once inside, pulled the doors shut. I flicked on my penlight and swept it across the dim interior. Pale centipedes and spiders dashed back into the dark corners, escaping from the painful flare of my light. Stone coffins lay against each of the side walls, one with its lid shoved aside. My light glanced off a jumble of brownish bones, not laid out in the usual symmetrical form. Cool in this tomb and damp. Aside from the bones and a net of cobwebs nothing else was there. The second coffin held an intact, undisturbed skeleton. The engraving was gone.

I felt numb with despair, the last hope I had of freeing Laurel swept away.

As I emerged from the tomb, a voice pierced the air. "Just one minute. You were here yesterday. I thought I made myself clear then." The caretaker walked down the rise behind the mausoleum, no friendly smile on his face this time.

Angling my body so he couldn't see the missing padlock, I said, "After you directed me to the columbarium I learned they had no record of my great-aunt's name. So I came back here, where my cousin had originally said to look."

"A little odd since this particular mausoleum isn't even identified."

"I thought there may have been some indication, something I'd missed."

"And you conveniently forgot you're not supposed to be in here."

"Something like that."

He eyed me for a few seconds. "What is it with you people? I had to throw someone else out early this morning. Some tourist with a backpack. Nobody can read I guess."

"What did he look like?"

"A bit like you but shorter and skinnier. Dark hair."

"Did he have an accent?"

"Yes, but his English was good."

Tomas. I apologized for the intrusion and hustled away from his angry glare.

I racked my brains trying to understand how Tomas had figured this out. He said he'd taken some courses at Columbia, so it was possible he'd solved the anagram. Except the ring was intact and in my possession. He didn't have the benefit of Hal's final clue. Could it have been my conversation last night when I'd opened up to Ari? I'd told him about my visit to the cemetery. Had he passed that along to his brother? He must have. I knew in my gut that I couldn't trust Tomas.

Whatever. Tomas had Nahum's engraving now. The enormity of his duplicity staggered me. He'd betrayed me and left Laurel to die. I'd tear him apart if I ever got near him again.

Anger is a useless ally. It fogs the mind. But even with my senses on full alert I wouldn't have seen it coming. As I passed through the Amsterdam entrance the jester, lurking behind the high stone wall, jammed a gun into my belly.

He pulled the trigger.

Pain roared through my gut and then seemed to expand, turning my whole body into one gigantic, throbbing wave of hurt. I fell, twitching on the sidewalk like a slaughtered lamb. I couldn't breathe. I had a vague memory of being dragged into a vehicle, the stink of exhaust, a woman's voice. When I tried to move, my body lay like a dead weight.

"Where is it?" Eris glared at me. She yanked open my bag, and swore when she realized it was empty.

"He shot me." I tried to raise my hand and press it to my abdomen.

"*Tasered* you," she corrected. "What did you do with the engraving?"

Still groggy, I raised myself up to a sitting position, sucked in a couple of deep breaths, and closing my trembling fist, took a violent swing at her. She easily deflected it and twisted my arm painfully behind my back. She pulled out the Taser.

"You'd like more of this? Fifteen hundred volts straight to your temple this time?"

"Then you'll *never* find it."

She frowned in exasperation. "Okay, I'm repeating myself here. Where did you put it?"

"It wasn't there."

"You're lying." She clicked something on the stun gun and pressed it against my temple.

A phone rang. Eris reached into her purse and pulled it out. After a brief, terse conversation, she looked out the window and then turned to me, smiling. "We're just about there," she said. "He's going to come down to see you."

"Whoever he is, he can screw off too."

"We'll dig it out of you then."

Twenty-six

The car pulled into a sizeable parking garage that I assumed belonged to the building on West Thirty-fourth Street. We stopped at a loading platform. Eris and the jester hustled me roughly through the gloomy space and up a few steps to a steel door.

At first glance the room we entered reminded me of a funeral parlor, a ritzy one dressed up for rich folk. Plush mushroom-colored broadloom covered every inch of the floor. A large silver vase sat on a Queen Anne buffet, the top so glossy it reflected the vessel perfectly. Embossed around its base were the signs of the five ancient planets I'd seen on the Alchemy Archives website: Jupiter, Venus, Mars, Saturn, and Mercury. A cloying scent hung in the air, as if someone had tried to cover up a bad odor with cheap floral spray. The place carried with it a kind of hush, of breath caught in the throat, like you find in an emergency waiting room or at the side of a grave.

"Sit here." Eris motioned to a row of upholstered chairs.

I glanced around the room, trying to find some way to make a break for it, and heard a voice behind me.

"I think this time we'll have a more honest conversation."

When I turned, Jacob Ward was standing a few feet away. My momentary surprise faded. Here, I had no doubt, was Jupiter. I couldn't imagine him in any role but that of kingpin. My mind raced. Jacob Ward was Tomas's contact. Had this whole thing been a setup? Ward had a keen enough interest in the period and deep enough pockets to buy the artifact. But if he and Tomas had Nahum's engraving, why was Ward strong-arming me now?

"I'll say one thing for you, Ward, you've got talent. How have you managed to hide the fact that you're no better than some deadbeat killer in Rikers?"

He reddened slightly and ran a hand over his jaw as though I'd just spit on his face.

"Where's Laurel? Take me to her right now."

The way he was dressed, black bespoke suit, plain white shirt, conservative tie, made him look like a funeral director. I saw him twitch, the only hint at the tension he carried.

"I quite enjoyed your company at my home, John. Let's avoid getting off on the wrong foot today." He took a few steps forward and gave me a pat on the shoulder, the kind of gesture an uncle would make toward a favored nephew.

I jerked away from his pudgy hand, in no frame of mind for any pretense of politeness. "You didn't answer me. I said I want to see her."

"And what if we refuse? You'll come out swinging, both gun barrels blazing?" He laughed. "Madison, think of this as a dogfight. We're the rottweilers and you're the poodle—one of the small ones. It's no contest. Let's go somewhere else to talk; people are always coming and going through here."

Venting my rage might make me feel better, but it wouldn't help Laurel. I'd be further ahead playing along with them and finding some angle I could exploit. We walked down the corridor to an elevator. The jester wandered off, leaving Eris as rearguard behind us. Ward pressed the button for the fifth floor and we exited into a huge room. Floor to ceiling, the height of the place rose almost two stories. The space was circular and vast. It had no windows; I assumed the ones I'd seen on the exterior had been blocked off. The walls were finished with expensive paper in lustrous white. The ceiling, a gentle dome, was topped with an oval central skylight framed in bronze. I could see an ellipse of sky overhead but most of the light came indirectly, the actual fixtures probably hidden behind the rolled cornice. The room had an other-worldly cold, flat tone. Around its circumference was a series of glass-fronted cases customized for the circular walls.

Ward swept his arm in a wide arc. "Our gallery," he said.

White plastic monitors, each with a row of winking green lights, were affixed to the cases. Almost two-thirds contained artifacts, and the rest books and manuscripts. I assumed not all of them were legitimate, having either been looted or fabricated. I thought I could identify a statue stolen from the National Museum. With one phone call, I could probably clear up a significant number of open FBI files.

"The glass is shatterproof," Ward said. "You could set off a grenade in here and it wouldn't break. The whole thing is screened against ultraviolet light. Inside there's even a separate airflow system; it keeps the atmosphere humid and at a constant temperature. As you probably know, Iraqi soil is very salty. When clay objects are removed from the earth they dry out, crack, and disintegrate. I make time every day to come in here. You can feel them, you know, the ancient craftsmen speaking to you through the glass."

Many of the books and manuscripts had pages that were parchment thin and brownish, the pages almost transparent, fragile as elderly skin. They perched on small wooden platforms or custom frames like minia-ture lecterns. I pressed my hand against the glass to slide it open, forgetting it would have been locked.

"The artifacts are available to buyers but this section is my own collection. Some of them are very rare. I can get one out if you want to see it." Ward pointed to a leather-bound tome with clasps like I'd seen on the *Picatrix*. "That's *Secretum Secretorum*, *The Secrets of Secrets*. Goes back to the twelfth century."

He gestured to the right. "*The Munich Manual of Demonic Magic*, a German book about forbidden rites. It's in Latin. The volume beside it is a work on astrology by the Russian Vladimir Apriagnev. And here's my pride and joy—a French title, *Le Mystère des Cathédrales*. The author vanished in 1953; no one knows what happened to him. Some speculate he found the key to immortality." Ward tapped the glass in front of the book. "Only three hundred copies originally printed. Considerably fewer in circulation now."

"You really believe in all those preposterous fairy stories? Immortality? Alchemy?"

Ward colored. "Explain why Himmler took it seriously then. He planned to use alchemical gold to finance the Nazi Party."

"You're expecting the engraving to lead you to, what, some kind of formula to make gold?"

Eris, who'd been uncharacteristically quiet, butted in. "We don't have to justify ourselves to you, Madison."

I decided right then to puncture their balloon. "No, you don't. But you're not completely up to date. Vanderlin's game has been solved and Tomas Zakar has the engraving."

I'd taken a bold step telling them Tomas had it, but I got the response I was hoping for. The news came as a shock. To Ward especially. His inability to hide his anxiety told me how hard the information had hit him. He rubbed the side of his cheek as though he'd just been stung by a wasp. When he spoke, his voice sounded weak. "Where is he?"

I looked straight at him and tried to force a smile. "Your guess is as good as mine. Somewhere over the Atlantic I assume. He left Laurel and me out to dry. You've wasted your time by hauling us in here."

"Don't think, Madison, that my current good humor toward you means anything." Ward nodded toward Eris. "Laurel's already had a taste of Eris's talents. She's quite effective at teasing out people's secrets."

"Right. Like Hal's. She certainly blew that."

"He tried to end-run us," Eris said defensively.

I masked my surprise. The pieces were finally falling into place. Laurel had been right. Hal *had* been part of their group and ended up paying for that with the same sickening fate as Hanna Jaffrey. *Jesus, Hal. What did you get yourself tangled up in?*

"He was willing to sell the piece. You didn't have to kill him."

"He wanted six million. Far too much. I didn't achieve all this by being a fool," Ward said.

"The engraving is worth way more than that."

"Undoubtedly, but I like to be the one to maximize profits."

I felt the fear. But you can't be good at sales without reading people well, and something told me there was bluff mixed in with his threats. "A word of advice. Your time would be better spent tracking Tomas and letting Laurel and me go. Squeezing us won't get you any further."

He rounded on me, the supercilious smile finally wiped off his face. "I guess the afternoon we spent at my house gave you the wrong impression. The purpose of that cordial interlude was simply to allow me to size you up. You can buy your freedom only by telling us where Tomas is."

I reared back from him. The sudden motion sent jolts of pain through my stomach.

"Tomas deceived me. I imagine he's heading for Iraq but I don't know for sure."

Eris focused her cold gaze on me. "How did he get out of the country? He didn't buy an airline ticket."

"He flew in to a private airstrip in the States and probably left the same way." I was still furious about the Zakars' deception and wanted any repercussions aimed straight at them. Ward eyeballed me for a few seconds, trying to sort out whether I was telling the truth.

"I thought you had everyone under constant watch. How did he and Ari slip past you?"

"We gave you maximum latitude to find the engraving. We don't have limitless resources, so most of our surveillance had to be focused on you. We knew Ari Zakar flew solo back to London and we lost track of Tomas."

"You people are fools."

Ward moved surprisingly fast for a heavy man. His backhand whipped my head around.

The room wavered. My brain felt like it had been shaken loose from my skull. I had to wait until the ringing in my ears faded before I could hear what he had to say next.

"Now, we have some business to finish. Tell me where Tomas took the engraving."

"Not until I'm released *with* Laurel."

"I don't think so," he said. They herded me back to the elevator. We dropped to the basement. He and Eris marched me down a hallway and stopped when they reached the doorway to a small room. "Up to now we've been playing along with your puzzles. We had no intention of harming you, at least not irrevocably. You had your chance. That phase is done."

They threw me inside. The room had a tiled floor and walls, no window, similar to the room in the video of Laurel. A weak light came from a fixture high up on the wall in one corner. The only feature giving the place any distinction was a niche cut into the back wall, arched at the top, about eight feet at its summit and four feet wide. It looked tailor-made to contain a life-sized sculpture. Inside it stood Shim, massive and silent. My own personal wrecking ball.

The door slammed shut with a clang of metal against concrete. I backed up to the wall farthest away from the Cyclops. He didn't move a muscle. He just stared. The room was completely silent except for the jackhammering of my own pulse. I had no idea how long we stood like that, but we stayed in those positions, locked into a stalemate like the last two pieces on a chessboard.

They'd taken my phone and wallet, and with no

watch or window to track the fading sunlight I quickly lost all sense of time. A few hours could have passed or the better part of the day. I focused on the tile floor and counted the squares, hoping to stem the messages of fright pummeling my mind. I noticed it was clean, almost too clean for a basement floor, and it smelled of bleach. I could see faint stains in the grout between the tiles.

At one point, my mind tricked me into thinking the brute really was made of stone. Shim was able to hold himself completely motionless. When not called upon to act, his mind simply shut down as if he were some giant windup toy. His one good eye stared unblinkingly straight at me like the homicidal gaze of a giant prehistoric bird of prey. I'd find myself dropping off, starting to slide down the wall I was propped against, when a surge of adrenalin would jolt me awake and I'd catch sight of Shim, who remained static, never uttering a sound.

I wondered what he'd been like before the explosion in his lab. A young genius anxious to make his mark on the world. Perhaps not even a bad man. He'd retained something of an emotional life. I saw that in his fierce attachment to Ward and Eris.

Every now and then I'd hear muffled sounds outside. Footsteps echoing down the corridor, two men's voices in conversation, someone clearing his throat. Eerie, to hear those sounds of normalcy, imprisoned in this cell. What could be gained by prolonging my misery? Was this some kind of breaking-in exercise before they bled out every last drop of information they thought I had?

I heard the lock turning. Shim reached me in one giant step, forcing me against the wall, pinning my arms back. My shoulder screamed and my eyes teared up. I tried to prepare myself mentally for the torture I knew was coming. I was young and in reasonably decent physical shape. That would give them a fair amount of time before I broke down for good.

The door banged against the wall as Jacob Ward entered. "Let's get started. You've had some time to think about your situation, so tell me where Tomas has gone."

"I want to see Laurel first."

"I thought we'd already dealt with that."

"Not to my liking."

A disabling pain hit my arm when Shim jerked it up. A gesture from Ward told him to ease off. "I'm willing to show some good faith," he said. He motioned to Shim. The two of them led me out of the room and along a basement corridor to a similar room, but one with a cheap-looking cot and single chair.

Laurel lay on the cot. Eris rose from the chair beside the cot when I walked into the room.

I rushed over to Laurel, who lay face down, not moving.

"It's John, Laurel."

She stirred and rolled onto her side. I put my arm around her and helped her sit up, or rather, she slouched against my side, my body propping her up.

Her eyes looked hazy; she blinked and peered at me as though she didn't believe I was really there. I took her hand. It felt cold and sweaty. "Is it really you?" she said. "How did you get here?"

"They brought me here. I refused to talk to them unless I'd seen you first."

She pulled away. "Don't touch me."

I remembered too late that her hands had been tied. "Your wrists must still be so sore."

When she faced me I could see how angry she was. "What did you think seeing *me* would accomplish? You've taken everything away from me now. At least believing you were still out there gave me some hope. I wish I'd never opened the door to you that first time when you came, full of sympathy. So solicitous. Comforting me about Hal. Swearing you'd protect me. I can't even stand to look at you."

I wanted to tell her she was wrong, that she would have probably been killed by Eris had it not been for my efforts, but she was in no frame of mind to hear this. Besides, hadn't I already berated myself for bringing bad luck to everyone I cared about?

I stood up and tried to think of a last word to give her some reassurance. "Try to keep up your strength, Laurie. I'll find a way to get us out. All they want is the engraving." I didn't want to frighten her even more by telling her Tomas had made sure we'd never get it back.

A shudder spread through her body. She had one more bitter remark left for me. "Don't fool yourself.

We'll never see each other again. That's some kind of blessing, anyway."

"She needs medical attention," I said to Eris. "You have to release her."

"Doctors are in short supply around here," Eris shot back. "Time to go."

Ward and the jester were waiting for us outside Laurel's makeshift prison cell. "So, your part of the bargain is due now. Where is Tomas?"

I wasn't about to give in that easily. "Tell me something first. It was Eris who picked Laurel up, right? I assume Laurel was drugged?"

Ward nodded.

"So she probably hasn't any memory of where this place is."

"Yes," Ward replied.

I was steaming, but I tried to keep a lid on it for Laurel's sake. "And my guess is, she doesn't know about you. Eris is probably the only person she's seen."

Eris let out an annoyed huff. "Forget it, Madison. We can see where you're going with this."

"We're not letting her go." Ward said this in such a matter-of-fact tone he may as well have been ordering up pizza. "At least not now. But I understand your thinking and you're right, she'll have next to nothing for the police to go on when we do release her. That should give you some encouragement. So you have a heaven-or-hell choice. It's good to keep things simple. Cooperate with us and she'll be free; don't and she'll end up dead."

I had to admit my arsenal was empty. My only option was to wait for a new opportunity to open up. "He's in Baghdad—I've got the address." I felt in my pocket for the crinkled hotel memo on which I'd written the address I'd taken from Tomas's room and handed it to Ward. He looked at it and passed it immediately to Eris. "Check this out," he said.

Once Ward was certain I'd told all I knew, they took me back to Shim. An hour or so later, Ward and Eris returned and hurried me back along the corridor, the jester pressing my head down so I could see only Ward's broad back, the muscles making his black suit jacket ripple as we followed in his tracks. "Where are we going now?" I asked him.

"To Babylon," he said. "Lucky you."

Twenty-seven

Thursday, August 7, 2003, 10:30 P.M.

We drove to an airfield in what I guessed was New Jersey. Laurel remained captive in New York to ensure my cooperation.

I could smell the tang of gasoline and glimpse pavement glistening after the rainfall. We'd stopped beside a small jet. Our destination was Baghdad, not the actual site of old Babylon. But Ward didn't need me to locate the address I'd given him. Why go to the trouble of sending me to a country I was totally unfamiliar with in the midst of a war? I got absolutely nowhere with Ward when I lobbed questions at him about why he was taking me there. The fact that they'd held off torturing me implied they needed my cooperation for some future plan. What was it?

They hustled me into the rear of a Learjet 35.

Ironic that I'd flown in a similar plane a couple of
months ago to babysit an Italian ceramic one of my
clients had purchased. In this one the back of the
cabin was closed off with drapery and some seats had
been removed. The windows were painted black. It
looked as if I wasn't the first person forced to travel in
this plane against his will.

The jester snapped a metal cuff onto my right
wrist, fastening it to a handle jutting out from the
wall. My body ached nonstop. I sagged against the
wall. The man buckled himself in. He wore a suit
now, but it did nothing to improve on his lank black
hair and deadly pale skin. He had the strangest eyes—
almost yellow.

I could see the red tattoo on his wrist, but his
sleeve hid almost half of it and I couldn't tell what sign
it was meant to be. I assumed Eris and Shim were up
front with Ward. I mentally ticked them off: Venus,
Mars, Jupiter. I'd concluded that Ward was Jupiter, the
boss; Eris, Venus; and Shim, Mars. Laurel said that
Hal was Saturn. By default, then, the jester must be
Mercury. A very unlikely messenger of the gods.

Since I was going to be spending more than a day
with this man, I decided to try lowering the threshold
of hostility. "Which one are you?" I asked.

He misunderstood me and grunted, "Lazarus."

"Is that your real name?"

"It is now."

"How did you come by it?"

"Doctors brought me back from the dead.

Sometime I'll give you a description so you'll know what to look forward to."

What a shitface.

"Where?"

"Chechnya."

"Why would you be involved there?"

"You don't know anything, do you? We're in all those holes. You flit around with your lattes and martinis selling your highbrow art and you know nothing about the real world."

"You caused that accident in front of the café, didn't you?"

"Ward said to make you afraid, not kill you."

"Someone got badly injured. Doesn't that even bother you?"

"You said it yourself—it was an accident. I was just trying to knock out the truck's tire. Anyway, we're not supposed to be talking."

I was in here with him for the long haul. With one stopover the trip on a commercial jet would take almost a day. This smaller plane would need more refueling stops and at a lower speed the flight would take longer. Before, I'd faced a threat only from a specific group of people. In Iraq the danger would increase tenfold. There were no safe places in Baghdad.

Lazarus reached inside his suit jacket and pulled out a knife. It had a cruel-looking, fat serrated blade. He played around with it, pretending to aim it at me and throw. When he tired of his stupid game he gave me a couple of cans of warm Dr Pepper, a soggy corned beef sandwich, and an empty plastic bottle to piss in. I was expected to manage all this with my free left hand.

I pictured the others: Ari dining in an upscale London restaurant; Tomas in Iraq, ensconced in some comfortable hideaway; the soothsayer, Diane Chen, humming along with the music, kibitzing with her customers. Her predictions were so accurate, she should go into the fortune-telling business. I felt the weight of Ari's talisman on my chest. Even the sun god had failed me.

I slept fitfully and finally woke up completely disoriented and woozy. I knew we'd been in the air for many hours and had a vague memory of landing and taking off again at some point—that was all. My drink must have been spiked with a sedative.

The aircraft began its stomach-heaving drops. I listened to the thud of the landing gear engaging and soon after felt the contact with terra firma and heard the whine of the jets reversing. While we taxied to our destination, Lazarus undid my shackles. When I unwound my legs and tried to stand I almost fell. My joints protested like those of an eighty-year-old man. He opened the curtains. "Go up front. Ward's there."

Ward waved me over when he saw me and indicated a seat across the table from him. Lazarus posted himself behind me. No one else was in the cabin. I tried to get a glimpse out the windows but could see only a blank whitish wall and concluded we must be in some kind of hangar. Ward dug in his pocket and took out a wallet and a dark blue passport, the Great Seal of the United States on its cover.

He dropped it on my lap. "There are credit cards and ID in the wallet too."

I opened the passport and was shocked to see that it was my own. "Where did you get this?"

"Eris took it when you two had that little chat in your condo. At the time we thought it might be preventative, to make it harder for you to leave the country."

"I'm going in under my own name?"

"Can't take any chances with customs. Authorities are strict around here."

I could hardly believe what he'd said. Taking me through customs would be a gift to me, an easy opportunity to break away from them.

As if reading my thoughts, Ward picked up a phone from the table in front of us. It was a large, clunky-looking piece, like a TV remote with an antenna.

Ward noted me looking at it and held it up. "A sat phone. Not too many viable cell towers where we're going." He punched in some numbers, waited for a minute or so, and greeted the voice on the other end. "Put her on now," he said and held out the phone. "Someone wants to say hi to you."

I snatched the phone from his hand and put it up to my ear. "John Madison here." I waited but got no answer, only the sound of static across the airwaves. I held the phone out for Ward. "Nothing on the other end. Is this another one of your games?"

Ward grabbed it and almost shouted into it. "Talk to him as you were instructed to do or it will get even worse for you."

Laurel had to be on the other end. It was a relief to know she still had the will to resist them.

She spoke to me when I took the phone back. "They're making me talk to you. It's not my idea."

"It's still good to hear you," I said.

"Your voice is kind of funny. Like there's a delay between when you say the words and I hear them."

She'd freak out if she knew how far away I was. "I'm in a very large room on the top floor of the building. It's cavernous. That must be causing an echo. You holding up okay?"

"Are you serious? Sure, I'm fine. I spend every minute wond-ering how they're going to do it. Maybe they'll do something to make it look like an accident." Her voice broke off at that point.

"Laurel, if they were going to get rid of us, it would have happened by now. Try to think that way instead."

I heard her laugh, but it was the kind of response that came from a deep gulf of disbelief and despair.

Ward held up his pudgy hand, indicating he wanted me to stop talking. I ignored him. "It won't be long now, Laurie. They're close to getting what they want. And I still have information to trade."

I didn't hear her reply because Lazarus yanked the phone out of my hand and gave it back to Ward, who shut it off and put it into the briefcase at his feet. He stood up. "You still have information to trade, do you? I'd like to hear it."

"I said that to comfort her."

"For once, I think I believe you. Anything happens in customs or anywhere in the airport and her life is gone. Yours too, of course. Eris has kept her drug supply with her."

"You're trying to suggest she'd inject me with heroin in the middle of an airport?"

"She has lots of other effective chemicals. You know what a taipan is?"

"A snake."

"The deadliest land-based snake in the world. Its venom will shut down your respiratory system in less than a minute. Eris has a supply of it, along with a very effective delivery system." He brushed off his jacket and fiddled with his tie. "Now, the reason for our visit here. We're headed to a place called Afyon. Heard of it?"

"No."

"It's a famous carpet-weaving town. We're on a business trip to buy some rare rugs. You can talk knowledgeably about that if you're asked, can't you?"

"You're crazy. This is the middle of a war zone and you're giving them some cocked-up story about buying carpets?"

"Let me be the judge of that." Ward shut down any further conversation by walking to the exit. I followed with Lazarus stalking behind.

There was no sign of Shim or the pilots. We'd

entered a hangar as I'd suspected and only Eris was waiting for us. She appeared wan and exhausted. Her usually perfect platinum hair was a mess; puffy dark circles ringed her eyes. Had Ward reamed her out for her mistakes? Or perhaps she had a conscience after all. Maybe it cost her something to do harm to other people.

A black Mercedes sedan was parked outside the hangar. But that wasn't what brought me to a halt. In the mid-distance stood a gleaming contemporary building, international aircraft flanked like the spokes of a wheel around its exterior. Not an army vehicle in sight. Before Eris or Lazarus could lay a hand on me, I grabbed Ward's shoulder and forcibly turned him around to face me. "This obviously isn't Baghdad. Where are we?"

He laughed in a mocking tone. "Atatürk International Airport. Welcome to your homeland, Madison."

Twenty-eight

"We're supposed to be going to Baghdad, to that address I gave you."

"You're complaining about a visit to the land of your birth?"

Lazarus chuckled at Ward's remark. I told him to eat it. "What's going on, Ward?"

"Just a short detour," he replied. "Enjoy it while it lasts."

Customs went smoothly. I cooperated because of the memory of Laurel's voice, stretched thin with fear. Nor did I doubt Eris was capable of deploying the poison. I had to find the right opportunity and some way to make sure Laurel was protected before I tried to escape. That meant waiting to make my move when they were distracted or I was alone with one of them.

According to the airport clock we arrived at 10 P.M. At night through the car's windows I could see little more than quick slices of the city. I thought

I glimpsed the dome and exotic spiked minarets of Istanbul's magnificent Blue Mosque, but that may have been just my imagination.

A couple of weeks before my ninth birthday, Samuel had written to say that he'd be leaving his work site in Mosul to spend a few weeks in Turkey. I pleaded with him to let me join him. Evelyn warned me not to get my hopes up, but, as a surprise to us both, he said yes, I could come. She bought me a book filled with pictures of Turkey and I pored over it again and again until I swear I had all the words memorized. I still remember the image of the green pools of Hierapolis, white marble Roman columns submerged beneath the pond surfaces like watery ghosts from a dim past. Days before I was due to fly over, Samuel wired to say he'd had a change of plans. I felt as though he'd slammed a door in my face. It took me months to recover from the disappointment.

That experience had played a major role in my lack of interest in my birthplace. From then on, it meant little more to me than a line or so on my naturalized American citizenship papers. Added to that was the sour aftertaste of the story I'd been told about the relatives who'd abandoned me. So the burst of pride I felt at seeing Istanbul for the first time, even as a blurred cityscape through a car window, caught me by surprise. And now my first reunion with the country was marred by its brutal circumstances.

The Mercedes eventually pulled up in front of an exceptionally beautiful building of ivory limestone, its facade richly ornamented with sculpture and decorative flourishes.

"The Grand Hotel de Londres," Ward announced. "We're stopping here."

One step into the hotel transported us back to the previous century—elaborate leaded-crystal chandeliers, Victorian wallpaper, golden art deco statuettes poised on either side of a grand staircase. Once a rich burgundy, the velvet upholstery of the furnishings had faded with time.

Ward gave the room a quick once-over when we entered the lounge, glanced at his watch, and barked at Eris, "I don't see our contacts. I thought they were supposed to meet us here."

"They'll show. Must have been held up by the traffic or something," she said.

"We're paying them enough to be on time," Ward snapped. "Let's get a table then—I'm starving."

He went over to the bar while we settled into chairs. I saw him talk to the bartender and hand over a sheaf of bills. The room maintained the Victorian theme, so much so that it could double for an English colonial movie set. Live parrots fluffing their brilliant chartreuse feathers swung in bamboo cages. Every now and then the birds would let out a squawk, but whatever they had to say, it wasn't in English. I half expected to see Graham Greene's Myatt from *Stamboul Train* perched on a bar stool, sampling a gin and tonic.

Ward's mood had improved when he returned.

The expansive personality of the jovial professor was back. I thought it a talent of his, this ability to flip so quickly out of the dark side where his natural personality lay. "Our contact phoned the hotel. He'll be here soon. I was told it isn't customary to eat in the bar but I managed to persuade the bartender. I ordered us some food and drinks."

"We're staying here tonight?"

"No. Just here for a while then we're off. It'll take five hours to reach our destination."

"Afyon—that town you mentioned?"

"North of it." The bartender interrupted with a tray of drinks and served Ward first instead of Eris. He almost bowed in deference, appreciative no doubt of the very large tip Ward must have passed his way. I played with the idea of getting a message to the New York police through him but doubted I'd manage to talk with him alone.

Ward decided to show off, still in full professor mode. "The hotel has one of the best views of the Golden Horn in the city. It's off the beaten path now, which is why I like coming here. This place was built in 1892, soon after the Orient Express line came to Istanbul. The trains brought a new wave of invaders, English tourists in search of Near East mystique. Agatha Christie wrote *Murder on the Orient Express* at the Pera Palace Hotel just down the street, and in the 1920s Ernest Hemingway sat in this very bar."

"It seems a bit genteel here for Hemingway. I remember reading that in China he drank wine from a

jar with eight snakes in it." I enjoyed the look of irritation on Ward's face after I butted in.

Two men appeared in the entrance. Eris smiled,
with a touch of relief I thought, and beckoned to them.
I guessed one was somewhere in his thirties; the other,
with a peppering of gray in his dark hair, close to fifty.
They wore casual suits, no ties, and sunglasses, even
though it was long past sunset. The younger guy had a
gold watch with a heavy linked band. They looked as
though they'd just stepped out of *Godfather III*.

Ward made a show of offering them drinks, which
they declined. Eris didn't bother with introductions,
or at least it seemed that way because she launched
into a short speech in what I gathered was Turkish.
When she finished, the gray-haired man glanced at
Ward and nodded.

"Ask how long ago it was when they saw him,"
Ward said to Eris.

She translated, got an answer, and said, "Last
night at the tomb. Mazare"—she indicated the older
man—"confirmed he's still in the area."

Who were they talking about—Tomas? He'd told
me the treasure originally came from Anatolia, and we
knew there was a Phrygian connection, but I couldn't
believe they'd find anything in Turkey. Ashurbanipal's
plunder was supposed to have been removed to Assyria
thousands of years ago. I couldn't be certain, though,
that Tomas had told me the truth.

"Where exactly are we going then? I don't want to
head off on some wild goose chase," Ward said.

Eris spoke to the older man. He got out his cellphone and placed a call, speaking rapidly in Turkish, and spoke to Eris again.

"He's in one of two places," Eris said, "the villages of Yazilikaya or Ayazinköyu. Mazare has watchers in both locations. They think he's holed up somewhere for the night and won't make a move until morning. If he tries to leave they'll keep him captive until you arrive."

Ward's face reddened in annoyance at the vagueness of the answer and at having to cede control to Eris, who had command of the language.

"You're referring to Tomas Zakar?" I directed this to Ward.

He hesitated then decided to give me the truth. "He's here, not in Iraq as you believed. Thought he could put one over on us I guess."

I still had strong doubts about this but kept them to myself.

The food arrived. A couple of appetizers, one served with cacik, a yogurt dip, along with stuffed eggplant, pilav, and doner kebab, a phenomenally tasty grilled lamb dish. We raced through the meal, as Ward was anxious to get away.

Back in the car I was once again stuck in the middle between Eris and Lazarus. Our original driver had disappeared and Mazare took the wheel, pushing the car to top speed. His companion followed behind in a blue Ford Econoline van. It would never keep up with our Merc, I thought.

I hated the scent of Eris's spicy perfume and the unpleasant proximity of the jester's hard, angular form. I remained wide awake for the entire ride despite the late hour, my internal clock thoroughly blown from the flight.

Through the front windshield I could see light beginning to filter through the eastern sky with the approach of dawn. We were in hilly country—reddish ground, tufts of dark green scrub, and vegetation punctuated by ravines and occasional stretches of fruit orchards and farms. I felt another tug at my heart. What I wouldn't give to have the freedom to get to know the country.

I kept my eye out for road signs, trying to get a sense of where we were headed. At one point we skirted a major city, Eski̧sehir, then continued east on the E90 highway. I realized soon after that we'd lost the van. As we approached a town about twenty minutes later, our driver turned around and spoke to Eris. "We've reached Çifteler," she said to the rest of us. "We turn here."

We veered off to the right onto a one-lane paved road until we reached a settlement. The car jerked to a halt, and Mazare pointed to a clutch of buildings ahead. "Yazilikaya," he said. We got out of the car.

"Which way?" Ward asked testily. Mazare must have understood some English because he again pointed ahead. The sight took my breath away. A gently sloping hill rose before us, dotted with rustic, tile-roofed houses and outbuildings. Behind them reared a high ridge of cliffs made up of rock towers, soft volcanic stone shaped by wind and water over millennia into gigantic sculptures. Centered in the ridge and rising almost the full height of the cliffs, at least sixty feet, a magnificent tomb face had been carved into the rock. It took the form of a simple rectangle with a peaked roofline. The rising sun shone directly on its surface, the pink tones of the stone dazzling my eyes. With the special effects of the morning light and the contrast between the tomb and the rough surrounding stone, it looked as though a magic doorway had just appeared on the cliff face.

We circumvented the village, the few people about at this hour paying us no heed. I assumed they'd long grown used to tourists. As we got closer I could see the structure was covered with intricate geometric designs and at its base was a deep niche. There was only this facade; the interior had never been completed.

Ward couldn't resist stopping in front of it. "The tomb of Cybele," he said, indicating a series of markings. "This is one of the best examples of Phrygian writing to be found." He turned to me. "You know the story of Cybele?"

"Some of it," I said, remembering what Phillip Anthony had told Laurel and me.

"She was a sister goddess to Ishtar, and like her, an emblem of fertility and blood lust. In a jealous rage Cybele slaughtered the woman her lover Attis desired. Attis severed his own genitals with a sharp flint in despair." Ward smiled. "Not a lady you'd want to tangle with."

We left the monument behind and walked toward a staircase hewn into the rock face. Eris walked beside Mazare, speaking quickly to him. Lazarus positioned himself at the rear of our little delegation. We reached the staircase and began to ascend. The stairs were uneven, crumbling in many places, and no handrails had been provided. Corrugated walls of rock towers hemmed us in on either side, making the path seem like a cathedral aisle. The scene resembled some wild, inspired Gaudi fantasy.

Even this early in the morning the heat was sweltering and Ward, the least agile of us, huffed and puffed. I'd taken a position directly behind him and noticed his legs shaking, either because of the physical effort or, more likely, fear of the height. Every so often a gap in the rock walls would open, the path dropping away sharply. One little push, that's all it would take and he'd plummet over the side. I could scramble down after him, get his phone, and try to run. Maybe. But Eris and Lazarus would be after me like a pack of dogs.

The stairs led to a natural archway in the cliff and through it shone a circle of azure sky. When we emerged out the other side we found ourselves on the flat crest of the ridge. Ruins of an acropolis stretched before us. Stone altars and strange robed figures with conical hats had been carved in relief out of the rock face. A faint wind ruffled my hair. I was awestruck by the enchantment of the place.

Our guide waved us over and crouched beside another section of cliff edge. Eris bent down and peered over. "There's a ledge jutting out from another tomb entrance about thirty feet down. Lazarus and I can check it out."

Ward flicked a glance my way and said, "No. One of you has to stay with me."

I swore silently under my breath. For a fraction of a second I'd hoped the group would divide and I'd be left alone with him.

We watched as Eris picked her way down. With her strong, athletic body it took her no time at all to reach the extension of rock. As she stepped on the platform the guide's phone rang. He had a short, terse-sounding conversation then yelled down to Eris.

She swore and began climbing back. "Mazare's told me they've just sighted Tomas at the other village," she shouted up to us.

Ward rounded on Mazare and hurled a series of accusations at him, punctuated by some choice obscenities. The guide spit words back at him in Turkish.

"I'm getting sick of this." Ward glared at Eris when she reached the top. He looked ready to hit her. "They told us Zakar was here."

She'd had enough and laid right back into him. "What he actually said was Tomas had been seen here last night. Look at this land—it's full of caves and twisted rock formations; Tomas could easily have slipped away. At least they've found him again. Dump your tantrums and focus on us getting over there before we miss him a second time."

Seeing the sense of this, Ward swallowed his rage and we hurried back to the cars.

Mazare drove again. The big Merc tore along unpaved roads, rocks and grit slamming into the under-carriage, the vehicle swinging wildly and spraying dirt at the turns. Soon we arrived at another village much like the one we'd just left. The van had somehow made it here before us. It was parked, empty, at the side of the road. Eris, Ward, and our guide huddled together for a few minutes, talking among themselves.

This area too was peppered with cliffs and strange volcanic rock chimneys. Holes and shrines had been hollowed out in a number of places. I assumed we'd head straight for the cliffs, but instead we took a steep, winding path of cobblestones running through the village. As we turned a corner a massive shadow darkened our path. Shim stepped out of a recess between two buildings. Behind him was the man who'd accompanied Mazare. He'd gone somewhere to pick up Shim. I cursed. It had just become that much harder for me to get away. Six of them now against one of me.

We walked to one of the houses on the outskirts of the village. The two-story home, painted a bright canary yellow, was built into the soaring rock face behind it and surrounded on its other three sides by a six-foot-high wall. An abundance of flowering vines spilled over the top. Our guide banged on a wooden door built into the wall and called out. A few minutes later we heard steps scraping toward us and the door unlocking. It swung open to reveal an elderly white-haired man who gave us a broad, warm smile. He welcomed us in Turkish and held the door as we entered. The courtyard we passed through was cool, shaded by fruit trees; I could hear the sound of a fountain somewhere.

When Shim passed by him as we went into his home, the old man took a good look and then cowered and threw his hands up, screeching something. Fear darted from his eyes.

"He doesn't want Shim in here," Eris told us. "Bringer of bad luck into the house."

"Ask him if he wants our money or not." Ward pulled out his wallet, peeled off a couple of hundred-dollar bills. He'd undone the top buttons of his shirt and was perspiring profusely. He was moments away from another blow-up.

Mazare took the old man aside and spoke to him quietly, then motioned for Ward to hand over the money. Our host grabbed the bills and hurried off. "Fucking creep," Lazarus said.

Eris was closest to the door. The elderly man reached for the handle, turned it. Eris moved nearer to him. I assumed she was going to bid him goodbye in Turkish. He looked up at her, smiling at the pretty woman, and began to edge the door open. Grasping something between her thumb and forefinger, she made a rapid movement, appearing to clutch his neck in an odd gesture of farewell. A startled look flared in his eyes. Then he clasped his neck and tried to say something. He dragged in one deep breath and didn't fall immediately but seemed to fold into himself, putting one hand out to stop the impact with the floor. The first spasm of his body hit. His legs jerked out. I think he bit his tongue. The seizures came fast then, one on top of the other.

Twenty-nine

Shim smashed me against the wall when I tried to run over to help the old man. Mazare was shouting. I didn't need to understand Turkish to read the anger in his voice.

"Tell Mazare to calm down, Eris," Ward said.

When Shim released me Lazarus and Eris had their pistols out. Mazare and his companion fixed the group of us with a hostile glare. Ward ignored them and rummaged in a bag and pulled out jacklights.

I was panting with fury. "Why kill the man?" I yelled. "You people are pigs."

"The minute he'd left with his money, half the village would know we were here."

"You murdered him for no reason. If Tomas is in this house he's being damn quiet about it."

"You've heard of Cappadocia?" Ward asked. "You know about the underground cities there, the ancient rooms and halls that descend eight stories under the earth?"

"What about them? We're far away from there."

"There's a network like it here, although much smaller in size. Tomas has located a tomb by reading the engraving correctly. We can get to it through the cellar of this house."

I almost laughed in disbelief but caught myself in time. If Ward wanted to think he'd find some treasure trove underneath us he was welcome to his fantasy. "What's your source for this?" I asked him.

Ward jerked his hand in Mazare's direction. "He's a confederate of Tomas's. He approached us through an intermediary, one of Eris's trusted contacts. The tomb Tomas has located here has been sealed off since the fall of the Phrygian empire."

"And you think the old man knew about this?"

"Of course not. He just thought we wanted to see the Christian shrines down there."

"And exactly why has Mazare chosen to come over to the dark side?"

"The most convincing reason of all. Tomas has been stingy with him. I'm offering a sizeable cut of the proceeds."

When Tomas told me about the notion of a hidden Assyrian treasure it had seemed like a stretch, but this new revelation of Ward's entered the realm of make-believe. People had combed these passages for thousands of years; a hidden tomb would have been found long ago. There was as much likelihood of an undiscovered tomb filled with treasure existing in an underground Turkish city as of the Grail turning up in Cleveland. A fanatical desperation to make a colossal find had caused him to lose his grasp of reality.

An idea occurred to me, however. The honeycomb of chambers and passages these underground cities were famous for had many connecting stairways and holes in the floors. Some of the holes had served as latrines or wells, but ladders had been used in others to climb down to more hallways below. If I kept on the alert I might be able to drop down into one of them as I passed it and get away. It offered me a slim chance.

"What's the point of taking me?"

"You're our insurance policy," Ward said.

"Tomas would be happy to see the end of me. I told you that before."

"He's down there with two other men and they're all armed. We'll put you out in front to bargain with him. If they start shooting, you're our cover."

And you'll never get that far.

Ward looked at his watch. "Tomas has been down there for almost two hours. We have to leave." He pointed in the direction of the old man, lying still on the floor. "Pick him up," he said to me. "We can't leave him here."

"Do your own dirty work. I'm not touching him."

Ward glared at me. "Choose your poison then. Eris's potion or Lazarus's knife. I'd recommend Eris. She'll give you a quicker death."

Mazare spat some more words out and walked over to where the old man lay.

"Mazare says he'll carry the old man," Eris said as Mazare lifted the body effortlessly, the old man weighing little more than a boy. His lips had turned blue and his head swung awkwardly. I turned my eyes away. Mazare's partner stayed above to watch out for any inquisitive neighbors.

In the cellar, a rough doorway had been cut into the stucco wall. We pushed the door open and entered a tunnel. A string of white Christmas lights had been tied to hooks in the ceiling, providing a dim illumination. Shelves had been stacked on either side of the passage, piled with round cheeses wrapped in burlap, dusty jars of olives, and preserves. It was noticeably cooler down here.

The shelves also held an assortment of clay vessels. I recognized them immediately as antiquities and guessed that the elderly man had found them in the course of making this corridor and stashed away a few valuable finds of his own. The tunnel had been shored up with timbers. Every ten feet or so, sprays of grit dropped from the ceiling as Shim's heavy tread hit the ground. I wondered how stable the structure was.

The passage ended abruptly. A circular rock, like a large millstone with a hole dead center, blocked our way. The object was clearly man-made. "The original doors," Ward said. "They used those holes to shoot arrows through."

We stood back while Shim, grunting with the

effort, rolled the door to one side, revealing a second corridor. Here, the electric light ended. When Ward flicked on his jacklight a rat scurried into a fissure in the wall, its long, naked tail looking like a snake sliding into its hole. The stone walls here were rougher and the ceiling lower. The tunnel smelled of ancient spores and fungal growths, the scents of decay. A primitive trench had been cut along one side of the floor. Shim was forced to walk stooped over. We'd entered the underground city.

Farther along, the wall had been sanded smooth. A mosaic had been applied to it, considerably damaged but still intact. It was composed of Byzantine Christian symbols and themes, among them a prominent cross. Below it a square hole had been chipped out of the rock. I figured it had once served as a primitive altar. I knew that in Cappadocia, these settlements went back 3500 years to the Hittite empire and possibly even earlier. Over the centuries many cultures had used them, added on to them, left their own indelible mark. The labyrinth of rooms and halls provided an excellent defense system and could offer protection from sieges above ground for months. I thought I could see the carbon imprint of smoky torches that had once been fixed into these walls.

Eventually we came across several empty chambers. We halted at one of them and waited while Mazare carried the old man in and laid his body on the floor.

In the next chamber Ward pointed to a lioness carved in relief on the back wall. It was so well executed that when Ward played his light on the image, the lioness appeared to leap out of the rock face. The artist had deliberately used the natural contours of the rock to define the animal's body. The lion reared on her hind legs, her open mouth displaying a row of ferocious teeth. On her stomach was a carefully depicted row of teats.

"That's Phrygian," Ward said, his excitement palpable. His mood had changed again. He seemed exultant now, as if the sight of the lion had confirmed all his hopes, and his previous bad temper had channeled into elation. I thought I could even detect a hopeful gleam in Lazarus's dead eyes.

Nahum's words came back to me. *"Where is the den of lions?"* Had I been wrong? Were we on the right track after all? If so, how did Nahum, a scribe living in Assyria, learn about the hidden tomb? I supposed it was possible he could have accompanied the Assyrian king on his campaign into Anatolia.

As we made our way down the corridor, Mazare spun around suddenly and motioned for us to stop. We'd arrived at two small rooms cut into the walls, facing each other. About a hundred feet ahead the passageway ended in a T-shaped intersection. Mazare whispered to Eris. "He wants us to turn off our lights," she said. "The tomb is to the left."

The lights clicked off, leaving us in total blackness. As our eyes adjusted, we could see a faint glimmer coming from the left branch of the intersection.

Mazare clicked his light back on and directed the

beam toward the floor. He spoke again to Eris. "He'll go up first," she said. Ward directed all the others into the rooms but insisted I stand out in the passageway in plain sight. Ward and Eris got behind Shim in one of the rooms; Lazarus took the other. When I tried to force my way in, he pulled out his knife.

If Tomas was here after all and a hail of bullets came my way, all I could do to protect myself was flatten my body against a wall. Mazare inched along the left wall until he'd almost reached the arch of the intersection. He beckoned to me. I stayed put. Then he said something—"Come," I thought. But I must have imagined it. He shrugged and holding his flashlight with one hand, dug into his pocket, pulled out his phone, and punched in a number.

For a second I wondered why he would try to make a call down here. In the next instant I realized what was about to happen and ran full tilt toward him.

Thirty

A blinding flash lit up the corridor, followed by a long boom. I heard Ward yell in the second before the ceiling blew up. Moments later I was thrown face down on the floor. I tried to move but my left leg was caught under something. I twisted my upper body and feeling with my hand could tell that the object pinning me down was a coffee table–sized chunk of rock that had sheared off and dropped on me. My leg had been cradled by the trench and so hadn't been smashed to smithereens when the rock fell. There was no pain and I could move my foot. I tried to grip the edge of the stone with both hands. But my position gave me little leverage and I couldn't shift it even an inch.

I wasn't able to see a thing. The rock dust was so thick I could barely breathe. I undid my shirt and tugged it off, wrapping it around my nose and mouth.

When we'd first entered the tunnel I'd tried to

keep track of our direction and figured the passageway extended under the cliffs the old man's house backed on to. That meant there was little chance anyone in the village would have heard the explosion. Eventually someone would venture into the tunnels and see the rockfall, but it would be far too late for me. Fate had already delivered so many low blows I'd lost count. And now, when I was finally free of my tormentors, I was condemned to die in this dusty hell.

Probably no more than ten minutes had passed, although it seemed much longer, when I heard the first sounds. A kind of groaning and babbling. I recognized the torturous attempts to speak that could only have come from Shim.

A dim light shone above me. Through the drifting dust I saw that the epicenter of the blast had occurred near the two small rooms. The force had been so strong, it had pulverized the rock. Stones the size of eggs up to small boulders jammed the passageway, extending up to a yawning hole in the roof. I couldn't see how far back the pile of rubble went. Had I not run when I did, it would have buried me alive.

At the top of the rock pile a spray of stones shot out. I yelled at Shim to stop before another landslide hit me. More stones dropped but this time slowly, and eventually his meaty hand pushed through. He cleared a larger space and then his hand disappeared. Eris squeezed through the gap and clambered down the pile, soon followed by Ward. Both of them were covered with the yellowish rock dust.

There was no sign of Lazarus. Ward looked at me and said, "Now, that suits you, Madison, pinned like a dead insect to the floor."

"How did you survive?"

"The main thrust of the rockfall hit the other room. It blocked us off too, but Shim could move a mountain if he wanted to."

"Lift this thing off me. My leg's caught."

"In your dreams," he said.

Somewhere along the line, I'd persuaded myself that I had some value to them, for what future agenda, I still didn't know. Using me as a shield from Tomas and his men was no longer an issue. Ward knew he'd exhausted any information I could give him. That meant Laurel was history too. I closed my hand over a sharp piece of rock. I'd think of some reason to get Ward close and smash it into his head. If I was going to die down here, so would he.

Shim cleared a much larger space and squeezed through the pile of rocks. Ward shone his light in the direction of the entrance to the other room. I thought I could see a dark crack that may have been the outline of the doorway. While the other two stood back, Shim got to work pulling away the stones. Eris called out for Lazarus but received no response.

Shim managed to shift a huge slab, throwing it to one side like a feather pillow. A cry emerged from his throat and he fell back from the stomach-turning sight as if he'd been smacked. Lazarus's head and shoulders were revealed, one side of his face caved in, the white bones of his skull exposed, his blood-smeared mouth open as if he'd just yawned. It was filled with rock dust. His knife blade had pierced the soft tissue under his jaw, the rockfall coming down with such force it had pushed the knife in up to its hilt.

The memory of what Corinne had told me about Hanna Jaffrey came back to me. That she'd been stoned, her face battered almost beyond recognition. And now Lazarus, entombed in his pyramid of rocks, had met the same fate.

"Throw the stones back, Shim. Might as well give him a decent burial," Ward said grimly.

They did pry me loose after all. I was too emotionally drained at that point to wonder why. I limped behind them. We turned left at the T-shaped intersection and saw the source of Mazare's light, the one he'd persuaded us had been used by Tomas. It was a large floodlight sitting on the floor. I saw no electric wires so assumed it had a powerful battery. Mazare had destroyed it by kicking the glass in when he fled.

This tunnel ran at what I judged was a forty-five-degree angle to the main passageway we'd followed. We had no idea where it led, but Mazare had taken it so an exit had to be ahead. Ward coughed continuously on our way back. Our one jacklight began to flicker. If we found no way out, soon we'd have to feel our way through. After trudging along for a stretch,

Eris pointed to a faint circle of illumination ahead that grew brighter as we approached. It turned out to be one of the holes we'd seen in the cliffs when we first arrived at the village. We burst into the sunlight, took a moment to get our bearings, and made for the car.

The Merc was gone, of course. They'd left the blue van but we had no keys. Eris got to work breaking into the van and hot-wiring the ignition while Ward fumed and Shim stood guard over me. Ward's sat phone had survived the ordeal unscathed; he made a quick call on it before we left. He told Eris to get in the passenger side while he drove. Shim waited until I got in the back and stuffed himself in beside me. I wondered whether Eris had lost her little trove of chemicals but decided I'd rather not find out at this point.

Ward's white-hot rage at being bested by Tomas was so pronounced you could cut the atmosphere inside the car with a knife. Mazare had lied, double-crossed Ward, and remained loyal to Tomas after all. The prospect of gaining a lot of money had been a ruse that he and Tomas knew Ward would swallow. It gave me some satisfaction to see the confident professor, always in control, coming apart at the seams. Away from his comfortable life in New York he was on shaky ground and he knew it.

Deeply ashamed over falling into the trap, Ward kept an angry silence all the way, breaking it only once to comment, "Once we're in Iraq everything will change. We're the ones holding the cards there."

He'd made one gargantuan mistake with this foray into Turkey. I hoped his certainty that he'd succeed in Iraq would prove as baseless.

We drove to Erkilet Airport outside the city of Kayseri, where the plane was waiting for us, and flew into Amman. After a couple of hours stalled there we got the go-ahead to proceed to Baghdad. This surprised me. I'd assumed we'd drive in from Jordan. Ward's connections with the powers that be must have been in pretty good shape.

When we arrived in Baghdad the plane sat for at least an hour on the landing strip. A stern American official in uniform entered, took a good look at me, checked my passport, and left. I assumed he was clearing me to enter the country. We stepped off the plane into a blast furnace and onto a paved area full of cracks and peppered with weeds. It had to be over one hundred degrees. How soldiers could bear this heat in full battle dress, carrying eighty pounds of gear, I couldn't imagine. I sucked in a breath and got a mouthful of grit. A white Humvee with tinted windows waited for us, the vehicle dented and battered and covered with dust.

Two musclemen occupied the front seat, modern barbarians wearing helmets and ACU jackets over sweat-stained undershirts and khaki jeans. ID tags flopped on chains around their necks. Both were clean-shaven and had buzz cuts. One wore a series of patches in a row on his left sleeve. They carried weapons that looked dangerous enough to destroy whole buildings.

I glanced over at Ward. "Who's the advance guard?"

"Private contractors. You can't survive around here without them."

"They look kind of young."

"What are they going to do, get some low-life job back home? You're looking at a thousand a day here."

"So exactly where are we going?"

"To the al-Mansour Hotel. You can't complain. It's a five star."

A hotel? That was a surprise. I'd feared it would be some kind of detention center. If Ward was forced to be my jail warden, I guessed he wanted as much comfort as possible.

"You won't be cuffed when we go into the hotel. Stay beside us. Our friends here will walk behind all the time, so it definitely isn't worth making any stupid moves. If you try to venture out anywhere beyond the hotel you'll walk straight into a firefight."

We roared out of the airport onto a stretch of highway. How many times had Samuel traveled this exact route into the city? I pictured him whiling away the night in the teahouses, drinking chai, eating sweet flatbread and sizzling kabobs. Admiring the glittering domes of the mosques. Sauntering beside the slow-moving brown waters of the Tigris, sitting out in the *sharayua*—the little riverside parks. Spending time with his cherished friends in the souks and the old Jewish quarter.

"The city has a way of seducing you," he once wrote to me. "When you leave her you think of your acquaintance as a brief fling, a transient attachment. But you find her returning again and again to your thoughts. Before long you're devising ways to get back. She appeals only superficially to the intellect; her real attraction is carnal. Like a mistress you're incapable of releasing no matter how much trouble she causes. And for me there is also the history."

I wondered what he would say now, seeing the wreck she had become.

The window looked out onto stretches of bleak terrain interspersed with islands of greenery, each one with a clutch of farm buildings. Closer to the road, the landscape resembled the backdrop for a *Mad Max* movie. Mangled guardrails; craters; piles of cinder and rubble from holes blown in the asphalt; a dead donkey, the stink of the carcass reaching us even through our closed windows; crumpled trucks and cars; the hulls of destroyed tanks. Dust and ash covered everything. People in traditional dress shuffled tired feet along the ditches, searching for God knows what. At one point I thought I could see a patch of blackened, dried blood on the pavement.

We drove through the outskirts of the city to its denser core, passing many ruined buildings. In some the first floor was perfectly intact, the large Moorish windows and buff bricks entirely unscathed. In stark contrast, the upper floors were a nightmare tangle of charred wood and tortured girders. I'd see long lines of buildings mostly intact punctuated by one that had been completely destroyed, like a missing tooth in a perfect row. Fetid heaps of garbage lay everywhere.

We entered what must have once been a Parisian-style roadway with a grand boulevard separating the lanes. The center partition had at one time been graced with rows of majestic date palms. Most of them had been hacked apart, their trunks sticking up like javelins rammed into the ground, their brown fronds rotting in piles. I noticed Ward looking at them too. "What happened there?" I asked.

"They had to take them down. Too much cover for the insurgents. This route from the airport is one of the most dangerous strips of highway in the entire city."

"What a shame."

Ward rolled his eyes. "Try having your legs blown off. You'd be chopping down a few trees too if you thought it would save you."

With checkpoint stops, it took us almost an hour to travel to our destination. Concrete barriers thrown up to prevent truck bombs from getting through and a heavy military presence stopped us from driving right up to the hotel. We parked and walked to the entrance.

Stocky, tough-looking soldiers dressed in black uniforms patrolled the hotel. They carried enough firepower to take over a small country. I was surprised to see they weren't Americans. *"Peshmergas,"* Ward told me. "Kurdish soldiers; they're working with the American military. You don't want to fool around with those guys."

After being checked out by the guards, we proceeded to our suite—one bedroom with a sitting area and bathroom. The hotel looked to be in very rough shape and Ward told me it had been looted when the occupation forces had entered Baghdad. He ushered me into the bedroom and ended my brief flirtation with freedom by cuffing my wrist to the bed frame. This time he left my right hand free.

"I've got to go out to make some arrangements. I'll order you something to eat. When I'm back we can talk." Ward said this on his way out the door. Eris accompanied him. The two mercenaries made themselves comfortable in the sitting room and immediately popped a movie into the DVD player.

I found I could slide the bracelet of the cuff a little way along the bedrail so I maneuvered over to the side near the window and looked out. Off in the distance I could see the turquoise dome of the Fourteenth of Ramadan Mosque, one of Hussein's last megaprojects. He was a great one for building monuments, most of them in praise of himself.

I looked down to the hotel grounds and could make out a pack of dogs, once family pets, now forced by hunger to return to their wild roots and forage in the urban landscape. They tore at some whitish lumps on the ground. I shifted my eyes away, not wanting a clear picture of what they were eating.

Traffic noise died down. The lyrical notes of the
Adhan cut through the evening air. This would be the
fifth and last call to prayer for the day, coming between
the fall of darkness and midnight. I felt the beauty of
his song, tried to loosen up and let the halftones float
through me. Then came the *tat-tat-tat* of gunshots.
The dogs howled, the muezzin's call shattered by their
song of despair. Laurel was now so far away I couldn't
imagine how to help her. My own prospects were
barely any better.

When we'd passed through the lobby, I'd noticed
a number of Westerners and judged by their easy
camaraderie and casual dress that most of them were
journalists. The thought occurred to me that if I could
get free, one of them might lend me a hand to get
away. But with no money or papers I'd have no means
to get out of the country. And even if I'd found a way
around that, Ward would take it out on Laurel.

I used the time to do some thinking and believed
I knew why he'd brought me to Iraq. If I was right it
would soon be obvious.

I called out to one of the guards. He stuck his
head around the door. "What?"

"I want a drink. Can you get me something from
the minibar?"

"We're not your waiters."

I could smell the hot dogs he'd just heated up in
the microwave. "How did you get hot dogs?"

"It all comes in from Kuwait. We don't eat the
eye-raki shit."

Despite his claim that he wasn't a waiter, when my food came he brought the tray in and placed it on the bedside table. Chicken tikka, rice, and something vaguely greenish that I guessed had originally been a vegetable. Along with that, a carafe of sweet chai with a screwtop lid that could be used as a cup. I wolfed down the entire meal as if it were cordon bleu.

After Ward returned he undid the cuffs so I could use the can. I took my time, soaping and splashing water over my arms and hands, running a washcloth under the steaming hot water and pressing it to my face, giving my hair a comb. My beard was starting to look unruly.

Walking back into the bedroom, I told Ward I wanted a drink.

"Help yourself," he said.

It was a measure of how low I'd fallen that I felt elated when he let me go unaccompanied into the sitting room to reach the minibar. His guards kept their eyes trained on me as I grabbed a mini bottle of Scotch and poured it into a glass before returning to the bedroom.

I dangled my legs over the edge of the bed while Ward pulled up a chair. He seemed more relaxed, a little brighter.

"Eris checked out the address you gave us. It looks credible. Actually, it's in this neighborhood, al-Mansour. The owner of the house is Assyrian like the Zakar brothers. Tomas may very well be hoarding the engraving there."

"So why not just raid it? You have the means. Why involve me?"

"I don't want to risk damaging it in a raid. And I need to know more before we go in. We've had them under continual surveillance. Whatever was in there a few days ago still is."

"Would Tomas have had time to get back here? He could hardly sail in through the airport."

"It's been what—over three days since you last saw him?"

"Pretty close."

"I doubt he ever entered Turkey. Mazare set all that up for him. That left more than enough time to fly to Syria or Jordan and drive in. The borders are like a sieve now, millions of holes for anyone to crawl through, and it's only half a day's drive to the city."

He tilted back and stretched. Despite the heat he was dressed in a relatively formal suit, white shirt, and tie. Perhaps to appear more casual and set me at ease, he took off his jacket, loosened his tie, and rolled up his sleeves.

The tattoo on his forearm stood out like a neon sign. A lowercase *h* with a short bar at its top.

Ward bent forward and rested his elbows on his knees and his chin on his fists. "Tomorrow morning we're sending you to the address you gave us. We want you to get inside."

"Why me? There must be any number of people you could call on."

"Shock value. You're absolutely the last person

Tomas Zakar would expect to see in Baghdad. We'll be able to flush him out that way." He paused to make sure I got the full impact of his next words. "Also, you're expendable. I don't want one of my own people dying in there."

"And after what happened in Turkey, exactly how am I going to explain how I got here, or why I even went to the trouble of coming?"

"You won't have to. Tomas is hardly going to answer the door, but whoever does will be reporting back to him. He'll be feeling very pleased with himself. Resting on his laurels. It will shake him up hard just knowing you're alive and made your way here. He'll want to know whether you're alone or if we all escaped. That's the state we want him in. Uncertain and knowing his plans have been shot to hell."

I got up and walked over to the window. Ward made no move to stop me. In the distance, the palms stirred slightly in the breeze; the air shimmered in the heat and haze. I felt as though I were part of the mirage, that none of this could actually be happening to me.

I faced Ward. "I won't do it. What's the point anyway? You'll kill Laurel and me anyhow."

Ward smiled, got up, and went into the sitting room. He came back seconds later carrying a suitcase, which he plopped on the bed and opened. He dug into the fabric sleeve inside the case and pulled out a manila envelope, spilling its contents onto the bedspread. I moved over to look.

A roll of about a hundred American dollar bills and my Visa card, along with my passport that he'd shown me before.

Ward pointed to the card. "The balance has been taken care of; you can use it now."

He reached into the case and lifted out a large black velvet bag. Loosening the braided gold drawstring, he gently lifted out a sculpted object. The copper head of Victory from Hatra.

I was stunned momentarily by the natural beauty of her face. Her eyes were intact, unlike the Mask of Warka, whose missing eyes made her resemble a blind sibyl. Victory's eyes, the irises crafted from obsidian and the corneas from pearly-white shell, gave her a startling lifelike appearance.

"Like I could ever get that into America."

"When the job's done we'll fly you from here to Belgrade. From there we'll drive you to Zurich. A dealer there will be happy to take it off your hands."

"I know who you are. You can't afford to let me go free."

Ward avoided my gaze and let out a manufactured laugh. "We're not interested in either you or Laurel. You're not the center of our universe. Just get us what we want."

This was another one of his cooked-up stories. There may as well have been a hook twisted into my lip with Ward jerking the other end of the line, the money and promise of freedom made simply to secure my cooperation. And I didn't believe his tale about not wanting to storm the house. Once I'd confirmed Tomas's presence the raid would start. The Victory sculpture was hotter than a blowtorch and would play a starring role. The blame for the carnage would be laid at my doorstep, the disgraced American art dealer. There'd be nothing I could do about it because I'd be dead too. His offer was made purely to ensure I'd play the role he'd created for me.

Ward gave a little jump, showing how wound up he was. I realized his phone must have gone off, vibrating on his hip. He fished it out and started talking then turned around and stood in the doorway, keeping his voice low. His form filled most of the door so the two guards couldn't see a thing. I scooped up the roll of bills, slid a couple into my pocket, and hastily put it back in exactly the same spot. It was agonizing to have to leave the passport and Visa card.

When he shut his phone off and turned back he was all business. He took the case and its contents off the bed and clipped my wrist back onto the rail. "I won't return until late and we're going to make an early start."

"I haven't agreed to anything yet."

"You don't have a choice." He mumbled something to the guards and banged the door on his way out.

I felt for the Scotch I'd put on the tray with the dirty plate from the meal. I closed my hand around the glass tumbler and brought it to my lips. A volley of shots exploded again, so loud they could have been aimed right at our window. I dropped my glass, spilling the liquor all over my shirt. I lay there reeking of booze, swamped in misery.

I must have drifted off because I woke with a start in the middle of the night. My arm ached from being locked onto the bedrail in an unnatural position and from all the punishment over the last couple of days. The light was still on in the guards' room, casting a dim glow into mine. Over the blaring movie and their snores I thought I could hear a rustling at the foot of my bed. I sat up and peered toward the source of the noise.

What was this—a hallucination? Some kind of strange insect crawled on the bedcover. It had a body as big as a hunting knife, the same unearthly, pale coloring of those underwater creatures that never see light. At its head, reddish mandibles opened like the beak on a squid. The thing was huge. I kicked at it and yelled. It scurried over to the wall. I grabbed for the empty glass and threw it. The tumbler splintered when it hit the wall, but the thing escaped into the dark crevice between the bed and the wall. Then it reappeared even closer. It raised its forelegs, waving them in the air as if trying to hone in on the vibrations from its enemy.

"What the hell's going on?" The figure of the guard materialized in the doorway, blocking out all the light. Now I couldn't see the thing.

"There's some kind of scorpion or something on the bed. Kill it. For God's sake hurry up."

He flicked on the light and I could see it was now only a foot away from my bare arm. "Shit. How did that get in here?" he said. "It's a camel spider. I'm not touching it. They hide in the sand and then spring up. Use their mouth to rip into the camel's soft belly. That's how they get their name. The bite's really poisonous; it's worse than a scorpion's."

In full panic mode now I yanked my body away as far as possible off the bed, but my arm was still firmly locked onto the rail. I could feel the feathery touch of forelegs beginning to probe my bare skin.

"Throw me the key then, you ass."

The second guard elbowed his way into the room, took one look, and doubled over laughing. "You should see yourself, Madison. You look ready to piss your pants." He grabbed the dinner tray, dumped the empty dishes on the floor, and batted the spider. It flipped over on its back, legs flailing uselessly in the air. He brought the tray down hard and I heard a crunch. With the coverlet he wrapped the carcass up.

I shifted back onto the bed. "You jerks let that thing in here on purpose."

"Shove it where the sun don't shine and think again before you treat us like servants then," the second guard said. "We needed a laugh. It's boring watching movies all the time. Arm hurt?"

The cuff bracelet had scraped the skin around my wrist raw when I'd pulled away. The two of them disappeared back into their den. I lay awake for the rest of the night wary of any more of their ugly stunts.

Thirty-one

Saturday, August 10, 2003, 9 A.M.

Next morning we walked out of the hotel into white-hot sunshine. Even the palms appeared to wilt in the corrosive heat. Patrolling soldiers gave us the once-over and looked away. As for our little group, tension all around—Ward's temper was particularly short once again. He kept snapping at his cohorts.

My chariot awaited. A battered orange taxi, a Datsun that had to be mid-eighties. Amazing the driver could even get it going.

Eris led the way, driving a sedan with Ward beside her, the taxi wedged in between that and the white Humvee bringing up the rear, commandeered by the two mercenaries.

Ward had been right when he'd said the address was close. Once we entered the residential zone it took about ten minutes before we pulled to a stop at an intersection. The homes in the area were palatial—at least that's what I imagined because a good many of them were concealed behind walled compounds. Many had tough-looking armed guards posted outside. A lot of heavy movers and shakers apparently lived here. But even in this area, one of the wealthiest sections of Baghdad, I could see bombed-out hulks. I remembered hearing on the news that two homes full of people had been obliterated after a nearby restaurant was mistakenly pinpointed as a location for Saddam Hussein.

Ward got out and leaned in my window. "The taxi will pull up in front of the house; it's about half a block up. The Humvee will stay here and my car will stop farther up the street. The rest is up to you."

My destination was hidden behind a substantial wall of basalt blocks. I stood in front of the gate, an elaborate metalwork grille. Through it I could see a cobblestone courtyard and a Mercedes parked in front of a two-story home. The car was silver and therefore not the one we'd used in Turkey. Young trees and vines grew lushly over the top of the wall. I pushed the button fixed into a brass plate and prayed for a miracle.

Nothing happened. I swore. Could this end up as some tragic-comic anticlimax when it turned out no one was home? I pressed the button again and heard the front door click open. A diminutive figure dressed in slacks and a polo shirt peeked out at me. A man, but not Tomas.

He turned and said something to whoever stood behind the door then walked toward me. He waited about eight feet away, making no move to open the gate, and jabbered on; it sounded like the Assyrian Tomas spoke. I smiled and shrugged my shoulders. "Tomas Zakar," I said. "Is he here?"

The man glanced over to the front door once more then pressed a remote he held. The gate swung open, closing automatically the second I walked through. He motioned for me to follow him inside and indicated a seat in the vestibule. Minutes ticked by. The room broadcast an air of elegance despite its sparse furnishings. Several kilims in gorgeous reds and ivories hung on the walls. A spray of roses sat in a tall alabaster urn placed on the floor. Imagine finding fresh flowers in this beleaguered city.

A second man entered, dressed in the long black cassock of a priest. His hair was dark but he had light blue eyes that gave him an ethereal look. He tilted his head forward in a slight bow. "How may I assist you?" I detected a hint of a British accent.

I put on my best face. "My name is John Madison. I just arrived in Baghdad with a cultural delegation. Tomas Zakar gave me this address and asked me to contact him when I arrived. Is he here by any chance?"

"Zakar? How do you spell that?"

"Z-A-K-A-R. Zakar," I said again.

He shook his head slowly. "I'm awfully sorry. I can't help you. There's no one here by that name. A misunderstanding, no doubt?"

"I don't think so. He gave me his card."

The man responded with a weak smile. "That is strange. My father has owned this property for years; I can't imagine how anyone could make such an error. Have you come here alone?"

"Yes."

"I'd advise you to take great care then." He gestured gracefully toward the window. "Hostages are taken every day in the city. Two doctors live on this street. The son of one of them was kidnapped three weeks ago. They still don't have him back. The other doctor is so frightened he's barricaded himself and his family inside his house. It's a miracle you even made it alive from your hotel to my home."

I was growing impatient. I had to take something back to Ward. "Look, I appreciate your concern for my welfare and any privacy worries you may have, but it's imperative that I speak to Tomas. I know his brother, Ari, is in London. We were together recently in New York. I can be trusted."

A flash of irritation crossed his features. "Sir, I will allow that someone has misled you, but I assure you, I've never heard of these individuals. If you don't mind, I think it is best you depart." He hesitated. "You're staying at a hotel?"

"Yes. Al-Mansour."

"I presume you don't speak Arabic?"

I shook my head.

"Their staff are very competent and speak English. I'd suggest you enlist their help in your search. They will have directories and other resources." He moved over to the door. "I'm afraid you've caught me at a busy moment. You'll excuse me now, I hope."

I thanked him and walked away. What else could I do? I had about two minutes to forge a story that would satisfy Ward. I desperately searched for ideas and came up with something that might work.

Ward and Eris met me when I reached the taxi. "Well?" he asked.

"Tomas didn't show up, as you predicted. The man I spoke to claimed he'd never heard of him. But I saw something."

"What?" Ward thrust his face closer to mine. Streaks of sweat ran from his temples to his chin.

"The guy was lying. At least Ari's there—that much I'm sure of."

"Why do you think so?"

"I saw his camera propped up against a cabinet in the front room. The same one he carried in New York. If he's here, Tomas has to be close by." I decided this sounded more convincing than saying I'd seen either of them in person.

The flush left his skin; the tension that had produced crevices of worry between his brows and around his mouth subsided. Ward was clearly not prepared to raid the house right now. By the time they stormed the place, interrogated the owner, and discovered there was nothing of substance to my story, I might have found a way to extricate myself from this nightmare.

Eris pulled out her phone.

"Who are you calling?" I asked.

"There are people who need to be alerted if Ari Zakar is back," she responded. She saw the question mark on my face. "It's nothing to do with our little venture. Just a quid pro quo for some important people."

"Why do they care?"

"A story he's working on. Something about Abu Ghraib. Nothing to do with us." She punched in a few numbers and delivered the information I'd just given her to the voice on the other end. I smiled inwardly. Ari had that prison story to thank for being safely holed up in London.

When we reached the hotel room we saw the button on the hotel phone flashing. Ward picked it up while Eris went back into the bedroom. Just as she was about to lock me up again Ward called out. "Hold on, we've got a new development."

I pushed my way past Eris. Ward beamed. "Congratulations, you delivered."

I managed to cloak my shock at this news.

"We just missed a message for you."

"I'm officially registered here?"

"We had to."

"What's the message?"

"You're to meet a contact of Tomas's at the museum. Three o'clock."

Thirty-two

The instantly recognizable facade of the Children's Museum, featured on the front pages of the international press this spring, sat at the intersection of Qahira and Nasir streets behind a high wrought-iron fence. Its sand-colored limestone structure—two square towers joined by a bridge over the central arch—was a handsome example of museum architecture. Distinctly Islamic with classical grace.

Between the central frieze and the roof of the arch, a black circle—a shot from an American cannon—looked like the point on an exclamation mark. The arch was impassable now, the space taken up by a tank.

A little late, I thought grimly. Probably just there for show. The place looked forlorn. It reminded me of those abandoned factories in the Rust Belt, once thriving concerns built at the turn of the century, now lonely outposts without a purpose.

The museum's story was familiar to me. Founded

at the zenith of British power in the Middle East, when the boundaries of modern Iraq were carved out, it was at first only one room in a Baghdad building. When more space was needed a small museum was built overlooking the Tigris. Inaugurated in 1926, the museum resulted from a collaboration between the Iraqi king Faisal and a remarkable Englishwoman, Gertrude Bell. Al-Khatun, they'd called her. An explorer, writer, and archaeologist, she'd dedicated a good part of her life to protecting Mesopotamian culture.

The present site, a complex of buildings, was established in the sixties. The main galleries were housed in a rectangular structure with an inner courtyard. Since the museum's establishment, periodic bouts of looting had broken out, the most notorious occurring during the Gulf War. It had been shut off to the public since then.

After I walked through the gate I handed the passport Ward had restored to me to an American Marine, who helped me locate the right entrance. I was met by an older woman wearing black-rimmed glasses and a hijab who introduced herself as Hanifa al-Majid. This was Tomas's colleague; I'd imagined someone much younger. "Much welcome, sir," she said after I greeted her. Her English was rocky but we managed to communicate well enough.

I recalled all the times in my youth when I'd daydreamed about walking these corridors with Samuel. The thrill of actually being here momentarily overwhelmed me. Our route took us through the Assyrian gallery. At its entrance loomed the massive Lamassu, with their bull bodies, wings, human-like heads, braided hair, and horned helmets. Each statue had five legs positioned so they could be seen as four-legged from either the front or the side. Inside the gallery the floor was strewn with debris, but the life-sized reliefs of Assyrian royal figures and Apkallu around the perimeter were blessedly intact. I paused in front of a magnificent portrayal of a man grasping the bridles of two horses, sculpted as beautifully as anything done by the Greeks and Romans.

My guide summoned me. As we hurried away our footsteps echoed in the emptiness of the hallways. I felt saddened by what had been stolen, trampled underfoot, lost forever. *Nothing really changes.* All the great Mesopotamian cities had been destroyed in antiquity. More than two millennia later it was happening all over again.

I could see efforts underway to clean up some of the disorder, although many areas were still in a shambles. We traipsed through a wide hallway, one side patterned with small squares of openings to admit natural light. On a low podium a headless statue stood to one side. When she saw me glance at it, Hanifa flushed and said, "Always the head was gone. Done in the past, not looters." I sympathized with her obvious distress over the state of the museum.

An Iraqi guard with an AK-47 sat at a small desk in one of the restoration rooms, surrounded by banks of shelving holding hundreds of dusty clay vessels and jars. Broken bits lay heaped in piles on the floor, some shards with the museum ident marks still visible, all of them crushed by the looters. I wondered whether this was the room where Samuel had kept the engraving.

She pointed to the piles. "I'm sorry for it—how it looks. No electricity is here. Most staff are gone. No security system. It takes us long time to fix up because of this." The poor woman looked as if she carried the weight of the entire building on her shoulders.

I moved closer to her. "Do you have a phone? I have to make a call urgently." From the look on her face I could see she hadn't understood. I mimicked making a call and she got the idea. She shook her head. "No—sorry."

My hopes sank again. It had been a long shot anyway. Even if she had a working phone, putting a call through to New York would probably be impossible.

She took paper and a ballpoint pen from the desk and scribbled a note, passing it to me. It read *Follow me, please*. I started to speak, but she put two fingers up to my lips to signal silence. She grabbed the paper, turned it over, and wrote, *Someone else waits for you*. She stood up and said in a voice loud enough for the guard to hear, "Please come. I will get us tea."

Several hallways and rooms later, we met up with a Middle Eastern man wearing sunglasses, his dark hair shot with gray. The woman gestured toward him as if she were offering me up as a gift, and giving me a weak smile scurried away. Mazare extended his hand and said hello.

I stepped back from him. "You're not carrying any explosives today, I hope. And what a surprise. You speak English."

He grinned. "Sorry for that."

"You're sorry? You almost fucking killed me."

"I tried to tell you. Make you come closer to me. You didn't read my signs soon enough."

"It was a touch difficult to appreciate nuances with four people at my back looking for an excuse to shoot me."

His good humor faded. He checked his watch and said, "Tomas and I are taking many chances to save you now. Stay with Ward and you'll be dead by tomorrow. Come with me or not. I caution you to make up your mind fast."

I cast my memory back to the tunnel in the underground city and remembered Mazare gesturing for me to come forward, murmuring something. It was possible he'd been trying to alert me.

"I can't go with you. They're holding a woman back in New York. They'll kill her if I escape."

Mazare's face fell and I could read sympathy in his expression loud and clear. "That woman—Laurel, is it her name?"

"Yes."

"I feel in my heart this sad for you. She is dead. Drowned in the river."

Oh God. It can't be true. "Are you sure? How do you know that? Did Tomas tell you?"

"Not Tomas. Ari. He found it out. Just today. The news said she went onto a high bridge and jumped in Harlem's river, sick because of losing her husband."

Scrambled though his expression was, there was no way he could have made up the reference to the High Bridge and the Harlem River. And the story had logic. When Ward and Eris spirited me away to Baghdad she was nothing but a liability. Ward could still threaten me about harming her because I'd have no way of knowing her fate. Mazare said something. I barely heard him, the news about Laurel bearing down on me like a thundercloud.

He grabbed me by the shoulders and shook me hard. "I said we have to go. Now." He half dragged me to the dusty Toyota van parked in the shaded lane outside. He opened the back doors and pushed me inside before climbing in himself and putting the key in the ignition.

"Stay in the back where no one can see you. I'm taking you to Tomas."

I slumped against the side of the van, not caring where we were headed. He drove for a few minutes then braked, rolled down the window, and spoke a few words in Arabic to a guard. An anxious minute of silence passed before he stepped on the accelerator and took off.

I tried to pull myself together. Mazare wasn't

tearing up the pavement. That is to say he was speeding like crazy but no faster than most Iraqi drivers. Fifteen minutes later we halted again. "Come into the front now," he said. I sighed and clambered onto the passenger seat beside him. We were parked behind a strip of bombed-out buildings. The stench from the garbage outside was overwhelming. Rotting fish parts and bones were scattered everywhere.

"Are these clothes yours?"

"The pants are mine and the shoes. They gave me the jacket and shirt back in New York."

He opened the glove compartment and extracted something that looked like a cellphone. Pressing one of the buttons, he ran it over the arms, lapels, and back of the jacket.

"Take your jacket off and pull the shirt out at the waist." He repeated the exercise over my shirt then looked at the screen, clicked the device off, and put it back.

"What were you looking for?"

"They can weave those tracers into material now. We have to be careful."

I took in a few deep breaths, tried to calm down and remember the risks the guy was taking on my behalf. "Thank you. I know how dangerous it is, doing this."

He shrugged. "Whatever Tomas wants we do."

His dark eyes bored into mine and he pointed his index finger at me like a teacher getting ready to scold. "The places we're going, you'll only be safe with me. Speak to no one."

We crossed a bridge and turned onto al-Rashid, Baghdad's main commercial street. Closer to the bridge buildings showed the impact of the war, windows blown out with ragged frames, starbursts of soot on facades, blackened wounds on the cladding.

The street was thick with traffic. Leaning on the horn was simply a normal part of driving, like hitting the brakes or changing gears. Buses jockeyed for space, boys staggered under carts flush with goods, vehicles fought for every inch of pavement. I could have been back on Broadway.

We jerked to a stop, cars pressing in on all sides. Exhaust fumes swirled in a suffocating haze. Mazare threw up his hands and swore.

He finally located a side street and parked the van. "We walk from here," he said. Heat beat down on us unmercifully. I shuffled along beside him, images of Laurel flaunting themselves in my brain. They would have drugged her probably with some kind of tranquilizer to make her suicide more convincing. Had one of Ward's men clasped her in his arms, lifted her cleanly over the rail, and cast her body down? Even with drugs in her system, a minute or so of total panic would have taken hold as she plunged toward the murky river. What a desolate way to die.

Was there anything I could have done differently? Had she simply been condemned the minute we began working on Hal's game? Everything I touched withered and died.

Mazare seemed to grow less tense as we mingled

with the crowds, although he looked back every couple of minutes.

He waved his hand. "This is al-Mutannabi Street; you'll see the book bazaar. We still have culture here, no matter how hard you Americans try to kill it." If he was trying to shame me, he was doing a good job.

"Did you know my brother Samuel?" I asked indignantly.

"I met him once."

"He was an American and did everything he could to save Iraqi culture. He loved this city."

"Well, he failed then."

"It's not his failing only."

Mazare gave a disdainful laugh and I looked away. There were no vehicles on al-Mutannabi, at least not while the bazaar was on. It was a little crescent of peace compared to what we'd just driven through. Antiquated buildings, a number of them housing bookstores, walled off the street. Towering stacks of volumes lined their dim interiors. Outside, cheap plastic tarps were covered with periodicals, pamphlets, pirated DVDs, and tomes in English and Arabic. High metal filing cases, their doors propped open, burst with musty old pages.

Above a poster stand, an image of Saddam Hussein had his face crossed out. A neighboring stand displayed a framed portrait with Arabic script. "Who's that?" I asked Mazare.

"Ayatollah   Muhammad   Muhammad   Sadiq

al-Sadr. Assassinated in Najaf in February of 1999. A very revered man in Iraq," he said.

Almost all the shoppers were male; very few women ventured out onto the street. We walked past a cleared space occupied by three men standing on a wooden platform. Two were on their knees; the third stood over them with a baton, pretending to hit them. An enthusiastic audience yelled out comments. "Actors," Mazare said. "This is an old tradition."

We followed a bend in the road. I could see the glassy water of the Tigris at the end of the street. A little farther on Mazare pointed to a semi-circular, single-story building with tables strung along its front. "The al-Shabandar. A famous place in Baghdad."

The café was filled to the brim, again with men, almost all of them smoking. Some pulled sweet oriental tobacco through their narghile pipes, others smoked cigarettes. I thought I could detect the vanilla perfume of hashish. You could almost taste the mingling scents in the air. Tumblers of steaming tea sat on the tables. A fan revolved slowly from the high ceiling. Framed paintings and photographs in all sizes crowded the walls—portraits, landscapes, still lifes. A generator buzzed. Dominoes clacked. A couple of backgammon games were in progress.

A helicopter passed overhead the moment we sat down, its big rotors making the building shake. Mere seconds later we heard a terrific explosion. A mortar going off, I guessed.

The room froze.

Mazare frowned and shook his head. "Look at us," he said. "We stink of fear."

I leaned over, lowering my voice. Knowing Laurel was dead had put an end to everything. I just wanted to escape. "Listen. Can't you get me out of Baghdad? To Jordan or Turkey? Anywhere, I don't care. I don't need to see Tomas and I'm sure he'd be just as happy not to see me. I was forced to come here."

He dismissed this idea quickly. "Tomas said nothing about that. I'll get some coffees."

He brought back two and set them on the table. The rich mocha scent should have been appealing but did not tempt me. Mazare checked his watch for what seemed like the hundredth time and looked outside, scanning the faces. Was someone else out there scouting for him? His coffee sat on the table, untouched.

I fumbled around for something to say. "You were speaking Turkish to Eris?"

"I am Assyrian but I grew up in Istanbul. We Assyrians are spread out in many places. Even in Europe. Even in your country."

A whistle sounded from somewhere in the street. Mazare jumped up abruptly.

"Come. Leave your drink. We must go right now."

He walked rapidly. I had a hard time keeping up with him. He wouldn't speak to me, his lips pressed together so hard they'd turned white. His eyes darted from side to side, checking out the street. We took a circuitous route back to the van.

When we drove away I said, "I appreciate the tour and all, but why bother going there?"

"Escaping Ward's people is not easy. They're trailing us. We need to lose them somehow."

"Where are we going now?"

"Suq al-Haramia, the Thieves Market. Do you know it?"

"I've heard of it."

We headed north on Khulfafa Street, away from the city core. On the outskirts of Sadr City, we ran into an American patrol. Mazare pulled over while they passed. "Things are bad again after the Jordanian embassy." He let out a cynical laugh. "No, that is wrong. Bad is what every day is like here. Is there a word in your language for something worse than hell? If there is, we are inside it."

The thought occurred to me that I'd been living in that domain for the last week. "What happened?"

"A truck bomb killed seventeen people. It blew cars onto roofs. And yesterday they attacked an American Humvee outside the Rabiya Hotel. Then the soldiers came to this market. Some men were testing guns to buy, shooting them in the air, and the soldiers fired, thinking the shots to be aimed at them. We have much fury over that. There will be no fast end to this war."

We left the van once more and proceeded on foot. The place seemed to go on forever. A black market version of London's Portobello Road. Samuel had said you could buy almost anything here, and he was right. Despite yesterday's events, an arms seller had filled the cargo bed of his pickup with guns. A clutch of men checked them out, but no one seemed inclined to test shoot today.

Another vendor stood over two large containers—rusted oil drums cut in half and filled with water, turbulent with the writhing bodies of fish. Mazgouf, the green carp caught in the sluggish Tigris. "Poison fish," Mazare said. "Once they were good. Now this war has filled the river with filth."

A strange assortment of things lay on a dirty carpet: squeezed toothpaste tubes, women's pink razors, half-full bottles of Detol, small one-serving containers of peanut butter and MREs—the army's meals ready to eat. Mazare gestured toward the wares. "They sift through the garbage from the army bases and take this stuff to sell."

A nearby table was piled with phones, DVD players, TV sets, computers—products of the looting or goods stolen from people's homes. The next vendor displayed strange-looking chunks of meat. Mazare told me they were sheep's lungs. A cloud of flies buzzed over the mutton. The raw flesh had a greenish tinge and steamed in the heat. When I expressed my distaste he shrugged. "People are starving. What do you expect?"

Another whistle sounded. No one else paid it any heed, but Mazare whipped out his phone and made a call. After a short burst of words he clutched my arm and hustled us along a different route back to the van. I could tell this was going badly and thought he must be running out of options, so it was a surprise when he said, "Tomas will come to us at our next stop. God willing."

This time as Mazare drove he didn't enlighten me about where we were. We'd turned southwest and traveled to a busy street, that's all I knew. He swung off the road onto a driveway and we slowed down. A sign announced the North Gate Cemetery, burial ground for Commonwealth soldiers of the 1917 campaign against the Ottoman Turks. Had Tomas taken a page out of Hal's book and chosen a hiding place similar to the one in New York?

Rusted metal gates hung open. We drove through on a path intended only for walking. He turned the van around and parked then yanked out his phone to make another call. After hanging up he said, "We wait for Tomas now. He'll come soon."

A broad center aisle was flanked by tall, scruffy palms; around the perimeter, grasses grew as tall as a man. The aisle led to a mausoleum, a four-pillared stone canopy erected over a base, clearly intended for someone important in contrast to the simple crosses and eroded headstones of the rank-and-file graves.

"This is a British cemetery? So many graves, it must have been a terrible battle."

Mazare shook his head. "Not all died from bullets and swords."

"What then?"

"The cholera." He pointed toward the rows of white crosses. "They got so sick they coughed their own guts up. So far away from home. Why did they even come?"

I had no answer for that.

Perhaps it was just the contrast between the quiet in the cemetery and the traffic noise in the rest of the city, but there was a stillness here that felt anything but peaceful. No birds chirped their evensong; no small animals scampered in the grass. We waited.

Near dusk, the sun limped lower in the sky. My attention was caught by a shadow out of keeping with the forms surrounding it. It seemed too tall and appeared to move toward us. It was as if a stone monument had suddenly come alive. Shim moved into view.

The white Humvee burst into the cemetery. On its tail, Ward's sedan. Mazare yelled and dove for the floor. He pulled out a semi-automatic from underneath the seat. I lunged for the door handle. Mazare grabbed me and pulled me back.

Truly lethal sounds have a soft edge. I heard a pop off in the distance, followed by a crump. The shock wave of a blast blew me against the door. A second wave resonated and held me there. The metal window frame of our van glowed, the heat scorching my arm. I yanked it back. The white Humvee exploded into a cauldron of orange flame. Its doors burst open and Eris's body tumbled out, a bloody hole in her ravaged torso, her hair on fire. A bloom of oily smoke gushed into the air.

Shim reached the sedan, flung open the door, and hauled Ward out, keeping his massive body between

Ward and the locus of the attack. With the force of a pneumatic drill, a series of shots tore up the grass in front of him. One of the guards spilled out of the sedan, spraying gunfire toward the mausoleum. Mazare hit the handle on his side, kicked open the door, and got off a few rounds. The shots tore into the guard's left side; his body bucked under the force of the bullets and he collapsed.

My own arteries felt close to bursting, my heart was pumping so hard. At the same time it seemed strange, as though I were watching all this happening to someone else.

A second missile hit the front of the sedan, throwing it into the air like a toy. It landed on its roof, shrapnel from the car whipping into us. Out of instinct I flung my hands up. Mazare jerked his body back when our windows shattered. I could smell burning rubber. I tried the door again; my hands shook so badly I could barely grasp the handle. I slammed against it and fell out. Mazare followed. I tried to get up but suddenly felt too weak to rise. Mazare looked at me for an instant, his face splintered with cuts, then ran.

Shim reversed course, trying to drag Ward behind the wrecked hulk of the sedan. More shots rang out. He shuddered and swayed but kept going, the bullets having about as much effect on him as if they'd been aimed at gravestones. But the sedan's gas tank blew and Shim was too close. The explosion showered them with fire. Ward's clothes burned; he screamed and flailed on the ground. Shim twisted and turned, caught in a violence of flame. He appeared to shrink and grow black, stone turning into cinder, and toppled to the ground.

I tried to stand up again. Another volley of shots hit the front of our van. A blinding pain ripped through my head. I became oddly aware of gravestones glowing with a white radiance as if they were embedded with internal lights. I remember forcing myself to breathe. Someone leaned over me, trying to say something. I could see a mouth moving but couldn't hear the words, as if I'd been submerged under fifty feet of water. The person faded away. And then I *was* underwater, green fish coiling around my legs, blankets of emerald seaweed wrapping my arms, Laurel's body rolling in the current, her skin silver like a mermaid's, her brown hair fanning out, her limbs moving as if she were dancing in the stream. My last thought—surprise—that a river could spring up so suddenly in a graveyard.

Thirty-three

Two spears of pain drilled through my temples. I opened my eyes and saw only the gray, amorphous screen that is the landscape of the blind. I blinked and rubbed my eyes, trying to force my vision back. My sight cleared and I could tell the environment actually was gray: concrete block walls, a floor painted prison gray, no furniture, the only daylight coming from a small window near the ceiling.

I lay on a foam rubber mat wedged into a corner of the room. I could hear nothing and prayed that didn't mean the explosion had destroyed my eardrums. A rough bandage applied to my forearm covered the burn from the hot metal of the van.

When I tried to get up I collapsed on legs so weak it felt as though my bones had been somehow extracted, leaving the flesh intact. I raised myself to my knees and crawled to the outline of a door on the opposite wall. There was no handle or lock so I struggled back, slumping once more onto the foam mat.

When the door did open, a beam of light hit me full in the face. I gave my head a shake and saw Tomas standing in the doorway. "Well, John," he said, "welcome back to the world." It sounded as though he were speaking from far away, but I was relieved that my ears hadn't been deafened in the firefight.

One of his men had to help me upstairs. It felt like I was climbing a small mountain of mud. On the second floor we went up another staircase to a little rooftop terrace with a stone statuette of a faun, a rust stain marking the path where the water would have tinkled out from his set of pan pipes. I slumped into a plastic chair.

Tomas handed me a glass of tea. "Drink this," he said. "It will refresh you."

Any resistance I might have summoned had been wiped out by the trauma of the blast. The cool menthol of the tea slipped agreeably down my throat. Over the wall I could see other rooftop terraces crowning modest buildings in shades of butterscotch, peach, and henna against the backdrop of an azure sky. Clumps of palms waved in the distance. I felt the sun on my face, soft in the cool breeze. I could have been sitting in a *pension* on the Côte d'Azur. I wanted to stay here forever.

Tomas had acquired a bit of a tan. He looked relaxed and settled, glad to be home.

I finished my tea and set the cup down. Tomas

reached for a tray of dates and nuts, asking if I'd like something to eat. I shook my head. Just drinking the tea had produced little spurts of nausea. I didn't want to push it.

"You'll feel better in a while," he said, "no serious damage done."

"Is it true about Laurel?"

Tomas's air of comfort lessened; he tightened up again. "She's dead, John."

Weak though I was, I pushed myself out of the chair and threw myself at him. "You piece of shit. You betrayed us. You may as well have killed her yourself."

His men dragged me away. One of them pulled out a gun. Tomas waved him off and rubbed the spot where my fist had connected with his jaw. "Put that away; it will not be necessary." His gaze shifted to me. "You aren't doing yourself any favors, Madison."

Silence reigned for a few minutes before Tomas spoke again. "They'd already taken her by the time I picked up the engraving. There was nothing I could have done."

"Ward wanted it. He was willing to make an exchange."

"You don't really believe they would have gone through with that, do you?"

"It was my only hope to save her. I was trying to work out a way I could involve the police without Ward finding out. You blew that all to hell and took any chance I had away. How did you know enough to look in the mausoleum anyway?"

"Laurel mentioned Hal's attachment to his mother. Then Ari passed on what you'd said about the tomb at Trinity. I remembered that place because I'd lived nearby when I went to Columbia. You'd told him you couldn't get into it. I found the mausoleum with no name and brought a cutting tool with me."

"And what about me? You abandoned me."

Tomas did not have a large measure of tolerance at the best of times; it didn't take much for his patience to break. He yelled, "What did you expect me to do? I had one of Ward's thugs on my back and barely made it out of the country as it was. Mazare and I took huge risks to bring you here. Consider yourself fortunate. We could have left you to die."

"Why did you bother?"

Tomas allowed himself a smile. "Perhaps I'm not as bad a man as you like to think."

"Really? After you killed people in cold blood."

"Like they were getting ready to do to us, you mean?"

"Did they all die?"

"Eris and Shim did. And the two contractors. About Ward, we're not sure. He was seriously injured, at least. You can appreciate my men didn't want to linger."

"How did they find us?"

"The jacket they gave you had tracers sewn into it."

"They let me escape so they could follow you?"

"Yes."

"But Mazare checked my jacket and found nothing."

Tomas smiled again. "Yes, he did check it."

Seconds elapsed before it dawned on me what he'd done. "Mazare knew the tracers were there. You wanted them to chase us."

Tomas was actually beaming now. "We trawled for them and they fell for it."

Anger broke through my exhaustion again. "You and Ward are the same, you know. Human lives mean absolutely nothing to you."

Tomas dismissed this with a flick of his hand. "Not nothing. But not the most important thing either."

I let that hang in the air for a minute. "Someone needs to tell the New York police what really happened."

"When you get back, feel free to tell anyone you like. I certainly won't. Be careful, though. You were one of the last people seen with both Hal and Laurel. You could be stepping onto a minefield."

"I'll take my chances. Where's Nahum's engraving? At least let me see that."

"In due time."

"What are you talking about—due time? You must have it here. You wouldn't let it out of your sight."

Tomas flipped his hand back and forth as if he were swishing away a bothersome fly. "Even this place isn't safe enough. It must be protected."

My temper surged again. "I don't believe a word of that."

My only answer was his contempt. He knew he was in the position of power.

"After what happened to Samuel, everything he went through, you have no right to keep it from me."

This touched a nerve. "Don't lecture me about Samuel. I was the one he could count on. You were nothing but a thorn in his side. People felt sorry for him having to put up with you. Laurel told me that back in New York."

Had she really said that or was he making it up? My own hot shame told me all I needed to know.

His men moved between the two of us. Tomas turned to leave, making it clear our yelling match had come to an end. He'd kept himself under better control than I had. It seemed the city had somehow transformed him. Or perhaps it was simply the luxury of seeing an enemy vanquished. "I have to go out for the rest of the day," he said casually as he went down the stairs. "My men will care for you while I'm gone."

He had no need to issue threats about what would happen if I tried to leave.

Not much was left of the afternoon. I struggled up, dragged my chair over to the parapet, and sat there until the sky took on flamboyant pinks and violets, grew murky and then dark. I was glad they left me alone. Despairing thoughts crowded in, reminders of all my failures. The car crash had set off the downward plunge. Even if I managed to stay alive, I didn't believe I'd ever recover.

Toward the end of the evening my thoughts

turned to Samuel. I remembered a train trip we'd taken after one of his long absences to visit friends living near Utica. I'd sat, my face pressed against the glass most of the time, taking in the country landscape. We passed farmers' fields turning golden in the sun; long-forgotten waterways, their still surfaces covered with verdant water plants; luxuriant vines draped over telephone lines; roads leading to nowhere; stands of forest; brown deer nuzzling grass on stream banks. I'd imagined on that day I was the last human left on the planet, watching the earth reclaim itself.

At one point we crossed a vast plain of marshes, the rushes standing straight as swords, pointing to the sky. Idyllic days, those times I'd spent with him in my youth. How had it gone wrong? What flaw had produced a personality that brought harm to everyone I cared for?

I recuperated for the next six days. My hearing gradually returned to normal. The burn on my arm became less painful. My memory of the attacks and the fight at the cemetery began to fade like a bad dream. Physically, I gained strength. Emotionally, I veered from self-recrimination over Laurel's death to deep depression, some of the blackest moods I'd ever experienced.

They had no TV or radio. The terrace quickly became my own private refuge; here at least I was blessedly cut off from the world. The only sliver of happiness, weak though it was, came through a developing affection for the city. Out of character for me, I'd get up early in the morning so I could see the boxy forms of its buildings emerge along with the first shafts of sunlight. Night animal though I was, my patterns became almost rural, rising at dawn and retiring at sunset so that when there were brown-outs or, frequently, no power at all, I barely noticed. Central Baghdad had many high-rises and I could see few, so I guessed our location to be well into the outskirts.

Reminders of the war intruded, of course. The sky would occasionally buzz with military helicopters, circling like angry wasps overhead. One day a bright arc of fire flared on the horizon, followed by a loud boom that seemed to go on forever. That did not cause me any real concern. Like a moth wrapped securely in its cocoon, I felt safe from the tempest raging outside. The next morning I noticed the rooftop furniture coated with grime. I got a cloth and wiped everything clean again. It seemed that easy, banishing the horror of a bomb with a flick of my hand. Perhaps that was my way of trying to regain some sense of stability.

Once, I thought I heard Laurel's voice. I rushed over to the parapet. In places the street was so narrow it looked as though you could touch the facades of opposite buildings just by stretching out your hands. I saw three women, each wearing a black chador, walking at a leisurely pace down the street. Their laughter rose up to me, bell-like. One extended a delicate foot; a filigree of silver circled her ankle. Her headscarf slipped back, revealing glossy dark hair. She looked up, sensing me watching from above. Not Laurel, of course. Just my mind playing a vicious trick.

Whether it was the new connection with the city Samuel had loved, my near-death experience, or my somber thoughts about Laurel, this was when I took my first faltering steps toward making peace with Samuel's death. I did not forgive myself for the accident, but the ceaseless voice of denial stopped and I more readily accepted that my own actions had played a role.

I saw Tomas only occasionally after that first meeting. When I asked why he didn't just help me to get out of the country he deflected my question with a joke, saying, "Why? Aren't you being well looked after here?" And when I demanded to see Nahum's engraving or tried to find out what progress he'd made in deciphering it, he gave me vague and unsatisfactory answers. Otherwise he behaved courteously enough, was even solicitous at times, but kept his distance. He opened up to me only on one occasion. Very late one evening I heard his footsteps climbing the stairs to the terrace. He'd brought glasses and a carafe of sweet wine with him. He sat down and poured us our drinks. He seemed in a very collegial mood. I couldn't imagine what had caused this change of heart.

"You've been through a difficult time, Madison," he said. "I can't see how I could have done things any differently, but I owe you some thanks for the role you've played."

I almost dropped my wineglass. Next thing you knew he'd be asking to be best man at my wedding. I'd gotten so used to his prickly, resentful attitude that I wasn't sure how to react.

"I hope you understand what it's been like trying to survive over here," he continued. "Over the last months, there've been many times I've wondered if I'd make it this far. When the invasion began I was convinced we'd all be killed."

I remembered what Ari had told me about his fiancée. "It must have been hell just trying to get out of Baghdad."

"I don't recall a great deal about fleeing the city. It was chaotic, I remember that much. People panicking, piling into vehicles, boxes and mattresses stacked on car roofs, traffic strangling all the major roads, looters going mad over the stuff they were grabbing. I spotted one man, by himself, dragging a fridge he'd stolen. When it tilted the door swung open. You could see the food and things still inside. People took anything they could get their hands on—plastic piping, hoses, even cables they'd strip to gouge out the copper. Looters sailed right through checkpoints. No one tried to stop them.

"On our last day we went to a friend's place to borrow some petrol. I waited with the van while the others saw to getting the tank filled. I noticed a woman on the street who looked to be in her late forties, wearing traditional dress, but the hijab was missing. Her hair hung loose, falling in a jumble down her back. In one hand she held a running shoe.

"She behaved very strangely, bending down and rooting through a pile of litter, then turning in the opposite direction, she'd take a few steps and kick through a mound of dirt. A younger couple came up to her, grabbed her arm, and tried to haul her away, but she screamed at them and shook them off.

"Our friend told us she'd been hanging around for over a day like that. Apparently her three sons had been on their way home when a missile struck, killing them all instantly. Her youngest had his leg blown off. The woman had convinced herself that if she found his other running shoe, his leg would be restored and he'd come back to life. She'd simply turned mad with grief."

I felt a stab of guilt, listening to him, even though I'd never supported the invasion. "That sounds like one of Ari's stories."

"He caught some of it on film, but I think it ended up on the proverbial cutting-room floor."

"Laurel told me he's won a lot of awards. So he doesn't have to prove anything anymore. He could easily get a safer post somewhere else in the Middle East. Why does he want to stay here?"

Tomas leaned back in his chair, swilling the wine in his glass absentmindedly. "I wish I could answer that. For a long time I thought he was attracted to the action, like a soldier getting high on danger. I don't think that anymore. Now I believe he just started in the business too young. When he was too impressionable."

"What do you mean?"

"In his first year of university, a news outlet hired him to cover events inside Iraq during the Gulf War." Tomas gave me a sardonic grin. "You can imagine there weren't a lot of volunteers for that with Hussein in power. Ari had wanted to be a portrait photographer; he wasn't even thinking about journalism. But he accepted. I wish he hadn't. He saw things that broke his heart. Hospitals where entire floors were slick with blood, people burned so badly pieces of their skin slid off where you touched them. That changed him forever."

He drained his glass and stood up. "Ari's a survivor though. He doesn't take stupid risks." He glanced at his watch. "I have to go now. Let's talk again over lunch tomorrow."

"Fine," I said. "What's happened to put you in such a good mood?"

He gave me a sly smile and turned away. "Tomorrow. You'll know then."

The room where we had lunch the next day was spotlessly clean and bare, holding only a large rectangular table covered with a cheap plastic tablecloth, patio chairs, and a canvas stool with a Bible lying on it. A crucifix hung on one wall, along with pictures—inexpensive prints in faux gold frames, all with Christian themes: Jesus turning water into wine, a scene from the Garden of Gethsemane, the Last Supper. He said grace before we started and seemed agitated throughout the meal. Not in a bad way, but as though he was trying to keep the lid on some kind of suppressed excitement. I tried several times to get him to tell me his news, but he put me off.

After we finished and were sitting with our coffee he dropped his bombshell. "I've found the Assyrian treasure cache," he said.

Thirty-four

I stumbled out of my chair. "What?"

"I've found it. King Ashurbanipal's treasure."

Given my experience in Turkey, for an instant I wondered whether he was being truthful, but he looked like a kid getting ready to dive into a mountain of Christmas gifts. I'd been totally caught off guard.

"That's incredible. Where?"

He held up his hand. "Sit, sit. I'll tell you everything. But first let me show you how I worked it out. You'll recall one of Nahum's verses, 'And the queen is uncovered, she is carried away, and her handmaids moan as with the voice of doves; tabering upon their breasts.'

"Nahum's writing is extremely clever; these lines have more than one meaning. Does this refer to the historical Assyrian queen, or is he playing with the metaphor of Nineveh as a woman? The reference to being 'uncovered' is a device. In ancient Assyria prostitutes were forbidden to wear head coverings on pain of death. That form of dress was permitted only for chaste and married women. And the worship of Ishtar was associated with prostitution. So the uncovered queen is a reference to the Assyrian goddess Ishtar. Nahum uses it to condemn the goddess."

"You're saying those lines are about Ishtar?"

He was too excited to sit for long so he got up and began pacing the room. "The first signal in the verses points to the queen as Ishtar, who's been revealed and carried away to a secret spot. Doves are also commonly associated with her. Nahum was directing his collaborators to look for Ishtar's resting place. That could only mean her temple."

"That's what you've found—a temple?"

His expression was jubilant. "A spectacular one."

"That's amazing. But it can't be intact." I thought of the Mayan temples still being discovered under the heavy shrouds of jungle in Mexico. That would be impossible here. All the historical buildings were known.

Tomas walked over and lifted up the Bible. "You're right, if the temple was above ground."

"How did you find it? What does it contain?"

He fanned through some pages. "That's what I'm about to tell you. Ah! Here it is. Read Nahum's text again. In chapter two he describes the actual battle, and then suddenly we're sideswiped by verse 2:10. It's totally out of place. 'Take ye the spoil of silver, take the spoil of gold; for there is no end of the store, rich with all precious vessels.'"

"You're saying Nahum wanted the verse about plunder to stand out," I replied.

"That's right. Where is the temple? Let's turn to another passage: 'Where is the den of lions, which was the feeding-place of the young lions, where the lion and the lioness walked, and the lion's whelp, and none made them afraid? / The lion did tear in pieces enough for his whelps, and strangled for his lionesses, and filled his caves with prey, and his dens with ravin.'"

He checked to make sure I was taking all this in, boyish enthusiasm written all over his face. "The lion's a key with a double meaning. It represents the King of Assyria but was also closely associated with the goddess. Hence the lioness. Nahum is reinforcing his message to seek out Ishtar's temple.

"This is a place where the lions walk unafraid. So it's concealed. And a few lines further down, he mentions a cave. Nahum is telling us the temple location is unusual. We're looking for a secret spot near or within a cave."

The prospect of a find like this cracked my permanently black mood. "That's phenomenal. Are you sure you know what you have? I've never heard of Mesopotamians putting temples underground."

"We do know of some, even though the actual temple structures have long since deteriorated. One site in particular, devoted to the moon god Sîn, is located in a cave called the Shwetha D'Ganowe, the sleeping bed of the robbers."

I thought about what he'd said. Aššurbanipal knew his empire was failing. If the king had something he regarded as excessively valuable, it made sense that he'd choose a location next to impossible to find.

Tomas held up a finger. "One more consideration. After the tirade against Ishtar, Nahum compares Nineveh to No-Amon. That is the Egyptian Thebes, also sacked by King Aššurbanipal and plundered for its treasure."

"That's what you found then? The lost treasures of Thebes?" Sensational headlines would result from something of that magnitude. "But I thought it came from Anatolia."

"I meant only that Nahum says Nineveh has been destroyed just like Thebes. But again there's a double meaning. The Dead Sea Scroll fragment for the Book of Nahum actually drops the 'No' and simply refers to 'Amon.' Amon is Amun, a chief Egyptian god. His name means to conceal. He's associated with hidden things.

"It's clear that Nahum or his trusted friends among the community of deportees in Nineveh successfully smuggled his work to Judah, or we wouldn't have the Old Testament book. There was likely a secondary copy on a papyrus scroll or parchment that could have been transported with relative ease.

"In the dying days of the Assyrian empire, the entire area was very unstable and dangerous. The

Hebrew king Josiah was murdered at Megiddo by the Egyptians. Not long after that Judah plunged into chaos and was eventually conquered by the Babylonians. Under those circumstances, mounting a caravan with an armed escort to travel hundreds of miles to Assyria would have been impossible. So the Judeans may well have correctly interpreted the location of Ishtar's temple but historical events interceded, preventing them from reaching their quarry."

"Where is it?"

"Near a village not far away." Tomas allowed himself a broad smile. "So. Would you like to see Nahum's secret?"

Thirty-five

"**W**hy are you willing to share it with me?"
"Your curiosity is dangerous and you have a tenacious side. Eventually you'd find it hard to accept you'd never seen it and might try to seek us out again. I don't want that to happen."

"That's still a startling change of heart."

"It's safe from you now." He reached for a plastic bag. My credit card, passport, and Ward's roll of bills tumbled onto the table.

"How did you get these?"

"We have contacts. They gave Ward's room a sweep." His next words were an almost equal surprise. "I'm arranging to get you out of Iraq. You'll be taken to the Palestine Hotel, where someone will meet you and make sure you leave the city unharmed."

And why, I wondered again, when the man had betrayed me, was he even bothering to help me? I grabbed the card, passport, and money, stuffing them into my pants pockets. "Where's the Victory sculpture?"

"It will be returned to the museum."

"Ward would never have left it in his room."

"We have good networks here. That should be obvious by now."

Glad though I was at the prospect of returning home, I'd developed an attachment to the city. "I'll miss Baghdad. I understand now why Samuel loved it so much."

"You're not in Baghdad. You're in Mosul, in northern Iraq, not far from the site of Nineveh. This is our home. You were unconscious for a whole day—the time it took us to bring you here. If you'd been in Baghdad, the military presence, aircraft overhead, gunfire, and explosions would have been much greater. Come now, if you want to see what we've found."

Mazare, his face still a rash of cuts, drove; Tomas sat beside him and a third man got in the back with me.

"Before we go to the temple, we're taking a short detour," Tomas said.

"Why's that?"

"When we first met, you questioned whether the prophet Nahum lived in Assyria. I'll prove it to you."

He could read the skepticism in my voice. "And how are you going to pull that off?"

In answer, he gave a self-satisfied smile. "You'll see."

Half an hour later we entered a town nestled against a small mountain. "The village of Alqosh," Tomas said.

"I thought we'd be going somewhere near the Nineveh site."

"A thriving Jewish community existed here for thousands of years. Originally, Hebrew people the Assyrian kings had forced into exile. It was Nahum's community, among them his confidants, the ones he hoped would lead the caravan from Judah to Ashurbanipal's treasure."

We entered the town and negotiated successively smaller streets, eventually bumping down a narrow lane enclosed on either side by buildings. We pulled up near an ancient building constructed of masonry and small boulders similar to the honey-colored stone in the rest of the town. The structure looked so old you'd almost think it had grown out of the underlying rock. Deep arches along one side formed a sort of rough cloister; rectangular holes in the walls had once been windows. One side had caved in. "When our country is stable again our State Board of Antiquities will protect this site and restore it," Tomas stated with a clear note of pride.

Tomas went next door and knocked. A man greeted him and handed him something. When he returned he held up a ring of keys. "This is an ancient synagogue," he said. "The last Jewish people left in 1948, and their rabbi entrusted the keys to their next-door neighbor. The family has acted as caretakers ever since."

He took us to a wooden doorway banded by corroded metal with a green patina. Carved stone reliefs framed the door, but they had been so eroded that I couldn't make out the designs. Inside, daylight filtered through the window openings, allowing us to see a large worship space. Tomas showed us various inscriptions, plaques, and Judaic symbols on the walls. He translated one of them: "He who has not witnessed the celebration of pilgrimage to Nahum's tomb has not seen real joy."

"Nahum's actual tomb is here? I can't believe that."

"Ever the skeptic, Madison. Look a little further."

In the center of a small room leading off the main worship area sat a simple plaster sarcophagus draped with a pleated green silk cover. "The prophet's tomb," Tomas said. "The Book of Nahum refers to him as Nahum the Elkoshite. That's a variation of the name of this place. You could just as easily say, 'Nahum of Alqosh.'"

One thing Samuel had always impressed upon me was the value of local narratives. Science had allowed for great advances in archaeology, but that was only one tool. The historic memory of village people carried its own kernel of truth. Nahum may well have found his final resting place here, and it seemed a fitting end in this peaceful old synagogue.

Back on the road we climbed hills, making sharp turns and stopping abruptly to negotiate steep drops. At one point we turned off the smoother surface of asphalt and slowed to enter a bumpy road. Mazare brought the car to a halt. The light had dimmed. Evening was fast approaching.

We'd stopped on a rough track cut into the side of a small mountain. Huge outcroppings of rock broken up by sage-hued swaths of vegetation had turned rosy in the sunset.

"We'll walk from here," Tomas said. "Not so long ago, you couldn't even reach this destination by road. It's dry here now. In the spring when the rains come it's beautiful; wildflowers grow everywhere."

He pulled out a heavy gold chain with a pendant in the shape of a cross, its horizontal and vertical bars ending in three-pointed flutes. "Put this on. It's the *Salib-Siryani*, the Assyrian cross, like the ones we wear." He undid the top buttons of his shirt. "Do likewise, so if we come across anyone, they'll see it dangling. I'll explain that we're pilgrims. Don't under any circumstances speak yourself."

"Wouldn't people know you anyway?"

"Farther south, not around here."

The steep, uneven path would have challenged a nimble goat. In places it had crumbled away and we had to use our hands and feet to scramble up. After about half an hour we rounded a high rock face. The vision greeting us stopped me in my tracks.

Close to its crown, an ancient citadel clung to the mountain's face. It looked like a crusader's fort or one of those age-old Tibetan monasteries. Masonry walls at least sixty feet high formed the base. Above, Moorish-arched stone buildings soared, pink in the last glimmers of sunset. High in the sky a pair of vultures wheeled, their outstretched wings black shapes against pale violet.

"Dair Rabban Hurmiz," Tomas said, sweeping his arm toward it, "the most famous monastery in Iraq. It dates to A.D. 640, built on the ruins of an ancient pagan cult center by two princes who witnessed the miracles of our legendary healer and spiritual leader Rabban Hurmiz. Over the ages the monastery has changed hands between the Syriac Church of the East and we Catholic Chaldeans."

I couldn't take my eyes off it. It looked like a phantom castle, like something out of *One Thousand and One Nights.*

"The monastery has literally been carved into the mountainside. Inside, a great dining hall was hewn out of the mountain, its pillars formed from verticals of uncut rock. The church has five altars, one room with a floor of stone coffins, and a saint's burial chamber. The library has documents going back to the fifteenth century."

"Is it still occupied?"

"The Chaldean Church reclaimed it in 1975. A caretaker community lives on here."

"Is this where you studied for the priesthood?"

"No, in Baghdad. My grandparents lived in Alqosh. As boys, Ari and I often played among the grottos here, secretly, of course. You couldn't imagine a better place for hide-and-seek. When I saw the inscriptions on Nahum's engraving, I recalled seeing the same ones on the wall of one of the caves."

He indicated the terrain below the structure, a scattering of boulders, plants, and small cave-like openings. The monks had probably meditated and fasted in the black holes of these grottos. In the distance a phantom-like figure robed in black appeared for a moment in an arched doorway, then turned and vanished. Otherwise, I could see no one else around.

Before approaching the monastery grounds, Tomas and his men knelt and bent their heads in prayer. I felt awkward, wanting to respect their faith but unsure of what to do. I crossed a patch of sandy soil to lean against an outcropping of rock. After a few minutes Tomas rose and beckoned to me.

I could make out a shadowy hole in front of us. Was I marching toward my execution? My rational side argued against that. They could have killed me any number of times, any number of ways, at Tomas's house. I crept forward into the recess.

We'd gone about thirty feet when a light suddenly flared ahead. Turning a corner, I found a cavity with a roughly rounded ceiling and square-cut stone floor. Tomas held a jacklight with a beam as strong as a searchlight; it lit up every crevice and cranny. I could see niches cut into the rocky surface and sanded smooth. They must have once held figurines, perhaps magical talismans, but now they were empty.

Tomas pointed to one of them. "This once held a small relief of a lion and his cubs. It was plastered over a long time ago. Below it, a cuneiform inscription has been incised into the rock." He shone his light so I could see. "On Nahum's engraving an inscription appears after the words 'Take ye the spoil of silver, take the spoil of gold.' It says, 'By the bond of heaven and earth, from the great above to the great below.'"

"Like the quote used by the Hermetics—as above, so below. But that was Egyptian I thought."

"Indeed it is the Hermetic quote," Tomas said. "But the phrase is a magical Mesopotamian incantation seen on many tablets and used to introduce their texts. It goes back to early written documents. Orally probably longer. The quotation came originally from Mesopotamia, not Egypt."

"Why was it attributed to the Egyptians then?"

"Because it first became known to the Greeks in Alexandria. Active trade between Egypt and Mesopotamia grew enormously in the Neo-Assyrian period. Caravans brought Arabian spices, the frankincense and myrrh of the Magi, prized commodities. It's not hard to see how such a common phrase could have been transported to Egypt. An inscription like that should have appeared right at the beginning of Nahum's book. Deliberately putting it where he did— incorrectly in the middle—was meant to be a signal. And to emphasize the point, Ishtar's eight-pointed stars terminated the inscription."

I bent down and ran my hand over the inscription. I recognized Ishtar's eight-pointed stars but couldn't read the cuneiform markings. "What does it say?"

Tomas's face lit up. "*Dur-An-Ki*, 'By the bond of heaven and earth.' And following that it says, 'From the great above to the great below.' Those two phrases are the beginning of a Mesopotamian incantation." He bent down beside me and traced the inscription with his finger. "It's immensely ironic. A mark of Nahum's genius."

"You're saying he inscribed it?"

"Yes. Nahum was here; he saw the grotto and left signs to show the way to the temple. The grottos were originally natural caves, here long before the monastery. Nahum added his mark for his people to see. And he meant it literally. The brightest stars of the Renaissance passed this phrase along to each other. But many centuries before that, Nahum used the same phrase to point the way to our Assyrian temple."

"You're saying the temple lies underneath us?" Had he allowed himself to be carried away over the excitement of a new find? How could an underground temple rival the glories of the Nineveh palaces and their treasures?

He motioned for me to stand back. "Press yourself against the wall. There's little room to maneuver here." I stood at the side of the cavity while Mazare used a large chisel to pry one of the floor stones loose. He shoved it aside, revealing a deep black hole.

Tomas turned toward me. "You go first. Take great care—it's almost fifty feet down."

"You've done it before. Wouldn't it make more sense for you to go first?"

"If you fall I don't want you taking us with you." Tomas shone the light down the hole. At the lip I could see crude wedges carved into the side of the tunnel, a rudimentary ladder.

Light from above cast ominous shapes and shadows as I inched my way down. The steps were slick with ancient slime and dripping water, my clothes picking up a greenish-black stain. It smelled like the bottom of a well where a stew of water and rotting things had lingered for centuries.

Only by gripping the upper wedges as tightly as possible with my hands could I stop myself from falling. My foot would slip and I'd hug my body to the rough stone wall like a lover. Once more I felt my foot give way. I gripped my handhold, a crack, and the chunk of rock split off the wall. I let out a yell and dropped.

"Going up is easier." Mazare laughed when he reached me and switched on his own flashlight, holding it up to guide the way for Tomas. I'd been close enough to the bottom that I'd suffered nothing more than embarrassment.

The third man posted at the top stood ready to slide the floor stone back into place at any sign of trouble. While Tomas made his way down I looked around. By the light of the flashlight, I could see two tunnels at the bottom of the shaft. Rock debris blocked the first one a few feet in. The second, which we'd have to stoop to enter, trailed off into inky shadow.

When he reached us, Tomas flicked on his light again and shone it toward the blocked aperture. "We think it was once the actual entrance to the temple and they cut the shaft we climbed down for ventilation. King Sennacherib was the grand developer of Nineveh, and that included a magnificent park. For irrigation his workmen diverted mountain streams to increase the flow of water into the River Khosr that bisected the Nineveh precinct. This tunnel was once the path of one of those underground streams."

Blackened stone glistened in the light. Water dripped off the roof, slithering down the walls, forming little rivulets that disappeared into the floor crevices. We descended, how far I couldn't guess, but it seemed like a long way. All of us were forced to crouch, the tunnel roof being about five feet in height. "Men then were much shorter," Tomas said.

We crept along for the better part of an hour, my knees and back aching with the awkward position, the various sites of my injuries reawakening in pain. As our lights receded, the tunnel closed in again to black and it began to feel as if the darkness were a material thing pursuing us.

I was on the verge of asking for a rest stop when Mazare, who'd taken the lead, waved his flashlight. "Up ahead now. Here it is."

The cavity abruptly widened and grew higher. His jacklight shone on a flight of stairs angling up into the darkness. As we climbed, our surroundings grew noticeably drier. I was beginning to think the steps were endless when the floor leveled out abruptly. This section was man-made, surfaced with enormous limestone blocks. Every three rows of blocks bore cuneiform words etched in the stone. Tomas pointed to one of them. "King Ashurbanipal's royal inscription. The treasure lies ahead."

Interesting, the formal title he always used when referring to the Assyrian kings. National pride had a long shelf life.

The treasure lies ahead. He made it sound like some Indiana Jones hoard of caskets brimming with gold coins, ruby-eyed idols, and ropes of fat pearls.

The half-rotted wooden timbers of what I guessed had once been magnificent cedar doors partially blocked the tunnel. I pressed one of the planks and it collapsed into a powdery wood dust.

They asked me to wait. Mazare handed me his light, then he and Tomas clambered over the wood and vanished into the gloom beyond. I'd stay a couple of minutes, no more. Even that much time was a trial.

Soft patches of light materialized ahead. When I heard Tomas call my name I scrambled over the timbers and emerged into an enormous cavern.

The place was vast. Big enough to easily hold the Great Court of the British Museum. In the middle of the cave was a magnificent temple. Not a ziggurat, but a rectangular building. Its roof must have risen forty feet. Undeniably Neo-Assyrian in design. Glazed tile friezes decorated the exterior in the iridescent blue, red, white, and black commonly used in Mesopotamian antiquity for high-status structures. This in itself was a major discovery, since it was the later Babylonians who'd been known to use this kind of tiling on exteriors. Two enormous stone Lamassu guarded the temple entrance.

"Come inside." Tomas's voice echoed strangely, as if he were the ancient king himself issuing an order to one of his subjects. I suddenly felt it had been wrong to come here, and I feared we'd pay a price for invading the goddess's precinct. But I walked through the entrance. It was far too late for any misgivings.

Tomas and Mazare had turned off their lights. Soft glimmers came from oil lamps set around the central room. My breath deserted me.

Shimmering with gold, a life-sized lion and lioness harnessed to a chariot faced me. I thought of Nahum's words. *Where the lion and the lioness walked.* Shell and ivory inlays of doves, rosettes, and stars embellished the harness and the chariot's booth. Ishtar's chariot. I walked around it, not touching it, just taking in the splendor of the work. The chariot was likely wooden and the lions would have been sculpted from stone, all of it coated with electrum, a gold-silver alloy. In places the electrum had flaked off, revealing the underlying material.

The interior temple walls—giant slabs of gypsum—were faced with life-sized images of Apkallu, the guardian spirits with human bodies, wings, and vulture heads. Their wrists sported rosette armbands; they held purification objects that looked like large pine cones.

Tomas watched as I toured the objects, pride lighting up his face. I thought of Samuel then—the sight of this would have brought him to tears. And no price could conceivably be attached to it. The value of Nahum's engraving paled in comparison. No wonder Ward and his people had killed for this.

Treasures like these would have graced a royal household. Crystal chalices; golden cups and bowls; amphorae for wine and olive oil; jewelry chests in gold, silver, and bronze. One of the chests was filled with necklaces, bead strings of alternating green malachite and banded agate, the agate carved to resemble fish eyes. The chests sat on small tables and chairs inlaid with ivory, shell, and precious stones. I saw alabaster statuettes; glass bottles for perfume; cylinder seals of chalcedony; ivory combs; copper hand mirrors, green now but originally burnished to a glassy shine.

One shallow silver bowl, black with tarnish, still held husks of grain. Nahum's script floated into my mind again: *Take ye the spoil of silver, take the spoil of gold; for there is no end of the store, rich with all precious vessels.* The oil lamps with their flickering flames looked just like the lamps genies sprang from in Arabian folk tales, the idea for the design inspired by the shape of the shells originally used as lamps. I recognized in the inlays the muddy rose of carnelian.

The rush of sensation almost overwhelmed me.

Tomas interrupted my thoughts. "These are typical of temple furnishings, all the items placed for the use of the goddess. Every day her human attendants would have brought real food and drink to her, clothed her in finery and jewels. The statue would have been taken out for processions on special days.

"Come over here." Tomas gestured toward an alcove. On the floor, an array of brown bones; I could make out a rib cage, a skull. Bracelets and anklets encircled the long bones of the arms and legs absurdly, as if the skeleton had wanted to dress up. A sword and an elongated gold helmet with elaborate designs lay a few feet from the skull.

"Look carefully," Tomas said. "This solves a 2600-year-old mystery."

Tangled in the rib bones I noticed a necklace. A hoop of gold with pendants dangling from it, each one embossed with symbols—a rosette, a sun, a lion.

"What you're seeing are the remains of the last King of Assyria, Ashur-uballit II."

"How could you know that?"

"When Nineveh was sacked and the king died, a few members of the royal family escaped. They fled to Harran but were routed from there and continued on to join their Egyptian allies at Carchemish. Ashur-uballit was declared Assyria's king at that time. But in 605 B.C. a brilliant young Babylonian general named Nebuchadnezzar decimated the combined Assyrian and Egyptian forces. There is no further account of Ashur-uballit's fate.

"Those accoutrements would only have belonged to the king. The necklace and the helmet, in particular. They're inscribed with royal symbols. No one knows what became of Ashur-uballit. That the king would seek refuge here makes sense. Do you recall Nahum's words, 'Where is the den of lions, which was the feeding-place of the young lions, where the lion and the lioness walked, and the lion's whelp, and none made them afraid'?"

"Yes," I said.

"At first I thought the rockfall closing off the main entrance had been caused by an earthquake, but when I took a second look I realized that none of the fissures and cracks you'd expect from earth tremors were present. I believe his enemies hunted him down and caused the rockfall. They sealed the king in."

"Surely he wouldn't have come here alone?"

Tomas pointed to the rear of the temple. "Behind that wall is his entourage. His queen, probably his personal guard, even the bones of children. But come, a much greater surprise awaits."

If this wasn't enough of a bombshell, I couldn't imagine what was.

He led me to a room. Inside were orderly rows of baked brick boxes. "The temple filing system. Each one is filled with tablets, although the clay is badly eroded now. King Ashurbanipal's library at Nineveh survived partly because the tablets were cooked in the high heat of the fires that destroyed the city. It's relatively dry here but not enough to preserve the clay."

On the way out he indicated an unusually shaped flask, a rounded bowl with a long snout projecting sideways, like some bizarre teapot. This was not metal but fired clay. "The first distillation apparatus, forerunner of the alembic still," he said. "For making perfume. The original model for alchemical vessels."

With great care I took it in my hands. A magical scent of rose and foreign spices seemed to cling to it. Only my imagination, I knew, but this place stimulated reveries. I knew also that I shouldn't touch a thing. Archaeologists rivaled forensics technicians in their insistence on the sanctity of a site. They'd photograph and measure the tiniest distance between objects before moving them. But for me it was impossible not to touch, not to make a direct connection with these lovely emblems of the past.

"So," Tomas said, "have you seen enough?"

"I want to stay here forever." I ran my hand over my forehead. "There's a certain irony here, don't you think?"

He frowned. "What's that?"

"It's now the property of the Chaldeans and the Roman Catholic Church."

"Not just us. It belongs to all the Iraqi people. The Church will do its best to safeguard it for everyone." He turned away. "Come. We have to leave soon. But before we do I promised you something truly amazing."

"What are you talking about? There's something else?"

"What we've just seen would have been temple property. King Ashurbanipal's plunder is hidden in Ishtar's shrine."

I'd completely forgotten about the shrine room, mesmerized as I was by the bones of the ancient king and all the temple treasure. His statement caught me off guard. "You're right. These are all Mesopotamian, so they couldn't be described as spoil."

"They may be Babylonian. Ashurbanipal destroyed Babylon and took everything of value."

"Technically that's not plunder because he controlled both Assyria and Babylon."

"Yes. The real prize is inside the shrine."

I looked to see whether Mazare was coming. He stayed back, a look on his face that could only be described as fear. What on earth was ahead of us?

I was not to make any discoveries immediately. In the shrine room a large tarp had been hung over a frame standing a few feet from the rear wall. The walls sported incredible paintings, some of the paint corrupted but the images still clearly readable. The first showed a winged Ishtar with her horned cap and war bow, surrounded by an arc of eight-pointed stars. The second pictured a lion disemboweling a man. Nahum's words came back to me again. *The lion did tear in pieces enough for his whelps, and strangled for his lionesses, and filled his caves with prey.*

A low stand held more pots. I knelt down and picked one up. Iron. Easy to see because it was coated with rust. Exceptional care would be necessary to remove the accumulation of rust without destroying the metal underneath. These had a beautiful form but were nothing compared to the poorest item outside. I looked at Tomas. "These are probably from Anatolia."

"Yes, you're correct. From Phrygia."

"There must be something pretty spectacular underneath the tarp."

Thirty-six

Tomas didn't reply. He turned on his light and positioned it to shine on whatever lay underneath. Then he moved over to one side of the tarp. "Stand back a little," he said, and gently tugged it off.

The glare blinded me for an instant. It was as if the air had turned to gold. I gave my head a shake and looked again. The goddess in all her glory. Her body from head to toe a stunning rosy gold. A life-sized statue of a woman. One leg forward, torso slightly bent, as if she was getting ready to greet someone, golden cup held casually in one hand. Her midriff and breasts were bare; on them were exquisite gold necklaces accented with lapis, turquoise, onyx, and pearls.

I moved closer to take a look and saw the lapis was an intense blue with specks of golden pyrite, like an indigo river saturated with particles of gold. She'd once worn a garment, visible now only by shreds of red and violet threads clinging to her upper arms, pelvis, and thighs. The verse from the Book of Revelation describing the Whore of Babylon flooded back: *And the woman was arrayed in purple and scarlet color, and decked with gold and precious stones and pearls, having a golden cup in her hand.*

The body of the statue had been modeled after a young woman, judging by her smooth skin and high, firm breasts. Her nipples had been painted a ruby red. But it was the expression on her face that stopped me in my tracks. Her lips getting ready for a warm smile, but in her eyes, a look of abject terror.

"What on earth is this?" I turned around to confront Tomas.

"See the helmet she wears? Ivory. The sign of divinity—seven furls of the finest horn. The helmet, like the robe, necklaces, arm and leg bands, was put on later by the Assyrians. She is both Ishtar and not Ishtar."

He was speaking in riddles now.

The statue stood on a low stone dais shaped like a sarcophagus. At her feet rested several golden objects. What looked like a branch, two small nuggets of something I couldn't place, some spears of wheat, a few tiny pieces shaped like teardrops, an apple, and another cup.

The portrayal was astounding, every detail consummate. Her eyebrows must have been shaved, but her eyelashes had been duplicated perfectly, the dimples in her cheeks. I looked closer and thought I could actually make out individual hairs on her arms.

"What you're seeing is the origin of the notion of transmutation," Tomas said.

I didn't understand. "You mean the sculpture was made of lead and somehow converted into gold? It's not Assyrian, that's clear. Not Mesopotamian at all. The workmanship is unbelievable."

"You don't understand, do you?"

I just stared at him, trying to decipher his words.

Tomas continued. "Every child knows this story. But let me prove it by quoting from Ovid's *Metamorphoses*. I know it off by heart now.

Upon the eleventh day,
When Lucifer had dimmed the lofty
multitude of stars,
[The King] and Silenius went from there,
Joyful together to the Lydian lands.

There [the King] put Silenius carefully,
Under the care of his loved foster-child,
Young Bacchus, he with great delight,
Because he had his foster-father once again,
Allowed the King to choose his own reward,
A welcome offer, but it led to harm.

And [the King] made this ill-advised reply,
'Cause whatsoever I shall touch to change
at once to yellow gold.'"

I stood rooted to the spot, almost at a loss

for words. "You can't possibly be talking about Midas?"

"Not him. That is his daughter you see. Her father, King Midas, touched her and she turned to gold. His sorrow was so great upon losing her as a result of his own greed that he begged to be rid of his wish. Bacchus instructed him to wash his hands in the River Pactolus, known for its gold deposits to this very day. As Claire told you."

"You can't really believe this."

"Remember what you said about Samuel's journal? It worried me. I was afraid you might uncover his meaning. A line about the Assyrians striking a treaty with King Mitta of the Mushki. The king's correct name was Mit-ta-a. That was Midas, King of Phrygia; it's historical fact. In Turkey today Midas's tomb has yet to be discovered. That acropolis you saw with Ward? It has stellae naming the location 'Midas city.'

"Midas was literally as rich as Croesus. Behind the back wall is another room stacked with more clay boxes; inside are hundreds of gold ingots stamped with Midas's seal. The Phrygians used these for trade," Tomas said, "because they had no actual currency. Lydia was the first to produce electrum-coated coins in 650 B.C.

"Midas needed protection from the Cimmerians, barbarian tribes who, like marauding Vikings, swept down from the Black Sea. King Ashurbanipal's great-grandfather, Sargon II, agreed to protect Gordium, the capital of Phrygia, because of its valuable precious metals. After Sargon died, tribes overran Phrygia and sacked it. Midas hid in the tomb he'd built for himself. They think he committed suicide by drinking bull's blood, a reference I believe to his worship of Mithras."

He pointed to the golden objects lying at the statue's feet. "There you see the twig, stone, grain, and apple that Ovid described in his poem; they were practice objects for the craftsmen."

"Have you figured out how they did it?"

"Pretty much." He slid one of the armbands down an inch or so. "It's next to impossible to see with the naked eye, but there's a faint seam just below the elbow. We think they used the lost wax-casting method to make a funeral mask of the head, forearms, hands, and feet. The rest of the body was sculpted, again originally in wax, and separate casts were made, one for the lead core and the second for its gold shell. Then all the pieces were expertly joined together. We even think we know how she died—suddenly, judging by the look on her face."

"How could you possibly guess that?"

Tomas gestured toward her feet. "It's written on that bier she's standing on. This isn't an exact translation, but it says, 'She drank from the golden wine to become one with the gods. The goddess became jealous and punished her.' I've learned high-ranking individuals in those times indulged in a strange rite. They drank water or wine infused with gold particles in the belief that they could achieve immortality. Combine a high concentration of gold particles with the right body metabolism, and the brew would react like a lethal poison. That's likely what happened to her. If you don't believe me, that's exactly how a mistress of the French king Henry II died.

"The myth of Midas's golden touch was born, no doubt, in part by this strange practice. King Midas, in anguish over his daughter's tragedy, must have ordered his craftsmen to preserve her image in the most lifelike way possible."

I could understand Mazare's fear. You'd swear she was actually alive.

"In 1995 it was thought the tomb of Midas had been found in Turkey at the site of Gordium, but that turned out to date to a time before his reign," Tomas said. "King Ashurbanipal must have known about the actual tomb location, and when his campaign into Anatolia provided the opportunity, he plundered its contents and took them back to Assyria. He honored Midas's daughter by converting her to Ishtar."

"So that's why you set up the trap for Ward in Turkey?"

"Yes. He suspected the Midas connection, so I knew he would buy into it."

"Why did Ashurbanipal hide the statue here?"

"His son assumed the reign several years before Ashurbanipal's actual death. The old king could see that the empire was failing and knew Nineveh would be savaged if the city fell. So he hid its most precious possessions."

"And Nahum, a scribe he must have trusted greatly,

was one of the few aware of the actual location," I said.

Tomas walked over to the back wall. "Nahum hated the royal Assyrian family. But he kept his anger concealed—like a coal fire simmering underground for years before it finally bursts into flame."

He touched the wall painting. "This is an image of the Musmahhu, a snake monster, the beast with a leopard body, the paws of a bear, the seven horned heads. Ishtar was later transformed by the last book of the Bible into the Whore of Babylon. This demon is a prototype for the Whore of Babylon's beast in Revelation: 'And the beast which I saw was like unto a leopard, and his feet were as the feet of a bear, and his mouth as the mouth of a lion: and the dragon gave him his power, and his seat, and great authority.'

Mušmahhu—The Snake Monster. Shell inlay, Mesopotamia, 2750–2315 B.C.

"Ward was correct about that. The Bible's authors portrayed sorcery and magic as exclusively evil practices and converted Ishtar, whom even the Hebrew people worshiped, into a witch and a harlot so that she'd be condemned rather than revered."

I agreed with him there. Ishtar and her sister goddess, the Phoenician Ashtoreth, had incredible power over ancient minds. Mesopotamian temples were centers of magic, sorcery, and divination involving whole ranks of specialists. Here Ashipu priests recited incantations to exorcize evil spirits; the Baru and Mahu were diviners.

"The King James Bible substitutes the word *whore* for *harlot*," Tomas continued, "making us think Nahum called Ishtar the most degraded form of prostitute. But the true meaning of harlot describes a temple prostitute. Many of those women enjoyed elevated status. The mother of one of the Assyrian kings was a temple prostitute. Again, Nahum is drawing a red circle around Ishtar.

"Jump ahead eight hundred years to the Revelation of John, when Ishtar becomes the Whore of Babylon. Many scholars acknowledge that Revelation portrays the goddess holding a golden cup and riding a seven-headed, horned beast. The cupbearer had high status among Assyrian courtiers.

"The theory of transmutation—turning lead into gold—originated in Phrygia with the death of Midas's daughter and the creation of this statue. Once temple priests performed the rituals to capture Ishtar's presence to animate the statue, the ancient Assyrians would have believed the goddess was alive within it. Through the centuries this originating event was forgotten, but the lifelike statue of the goddess grew into a legend. Myth took over and people came to believe it was possible to turn a material substance into gold. The great Arabic court scientists of the eighth and ninth centuries in the Baghdad caliphate would have been familiar with the myth. It was they who provided a scientific foundation for the legend."

I was only vaguely conscious of Mazare calling to us.

"Come," Tomas said. "Time to leave now."

I trailed behind him in a daze.

"So this will all end up in the Vatican?"

Tomas laughed when I said that. "You've been reading too many thrillers. Tomorrow I'll meet the patriarch of Babylon, the head of the Chaldean Church in Iraq. He'll do his best to ensure the temple and its contents are secure until the country is stable again."

We made it back more quickly this time. While we waited for the car, Tomas told me that once we got back to the house Mazare would take me to Baghdad. We said brief goodbyes. There was no point, I suppose, in pretending we shared any sadness at parting.

Thirty-seven

Tuesday, August 19, 2003, 11:15 A.M.

The car bumping along a dirt road woke me. Mazare drove. I'd been dreaming about Laurel, reaching out to touch her. When I did so, her skin turned to gold. The image shattered, breaking outward, sharp pieces of metal flying, slicing into my face.

A canvas of parched ochre earth stretched away on either side of us as far as the eye could see. The dry, hot atmosphere had given me a throat as rough as sandpaper. I asked Mazare for some water.

He picked up a Thermos from the cup holder separating our seats. "You've been asleep for a long time. Have this coffee. It will help you wake up fast."

I unscrewed the cap, poured some out, drank it all and poured a second. I squinted at the sun beating through the windshield. It had the sharp quality of morning sun. Aiming toward it meant we were headed east.

"We're south of Tikrit, east of Samarra," Mazare said. "All being well, we should make Baghdad soon. I'd take a more straightforward route but I have to avoid checkpoints and military vehicles."

A little ways on he pulled over to the side of the road beside a dilapidated shack. A herder's hut probably. "There are better clothes in the trunk." He gestured toward the shack. "You can go in that place and change." The smears of slime drying on my shirt and pants persuaded me he was right.

"Why does Tomas dislike me so much?" I asked him after I'd climbed back into the car and we'd taken off.

"He says you are not moral."

I could think of several comebacks to that but I let it ride; my differences were not with Mazare.

"So why bother to protect me then?"

Mazare stole a glance at me. "Ari was furious when he found out what Tomas did—taking Nahum's book and leaving you to be eaten by Ward and his vultures and then us almost blowing you up. He threatened Tomas. The first time I ever heard him do that. Ari said he would put the temple in the news and tell everyone its location unless Tomas saved you. That's why we kept you with us for so long. To make sure you were healed."

"When did you hear this?"

"Last week."

"Are you telling me Ari's here? I thought it was too unsafe; he's supposed to be in London."

"He came back. Tomas tried to stop him, but Ari refused to give up his reporting. He could not let it go. He said if he makes the tortures public that will end them. He's not coming with the English television. There are ways to slip into the country. The Americans won't find out."

I recalled Eris's phone call. *There are people here who need to be alerted if Ari Zakar is back.*

I swung around to face Mazare. "I've got to talk to Ari. They know he's back. They've had a lot of time to look for him."

Mazare raised his eyebrows. "How did you find out this?"

"Just get me to him. For God's sake."

"I'm supposed to drive you straight to the hotel."

I yelled at him then. "He'll be thrown into that prison. I don't want to think about what they'd do to him in there. You've got to take me."

Mazare shrugged his shoulders. I sensed it was an anxious gesture.

"Here, take this. I'll pay you." I pulled out the roll of bills Ward had given me and threw it in his lap.

"I don't want your money." He threw it back at me. He reached for his phone and punched in some numbers, keeping his left hand on the wheel. When he made the connection he spoke in Assyrian, waited to hear the response, and ended the call. "Tomas says the crew have permission to shoot there but we should try to find Ari anyway. Thanks to God. He'll try to call him too." He hit the accelerator, made a U-turn, and headed west.

Nearing a main highway, we narrowly missed being fired upon. We raced along roads that were no more than lanes, skirted potholes the size of craters. At one point we had to drive off-road around an enormous spread of reeking mud. For the routes we took Mazare drove dangerously fast, but all the same I would have put my foot down on the accelerator to push the vehicle faster if I could.

I was shaken out of the turmoil of my thoughts by the car hitting rises that felt like small hills. "Where are we going?" I asked Mazare. "I thought Ari was in Baghdad somewhere."

He took his eyes off the road for a moment. "He's at Abu Ghraib shooting film with RaiNews 24. Reporters from Italy. The prison's west of Baghdad. I need to be careful near it. I can't just drive up to the gate."

"Just get there as fast as you can." My face and neck poured with sweat. My heart actually hurt. I could only hope Ari had done a good job of hiding his identity and that the prison's military command was too far down the pecking order to be on the alert for him.

Mazare slowed the Toyota to a crawl. Ahead I could see dusty blocks of buildings. "This place is huge," I said.

"Abu Ghraib. It means place of ravens. It can hold fifteen thousand men. That's how many in Saddam's day. America has not that number, but the prison's evil raven soul is still the same." He took his right hand off the steering wheel and made the obscene sign for coitus. "They strip people naked and make them do things to each other. They even keep children in there."

"How will we ever find him?"

"Tomas told me where he's shooting."

Moments later we slowed. The vehicle inched along like the proverbial tortoise at the end of the race and then halted. "Too dangerous going any farther," Mazare said. He pointed to a clutch of vehicles in the distance. "That's them. I'll turn the car around. Make yourself ready to move fast when you come back."

I left the door swinging open and ran. A dirty white building with no windows ranged ahead on my right, a guard tower standing at its perimeter like the pilot's nest on a steamship, the shadow of a soldier inside. A long pole was raised at a forty-five-degree angle, painted red and white like a giant barber's pole. A mélange of huge concrete blocks, cement barriers, and miles of razor wire clustered around the entrance.

I could see press vehicles in the distance.

A figure emerged from one of the cars. I practically went down on my knees in gratitude. It was Ari. He took slow, measured steps back from the car, his camera balanced on his shoulder. I waved both arms and yelled his name. Either I was still too far away for him to hear me or he was too focused on what he was doing, because he didn't look up. I summoned all my energy and ran toward him.

Army vehicles approached Ari from the opposite direction. The convoy looked like a train of lumbering dinosaurs, a Bradley fighting vehicle in the lead. Probably just checking things out. In the bright morning light I could easily see the word *Press* emblazoned on the cars and Ari clearly held a camera.

I yelled again, only a hundred feet or so away now. Ari glanced toward me, a flood of joy lighting up his face mingled with surprise at seeing me there. He lifted his hand, waved, and then motioned for me to wait while he finished the shot. He didn't appear to be aware of the military vehicles behind him. Had seeing me distracted him? I called out once more and gestured emphatically, trying to draw his attention to the convoy. Ari waved again and smiled, not understanding me.

I put on speed.

I looked toward the lead Bradley again. It kept coming. Something about the body language of the soldier manning the gun alarmed me. Not much time left. Ari had almost no chance of escaping arrest now. I notched my voice up and shouted, "Turn around— they're at your back!" Ari's ginger hair ruffled in the breeze, the light making it look like spun gold. He began edging his camera off his shoulder, preparing to greet me. He grinned. Said something to me. I felt the warmth of his smile link the two of us. But I couldn't hear him and that meant he still hadn't heard me.

The gun on the Bradley fixed on him. They were getting ready to make a move.

Look behind you, Ari! Get back in the car and get the hell out of there.

What sounded like firecrackers went off. Ari buckled as if a missile had struck him. His camera toppled to the ground. He screamed and grabbed for his chest. One of the journalists lurched out of the press car, blurting out a volley of Italian. Ari crumpled into the dirt, a geyser of blood bursting over the front of his shirt.

"They shot him. They shot him!" I screamed this as I ran the last yards. I threw myself down beside him. Ari struggled for breath. Wheezing sounds rushed out of his throat. His eyelids flickered and his whole body shook with convulsions. I had no idea what to do.

Soldiers appeared on either side of me. It took two of them to pull me away. "Let me alone," I said. "I've got to do something; he's hurt, you can see that."

"There's other people coming," one of them said. "Let them take care of it. Who are you?"

I looked toward Ari, military men now crowding around him, attempting to stanch the flow of blood. I sank down on my knees, shuddering. "His friend," I said. "I'm his friend." I could no longer talk, the agony as great as if it were my own life draining away. The soldier set his gun aside and crouched down beside me, putting his hand on my shoulder. He said, not unkindly, "They'll try to save him. You can't make any difference now anyway."

When the team around Ari finally stepped back it was clear nothing more could be done. His body lay in the dust. The soldier guided me toward him, let me stand near Ari for a few moments to say goodbye. They assumed I was with the press team. I took off the sun medallion Ari had given me and wound it around his hand, recalling Diane Chen's prediction: *Only the sign of the sun can save you.*

The Italian crew eventually drove me back to the city. Mazare was nowhere to be found. I asked the journalists to take me to the al-Mansour Hotel. I got thoroughly tanked in the hotel bar and spent the rest of the night wandering the grounds, wishing the dogs would come to finish me off, the scene of Ari's last moments competing with the horror of Laurel's fate playing over and over again in my mind.

I finally came to my senses with the dawn.

A freelance journalist planning to leave for Kuwait City agreed to give me a ride late that afternoon. The day was an oven again, the heat so thick it seemed to take on a material form. As we drove out of Baghdad I took one look back. The waning sunlight had turned the buildings into orange flares. It looked like the city was burning.

Thirty-eight

Friday, August 22, 2003, 12 P.M.

Three days later I returned to New York. In three more days my grace period would be over and the new owner would be installed in the condo Samuel and I had shared.

Amir brightened up when he saw me. "You keep vanishing and then reappearing. I'm beginning to think you're a ghost."

I gave him a weak smile. He had no idea how close he was to the truth.

"How come you sold your place?" He looked a little hurt, as though my leaving was a personal affront. I rubbed my thumb and forefinger together in the universal sign for money.

He pursed his lips. "A lot of people came looking for you. I wrote them down."

He hunted for something under the front desk counter and retrieved a scrap of notepaper. "The first was a policeman, I'm guessing in his late fifties. He came on August 4, over two weeks ago. A man built like a wrestler with holes in his face." Amir peered at his handwriting. "Detective Gentle."

"Gentile," I said.

"Yes, that's it. He seemed mad. Like angry mad."

"Who else?"

"Next day the black lady came back again."

"You mean the lady who dresses in black."

He nodded. "Yes, her. A sad person."

"That was Evelyn."

"And last came a beautiful stranger. An angel woman. Hair shining like ice, blue eyes."

"When was this?"

"They all came in around the same time." He looked down at his paper again. "The light-haired woman showed up on August 5. Nobody since." He crinkled up the paper. "You have mysterious friends."

I explained I'd lost my keys and got a duplicate from him, then grabbed the armload of mail stuffed into my box. The elevator door had almost closed when he called out to me.

"I forgot one more thing. The carpet fitters came last week."

Carpet fitters? The new owners must have been in already. Since they came from Dubai, I wasn't sure whether they planned to rent the place out or keep it for occasional use. What if they'd already removed my property?

I opened my front door with great reluctance, expecting to see the place stripped bare. Instead it looked like a drunken football fan's hotel room.

Graffiti had been sprayed across the walls, quite unimaginative taunts like *up yours* and *your mom is a whore*. They were a careless bunch who did this, spraying right across the paintings when the mood struck them. The sofa was ripped to shreds with the stuffing left intact, so it was plain they weren't searching for anything. Huge gouges had been scraped in my teak media cabinet, a retro piece I was particularly fond of.

Bleach had been poured over every one of my precious Turkomen carpets, eating through the fabric in places. On the floor in front of the cabinet it looked as if a mirror had been smashed into tiny shards. All my CDs had been taken out of their cases, broken to pieces, and dropped on the floor.

It made me sick to see what they'd done. I bent down and found fragments of my Steve Vai DVD. I gathered them up in my hands, wishing them back together. This was his performance two years ago at London's Astoria; one cut, "Whispering a Prayer," was one of the best guitar solos ever recorded. A personal anthem for me.

"Watchtower" on the *Ali* soundtrack, Jimmy Page and John Mayall with Mick Taylor on lead. What a travesty. Some of those disks were irreplaceable.

I wandered from room to room. The kitchen counters of Brazilian black slate and the stainless steel cupboards had been criss-crossed with lurid green spray paint.

My bedroom was a similar mess. Scrawled on my mirror with Magic Marker were the words *Dear John, Thanks for your hospitality. Sorry for leaving things in such a mess … The Rap.* It would be impossible to tie him to the crime, of course, safely stashed away in jail as he was. His friends had done this job.

There was no way to set things right in three days. Our insurance had terminated with the sale. I assumed the new owners had some and hoped it would cover the damage. Visions of lawsuits danced before my eyes. I was heading for bankruptcy anyway—this would just get me there a bit faster. My emotional reservoir had already been drained dry, but I seemed to find room for another wave of despair.

I wasn't sure I had the guts to open the door to Samuel's suite. I pried it open a crack and peered in. More graffiti was sprayed on the walls, but their energy must have flagged at this point because other than the books pulled from the shelves, I couldn't see too much damage.

I hauled my treasure chest from the closet. All the items were still inside. Samuel's secretiveness about the engraving and the condo sale had blown a hole through my trust. Was the story about my origins perhaps a little too neat? There had never been any photographs, no long-lost relatives showing up at our door. Samuel and I didn't resemble each other at all.

I picked up the golden key. What was it meant for? What beautiful woman had inspired the portrait on the cameo? With Samuel gone, who could fill in these blanks? I pushed the chest back again, wondering how I'd ever find the answers now.

I stripped off and stood under the shower in Samuel's bathroom, turning the hot water to steaming and letting it cascade over me for as long as I could stand it. A map of my tribulations was etched all over my body. The cartography of my failures. Reddish welts still demarcating the ribs hurt in the accident, the burn and tenderness of my arm, yellowing bruises in the various places Shim had laid hands on me, blemishes on my lip, scrapes on my face, the herringbone scar the surgeon made when he sewed up my leg. I scrubbed hard to wash away my sins.

I had no choice but to put my old clothes back on because Samuel's were too small. All the garments in my dressing room had been torn to shreds. Using my landline, I called the police. The new owner's insurance company would expect me to report the vandalism right away. The clerk assured me someone would be sent over immediately.

An emphatic knock on my door came half an hour later. The police don't have to be buzzed up like the rest of us common folk. I opened it to see the detective built like a wrestler with pockmarked cheeks standing beside Vernon, his uniformed sidekick. "I see you're back from your travels, Madison," Gentile said and walked in.

He held up his hand. "Don't panic. I'm not here to arrest you."

He placed himself in the middle of my living room and revolved slowly as if he were at the Louvre and wanted to take in all the masterpieces while standing in one spot.

"Somebody doesn't like you," he said. "Why am I not surprised?"

"I came home to this. You've been demoted, I guess," I replied. "Chasing after B and Es?"

"Ever the smartass, Madison. That's healthy, actually. Meeting adversity with humor or something like that."

I swallowed a stinging retort. There was no point adding any more problems to my catalog of misery. "Why are you here?" I asked. I was afraid to hear his answer. Was he really telling the truth about not arresting me? Had they been asking questions about Laurel and suspected me of being involved?

"Just cleaning up some details," he said. "Let's have a talk."

We went into Samuel's study and sat around the worktable he'd used when he wanted to spread out maps or illustrations. Gentile asked to hear my version, again, of the events on the night Hal had been killed. I decided to tell him the whole story of the past weeks with two exceptions. I mentioned nothing about Laurel. If he wanted to raise it I'd answer truthfully, but I had no intention of offering myself up on a platter. Nor did I reveal the true nature of Tomas's discovery.

Occasionally Gentile would ask me to repeat something, but in the main he listened quietly. Vernon scribbled in his notebook. The detective seemed shocked only once when I described the cataclysm at the North Gate Cemetery. But he appeared to believe me; that surprised me.

"So he's dead then, Ward," he said.

"I don't know. They flew him to a burn unit. He's still in Kuwait."

"That reporter Ari Zakar died. It was all over the media here. He filmed his own death apparently."

His words brought back the image of Ari falling, the camera toppling off his shoulder. I pressed my hand to my eyes in a vain attempt to obliterate the sight.

Gentile took out a tissue and patted his forehead. I'd noticed earlier it was growing shiny with sweat. He got up and walked over to the window, stood there with his back to me.

"I did some looking into the woman, Eris Haines or Hansen. She's had a checkered history. She was the subject of an outstanding warrant for a criminal assault on another matter. And I believe she was likely responsible for your car accident."

If I'd been asked earlier whether anything else

could shock me I would have laughed in disbelief. But this did. I pushed back my chair and rushed over so I could look him in the face. "How did you find out?"

"Our people working the stolen vehicle rings. They seized a pickup in a body shop raid. Matched the paint and the collision marks to our alert. Your car was deliberately driven off the road. It was traced to her." He paused. "Mind you, your speed was excessive. Whether that was a contributing factor or not, we'll never know."

I wasn't responsible for Samuel's death. A huge sigh traveled through my frame and left me, as if an exorcist had just banished a demon. "Thank you for telling me," I said.

"We'll write this up. I'll want you to come in tomorrow to sign off on the report."

"That's fine," I said. "I'll do anything you want. What about Hal's murder?"

"It will probably end up in the cold case docket. I've got nothing but suspicions and your story at this point."

As I walked him to the front door Gentile pointed to the mess. "Vernon will stay for a bit and document the damage. Give your insurance company my name. I wouldn't hold my breath on finding the vandals."

The ensuing weeks were busy ones. A wire transfer arrived, authorized before Ari's death, for about seventy thousand, the amount he'd persuaded Tomas to part with from the proceeds of the condo sale. A fraction of what our place was worth. I hadn't expected to hear from Tomas, but I imagined his sorrow over Ari was extreme.

The greater portion of the money went toward the next year of Evelyn's care. As soon as I had my life somewhat back on track I went to see her. She lived in a Midtown studio apartment, in a featureless brown-brick housing complex. After I knocked at her door I could hear the creak of her wheelchair, then the door opened and before I even had a chance to step in, she leaned forward. I barely had time to crouch down to her level when she hugged me. I should really say clung to me, for it seemed long minutes before she was even willing to release me from her embrace.

She was already in her dressing gown and pajamas, so I'd almost come too late. As much as she could with her arthritis, she scrunched her knobby fingers and pressed them to her cheeks. Tears gathered in her eyes. Her words tumbled out. "I was afraid I might never see you again. I tried and tried. The hospital wouldn't let me in. Only close relatives, they said. I called so many times. Wrote a letter even. Did you find it?" She stopped almost in mid-sentence and peered at my face. "What's happened to you? Those marks on your face?"

"It's nothing, Evie. Don't worry about it. I'm here now. Everything's fine." I wheeled her over to the couch and sat beside her. I'm ashamed to admit this was the first time I'd been to her home. Samuel had cared for her, and when we got together it had always been on outings he'd arranged or for dinner or weekend afternoons at our place. The times he'd been away, he'd hired someone to help her out.

The apartment was cramped but neat as a pin. How she managed to keep it that way with her disability I couldn't imagine. On a table beside the couch sat a pill box sectioned into the days of the week, a glass half full of tea, and a box of tissues. She had a small TV, radio, books, and things on a wall unit; a simple kitchen and bathroom; and a recessed area for her bed. There was one piece of fine furniture, a buffet that once belonged to Samuel. The top was crowded with framed photographs, one picture of her and Samuel, all the rest of me—the two of us walking in Central Park, me as a toddler holding a dripping ice-cream cone, school pictures from elementary through to university. That came as a bit of a surprise.

I'd made up my mind to say nothing about Hal's game or my time in Iraq; it would only upset her. "Evie, sorry it's taken me this long to visit you. Getting over the accident and feeling lost without Samuel took its toll. I had to deal with it in my own way."

"You know he's sold your place? I wanted to warn you. Samuel was going to tell you when he came back, but of course he didn't get a chance. I begged him not to do it. It was your home but he wouldn't listen."

I wondered how much she knew about the whole affair. "Did he say why he wanted to sell it?"

"To help the museum. To protect its treasures. He was a good man but he went too far. He sold your birthright. That wasn't fair."

I smiled and said, "It's done now and I'm managing okay." Samuel and Evelyn had had such a long acquaintance, and I knew they'd often shared confidences. "Speaking of treasures, you remember my little casket, the one Samuel gave me on my birthday?"

"Of course. You played with it so many times."

"Samuel once said it was part of my inheritance. But I've gotten to thinking. Is there anything else? Did he talk to you about my parents? Are there any photos I didn't see? Letters? Anything like that?"

"There is nothing else."

"It's just, I've started to question ... to wonder about my past in Turkey."

In what seemed like an unconscious gesture, she rubbed her hand over her heart. "When I first came to this country I told myself, 'You have a new chance. If you keep remembering bad things about the past they will become like demons flying around inside you. Forget them.' That's what I did. Don't bring trouble to yourself by asking about these things, John. It will not help you." She'd kept her eyes averted from me as she spoke, which was quite unlike her. Perhaps another time, if there was anything to reveal, I'd find her more forthcoming.

We talked for a while longer but she started to fade. I got her settled in for the night, dismayed to see the little huffs of breath she let out with the pain of

moving off her wheelchair and getting into bed. I gave
her a kiss on the forehead and said goodnight.

A few days later we visited Samuel's grave
together. The balance had shifted. The appeal of the
bad-boy image had faded for me, and Samuel's saintly
aura had been modified by the very real repercussions
of the disaster he'd set in motion. I was thankful for
this reunion with him and for the restoration of good
memories, untarnished by guilt.

I rented a small apartment in Astoria and tried to revive
my business. I had limited success because the after-
math of the accident still clung to me. Once innuendo
stakes out its territory, it isn't readily vanquished by
facts. Commissions dribbled in, but not fast enough.
So much of the business is social. Hosting gatherings,
lunches at good restaurants, dressing the part. My
career looked unsalvageable unless I could magically
produce some cash.

One incident gave me a ray of hope. Among my
large backlog of mail was a letter I'd received from a
London solicitor at a prestigious Lincoln's Inn Fields
address. It came in a plain manila envelope; curious,
I tore it open. Out fell an auction house catalog and
a letter addressed to me on crisp white bond from
the solicitor—Arthur S. Newhouse. He'd written at
the behest of his client, who wanted me to represent
him at a Sherrods auction on October 13 to bid on
a seventeenth-century manuscript. When I saw the

commission—25 percent of a purchase price estimated to reach at least a hundred and fifty thousand pounds— my jaw dropped. And an advance would be given to cover expenses.

But there was a hitch. There always was with good things coming my way it seemed. Once I'd successfully bid on the manuscript, I was on no account to attempt to read it. "Apparently the document has a repellent history," Newhouse wrote. "This requirement is for your own protection."

The commission would put me back on my feet, no question, but I'd learned not to trust offers until I actually saw some green. Just as I was picking up my phone to contact the London office, a call came through. Corinne on the other end. And what she had to tell me drove all thoughts about strange seventeenth-century manuscripts from my mind.

Thirty-nine

The new information Corinne had gathered sent me into a frenzy of activity. All the time not spent getting my life up and running again I devoted to this new pursuit.

My endeavors bore fruit and reached their zenith on the evening of Wednesday, September 10. I walked through the doors at 8:30 P.M., a little early for the meeting I'd arranged. The gallery was empty, but I heard a rustling sound from the office adjacent to the showroom. Soon enough Phillip Anthony emerged, shutting the door behind him.

It amused me to see his shocked expression after he set eyes on me. His mouth flapped open and shut like a barn door in a spring storm. It took him a minute to find his voice.

"Why, John," he finally got out, "how charming to see you. This is unexpected." He snapped out of his momentary nervousness and peered at me through his thick glasses. "What's happened to your face? It looks like you've been losing at boxing matches, you poor fellow."

"I've been traveling a lot, Phillip, over some rough terrain."

"Pick up any goodies? I'm always in the market, as you know."

"Nothing that would interest you."

He feigned disappointment. "The rumor mill suggests you've met with some hard times. This business can be flighty, like women. You think you have things in hand and they end up deserting you." He paused to give me time to fully appreciate his wit.

"I'll manage. Thanks for your sympathy anyway."

"I know this is a delicate matter, but if you're inclined to dispose of anything from Samuel's collection, I'd like to be helpful."

Translation, you'll get a quarter of its real worth.

"Actually I'm doing everything possible to keep his collection intact. That's what Samuel would have wanted."

He mistook my words. "Ah, the entire body of work. Well, we'd have to consider a lower sum for that kind of volume."

"Phillip, I have no intention of selling it."

With an exaggerated flourish he stretched out his thin arm to look at his watch. His shirt cuff rode up, exposing liver spots and gray hairs sprouting on fish belly–white skin. "I'd love to have a good long chat, but I'm expecting a client. He'll be arriving any minute."

"I'm your client, Phillip."

A frown creased his brows and high, shiny forehead. "I thought you just turned me down."

"What I meant was, I arranged the meeting. The name was Bernard White, I believe."

"He's supposed to authenticate an object for a buyer. How do you know that? Are you representing the buyer?"

"There is no Bernard White. A bit of witchcraft on my part. I made the whole thing up."

He dropped the phony patter. "You bastard. I delayed two other bidders because I thought your phantom client would give us a better price. You've wasted my valuable time. Get out of here."

I suppose that was the moment my impression of the man underwent a permanent change. A kind of instant shift, the way the sun at dawn will suddenly pop over the horizon, revealing the landscape as it really is. The dilettante disappeared; inside lurked another personality. I recognized him in a few of the wealthiest collectors who'd crossed my path. Men, always. A ruthlessness at their core.

I started walking toward his office. "Why don't we go into your office for that long chat?"

"I see no need for that." With undignified haste he hurried toward the door and stood in front of me, arms folded, like a bull terrier guarding its bone.

"I know she's in there, Phillip. I've been waiting across the street for over an hour. I saw her come in."

"That's none of your business, John."

The door creaked open. Phillip glanced anxiously behind him then stepped aside. Laurel entered the room. "Don't be silly, Phillip. He obviously knows." There was a hint of tension around her eyes, but that was the only sign of stress. She'd dropped her hippie look and now resembled an Upper East Side matron— expensive fitted jacket, pencil skirt that stopped just short of her knees, Christian Louboutin pumps. A choker of opals and small rose-cut diamonds hugged her throat.

A burst of rage at seeing her nearly got the best of me, but I held it in and tried to concentrate on my end goal.

"Who would have thought, Laurel, your new career choice would be major crime?"

Phillip, ever the gallant, jumped in to defend her. "I don't think sarcasm is called for. You can leave now."

"I'll go when our business is concluded."

Laurel patted his arm. "Nothing will be achieved by quarreling. There's no point ending up with bad feelings."

Bad feelings? After all the deaths she's caused, what version of reality is she working with?

Phillip opened his mouth to object but thought better of it. He went to the front door and punched a code into the locking mechanism on the wall. A lattice-like grid of brass dropped down over the front window. He ushered us into his spacious office, a plush affair. Furniture designed by Gehry, a Bakhshaish rug covering most of the floor, and a Tintoretto resting on an easel in a corner of the room. A flat-screen TV mounted on the wall opposite his desk was probably a marketing aid for his sales.

"Nice bling," I said to Laurel.

She fingered the necklace. "An heirloom from Mina. Frankly, I think it suits me better."

An heirloom she never wanted you to have.

Phillip closed the door and went to his desk. He got out a bottle of Rabelais cognac and poured snifters for the three of us.

"So," I said, "a lot of this is guesswork, but I'll bet I'm pretty close to the mark. Hal hung around on the fringes of the alchemy group but never made it as a central player. I suspect he didn't know everyone's identities. Ward was Saturn; Eris, Venus; and Lazarus, Mars. Shim was too damaged to become a full member. You, Phillip, were Mercury. I'd thought Jupiter at first, but you don't have the creativity to run the whole show. Mina, the witch, was originally Jupiter. When she died you saw an opportunity, Laurel, and took over."

She fiddled with her necklace again. "Guess I'll have to take compliments wherever I can find them. How did you figure it out?"

"Eris had a Venus tattoo, and then in the Baghdad hotel room Ward rolled up his sleeves, revealing a tattoo on his arm too, a lowercase *h* with a cross on the vertical. The symbol for Saturn. You'd told me Hal was Saturn. In his letter to me Hal indicated five opponents. If he was Saturn, that meant he'd have to be including himself as one of them. A little too obtuse. Knowing Mina well, even if your relationship was conflicted, you were in an ideal position to control events. You were living in her house for Christ's sake! Gip told me Hal had never planned to get back with you. He just agreed to let you stay at the Sheridan Square location temporarily, that's all. Staff know every move the residents make. That's how they keep their jobs.

"Once I got back to New York, a friend of mine broke the barriers hiding your identities and confirmed everything. So you had the connection with Ward, not Tomas. How did Ward fit in?"

"That preposterous man," Phillip snorted. "Fancied himself some sort of grandee when he was no more than a cook and bottle washer for us. I'd occasionally broker some of his sales, that's how I got to know him. He took all that alchemy business seriously, as did his band of criminals. Can you imagine? Shim, the monster Eris traveled with, actually blew himself up trying to make gold from lead. Did Ward show off his private 'museum'? A mixed bag, the stuff in there. Several of the manuscripts were rare and he had a few nice Near Eastern objects, but in the main, it was pretty low grade, a good portion of it counterfeit."

Flattery always worked with Phillip. "Smart of you, then, pitching Ward's group first against Samuel, then Hal, and finally me, while you two hid behind them. And Tomas's talented plan to annihilate them in Iraq took them permanently out of the picture.

On home ground Tomas had a much better chance of defeating them. Once they were dead, nothing could be traced back to you. Quite impressive."

"That is conjecture, Madison," Phillip said. "You have nothing to base it on."

I sipped my cognac and savored the subtle flavours. "Hanna Jaffrey, who I learned was much closer to Ward than he let on, failed to steal the engraving after Samuel discovered it. Lazarus and Shim eventually dealt with her. Lazarus tried to steal the engraving from the Baghdad museum during the looting, but Samuel had anticipated that so you missed out a second time. It must have been tremendously frustrating not to get it after so much effort.

"When my brother died and I was incapacitated in the hospital, you conscripted Hal to search our condo. That's when everything really spun out of control. Hal lied. He said he'd found nothing, intending to sell the engraving and keep the proceeds for himself. Did he know what he really had?"

"He'd picked up on the idea that it had something to do with transforming base metals into gold. He knew the engraving was the Book of Nahum and realized how much money it would be worth."

"So you used Ward and his people to keep the maximum pressure on me, harassing me, making me think I was running for my life. And they'd always known where I was because of the tracking device. You removed it to gain my trust, Laurel. By then I was confiding in you, so it wasn't necessary anymore.

All those crocodile tears you shed over Hal. What a shock it must have been when you found out he was peddling the thing.

"Eris confronted him. He lied again, only the second time he threw me into the mix. His game came at you out of left field."

Laurel had been listening intently. "Latching onto you was our only option once we realized you genuinely did not know where the engraving was. Hal included some elements that only you would recognize, and we had no way of solving the game ourselves. Certainly not in a short time, anyway. It was easier to get you to do the work. Phillip thought you'd chase the engraving just so you could sell it, but I wasn't so sure."

I searched for any sign of guilt, a slight flush perhaps in her cheeks to suggest a hint of shame, but could find none.

"I must admit," Phillip said, "it was rather fun watching you getting battered."

"And yet here I am. I succeeded and you two failed. Were you actually going to go through the farce of an exchange at High Bridge Park?" I asked.

"Of course not," Laurel said.

Phillip peeked over his glasses at Laurel like an impatient schoolteacher. "What's the point of going on about this? We don't owe him any explanations. We beat you at the game in the end, Madison. It's your sour luck."

"Humor me, Phillip. I've earned some answers,

and unless you want a really nasty scene when you try to throw me out, I'll get them."

I turned back to Laurel. "You and Phillip set up a double sting, keeping Ward and his people occupied with stalking me. Unbeknownst to us you two also kept a check on Tomas. When he did an end run on me and picked up the engraving, you got lucky. How did you get it from him? Did you have a weapon?"

"Could you honestly picture me waving a gun around?" Laurel giggled. "Only a weapon of the monetary variety. Phillip had the connections, so we could get a much better price for the engraving. Tomas saw to reason quite rapidly. And we let him shoot a photo of it. That's all he really needed. This was your own fault."

"How's that?"

Laurel tapped the rim of her glass. "You didn't bother to tell us, John, about your plans to leave town. When you went to the Port Authority and Ward found out about it he freaked, thinking we'd pushed you too far and you were going to bolt. So we had to put the kidnapping into play. Tomas, on the other hand, actually believed you'd take the engraving to the FBI. If it weren't for that, he might not have given in to Phillip and me."

"While you kept Ward and Eris preoccupied with me, Tomas headed back to Iraq."

"Hal wasn't the only one who could stage a good trap."

"I can see how Tomas gained, but what was in it for Ari?"

"Ari was never involved. Ward and his people were chasing a dream. Finding the treasure was also what Tomas most wanted. Both saw the engraving as primarily a means to an end."

I threw back the rest of my drink and stood up. "After all the hardship I've gone through, the least you can do is show it to me."

"Dear boy," Phillip interjected, "we're under no obligation to do anything."

"Maybe you won't have any choice." He might be haughty but I hadn't come empty handed. I had my finger on a trigger and it was still waiting to be squeezed.

Laurel patted his hand. Phillip actually blushed with pleasure. "There's no point playing hardball, is there?" she said.

Phillip took a remote out of his desk and pressed a key. The TV screen slid silently to one side. Nahum's engraving sat in a shelved recess beside a Michelangelo drawing and what looked like a Vermeer.

The engraving had the typical greenish hue of olivine basalt, its color deepening from exposure to oxygen over the ages. It hadn't yet been cleaned. I could see reddish dust lodged in the impressions. That made sense. They wouldn't clean it because the dust could be analyzed to confirm the tablet's age and legitimacy.

I ran my hand over the eight-pointed stars Tomas had referred to. The piece had an air of majesty, as if Nahum's passion had somehow given life and spirit to the rock. I felt a moment of sadness for the prophet whose grand plan had come to nothing. After thousands of years, the riches he'd intended for the Kingdom of Judah would remain in Assyrian hands. "When you sell it, I suppose Tomas gets a cut?"

"Of course. The proceeds from Samuel's estate would never have been enough to finance all the restoration work on the temple and its objects." Phillip pressed the remote again to move the TV screen back into place.

"Well, for my end of things, I'll take the Vermeer."

Phillip let out a cynical laugh and held up the bottle of Rabelais, raising his eyebrows. I shook my head. Neither he nor Laurel had touched their drinks.

"I'm a bit surprised at your willingness to forgo the treasure cache. The engraving's worth twenty million, but the value of Midas's hoard is incalculable."

"Bird in hand, my friend, bird in hand," Phillip said.

"I'm not your friend."

I'd obviously succeeded in stirring Phillip up because he snapped back at me. "I thought we were having a civilized conversation. Let me finish. Ward deluded himself about how easy the hoard would be to move. Realistically, how could he get control of the temple treasures and transport them back here, even if he'd won his battle with Tomas?"

"He had a lot of muscle, private contractors."

"Not enough under the circumstances. The

museum looting turned out to be too great an embarrassment. After the FBI sent out alerts, getting caught even with a small item would land you in serious trouble. Not to mention local citizens. You don't think they'd know what was going on? You could hire a whole battalion of thieves without a prayer of getting past them. And the temple is on the property of the Chaldean Church. They'd just look the other way while Ward loaded up the trucks? Catholics don't part easily with their valuables. I predict the find will never be made public. Laurel and I are content with our paltry share."

"The Chaldean Church is doing its best to protect antiquities in the middle of a war. They're facing threats daily and still trying to restore Nahum's tomb and the synagogue. You don't have a decent bone in your body, Phillip."

He smiled and let my insult float away. "You'll be getting no cut, John, least of all that Vermeer. Good Lord, it's worth as much as Nahum's engraving."

"The engraving's stolen. You can't peddle it safely."

"There's no evidence to suggest that. No museum records, no identifying marks."

I supposed now was as good a time as any to turn the tables. I pulled my phone out of my pocket and held it up. "I made a call on this before I walked in here. The line has been open the entire time. On the other end, a friend has taped every single word."

This didn't produce the desired effect. Laurel let out a little grunt of amusement, and Phillip laughed outright. "That old trick. Did you really think I'd fall for it? I'm not brain dead. My office is for private conversations. I have clients for whom discretion is a necessity; you never know who may be trying to listen in. There are a lot of useful technologies these days, and I like to employ them. Wireless won't work in here."

When I checked my phone I saw the message that the network could not be found. "I'll go to the police then."

"They didn't even believe you about Hal. They'd need a warrant to search my gallery, and that has to be based on evidence. The engraving will be long gone before that eventuality."

Laurel lifted her shoulders slightly as if to say there was nothing she could do, the matter was out of her hands.

I could feel the dam cracking, my anger breaking out again. "Do Ari and Samuel mean nothing to you?"

"Don't start preaching, John. You just wanted it for yourself. You went to that cemetery the first time without anyone knowing. The caretaker described you." There was no malice in her tone, if anything, only a slight air of amusement that she'd put one over on me. It seemed schizophrenic, a kind of moral blankness, her ability to treat all this as a game, utterly oblivious to the consequences.

Phillip let me out. I walked a half block east to an electrician's van, checked to make sure neither Laurel nor Phillip were watching, and called out. The side door of the van cranked open. Gentile looked worried. "We got nothing but static," he said.

"Phillip Anthony blocked his office for wireless." I undid my shirt, pulled at the wires and tape, and handed him the tape recorder.

I didn't know the man well, but I'd have thought smiling was a foreign expression for him. He proved me wrong when a broad grin lit up his face. "I'll take the old-fashioned stuff any day. Smart of you to think about doing both; otherwise, he might have suspected something. Did you get it all?"

"Everything. They're hung, drawn, and quartered."

While he and an agent from the FBI's Art Theft Program listened to the recording, I watched the screen inside the van broadcasting views of the gallery's front door. Light filtered through the window grate, and I thought I could detect shadows of the two of them moving around inside. There was no back exit. Neither Laurel nor Phillip ventured out. With any luck this would turn out to be a triple win if the Vermeer and Michelangelo drawing shared equally dubious origins.

"Okay, that sounds great," Gentile said. The FBI agent signaled his agreement and made a call. Within minutes a couple of unmarked cars pulled up at the curb in front of the gallery. I stayed for the pleasure of seeing Phillip and Laurel hauled out in restraints.

✸

Before meeting Gentile at his office the next day for a full report, I decided I needed to cool down and trudged the eight or so blocks to Kenny's.

Diane was tending bar when I sauntered through the front door. She could manage only a weak smile after I sat down, which told me her feelings were still tender about the incident with the police.

"I came to make up," I said.

She acknowledged me with a curt nod, got a cloth from under the bar, and began zealously wiping down the counter. I noticed, though, that she hadn't moved very far away.

"Hey," I said. "Is this the end of a great relationship?"

"Lying. That's not my definition of a great relationship."

"There were extenuating circumstances."

"That's what they always say."

"Your fortune was dead on. Sadly for me."

This sparked her interest. "Why?" Then she noticed my face. "What happened to you?"

"I was hunted by five masked assassins, one of whom fried himself trying to make gold. I was shot at, Tasered, nearly bitten by a giant spider, kidnapped, and whisked away to a foreign land."

She had trouble suppressing a grin and tried to hide it by shaking her head. "John, you're too much. Dare I ask why you were singled out for such punishment?"

"They believed I held the secret to King Midas's treasure."

Diane couldn't hold it in anymore and burst out laughing. "Well, that's so off the wall it doesn't qualify as a lie. I've missed you despite everything, but we have to make a pact."

"I don't have any razors on me. We'd need that for the exchange of blood."

"Verbal is just fine. In all seriousness, I want your promise you won't lie to me again."

I held out my hand; she reached for it and closed her own over mine.

"And we'll have to agree on no more fortunes."

"Done," she said.

We chatted for a while longer before a flock of new customers took up her attention. I recalled her last prophecy: *happiness follows sorrow.* However much joy I got from achieving retribution, seeing Laurel and Phillip under arrest just plugged the hole temporarily. Losing my brother and Ari to them would always remain a searing wound.

From Iraq, I'd brought one memento home. I took it out and held it in the palm of my hand. A golden apple, every pucker in the skin, the creases, veins, and finely serrated edge of its one leaf so perfectly formed you would have sworn someone had, with the touch of a finger, turned a piece of real fruit into gold.

I stayed until closing time. Bleecker even at this late hour was teeming with people. Already I felt a little out of place here. Subtle changes. Like the slowing of a friendship when one of you moves on to other things. The night air had a touch of chill. A few leaves drifted onto the sidewalk, early harbingers of the year closing in on itself. I looked up to see the lighted windows of my old home. A stranger leaned on the balcony railing the way I used to, a drink in his hand. I waved to him. He tipped his glass to me. A small omen, I hoped, of better things to come.

Mesopotamian Culture

Mesopotamia is a Greek word describing the "land between two rivers"—the region bounded by the Tigris and Euphrates rivers approximately corresponding to modern-day Iraq. Professor Leo Oppenheim's highly regarded book *Ancient Mesopotamia: Portrait of a Dead Civilization* is recommended as a starting point for anyone interested in learning more about the early history of this region. What follows is the briefest of snapshots of the three pre-eminent Mesopotamian cultures.

SUMERIANS

It is not known whether Sumerians were indigenous to southern Mesopotamia or migrated there. Their language group is not Semitic and has no proven affiliates. Intensive agriculture, irrigation, and the specialization of labor created conditions for Sumerians to develop the first city-states ruled by priest-kings. Cities were temple-centered and under the protection of a specific deity.

Sumerian achievements were so exceptional as to represent almost an evolutionary advance in human accomplishment. The Sumerians developed geometry and the sexagesimal (base sixty) numeral system still used today (for example, measurement of angles, the minute); the lunar/solar calendar; the wheel; the early chariot; and cuneiform, the first writing system.

Periods of Sumerian Dominance (B.C.)

Early Dynastic	
(Sumerian city-states)	3100–2390
Neo-Sumerian	2168–2050

ASSYRIANS

The Assyrian homeland occupied the territory between the Tigris and Euphrates rivers in northern Mesopotamia (the area just north of Baghdad today), which had sufficient rainfall to carry out agriculture without need for intensive irrigation. Ancient Assyrians were Semitic-speaking tribes noted for their prowess with the bow and superb horsemanship. Assyrian dominance ebbed and flowed, but at the height of their power in the seventh century B.C., they controlled the entire Levant area of the Near East, Egypt, Phrygia, and what is now southwestern Iran. Assyrians developed a complex system of government and are considered to have built the first empire.

Periods of Assyrian Dominance (B.C.)

Old Assyrian Period	1869–1837
Middle Assyrian Period	1350–1000
Neo-Assyrian Period	883–612

Assyrian Kings, 722–609 B.C.

Sargon II	722–705
Sennacherib	705–681
Esarhaddon	c. 681–669
Ashurbanipal	c. 669–627
Ashur-etil-ilani	c. 631–627
Sîn-shar-iskkun	c. 627–612
Ashur-uballit II	c. 612–609

BABYLONIANS

Babylonians were also Semitic speakers; their name is derived from Babylon, where the kings resided. At its height the Babylonian empire controlled territory stretching from modern-day Egypt to Iran. The sixth king of Babylon, Hammurabi, developed the first code of law. Other achievements included advances in architecture, mathematics, astronomy, and astrology. Babylonians introduced the zodiac, and a Babylonian, Seleucus of Selecucia, may have been the first to propose the heliocentric model of astronomy, describing the earth and planets as revolving around the sun.

Periods of Babylonian Dominance (B.C.)	
Old Babylonian Period	1950–1651
Middle Babylonian Period	1651–1157
Neo-Babylonian Period	625–539

Notes

Prologue

1   *The Gods have abandoned us:* Alex Whitaker (trans.), Sumerian Home Page, www.ancient-wisdom.co.uk/iraqur.htm. "The Lamentation over the Destruction of Ur" was originally translated by Samuel Noah Kramer, 1940, University of Chicago.

Chapter 4

34   *Bruce Springsteen was headlining: Crawdaddy!* February 2005. From the Kenny's Castaways website describing a Bruce Springsteen performance at the pub.

Chapter 8

82   *Every stone in it has been soaked in blood:* Lieutenant-General George Molesworth, *Afghanistan, 1919: An Account of Operations in the Third Afghan War* (London and New York: Asia Publishing House, 1962).

Chapter 11

120   *As to Hezekiah, the Judahite:* Israel Finkelstein
      and Neil Asher Silberman, *The Bible Unearthed:
      Archaeology's New Vision of Ancient Israel and the
      Origin of Sacred Texts* (New York: Simon & Schuster,
      2002), 260.

122   *Ashurbanipal had beheaded:* H.W.F. Saggs, *The
      Might That Was Assyria* (London: Sidgwick &
      Jackson, 1984), 113.

122   *Whosoever shall carry off:* Sir Ernest Alfred Wallis
      Budge, *The Babylonian Story of the Deluge and
      the Epic of Gilgamesh with an Account of the Royal
      Libraries at Nineveh* (London: British Museum
      Dept. of Egyptian and Assyrian Antiquities, 1920).

123   *The Book of the Vision of Nahum the Elkoshite:*
      Nahum 2–3 (Jewish Publication Society Bible,
      1917).

Chapter 13

145   *That which is below:* Adam McLean, "The Emerald
      Tablet of Hermes," The Alchemy Web Site, www.
      levity.com/alchemy/emerald.html.

147   *It is we who through our glance:* Michael Baigent and
      Richard Leigh, *The Elixir and the Stone* (London:
      Random House, 1997), 19–26.

147   *As a humorous aside, our own King John of England:*
      Ibid., 70–71.

148   *The bell, for example, represents the correspondence:*
      Ibid., 62.

Chapter 20

200   *Who wrote* Mutus Liber*?:* Adam McLean, The Alchemy Web Site, www.levity.com/alchemy.

Chapter 21

208   *The Judean Hebrew people of that time:* Israel Finkelstein and Neil Asher Silberman, *The Bible Unearthed: Archaeology's New Vision of Ancient Israel and the Origin of Sacred Texts* (New York: Simon & Schuster, 2002), 153–54.

211   *The Book of Nahum was not a prophecy but an eyewitness account:* Laurel Lanner, *Who Will Lament Her? The Feminine and the Fantastic in the Book of Nahum* (New York: T&T Clark, 2006), 7.

Chapter 25

239   *Upon the eleventh day:* Brookes More (trans.), *Metamorphoses (Books 1–5)* (Boston: Cornhill, 1922), 19.

Chapter 34

325   *And the queen is uncovered:* Nahum 2:8 (Jewish Publication Society Bible, 1917).

326   *Take ye the spoil of silver:* Ibid.

326   *Where is the den of lions:* Ibid.

327   *This is a place where the lions walk:* Ibid.

Chapter 36

344   *And the woman was arrayed:* Revelation 17:4 (King James Study Bible).

349   *And the beast:* Revelation 13:2 (King James Study Bible).

Bibliography

The following books, newspaper articles, and websites have been instrumental to my research. I recommend them all as fascinating reads.

Books

Baigent, Michael, and Richard Leigh. *The Elixir and the Stone*. London: Random House, 1997.

Black, Jeremy, and Anthony Green; illustrations by Tessa Rickards. *Gods, Demons and Symbols of Ancient Mesopotamia: An Illustrated Dictionary*. Austin: University of Texas Press, 2003.

Blech, Benjamin, and Roy Doliner. *The Sistine Secrets: Michelangelo's Forbidden Messages in the Heart of the Vatican*. New York: HarperCollins, 2009.

Bogdanos, Matthew, with William Patrick. *Thieves of Baghdad*. New York: Bloomsbury, 2005.

Finkelstein, Israel, and Neil Asher Silberman. *The Bible Unearthed: Archaeology's New Vision of Ancient Israel and the Origin of Sacred Texts*. New York: Simon & Schuster, 2002.

García Martínez, Florentino. *The Dead Sea Scrolls Translated: The Qumran Texts in English.* Translated by W.G.E. Watson. Leiden, the Netherlands: E.J. Brill, 1996.

George, Donny, Micah Goren, and Marie Hélène Carleton. *The Looting of the Iraq Museum, Baghdad.* New York: Harry N. Abrams, 2005.

Grimal, Pierre. *Dictionary of Classical Mythology.* Edited by Stephen Kershaw from the translation by A.R. Maxwell-Hyslop. London: Penguin Group, 1991.

Hedges, Chris, and Laila Al-Arian. *Collateral Damage: America's War Against Iraqi Civilians.* New York: Nation Books, 2008.

Hersh, Seymour M. *Chain of Command: The Road from 9/11 to Abu Ghraib.* New York: HarperCollins, 2004.

Kuhrt, Amelie. *The Ancient Near East.* London: Routledge, 1995.

Lanner, Laurel. *Who Will Lament Her? The Feminine and the Fantastic in the Book of Nahum.* New York: T&T Clark, 2006.

More, Brookes, trans. *Metamorphoses (Books 1–5).* Boston: Cornhill, 1922.

Rhea Nemet-Nejat, Karen. *Daily Life in Mesopotamia.* Westport, CT; London: Greenwood Press, 1998.

Scaggs, H.W. *The Might That Was Assyria.* London: Sidgwick & Jackson, 1984.

Wallis Budge, E.A. *The Babylonian Story of the Deluge as Told by Assyrian Tablets from Nineveh.* London: British Museum, 1920.

Wayland Barber, Elizabeth, and Paul T. Barber. *When They Severed Earth from Sky: How the Human Mind Shapes Myth.* Princeton, NJ: Princeton University Press, 2004.

Weidener, Jay, and Vincent Bridges. *The Mysteries of the Great Cross of Hendaye, Alchemy and the End of Time*. Rochester, VT: Destiny Books, 1999.

Newspaper Articles and Websites

Aprim, Fred. "Alqosh—The Mother of Assyria," August 22, 2004, www.fredaprim.com/pdfs/2004/Alqosh.pdf.

Asser, Martin. "Baghdad Diary: British Cemetery," *BBC News Online*, April 24, 2003, http://news.bbc.co.uk/2/hi/middle_east/2974111.stm.

Bates, Clair. "Dying to Look Good: French King's Mistress Killed by Drinking Gold Elixir of Youth," *Mail Online*, December 22, 2009, www.dailymail.co.uk/sciencetech/article-1236916/Dying-look-good-French-kings-mistress-killed-gold-elixir-youth.html.

Bogdanos, Colonel Matthew. "U.S. Concludes Investigation of Looting of Iraqi National Museum in Baghdad," *Culture Kiosque Art and Archaeology News*, September 25, 2003, www.culturekiosque.com/art/news/baghdadmuseum.html.

Bowser, Jonathon Earl, from an article by Jerry Jeffries, "The Perfection of Number," *The Memorial Website of Jerry Wayne Jeffries*, October 27, 2009, www.jerryjeffries.net/jeb7.html.

Clarfield, Geoffrey. "Stop the Appeasement of Art and Antiquities Thieves," *The Globe and Mail*, July 5, 2008, A19.

Darby, Gary. *Durer's Magic Square*, May 18, 2009, http://delphiforfun.org/programs/durersSquare.htm.

Deblauwe, Francis. *The Iraq War and Archaeology Blog*, http://iwa.univie.ac.at/iraqarchive12.html.

"An Eye for an Eye," *Knowledgerush*, 2009, www.knowledgerush.com/kr/encyclopedia/An_eye_for_an_eye.

Filkins, Dexter. "Among the Ghosts: Heroes and Grand Plans," *The New York Times*, July 9, 2006, www.nytimes.com/2006/07/09/weekinreview/09filkins.html.

Fisk, Robert. "Untouchable Ministries," *The Independent*, April 14, 2003, www.independent.co.uk/opinion/commentators/fisk/americans-defend-two-untouchable-ministries-from-the-hordes-of-looters-594419.html.

Freer, Ian. "The Picatrix: Lunar Mansions in Western Astrology," *The Astrological Association of Great Britain*, 1994, www.astrologer.com/aanet/pub/journal/picatrix.html.

Grant, Paul J. "A Display of Heraldrie: by John Guillim," Paul Grant's home page, July 9, 2007, www.btinternet.com/~paul.j.grant/guillim.

Jastow Jr., Morris, and George A. Barton. "Astarte Worship Among the Hebrews," *Online Encyclopaedia of Mythology and Folklore*, August 7, 2010, www.themystica.com/mythical-folk/articles/ishtar.html.

"Kenny's Castaways: History," Kenny's Castaways home page, n.d., www.kennyscastaways.net/history.html.

MacLeod, Donald. "U.S. Lobby Could Threaten Iraqi Heritage," *The Guardian*, April 10, 2003, www.guardian.co.uk/education/2003/apr/10/highereducation.iraq.

McLean, Adam. "The Alchemy Web Site," *Levity.com*, n.d., www.levity.com/alchemy.

Moore, Tristana. "Death on the Road to Basra," *BBC News Online*, June 29, 2003, www.informationclearing house.info/article 3962.htm.

Nomanul Haq, Syed. "Jâbir ibn Hayyân al-Sûfî," *Center for Islam and Science*, May 25, 2001, http://cis-ca.org/voices/j/jabir-mn.htm.

O'Connor, J.J., and E.F. Robertson. *Albrecht Dürer*, December 2006, http://www-groups.dcs.st-and.ac.uk/~history/Biographies/Durer.html.

Pfeiffer, Robert A. "Review of Ziggurats et Tour de Babel," *American Journal of Archaeology*, 54: 431.

Read, John. "Interpretation of This Drawing," *Hermetic Art*, n.d., www.alchemylab.com/melancholia.htm.

Revelas-Canham, Louise. "Waldorf Astoria New York—Luxury Hotel with History," *EzineArticles.com*, November 5, 2009, http://ezinearticles.com/?Waldorf-Astoria-New-York-Luxury-Hotel-With-History&id=3214532.

Robertson, Phillip. "The Death of al-Mutanabbi Street," *Selected Stories*, July 8, 2005, http://phillip robertson.com/IRAQ/articles/muntanabbi/index.htm.

Shemer, Adam. "A Drive in the Country," *Baghdad Journal*, August 9, 2003, http://journalism.berkeley.edu/projects/baghdad/archives/2003_08.html.

University of California at Berkeley Archaeological Research Facility, "Nineveh Region," *CyArk*, 2009, http://archive.cyark.org/nineveh-region-info.

Credits

The Assyrian empire, seventh century B.C. (Dino Pulerà, Artery Studios, Toronto)

The Royal Game of Ur (The Trustees of the British Museum)

Alchemy Archives website, masks from left to right (Ella's Design, 2010, Used under license from Shutterstock.com; Arthur Tilley, 2010, Used under license from JupiterImages.com; Volk65, 2010, Used under license from Shutterstock.com; Rui Vale de Sousa, 2010, Used under license from Shutterstock.com; Studio 37, 2010, Used under license from Shutterstock.com)

Planetary symbols (Dino Pulerà, Artery Studios, Toronto)

Stone panel from the southwest palace of Sennacherib (The Trustees of the British Museum)

Melencolia 1, Albrecht Dürer (public domain, Wikipedia Images)

Woman of Babylon, Albrecht Dürer (public domain, Wikipedia Images)

Ishtar's eight-pointed star (Dino Pulerà, Artery Studios, Toronto)

Acknowledgments

Setting out to write *The Witch* seemed to me much like embarking on a journey, one I would take in my imagination, alone. What I discovered along the way was how false a notion that turned out to be. A book is the product of many people working together, and numerous welcome fellow travelers joined this journey as it gathered steam.

I'm immensely grateful to my literary agent, Denise Bukowski, whose superlative talents and international reach have made it all possible.

Much appreciation goes to Penguin Publisher Nicole Winstanley and Commissioning Editor Adrienne Kerr for that first exciting sale. Adrienne, you have been instrumental in shaping the book— thank you so much for your insight and great ideas.

It requires a very talented team to take a book from the early manuscript to the bookstore shelf and I've been really fortunate to work with some of the best in the business: Karen Alliston, Mary Ann Blair, Barbara Bower, Daniel Cullen, Marcia Gallego,

Yvonne Hunter, Lindsey Lowy, Mary Opper, Lisa Jager, Don Robinson, and Katherine West.

I will never forget the thrill of learning that *The Witch of Babylon* was shortlisted for the Crime Writers Association (U.K.) Debut Dagger. That one milestone gave me the confidence to carry on and the professional support every debut author needs. Equally, my fellow writers who make up Crime Writers of Canada have been admirable tutors on the art and business of writing, as well as great friends. Winning the Arthur Ellis Award for Best Unpublished Novel was another memorable step in the journey.

My sister, Ellen, and daughter, Kenlyn, have been my steadfast anchors through both the peaks and the troughs. As well, many thanks to Stephen Mader and Dino Pulerà of Artery Studios in Toronto for such excellent work in bringing the illustrations to life; to Robert Rafton for his photography; and to Helen Heller for her sage advice.

This novel is a work of fiction but one grounded in historical facts, and I'm indebted to Dr. Paul-Alain Beaulieu of the University of Toronto Department of Near and Middle Eastern Civilizations for his help with ancient Assyrian culture and terminology.

It was, of course, impossible for me to do "research on the ground" in Iraq, so I'm very thankful to the many journalists, bloggers, and photographers whose first-hand accounts proved so valuable.

Special gratitude goes to my friends and colleagues who've been so generous with their support and lent a much-appreciated critical eye: Max Allen, Cathy Astolfo, Pat Armstrong, Jan Armstrong, Joanne Bernstein-Cohen, Liz Brady, Jane Burfield, Melanie Campbell, Donna Carrick, Vicki Delany, Ron Dixon, Cheryl Freedman, Joseph Glazner, Madeleine Harris-Callway, Peggy Hughson, Alan Lennon, Lee Lofland, Judy and Fred Martin, Nancy McQueen, Charlotte Morgan, Eudora and John Pendergast, Jan Raymond, Linda Smith, Christine Von Aesch, Basil, Rob and Caroline Wall, and Richard Wright. As this book went to press, I was most saddened to learn that Dr. Donny George Youkhanna had passed away and would like to recognize his remarkable contribution to illuminating and safeguarding the magnificent legacy that Iraq and the Assyrians have given to the world.

The Witch and I thank you all.

An excerpt from

THE BOOK OF STOLEN TALES

the new antiquities thriller by

D.J. McIntosh

COMING IN 2013

THE BOOK OF STOLEN TALES

is Book Two of the Mesopotamian Trilogy. It takes place in November, symbolized by Nergal, Babylonian god of war and pestilence.

A European Estate
on All Souls' Day

Firelight on the faces of the villagers showed their lust for the burning as they held their torches proudly in front of the captain and his guard. Stunted and malnourished from years spent working in the mines, the villagers leapt at the chance to destroy the noble family's precious property. They fought over who would throw the first fire brand, yearning to see the great estate crumble and burn.

Encouraged by the count's guard, throughout the day the villagers had destroyed the garden. They'd ripped up a maze of boxed yew hedges, cedars clipped into shapes of unicorns and centaurs, and the carefully tended orange trees, and bunched them in a ring around the stately home.

The much admired statue of Eros and Psyche stood under a little arbour thronged with roses, their blossoms long turned a papery brown, but leaves still verdant thanks to a prolonged summer. The sculptor believed he'd seen the forms of the two lovers in the gray veins of the prized Brocatelle marble. In contrast to the other garden ornaments, this statue had a compelling authenticity. The villagers pried it from its base with brutal force and threw it against the massive doors at the head of the stairway.

They smashed stone outbuildings and piled the rocks on top of the sculpture, demolished the wooden stables and added the wreckage to the ring of uprooted trees and hedges. Hot pitch sealed doors and windows shut.

Enclosed in the circle of vegetation the great building loomed out of the fog like a pale monument.

The time had come. The captain brought his hand down swiftly and gave the order. His soldiers knelt and raised their muskets. They opened fire.

The villagers froze in shock, unable to comprehend how they had suddenly become targets. Cruel pikes impaled those not felled by bullets. One young man with the presence of mind to break away almost crashed through the gauntlet of the soldiers' line before a rapier punctured and gutted his belly. The massacre was over quickly. Bodies lay on the ground like slaughtered lambs. The soldiers heaved them onto the makeshift pyres. The captain's horse, a rare white Camargue tethered to a nearby tree, cried out in terror at the reek of blood.

Soldiers added oil-drenched faggots of wood onto the mounds of greenery, then joined their captain behind the ring and set it alight. Dense clouds of smoke from the fresh leaves and branches intermingled with the fog, obscuring the manor house entirely.

Pleased by their good service, the captain ordered his aide to gift a gold piece to each member of the guard along with generous servings of his finest cognac. The aide was permitted to join in, a privilege not normally granted him. The captain toasted his men. His soldiers threw back their drinks and cheered as the blaze tossed sparks heavenward.

One soldier gripped his throat and sucked in a breath. Cognac could burn when drunk too rapidly but surely not like this. He strained again for air then toppled onto the ground. The others followed, stumbling toward the fire, blinded by the poison. Within minutes the entire company lay dying, save one. A soldier who'd cursed aloud when he'd spilled his drink now stood dumbly, gazing at his fallen brothers. The captain shot him through the throat.

The horse flailed in panic, its gleaming white withers slick with sweat, its soft fleshy lips bloody and torn from wrenching at the bit. The captain lashed the animal into submission, then mounted the horse and galloped onto the dark forest trail. He smiled to himself, anticipating his reward from a count well pleased with the night's work.

The wood was abnormally silent. No rush of wings or predatory growls signalled the waking of its night creatures. The horse, usually a cautious animal alert to the signs of danger, kept up its frenzied pace, focused only on fleeing the smell of murder and fire.

A shape like a bloom of ink on parchment spread across their path, darker than the gloom of the night forest and foreign to the natural forms of the trees and plants surrounding it. Both the rider in his reverie and the frightened horse failed to notice the deepening shadow until it had them in its grip.

Part One

THE CROOKED MAN

"Of such great powers or beings there may be conceivably a survival ... a survival of a hugely remote period when ... consciousness was manifested, perhaps, in shapes and forms long since withdrawn before the tide of advancing humanity ... forms of which poetry and legend alone have caught a flying memory and called them gods, monsters, mythical beings...."

—ALGERNON BLACKWOOD

One

London, November 17, 2003

My brother Samuel kept his journals religiously and when he died I took up the habit. I'd left New York to take a commission in London and on the flight over began my new journal by describing my harrowing encounter with Samuel's killers and the treasure they coveted. I'd chosen a volume with handsome bronzed leather covers and when I jotted the first words down the harsh memories came tumbling back. Recording my experiences the way Samuel used to brought me nearer to him and I was inspired to write as though he were my reader. It was a fanciful thought, but one that comforted me, if only a little.

Arriving at my London hotel room I looked forward to the new commission and felt elated my life had taken such a positive turn. In a few short hours,

I would realize how fleeting this moment of satisfaction was. My good fortune wasn't destined to last very long.

Cold air wafted in through the window I'd opened for relief from the stifling combination of heat and poor air circulation. Rain fell gently outside on the pavement. The ancient radiators rattled and hissed. I'd kept the lights off even though dusk had fallen, in the hope that the man outside would give up his post and go away.

Shifting over to the window, I kept out of his sightline although I doubted he could see anything against the dim background of my room. Five floors down and across the street, the man lingered just outside the yellow arc of light cast by a street lamp. He hadn't moved for hours. Suddenly he looked up as if sensing my presence. What sixth sense did he possess, knowing I watched him?

I'd brushed past him on my way back to the hotel earlier that evening, after successfully acquiring the rare book I'd been hired to bid for at Sherrods auction house. The man had called out to me as I hurried past, "Mr. Madison, isn't it?"

At first glance he appeared elderly; both of his hands rested atop an ebony cane. A rearing white horse had been expertly carved into the shaft. The horse's rippling withers and powerful legs were meticulously rendered; its flashing mane, arched neck and head formed the curved handle. In an oddly formal gesture, he bowed and took a few steps toward me. His fluid movements and sure step belied my initial impression of frailty.

"Do I know you?" I asked.

"Not yet." His accent was hard to place, but I detected the faint suggestion of a threat in his tone. "My name is Gian Alesio Abattutis. Perhaps you have heard of me?"

"No, Sir. I have not." I pulled my trench coat up to my ears. A light rain had begun to fall.

He indicated my case with the ferrule of his cane. "I think you have in there something that belongs to me." He leaned in, and lowered his voice. "Those tales were stolen. I want them back."

When I didn't respond he added, "As compensation for your trouble, I will give you twice what you paid." He dug into his coat pocket and produced three gold coins. They lay in his palm, creased with deep lines.

I moved closer. The coins looked familiar. "May I see those?"

He snatched them away, as a magician might. "When you agree to our transaction."

I gripped my case harder. "This book belongs to my client. The sale was entirely legitimate. I couldn't sell it to you even if I wanted to."

It may have been a trick of the light, the street lamp playing strangely on his face, but his pupils seemed to narrow to sharp, bright pinpoints. "You'll wish you hadn't kept the book. You'll regret this," he paused. "Deeply."

"Good evening," I said curtly and spun on my heel, growing impatient with his hostile manner. I hastened to the hotel lobby feeling both a little unnerved at the exchange and annoyed at myself for caring.

The old brick hotel had seen better times. The ad neglected to mention shabby corridors, intermittent hot water, and constant gurgles and clangs from the radiators. But my stay was for a week—at most—and it came at a bargain rate.

I unlocked the door with an electronic key card and tossed my trench coat over a chair. Then I poured two fingers of scotch into a tumbler and put David Gray's *Babylon* on the CD player to take my mind off the menacing words of the strange man outside. The solicitor's letter that had originally proposed my commission lay in my pocket. I fingered it, and thinking it might shed some light on him, I pulled it out and read it again:

Dear Mr. Madison,

At the behest of my client who, for the time being wishes to remain unknown, I am writing to seek your services. On Monday, November 17 at 7:30 pm, Sherrods will offer at auction a rare book. You are being asked to represent my client to bid on it. Details about the item may be found in the enclosed catalogue on page 21, item #164. The owner has fixed a price and will not agree to sell the book below that figure. Nor is it available for public viewing beforehand.

Should you be willing to accept this task, funds will be forwarded by my office to cover your travel, accommodation, and ancillary expenses.

There is one further stipulation. Once you have concluded a successful purchase, do not attempt to read the book. I'm advised a repellent history is associated with it and my client maintains the precaution is for your own protection. Sherrods will deliver the item to the successful bidder in a wooden box. Do not attempt to disturb the contents.

We have set a maximum of £175,000. Beyond that my client is unwilling to go; however, we don't anticipate the final price will rise nearly that high. Assuming you are successful, 25% of that figure will be forwarded as your commission. Should you decide to accept these terms please reply by letter. You are welcome to contact my office should you have any further questions.

I thank you for your consideration.

Cordially,
Arthur S. Newhouse LLP

The solicitor had a fancy Lincoln's Inn address. I'd made a few inquiries, and after he'd checked out, I agreed to take on the job. Twenty-five percent was very generous and I'd jumped at the chance. After coming close to bankruptcy in recent months, I was in no position to turn it down.

Other than the reference to the book's dark history and the secrecy surrounding the identity of my client, there was no indication in the letter why the man who accosted me tonight would be interested. I thought of the infamous *Malleus Maleficarum*, a fifteenth century treatise on witchcraft. Such books could also be described as having a "repellent history" but his meaning was obscure and I could not imagine what would merit such a warning.

I returned the letter to its envelope. The book I'd just won at the auction now sat in its little wooden box on the hotel room coffee table. Most of my deals were conducted privately, in the climate controlled offices and homes of wealthy men and women. But if the truth be told, I relished auctions. They had the same drama as casinos. Reading the auctioneer's expressions and gestures, watching who he'd trade glances with and who he avoided, baiting the enemy—the psychological art of the auction shared a lot of similarities with poker. A false showing of your hand, a deadpan expression, the tension in the room as the bids rose to astronomical sums, the barely perceptible intake of breath before the coup de grace. All were the stuff of legends.

Sherrods was a smaller auction house located in the Royal Borough of Kensington and Chelsea that specialized in rare books and antiquities. The place had been buzzing due to a number of spectacular items on the block—a dozen leaves from the first edition of the Gutenberg Bible known in the business as "Noble Fragments," a gorgeous Abbotsford edition of Sir Walter Scott's twelve Waverly novels including 2,500 steel and wood engravings, and ten steatite Mesopotamian cylinder seals circa 800 BC.

Sleek, well dressed men and women milled about the Gutenberg display and the Waverly set, catalogues in hand. Some jotted notes in the margins of the item entries, others whispered into their iPhones.

In contrast, the object of my attention, ticket #164, garnered little interest. It sat in lonely splendour in its little wooden box adorned with a white cross. I was not surprised by its lack of admirers. Few details had been provided in the catalogue and its presentation was decidedly understated. For that, I was pleased. With fewer bidders I'd have an easier time.

To ensure a good audience the more popular items had been left until the end of the evening, so there was still a healthy crowd when my item went on the block. With the help of my friend Amy, who worked at Sherrods, I'd been able to identify those with interest in the book. The man with a mop of shocking red hair and wearing a bespoke suit lingered in front of the little wooden box for just a second more than I would have liked. Amy told me auctions were his preferred form of entertainment. Some people took in the opera, others liked the bar scene, he attended auctions. He was famous for bidding an object up and pulling out before he had to lay any money on the line.

Another agent, Marlee Scott, also expressed an interest. Amy said she often represented major rare book dealers in the U.S. and on the continent. She would be my major competitor and I caught a glimpse of her in pearls and classic black Dior.

The auctioneer announced ticket #164 and the reserve price of £80,000. Scott threw a glance my way so I knew someone had spilled the beans about me too. She picked up the bid at £85,000 and avoided my eye. The auctioneer raised it by a couple of thousand pounds and looked in my direction. Copperhead entered the fray for £90,000. This was fun; I could feel the adrenalin pumping.

I entered at £110,000 then the auctioneer pushed it up by another couple of thousand. Scott bit on that. I snapped up the next bid and out of the corner of my eye watched Copperhead take it after me. He was in a feisty mood tonight. When the auctioneer deliberately slowed his call Copperhead darted a nervous glance at me but I held off making a move. He was afraid he'd taken his game too far. Scott finally raised her paddle, stepping up just in time to rescue him. That was enough for our red-haired friend. He was out.

I took the next bid and noted a wrinkle of worry in Scott's expression. She was very close to her max. She whipped out her cell phone, stabbed a key with her red lacquered nail and talked rapidly. She pushed it to £120,000 and I went for it at £124,000 then held my breath.

"£124,000. Do I hear £125,000?" Quiet reigned throughout the room. I held my breath.

"Fair warning," he chimed and scanned the room.

"Last chance!" No one stepped up. The auctioneer waited a few more seconds, then gave me a nod and announced, "Sold! To number 78." I silently cheered. That was my bidding number. The book was mine.

Scott raised her delicate eyebrows and gave me a thumbs up to show there were no hard feelings. I smiled back, appreciating her grace. It had gone higher than I hoped but was still under my client's maximum. I assumed my unnamed client would be pleased with the night's work.

I closed the heavy hotel drapes and clicked on a small bedside lamp. I turned back to the book. The written warning not to open it only served to entice me. The antique cedar box inside my case bore no maker's mark except for a coat of arms stamped in its lid—a fat, white cross on a red shield. This was the standard of Count Amadeus 1 of the House of Savoy, ancestor to the Kings of Italy. That meant the box could date back as much as four hundred years. Its fitted lid was firmly secured by four small brass screws. I extracted them with my pen knife, lifted the lid and removed the contents.

The book covers were worked in gold leaf and studded with semi-precious stones lodged in metal housings, both faces entirely covered with geometric designs that looked vaguely Arabic. Two small silver clasps held the book shut. The spine, made of silver as well, was banded with gold.

It was in near perfect condition. The silver was barely tarnished; there were no dents or splits in the metallic finish you'd expect to see from it being handled over hundreds of years, and there was no foxing on the fore edges. No dust or moisture had been permitted to mar its perfection. And yet it felt old.

The clasps didn't appear to be locked nor would they budge, further suggesting the book hadn't been opened for some time. Not willing to risk scratching the metal with my penknife it took me over half an hour of fiddling before I succeeded in disengaging the covers. The actual volume turned out to be quite slim. I'd seen elaborate metallic covers like these before on literary Judaica, but nothing nearly so ornate for a book this small.

I slapped on latex gloves to protect the ancient pages from the oils of my skin. The leaves were handbound vellum and lay beautifully flat; the typeface, large, archaic and very elegant. I could see deep in the crease of the spine; the pages had once been a beautiful bone white and therefore were of the highest quality.

I carefully held it up to the light and spotted a Fabriano watermark—another sign of high value. A prestigious paper manufacturer in the Apennines, Fabriano had been in business as far back as the early Middle Ages. At one time, anyone who revealed their paper making secrets would have been sent into exile.

On the title page, above an illustration of the head of a noblewoman surrounded by elaborate scrollwork was the title: LO CVNTO, DELI CVNTE. Below the illustration: In Napoli. Appresso Ottauio Beltrano 1636. Conlicenza de Superiori.

Housed in an Italian box, printed on Italian paper, it made sense the book would be written in Italian. Even so, I groaned in disappointment. I'd hoped the book would be written in English. I understood a smattering of modern Italian—enough to have a limited conversation, or order a decent meal and a bottle of wine. Deciphering a Renaissance Italian dialect was beyond my abilities. Whatever secrets the book contained would remain hidden from me for now.

Using my phone I snapped photos of the covers and pages then sent the folder to my email address. It was only wise to keep a record of any item under my care, especially when it had so aroused the curiosity and ardour of others.

I returned to the illustrations accompanying the Italian text. They were superb black and white engravings. The first few seemed familiar, reminding me of a popular childhood fairy tale. From there, however, they depicted increasingly dark and horrifying scenes. The second last one showed a woman of middle age dressed in a flowing gown, being forced by two men into a large hearth burning brightly with fire. The woman's flailing movements and the look of sheer terror on her face was rendered so convincingly, I wondered whether the artist had witnessed a real event.

The last, equally gruesome image showed a man spearing a monster with a reptilian head and a raptor's claws. Under this image a note read: *Gracie a Lo*

Spagnoletto. My Italian was sufficient here. It said: *Thank you to the little Spaniard.*

The hairs rose on the back of my neck. Lo Spagnoletto was the Italian nickname for José de Ribera, premier print maker and painter of seventeenth-century Naples. Ribera was one of the Tenebrosi, the shadow painters, who used heavy contrast between dark and light in their work, inspired by Caravaggio. A sinister figure of those times, Ribera led the cabal of Naples, a small group of painters who harassed and threatened other artists to beat them out of lucrative commissions. If the prints were truly by Ribera, the book was worth far more than its auction value.

I returned to the title page to learn the name of the book's author, then remembered it contained no attribution. That appeared on the next page.

It had been signed *Gian Alesio Abbatutis, In the Year of our Lord, 1634.*